THE KISS SENT THEM SPINNING

The tentative, careful caress caused a slow, delicious meltdown in the pit of his stomach. He gently held her face to his, as one kiss moved into another, even better and endless.

She felt his body give inward and fit warmly against hers, holding her safe, sending her hands exploring around his neck. Time stopped. Nothing existed except him and the way he made her feel.

◇ ◇

ALWAYS

by Jeane Renick

Available from HarperPaperbacks

TRUST ME

JEANE RENICK

HarperPaperbacks
A Division of HarperCollins*Publishers*

Special edition printing: February 1994

If you purchased this book without a cover, you should be aware that this book is stolen property. It was reported as "unsold and destroyed" to the publisher and neither the author nor the publisher has received any payment for this "stripped book."

This is a work of fiction. The characters, incidents, and dialogues are products of the author's imagination and are not to be construed as real. Any resemblance to actual events or persons, living or dead, is entirely coincidental.

HarperPaperbacks *A Division of* HarperCollins*Publishers*
10 East 53rd Street, New York, N.Y. 10022

Cover illustration by Jim Griffin

First printing: September 1992

Printed in the United States of America

❖ 10 9 8 7 6 5 4 3 2 1

For my shrink,
and all the people who believed . . .

TRUST ME

Allison Shreve, shivering in a thick cashmere turtleneck, stared down at her new hiking boots cooling on two inches of snow in the taxi lane at O'Hare. Scar tissue pulled at her left shoulder, stiff and achy in the cold; her stomach threatened rebellion against an unwanted breakfast and the metallic weight of acid pumped into her insides. Blue airport shuttles, motley taxis, and snow-covered automobiles disgorging nervous flyers slid and skidded and honked around her—women doing double takes at the sight of Jake, while she huddled unrecognized in the freezing cold next to his silver-blue Mercedes.

A flurry of snow stung at her face, and the wind thrashed about, whipping her thick blond hair. Even with Jake's calfskin jacket, borrowed for the trip, her body heat dissipated rapidly into the icy cold. She lifted eyes haunted with dark circles to stare into his gorgeous face, maddeningly dour as he regarded her through the window.

"Maybe I shouldn't go. It's a short layover in Miami, I'll never make the connection." The wind tore away thin wisps of breath vapor as she searched frantically for other reasons. "I've studied Mayan culture—I won't learn that much on a dig. The sun will ruin my s-skin, I'll peel . . ."

Jake's implacable voice lifted out of the car to cut her short. "Since when do you worry about your skin? I've seen you work broiled as a Maine lobster. You're not going for the culture, and I didn't get my famous body out of bed at six A.M. to watch you change your mind." Even his pained smile was dazzling, denying the harsh words.

"I'm just not sure I'm ready," she said, stalling. "I had the dream again."

Jake refused to entertain further discussion. "It's D-Day, Lovely."

"I can forfeit the trip, the money, everything."

"You can't afford to cancel." Jake was brusque in his judgment, even when it hurt; she relied on his absolute honesty—one of the few things she trusted still—and he wouldn't fail her. Affording it had nothing to do with money, and they both knew it. He deliberately sought to divert her attention. "Where exactly is this place again?"

After a pause she released her breath and allowed it. "Belize. It used to b-be British Honduras." Her teeth began to chatter. "It's c-close to the southern border. Guatemala, I think." She breathed in through her mouth, and the icy air slicing off Lake Michigan made her eyes water. "I g-gave you a map. Didn't you even look at it?" she accused, blinking tears from the relentless cold.

Obviously he hadn't.

"You're catching pneumonia."

It was his turn to shiver as frigid gusts tore through the open window. From the glove compartment he extracted a tiny packet perfectly wrapped in turquoise foil with a pale green ribbon. "Open this in your hotel and not before," he instructed sourly as he handed it out to her. He forced himself to stifle worry. She'd be okay down there. She'd be fine. She'd be home in eleven days and he'd pick her up, brown and healthy and beautiful, at this curb a week from Sunday.

Her eyes threatened real tears as she pushed his present into her pack. "You promised you w-wouldn't make me cry," she quavered.

"Don't you dare—you'll ruin your face," he commanded, then hurried on. "Gain five pounds and get rid of those circles. I'll have work for you when you get back." He reached out the window to pull her drawn face down to his and kissed her soundly.

Her thin frame now shuddering in waves from the dry cold, she returned his kiss with feeling. What had started as a token attempt at rebellion had gotten out of hand; he'd put it right with his crusty, reassuringly normal reaction. Jake was her balance wheel, her touchstone. Had he said stay, she'd have scurried back into the warmth of the tiny car and broken pell-mell for home. But he was letting her go. It was going to be all right. She shouldered her carryon and walked rapidly through the automatic glass doors, which swept open to the frantic tangle of a Wednesday morning airport.

The skin on her shoulder was still touchy from the dermabrasion session. Yesterday, during her final checkup visit, Dr. Menzes had studied her stiff shoulder under a special light and triple lenses. "You're healing splendidly," he'd pronounced proudly. "Looks like we'll only need three more sessions. The tissue will be tight for a while, but that's normal. Use this while you're gone and don't expose the skin to much sun."

"I won't," she'd assured him. With the ugly new scar, sunbathing was out of the question.

"When you get back, we'll take another look at these." "These" were the lines in her face, creasing at either side of her wide mouth.

It had taken until nearly three-thirty this morning to defeat her anxieties about getting on the plane. This would be the first flight alone. And she'd had the dream again—his face as she . . . she wouldn't think beyond that.

Through the smoky plate-glass wall of the airport, Allison watched Jake ease his prized vintage Mercedes into slippery traffic. If it hadn't been for him these past months, she wouldn't be here at all. She wouldn't be anywhere. Probably still in the hospital, the nurses going all dithery every time he came to see her. Tom Selleck couldn't have caused more uproar.

Outwardly calm, his car out of sight, she stood alone in the swirl of executive commuters and post–New Year's travelers until she got her bearings, then joined the check-in line for the Eastern flight. When she took her turn at the counter, the harried agent glanced at her briefly without recognition, then busied himself with the official stamping and stapling required to check her sleeping bag and issue a boarding pass.

Awaiting the call to board, she caught her pale reflection in a Departures monitor. With Dr. Menzes's promise of a medical miracle, the lines were fixable and might not prevent future close-up work; but medical science had nothing to offer that would change the look in her eyes. The reflection in the screen was indistinct, but she knew what was not there. They no longer held her presence, or the depth and excitement cameras once captured.

Three years of not working had forced her to liquidate one investment after another to meet expenses, and after a disastrous bout with "Black Monday" on the stock market, when a margin call had destroyed more than half her portfolio, her assets were nearing depletion. She was terrified of going back to work, but dependency was driving her crazy and she longed for her former life. She couldn't cling to Jake forever; it was time to function on her own. And it started with this flight.

The Belize project provided something she'd wanted to do since she was fifteen—an archaeological dig. She'd been a member of OneEarth for several years, drawn to its activity of matching member/volunteers with research expeditions. Volunteers provided the labor for fieldwork to preserve endangered habitats and archaeological sites. It had been her haven from the highly pressured business of being beautiful, a place to drop out and unwind, go unrecognized. Now it would be a neutral place to mingle with benign strangers, make decisions, get a little more comfortable with the world.

Having listed her occupation as "Photographer," and leaving the volunteer questionnaire relatively blank, she'd been thrilled to receive notification of acceptance; but now it was here—the actuality of eleven days on her own—no Jake, no shrink, no hiding in sleep when the dream was hibernating. Only herself to sit in judgment if she failed. She felt equal parts fear and determination.

The airport voice broke through her thoughts to call the flight. She turned away from the too thin face in the glass and joined queuing passengers through the boarding gate.

She slept lightly in the winter-warm cabin, waking as the flight touched down in Florida. Lulled by muggy, tropical air seeping through the jetway, she was slapped alert by a cold wash of air-conditioning in the Miami terminal. Her new departure gate posted a delay, so she located a ladies' room to change from the sweater to a cooler OneEarth T-shirt. The logo helped team members identify each other en route. Emerging from the cubicle, she discovered a OneEarth jacket draped over a small suitcase, and she smiled. It was always a pleasant surprise when the system worked.

The owner of the jacket, a dead ringer for Woody Allen—with a decided limp—cast a cheerful look at Allison's shirt and introduced herself. "Ellen Woodrow. Call me Woodie. You can see why everyone does."

Caught off guard, Allison said her own name and focused with care on the woman's face, but Woodie smashed through her polite avoidance.

"Polio," she announced. "Came down with it while Dr. Salk was working on the vaccine." She plowed on before Allison could respond. "I'm a widow, seventy-eight my next birthday. Sixth trip for OneEarth, second time in Belize. I was with Tom Rider's group last year when he located that bunch of rocks. Thought I ought to go back to see what he found."

Allison was nonplussed. "I envy your independence," she managed at last, meaning it.

"Well. Retired ain't dead—contrary to what some people will tell you." The energetic little woman dried her hands as she talked, efficiently wiped the wet counter with the paper towel before tossing it into the trash container. Despite her withered limb, she turned smartly and stuck out her foot shod in a hiking boot with a thick, leveling sole. "I had this made special so I can climb up and down pyramids."

Allison's silent voice chimed in, *Seventy-seven and special hiking boots—if she can handle this trip, and I can't, I'm a turnip!* She trailed Woodie into the waiting area.

"George Edley, this is Allison Shreve."

George, standing tall in red cowboy boots, doffed his orange baseball cap with a OneEarth patch sewn squarely on the front, and summarily announced his status as a divorced probate attorney from Wisconsin. Two inches shorter than her five foot ten, with a florid complexion and cocker-spaniel eyes, he wore his straight black hair meticulously parted deep over one ear and combed across the top of a balding dome. He was resplendent in a green-and-yellow nylon windbreaker, a khaki OneEarth T-shirt, and gray Calvin Klein jeans.

He gave what he obviously considered a complimentary whistle, his face radiating one huge smile. "Headed into the jungle with two beautiful women. . ." He included a decidedly tolerant Woodie but kept his eyes on Allison's face. "You just consider yourself in good hands for the next coupla weeks."

A graduate years ago from the School of How to Handle George Edleys, Allison sent a bright professional smile in his direction. Thirteen years a model, including work in France and Italy, had provided a Grand Tour education in men who neither see beyond the features nature deeds beautiful women nor seek the intelligence waiting there. She was relieved to find herself behaving normally. It was the first test of a man's attention, albeit unwanted, and she was weathering it well. She turned to Woodie. "Would you like something from the candy counter? I need something sweet."

"So do I," said the lawyer, not quite under his breath, "and they don't stock it at the candy counter."

The women abandoned him to the waiting room. "On the whole," Woodie assured her dryly, "these expeditions tend to take the vinegar out of the flashier types." Woodie was from Maine; not much impressed her.

Following Woodie through the line at the counter, Allison carefully located her mother's wedding ring from an inside pocket of her purse and eased it onto her finger. On her return to the lounge, the sight of the gold band sent George hustling to his information sheet to discover that her space for marital status was blank.

On board the 727, she stored her carryon in the overhead compartment, then maneuvered her backpack neatly under the seat in front of her. The No Smoking indicator was a reminder that the flight was international and the uncomfortable smell of cigarettes would soon be inevitable. Finally she sat and buckled herself into the carefully chosen aisle seat near the galley and flight crew.

Listening subconsciously to the familiar sounds of bumps and shudders that told of cargo holds being loaded and secured, she reassessed her emotional condition. The jumps and flutters in her tummy were simply preflight jitters, not the beginnings of the grinding spasms she dreaded. The seat next to her was blessedly empty, and the fear was a great deal less than she had anticipated. It was going to be okay after all. Jake would be proud of her.

One last passenger swung through the cabin door just as the steward moved to close it off.

Safely inside, he searched out a boarding pass and the steward pointed to the seat next to an expensive-looking blonde staring out a starboard window. The rush to the boarding gate had aggravated a massive hangover. "That's a smoking seat?" Obviously it wasn't, and he wanted a cigarette in the worst way. "Nothing left in smoking?"

"It's a full flight, sir." The steward secured the door. "If you'll remind me, we'll work something out when we're airborne." Frustrated, Zachary Cross jammed the boarding pass into the envelope with his return ticket and shoved it into an opening in the backpack. He worked his gear down the aisle.

The blond woman, without looking directly at him, stood stiffly aside to give him access. He sized her up with the discipline of long-practiced witness, honed to fine art from thirteen years on the street: expensive hiking boots, tan linen slacks, and a man's pricey designer jacket. She was easily five ten, potentially great legs. Tense face under the makeup; no smile—probably hated flying. Good figure, too thin for his taste; possible natural blond with a salon haircut. Unusual pallor, like she'd been living under a rock. Somewhere in her thirties, although it was getting harder to tell these days. Heavy gold wedding band, high karat, finely worn. He'd guess an uptight secretary for somebody major, on vacation. A wife that expensive would be in first class.

He wondered irritably why she'd chosen to hike in Belize. He bashed his worn army duffel into the overhead, crunched the backpack under a forward seat. Hell, he didn't even know why he was going.

He sighed and lowered his six-foot frame heavily onto the cramped seat, already hating the midplane confinement and dreading the three hours of flight time. Late arrival had cost him the coveted legroom of an aisle seat in Smoking, adding to his irritation. Still, he'd managed to catch the flight against the odds, and the woman next to him looked . . . interesting, he decided. If she wasn't a total flake, things might look up. Maybe he could persuade her to give up the aisle seat. With those legs, probably not.

They sorted out seat belts without conversation, and the stewardess began the ritual explanation of emergency equipment.

◆ ◆ ◆

Other than to note that the flight had nearly left without him, Allison had watched without interest when the tall man with a bashed-in face stepped inside the aircraft. Switching her gaze out a window, she remembered in a searing flash the one time a flight had been held for her late arrival. Three years ago. The frantic limousine driver had delivered her seconds before the plane was scheduled to depart. He had persisted in alerting the floor supervisor, who in turn had called the gate, and while she'd delightedly ridden a speeding courtesy cart through a VIP tunnel to an elevator to the boarding gate, they'd held the plane until she'd arrived, luggage discreetly whisked from sight.

It had been a courtesy to her celebrity as one of Chicago's own, and she'd boarded the plane high with excitement, feeling special. She'd flown first class then, at the instance of Charles Gallé. Autographing cocktail napkins and photographs for airline personnel had been an ordinary part of her life.

She stared out the oval double glass window at the blurred service trucks and luggage carts going about their business. Maybe it was true that every instant of life affected every other—if she'd flown to New York an hour later, would her life be so different now? Had that ripple changed things or caused things? Would there have been another passenger instead of him, a different conversation, no talk of favorite hotels and Manhattan restaurants, no invitation to dinner . . . ?

A frostlike pattern was scratched on one of the windows, and she traced it with her eyes. Would fate have arranged it anyway? Had it been a destiny of some kind, something written down somewhere on a master plan? Why were people entering your life so totally out of your control? The questions numbed her mind.

Lost in thought, she was startled when the tardy man appeared next to her. Uncomfortable with his scrutiny, she kept her face averted as she moved into the aisle, unwilling to meet his eyes in simple acknowledgement

What if he was another someone who would change her life? He couldn't do it if she didn't admit he was there. When would she know again whom to allow in and whom to keep out?

Unconsciously she pushed her thumb against the unfamiliar ring and stole a glance at his profile as he settled in. A drawn and battered face.

In the rear of the plane, a young Mayan woman tried again to relax. She pulled a thin black shawl around shoulders taut with apprehension, then hugged a cheap plastic purse to her small bosom with both hands. Unremarkable in a neat red cotton skirt, white blouse and sturdy leather huaraches, she felt the plane lumber forward, then stop.

She held tightly to the armrests and tried to see out the windows if there was a reason. The plane inched forward, then stopped again. No one seemed alarmed, so she accepted this as normal.

When the captain announced they were fourth in line for takeoff, she refused to think about the package. She didn't know about such things. Maybe they didn't X-ray packages.

The plane shuddered around a tight curve without pause, gathered speed, and moved down the runway into takeoff. She prayed again to Balum, god of the Jaguar People. She was Jaguar *onen*, and Balum would listen. The man next to her shifted on his seat and she feigned sleep, placing her future into the hands of Balum and Hachäkyum, Lord of the Underworld, where it had always been.

During the steepest incline of the takeoff, Zachary restlessly leaned forward against the pull of gravity to extract a package of cigarettes from his pack. The adrenaline rush from the race to the plane had heightened his body's craving for rough-sweet nicotine. Compounding the need was the onset of a gnawing headache from the hangover, aggravated by latent anger at his addiction to the legal drug in the first place. Jerry, the athlete, who never smoked, had taken great delight in pointing out to his older brother that cigarettes would kill him. Balancing them on the armrest, he rooted perversely through the backpack for matches as the pull eased and the flight leveled out over the Atlantic.

Allison stared at the cigarettes, stomach muscles beginning small jerking contractions. She worked her shoulder blades to ease the growing panic. It was no use. "There's no smoking in this section," she stated tightly.

The tension in her voice was grating. Oh, great. A bitch. Whatever happened to "Hello, how are you?"

"Hey, I know, lady," he challenged with a deadly smile, in no mood to deal with an aggressive nonsmoker, however attractive. "You see me light up, you call the captain, okay?"

Unable to find the bloody matches, he managed to wait until the seat belt sign was turned off; then, collecting the cigarettes, he unceremoniously climbed over her ankles and worked his way up to the forward stew to hustle matches and get permission to smoke in the galley.

The stewardess gave him a break and seated him in the last smoking space in first class. He ignored the window passenger's mild disapproval of his Levi's, faded shirt, scruffy denim jacket, and sockless Reeboks, to work on calming his nerves with a huge drag and a sympathetic Scotch. Two puffs later he stubbed out the cigarette. It wasn't helping. He'd given up the goddamned habit once. Now he'd have to do it all over again. He'd promised Steffie. Christ, he wished he'd never started this.

The Scotch set loose the memory of Jerry's funeral, off and running before he could shut it down. Cold and dank dirty gray—everything Jerry had hated about Ohio in December. Wet, slushy snow that melted within hours of hitting the ground, usually in desolate, bone-chilling rain that soaked through leather soles and seeped through loose puttied windows, up from joints in the baseboards and into cold bedsheets at night, turning everything dark, muddy black, and miserable.

Two weeks before Christmas, he was walking the crunchy gravel toward another soggy hole in front of the white, family-size headstone marked CROSS in huge block letters. Maybe it was some kind of curse: everyone in the family had died in winter, Grandpa and Grandma Garrett on the other side of the hill, Dad, Mom next to him, and now Jerry.

He took a long swallow of the biting Scotch. Well, it would be spring soon. If he made it through March, he'd be good for another year.

He'd stared vacantly at the greasy snow, iced edges crusted on the huge chunk of marble Mom had insisted on when Dad had gone. Three years ago he and Jerry had shared this spot when she'd been lowered next to Dad. Now he stood alone, still trying not to concede it was his brother's body, cold and stiff, resewn, inside the slick, mock-pewter coffin. His mind spun out a hope that somewhere among those stark, naked trees, Jerry could read his thoughts and hear him. "I'm sorry, Jerry, I swear to God I am."

He reclined the seat, relit the cigarette. The surge of nicotine constricted blood vessels in his forehead, protracting the headache, while his mind stubbornly clung to the memory. The day of the funeral had been endless. He'd had maybe four hours' sleep since the autopsy, and he knew now he had been dangerous. The girlfriend's family, thankfully, had been busy burying her in Omaha. At least he hadn't had to deal with her. Stupid, dizzy bitch.

He remembered Lana's face as a silly, vacant grin. A sexy, not-too-bright, unnatural redhead, bone thin and perpetually braless, she had stared through him, smiling away while Jerry yelled at him, "Trust me, Brother Zacharia. Trust me for once! I know what I'm doing!"

Trust me had been Jerry's watchword; "Brother Zacharia" referred to an in-joke about being his brother's keeper since Mom had died. They were fighting because Jerry wanted to bail on his second year at Ohio State. Finally he admitted he'd been kicked off the football squad. "Grades," he'd said with a shrug. "No big deal."

Zachary had lost it after that, and their words had been laced with anger, punctuated with slammed doors. Bitch! He could still see the loopy smile. Now, too late, he knew why there'd been nothing behind her lying eyes. Jerry had been a first-class student with a brilliant future until he'd gotten messed up with her. An exceptional athlete, grades right up there . . . the summer he'd met Lana, his life had gone to hell in a bucket. She'd won, Zachary had lost, and he hated her for it—a deep, abiding, living hatred. Damn women, anyway. If she'd lived, he wasn't sure he wouldn't have killed her.

He ran his fingers up and down the condensation outside the glass of Scotch, stared vacantly at empty blue outside the oval window. Nothing on earth could bring his brother back. Hell, she was just as dead as Jerry—let them rest in peace. The hatred eased a moment before edging its way deeper into his heart. Because of her, someone was busy chiseling Jerry's name on white marble while he was on this jerkwater trip to Belize.

He finished the Scotch and asked for another. Fogged in, he'd run across the OneEarth ad in an abandoned travel magazine at the Columbus airport; the bar had been closed. The idea of time off, endless acres of it, was a nightmare; he couldn't face filling it up somewhere on a beach, fishing, skiing, sightseeing—everything reminded him of Jerry.

He shifted in pain, unable to quiet the images. He'd prepaid two months' rent and sealed Jerry's dark apartment, unable to go inside and deal with it. Part of the loathing was lack of choice. None of this had been his decision—but he was the one who had to clean it up. Eventually he'd go through the closets and the cabinets and the drawers and pay the bills and discover the secret things in his brother's life he didn't want to know. Nothing in the rules said he had to deal with it now.

Within days, unfortunately, it was clear that he'd have to get away from the situation for a while. He was no good to himself or his kid—or the department—unless he got his head back together. Christmas had been a brief light of his daughter's shining face, but the rest of the week and New Year's had disappeared into a haze he didn't exactly remember.

A week and a warning later, he'd sent a deposit check requesting any available trip, and four days ago the woman from OneEarth had called. Two weeks in Central America sounded like an answer: lots of physical work and no luxury in the field, how bad could it be? Answer. So far, his taxi had blown a tire exceeding the speed limit on the throughway, and he'd had to settle for the last seat in nonsmoking next to a neurotic female.

An upgraded meal and three hours later, he returned to his seat with the stew's Miami number in his pocket, carefully balancing a final Scotch. Ms. Hostility was sleeping. He tried, unsuccessfully, to ease past her for the descent into Belize City and succeeded in splashing Scotch on her face and jacket as the plane bumped through a small bank of clouds. Damn it, anyway!

She woke instantly. Frightened and shocked by the icy bath, she stared directly at him, wide eyes an odd liquid color, somewhere between dusty crystal blue and light brown. Hazel, he concluded foggily; hazel encircled with dark gray, and arresting.

"Hell, I'm sorry," he said, bracing himself for deserved but unpleasant hassle.

The announcement to be certain seat belts were fastened came blaring as the plane continued jumping and jolting through the cloud layer and the stews began to buckle themselves in for landing.

To his surprise, she dismissed the smelly bath as unimportant. "Don't worry about it." Her voice was soft, unreadable, as she moved deftly onto his seat. "You'll have more room on the aisle—we're almost down."

He fumbled with the belt, trying to decide the best way

to combine appreciation with apology, when she handed him the packet containing his return ticket, the missing matches, and the expedition information he'd intended to read on the flight. "This must be yours. I found it under my seat after you left."

"Sure is," he said, reassessing. Pretty, but too rigid; a possible seven. It was a game he and Jerry had played since teenagers, comparing evaluations—usually of attractive women—on a scale of one to ten. His brother had always been more generous. He shut down the painful thought. The plane ceased bucking and settled into a smooth downward glide.

"I guess we'll be working together on the dig. . . ." She gestured at the OneEarth logo on the packet.

Terrific. I'm blitzed. Now she wants to chitchat.

"Listen, about before," she offered, still not quite meeting his eyes, "I didn't mean to be difficult. It's just that cigarettes . . . make me very nervous. I guess I'm a little scared about traveling on my own. . . Central America seems so . . . unstable." Her voice trailed away.

"Where you from?" he demanded, finishing the Scotch. Nervous, high-strung, apologetic. Absolutely a six, working on a five.

"Chicago."

"Honey, you look like you do okay in Chicago. Anybody handles that City has nothing to worry about in Belize. Trust me." A bitter smile, as he realized what he'd said.

The plane touched down and slowed to a halt on the skinny, blacktopped strip at the rural Belize City airport.

Reunited with George and Woodie, Allison felt her nerves settle down a notch as they waited in the moist heat to claim their luggage. From there they proceeded to customs and immigration. The man from the plane stood impatiently in an adjacent line. Not particularly attractive compared with Jake, there was nevertheless something unusual about him, indefinable. Dangerous, she decided. His face was engraved with wear and tear from smoking and alcohol and an all-weather Miami tan—a hard mouth, dark hair slightly mixed with gray, in need of a haircut, no alcohol damage to his waistline, yet.

Unquestionably a man accustomed to being in charge, he used little effort helping a tiny Mayan woman with a bulky package. She marked his impatience as customs officials required the package to be opened in order to sort through the woman's belongings—various items of women's clothing, baby clothes, a large stuffed teddy bear, a giant jar of Skippy peanut butter, shoes. His open impatience seemed to move the officer along, and soon the woman was retying her parcel and repacking her suitcase.

Woodie signaled with raised eyebrows that she approved of his actions, and Allison reacted with surprise and mock horror. "I sat next to him on the plane. He's on the dig with us. He's very difficult."

After discreetly showing the customs official his police identification, Zachary watched as his backpack and cameras were cursorily examined, and then he was through the line, duffel rezipped and slung over his shoulder. At the immigration window, he overheard the officer's comment to the young Mayan girl. "You are aware your permit to return to the United States expires in two weeks."

"I am here to visit my sister. Four or five days."

The official stamped the papers and passed her through.

Uncomfortable without the weight of the Magnum under his left arm, Zachary hitched his shoulders, feeling not quite dressed. He produced his passport for the official's stamp, then walked on to the lobby, scouring the building for the inevitable bar. The airplane Scotch had faded in the heat, and he wanted another drink.

Inside the tiny airport, Allison, George, and Woodie met a fifth member of the team, Harold Knolls. Harold was a poor man's edition of Chuck Norris, butch-cut sandy hair, lean and freckled, with eyeglasses disclosing the poor sight that had cost him a pro career in baseball; Harold's Rambo image of himself was running rampant. Living his fantasy, he was decked out in Banana Republic's finest jungle fatigues, complete with bush hat.

Woodie eyed his outfit. "If you had a bullwhip, you could give Indiana Jones an argument."

Harold was momentarily deflated at her opinion of his efforts, then pleased with his new image. "Say, Woodie, you're all right." He crunched the diminutive woman in a jovial hug as Allison escaped to the ladies' room.

Inside, she slipped out of Jake's jacket, missing his acerbic, reassuring support. It was hard to remember life before Jake. He and his family had moved into the house next door when he was thirteen and she was thirteen, and the number of girlfriends who wanted to sleep over had tripled. They'd grown up together, gone to high school together; at fifteen, amid to-die envy from every girl in junior high, she'd shared her first kiss with him. They'd fallen in and out of love for the next two years before finally sharing their virginity at seventeen, swept the proms, and dazzled their rivals. No one had managed to come between them to this day—male or female.

His parents had been killed in an automobile accident six weeks before graduation; her mother had put him to bed, rocked his sorrow, shared his grief. Four months later he'd rocketed into an overnight career as a smashingly successful male model and was still in heavy national demand at thirty-three.

On his twentieth birthday she'd stopped by a shoot, and his agency had approached her with an offer that afternoon. Until her exclusive contract with Gallé, because of their obvious affinity in front of a camera, most of her work had been with him. Her mother, in an unflagging campaign, had repeatedly stated her opinion that they'd be an ideal union and berated them openly for not producing perfect grandchildren.

Loyal to his core, Jake had held her together through the nightmare of police lineups and interrogations, pressing charges, more lawyers, and the trial—and, at the last, her mother's death. She wouldn't have survived without him.

She lingered at the mirror, searching for a reason to delay going outside and joining the others.

Zachary ambled through the cement-block building, sizing up the airport. Midway down the room was a tired, four-table cafe with a guarantee of greasy food built into the menu, opposite, a glassed-in souvenir shop with carved fish, dusty, bellied-up flies, and peeling boxes of duty-free Arpège. In line at the bus ticket window was the young Mayan girl from the plane.

Battle-scarred, wooden benches—too short for sleeping—were strung along the wall facing TACA, Aero-Mexico, and Eastern ticket counters and ended with the object of his search: a small bar near the exit door. Rattling salsa music from an ancient Gibson radio filled up the space behind the counter. Zachary dumped his luggage midlobby in front of the bar and settled at one of the stools to locate a familiar Walker label among the dingy collection of bottles stacked along the back wall. In vain.

"Try the local beer, son." Woodie eased herself onto an adjacent stool. "It's pretty good."

"Actually, I had something stronger in mind." They introduced themselves, and Zachary resumed his scrutiny of the bottles.

Woodie ordered a beer and, giving up, Zachary nodded for two.

"Allison says you're one of our group. That so?"

"Apparently. Aren't you two a long way from Chicago?"

"I don't know about her. I'm a long way from Maine," Woodie responded.

So Chicago and her wedding band were flying solo. Dollars to doughnuts the ring was a prop. Not a bad idea for women traveling alone. He signaled the bartender. "What's your name?"

"Mario." The grin was wide.

"Mario, you want to bring us two more beers?"

"Not for me, son—I got to pace myself."

Harold wandered up with Woodie's luggage, and Zachary took in his flamboyant costume. Downtown Miami on a Friday night. "Make it three."

Mario grinned at his good fortune. Americans were drinkers and generous tippers. It would be a grand afternoon.

Allison emerged from the lavatory to find George waiting. "We're all at the bar." Seizing her luggage, he walked her through the room and tossed her things onto the growing pile in the lobby. Harold vacated his stool so she could sit next to Woodie.

"We'll have another beer for the lady," George called out to the bartender, establishing territory.

Zachary slid a waiting bottle down the bar. "On me."

It was a simple gesture. She glanced at him and, after the briefest hesitation, murmured a thank you. It was hot and the cold beer was welcome. She took a sip from the bottle and examined the label, the bar and the bartender, the patrons, the countertop, the souvenir shop across the way—anything and everything except Zachary Cross.

Without the jacket, he saw she was thinner than he'd originally appraised and studiously avoiding him, apparently still miffed about the Scotch. Tough-ola, he decided. One apology's enough.

"Cold beer's a luxury in this country," Woodie informed them. "All you'll get at the site will be warm beer and Coca-Cola."

"Yeah, I hear Coke has a monopoly down here. Pepsi loses again," said Harold. "'Course they got Russia in the Carter administration, but Coke got China. Thanks to Nixon."

Harold's voice and the conversation ebbed from Zachary's private hell. The beer wasn't getting it. He ordered a double Scotch from Mario and stared into nowhere; absently lighting a cigarette, he drew smoke deep into his lungs before he realized he was smoking. He'd started again sometime the week of the funeral. Probably with the call to Sue. The agony of deciding what to tell his ex and their eight-year-old Steffie about her idolized uncle Jerry.

He and Sue had been divorced long enough that rancor had pretty much disappeared from their conversations, but it lurked a very short depth below their dealings with each other. She was about to remarry. The guy was okay, owned a string of bakeries, had bucks, but Zachary was Steffie's father and he'd already had a conversation with hubby-to-be. "One hand on my kid and I'll break you in half" had been the essential message. To give him credit, the guy had held his gaze long enough to be convincing that there wouldn't be any problems.

Sue was another situation. He wished the guy luck. Their divorce would be final four years come November. Other than missing his little girl every night of his life, he knew no regrets. Maybe the baker could keep Sue home at night. He sure hadn't been able to.

In the end, he'd told Sue what had happened to Jerry, and she had decided not to attend the funeral. He didn't know if he was relieved or sorry. Too tired to think much of anything. Full of Johnny Walker, wearing his brother's winter coat over his Miami-weight blue suit, he had been rigidly cold from the inside out. Jeremy James Cross. Twenty-two years old. Girl-crazy with a dipsy, can't-catch-me grin. A change-of-life pregnancy, his mother had said to explain the eighteen years between them. Her miracle child. He was glad she hadn't lived to see this.

Jerry's face flowed through his thoughts, lips drawn back. . . . He drank the liquor quickly and forced himself to listen.

" . . . because the electricity to make it is too expensive." Woodie was still talking about ice.

Allison, too, was barely listening. The inner voice was taking assessment: *This isn't too bad. I can handle this. Except him. He's angry. Makes me nervous.* She kept her glance away.

George and Harold were vying determinedly to hold on to some vague territorial arena of their own definition where she was concerned. In her silence, they drifted in and out of conversation with Woodie. As the beer mellowed her stomach, she waited for a break in the commentary. "What's outside?" she asked Woodie.

"Not much. Taxis mostly."

It sounded safe enough, and it would get her away from the bar for a while.

Outside the back door of the airport, Luisita settled on a wooden bench to wait for the local bus. The buzz of conversation, loud and boisterous, was typically American; it had been one of the things hardest to adapt to in her life in Miami. Mayas treated serious things with calm and poise. Americans went at everything with energy and push and abandon. Still, hearing their voices gave her the comfort of familiar sound. Her heart was bumping heavily. She had managed it. She hadn't been discovered.

Watching her things closely, she bought sweet shaved ice from an old Creole vendor. His leather face smiled as she chose also an orange for the long ride on the bus, carefully paying in local coins. She must not be seen spending much money.

She composed her face not to be present. If she was not here, no one could see her. No one would remember. Waiting was the hardest part. Each passing minute might bring one of the officials out the door to demand her papers once again. "Luisita Chun, come with me." Returning to the bench, she sipped the melting ice, her heart straining in its division: part of her longed to be home among *häch winik*—True People—and she savored the sights and sounds of this loved country, the singsong cadence of mellow ladinos with their smiling eyes and wise faces.

Caught in the unspeakable horror of guerrilla warfare in Guatemala, orphaned at twelve, she had fled to a small village over the border into British Honduras, now Belize, carrying frail seven-year-old Sara. She had married José Guero at thirteen and life had been restored to the safe order of centuries—soaking corn, grinding the softened grains each morning for daily meals, the endless carrying of water, beating José's shirts on the river rocks until they were sparkling white, planting the milpas and gardens, everything in rhythm with the days of the seasons and the demands of the gods, as it had been since the time of Hachäkyum. José had not divorced her when no children were forthcoming. Life had been good for seven years.

Then, José's death from the fever and her decision to leave the village for America. The elder, the old *t'o'ohil*, had read her dreams and agreed she might go. But she knew she would not return to a life in her village. Fear was here now, and uncertainty was here, and things were no longer simple; she must not make mistakes. Mistakes would cost everything. Mistakes would keep her from getting Sara to the United States. The papers were safe in the lining of her handbag, good for two more weeks. Somehow in that time she would find her sister and get her out of trouble.

Finished with the beer, Allison walked outside to investigate. Sun-baked taxis were parked in the half shadow of the airport building. Drivers, shirts loose against the heat, reclined on hoods, propped against windshields, to doze in the shade. Without motion they called out hopefully, "Taxi, miss?" She shook her head. Her boots tossed up little puffs of dust as she ventured across the sunlit drive to a Creole vendor dispensing sweet ice to several local children.

She sat in the shade of a wonderful old mango tree, sucked the orangy ice, and watched an old-fashioned school bus, battered and dusty, roll up the airport roadway and groan to a stop. A family of passengers heaved themselves to the ground, visibly exhausted from their ride, and filed into the airport. The driver placed a piece of white cardboard hand-printed "Mango Creek" over the preceding "Belize City." A woman from the plane showed the driver her ticket and climbed into the bus with her suitcase and package to claim a seat.

Within seconds two disreputable station wagons with mud- splattered wheels pulled alongside the bus and six sunburned people efficiently managed themselves into the airport. She spotted a OneEarth logo on a departing backpack and followed the second driver inside to the bar, where he identified himself as Professor Tom Rider, University of Illinois.

"Hello, Woodie." She watched Rider enthusiastically kiss the little woman on her cheek. "Welcome back!"

The professor, she judged, was somewhere in his late thirties, newly sunburned, an attractive graying blond. Just under six feet, he had the energy of a liberated schoolboy, jauntily at home in baggy fatigues and obviously enjoying his leave of absence from professorhood to work in Belize. He addressed the group.

"I'm glad to see all of you, and I appreciate your volunteering for my project. Eve will check you in while I see that my outgoing team gets through departure procedures and on their flights. See you in a bit." With that, the professor took himself off.

"He looks dependable," Allison said to Woodie, who smiled and moved her semaphore eyebrows to indicate the distinct possibility. Woodie's seal of approval gave her license to steal a second glance, in which she discovered Tom Rider checking her out also.

Zachary Cross had not missed Allison's appraisal, nor Rider's double take of his former seatmate. Good luck, Professor, he decreed silently, you're gonna need it. A tap on his shoulder turned him around. She was sunbrowned, medium tall and twenty-two cute, and fully aware of herself. He met confident blue eyes.

"Hi," she said, "I'm Eve Kelsey." She consulted a list of names. You'll be either George or—"

"Zachary Cross."

"—or Zachary Cross is not on my list, which means you're the substitute from Miami," she rattled on without pause, giving him the benefit of a two-hundred-watt smile. "I'm Professor Rider's assistant on the dig."

As she radiated her pleasure with his "substitute from Miami" status, he was slightly at a loss. Not at her attention. Although he had few illusions about his looks and had long ago accepted that his was not a conventionally handsome face, he'd managed reasonable success over the years in attracting beautiful women, primarily because he'd never been intimidated by them.

It had not, however, occurred to him until this moment that there might be a social side to this trip. Admittedly he hadn't thought about much of anything except satisfying his lieutenant by taking some time off.

He watched Eve work the group and studied the remote, incongruous lady from Chicago—a mixture of expensive poise and massive insecurity. A highly unlikely candidate for this kind of expedition, in his view. If she expected Chicago-style care and feeding in this neighborhood, she was in for another think.

Eve moved on to Woodie. "I remember you from last year, don't I? Ellen Woodrow?" There was a minimum of warmth in her greeting.

"Yes." Woodie gave the word two syllables. "Hello, Eve."

"Which makes you Allison Shreve." Eve gave her a fatal inspection that did not miss the lines in the tired face, the expensive haircut, lingered an instant on the wedding band, then an abrupt dismissal to introduce herself to George and Harold with a bright smile for each.

Many rounds of local beer and three hours later Paul and Madeline Miller and Colonel William Sharp, USAF retired, the remaining members of the expedition, were gathered from the incoming Eastern and TACA flights from Houston. Mario ended his shift to go home a rich man, content in his anticipation of making his wife a happy woman.

After a greasy dinner at the airport cafe of fried fish, more beer, and something resembling yams, the group approached the ancient station wagons, prepared for the hundred-and-fifty mile drive to Mango Creek.

Allison was drifty from the beer. Last into the second car, she found herself relegated to the backseat between Woodie at one window and Zachary Cross, with a bottle of beer, at the other.

"Looks like we're still together," he said mildly, sipping the beer as she struggled past his long legs.

Settling onto the sagging cushion, she was instantly

conscious that the collapsed springs forced her body into sweaty contact with him. Her bare arm met his and was instantly slick with perspiration. She could not prevent her leg from pressing firmly against his thigh.

The car lurched out of the parking lot onto the graveled highway.

"We call this 'fat air' in Miami," he said companionably, enjoying in spite of himself the vague but pleasant scent of expensive perfume emanating from her hair. He assessed her rigid posture and frustrated determination not to come into contact with him. If she was already this uptight, he reasoned, she was never gonna survive the rest of this trip.

He finished the beer, slid the bottle to the floor, and looked out the window into the dying light. Once. Just once, he'd like to meet a woman with her style—without the neurotics—in a class he could afford.

Hours crawled by as the cars wound their way through the humid night. Every bounce and sway of the vehicle pressed her against his leg, and she was rigidly aware of his warmth through the Levi's; her skin was sticky under wrinkled linen slacks from trapped moisture where their bodies touched. A lingering smell of masculine perspiration and the vague odor of cigarette smoke clung to him, unsettling her completely. The ride was endless, air hard to breathe; her thoughts dissolved into impenetrable blackness. Finally, exhaustion prevailed and she slept.

Her head slid lightly against his shoulder. A strand of blond hair, glowing platinum in the frail moonlight, lifted with the flow of air to lick along his cheek. Zachary studied her hands—soft, fine-boned, well cared for, curled in sleep like a child, the old-fashioned wide gold band incongruous on the slender fingers. Definitely not a ring she would have chosen, he decided. If she was married, it had to be a sentimental choice from one of the families.

An hour later the station wagons came to a halt in the dark. Disoriented, Allison jerked away from his shoulder in moist confusion and attempted to consult her watch.

"It's past midnight," he said lazily, uninvolved in her distress. "Apparently we've arrived."

"It's the dock at Mango Creek," explained Woodie. "We'll pick up a boat to the hotel. It's out on one of the cays."

As her eyes adjusted from sleep to car headlights to darkness, and finally to light from half a moon—and an astounding sweep of stars—Allison finally saw boatmen standing in two low, narrow fishing boats on the river. The trip literature had indicated travel by boat to the site, but to a nonswimmer the fishing boats looked more like canoes. Oh, God, and she was terrified of water. "If she can do it, I can do it," she repeated numbly to herself.

Groggy, she fumbled for her luggage and deliberately preceded Woodie, lighting the way for the small woman's uneven gait on the treacherous wooden pilings. "If she can do it, I can do it."

Approving Allison's thoughtful treatment of the older woman, Zachary discreetly followed their progress, assuring their safety. At the edge of the dock, he tossed their luggage to the boatman, swung easily into the boat, lifted wispy little Woodie safely aboard, then steadied Allison's awkward entry.

The boatman handed her a life jacket from the bottom of the boat. He watched her slip it on, tie the strings, and carefully choose a seat precisely in the center of the boat, next to Woodie.

"This man is too big. He should be here." The boatman relocated him forward, seating him between the two women, moving Allison to one side, Woodie to the other.

In her new position at the edge of the narrow boat, Allison tried to leave a decent space between them and still avoid the edge.

"Afraid of getting wet?" Zachary observed dryly.

Before she could respond, the loaded boats were allowed to drift away from the dock, out into the river; the engines kicked to life and revved to full speed. At nearly one in the morning, the boatmen were anxious to get home.

In the thin moonlight the narrow, wooden boats flew full throttle, turning and gliding through calmed channels between the cays. Cold increased as they headed out into choppy water. The wind threw heavy, chilled spray over the bow, drenching her face and hair.

From the boat bottom, Zachary pulled a small canvas tarpaulin around her shoulder to shield her from the water.

She closed her eyes to ward off the stinging spray, then, licking her lips, tasted saltwater. They'd gone from the river out into the ocean. Wet and shivering, fear of the open ocean the only thing greater than her fear of him, she finally ducked her head under the canvas and desperately pressed her face into his denim jacket. Rigid with fright, she shut down her mind as the boat lurched through the waves.

Suddenly sobered, Zachary realized she was truly frightened. He reached under the tarpaulin and held her body tightly against his own. What the hell's she doing here, anyway, if she's so scared? he wondered. Probably soaking my cigarettes. Still, he maintained his tight hold, keeping her slight body warm and secure.

Near midnight, the gray bus paused at the Mango Creek crossing long enough for Luisita to climb down with her package and suitcase. Its taillights rumbled into the darkness, leaving her alone and exhausted at the wooden dock. She'd forgotten how difficult travel could be in the cays. Then she saw Tom Rider's waiting boatmen.

"Can you tell me where is the Reyes Hotel?"

"Over there, miss." The boatman pointed across the river. He ferried her to the opposite dock, and she walked the short distance to the small nontourist hotel.

The sleepy young boy who gave her the room key told her they had not heard from Sara. "She went away a long time ago," said the boy. "I think maybe she had the baby."

Luisita questioned him closely, then gave him a quarter to carry her things upstairs to a sparsely furnished room and to wake her very early in the morning. For so much money, he would remember. She lay awake, too anxious in her exhaustion to sleep. Premature birth was something she hadn't considered. The boy had quickly admitted he didn't know whether or not the baby had come. She prayed fervently to Balum that it wasn't true. She didn't have papers for a baby—only her sister.

She had received the panicky call from Sara nineteen days ago.

"Rufino has disappeared—three months now. He was working for some men in Guatemala. I don't know doing what, but two men came here last night. Ladinos. They think I know where he's hiding."

"What do you mean? What happened?"

"They say he stole money. I told them I know nothing, but they didn't believe me. They hit me and threatened to kill me. I'm afraid for the baby."

Luisita, stunned, hadn't known her sister was pregnant. She had been sending birth control pills regularly, but seventeen-year-old Sara must have sold them. It was far too late for recriminations; Sara was in trouble, and fear was pulsing in her voice. "Please, I want to stay with you—it is only two months before the baby is coming."

Two months! "It will take some time—maybe a few weeks." Luisita's mind was racing. She had no idea how long it would take. "You must call me again in three days."

"I have no money." Sara was sobbing.

"Where are you staying?"

"With the *evangelista*."

Luisita knew the man and didn't trust him; if she sent money, Sara might give it to him. And he would take it. "I will send you money tonight. General Delivery at the post office. Are you listening?"

"Yes—General Delivery. I understand."

"It is not for the missionary. Okay? When you call I will know more and we can make a plan. I have to talk to the authorities."

Sara had hung up in tears, and Luisita had been chilled with fright. How on earth could she get her sister into the United States in so short a time? The *t'o'ohil* in her village, old and ill when she'd left, was dead. His son, the new *t'o'ohil*, had little power. There was only the relentless *ts'ul* missionary who demanded one's soul before he would provide help.

José had once asked the missionary for medicine; the

medicine was offered, but traditional payment of corn and squash had been refused. The price for medicine was "He' *wah a na'ksik a wol ti' hesuklisto.*" Will you now lift your spirit to Jesus Christ? The missionary had patiently explained to José that once he became an *evangelista*, the medicine would be provided at no cost. José had refused, unable to imagine what kind of god Jesus Christ could be that he would demand a True Person denounce his gods for medicine to cure an illness. Gods were called upon to help in things men could not accomplish.

Then José had died. The missionary had come down from his house on the hill overlooking the village, had come down with his wife, and the two of them had sat gingerly on wooden stools in the hut José had built for her, to ask the same question again and again. "H*e' wah a na'ksik a wol ti' hesuklisto*?" They told her José would burn in hell because he had not agreed. Did she also want to burn in hell? "H*e' wah a na'ksik a wol ti' hesuklisto*?"

She had waited, politely silent until they left her home, then she had broken the pots and dishes and burned the hut and everything inside, and left to go to the United States. Three years ago. The old *t'o'ohil* had agreed it was best. Now he, too, was gone. There was no one to turn to.

Frail Sara should not travel alone in her condition the route Luisita had taken—a bus to Mexico, from Mexico to Texas, working in each city for fare to the next. Two years it had taken. Crossing into the United States at Brownsville, applying for her green card in Corpus Christi, she'd found employment as a domestic with Paul and Sylvia Goodell, who had sponsored her. They'd offered to sponsor Sara also, but Sara, in love with Rufino, had refused to come to Texas. When Paul Goodell was transferred to Miami, his wife pregnant with Danny, they had taken Luisita with them. She'd taken night courses in second-language English; the Goodells had given her a raise when she had graduated first in her class. Baby Danny was just a year old, and Mrs. Goodell was pregnant again, when the call came from Sara. Somehow she would have to get the money.

She had approached Paul Goodell, afraid to tell him about the men who were threatening her sister, sensing he wouldn't want his family involved. He had listened with sympathy that her sister had been abandoned in the seventh month of her pregnancy but had been upset that Luisita would leave his wife to go to Belize on such short notice. After all they'd tried to do for her, he was sorry, but he would not agree to lend her the money for two airfares. He was, however, willing to employ Sara when she arrived in Miami and would provide a plane ticket.

That evening she had sealed twenty dollars into one of his heavy manila business envelopes and mailed it to Sara.

Sara did not call back. After a week Luisita knew she would have to go to Belize to find her. Without telling the Goodells, she'd applied to the passport office and obtained permission for Sara Luisita Chun to travel to Belize and return to the United States within four weeks. A few days later she'd lied to the clerk that the papers had not arrived in the mail. It had taken ten precious days to convince the woman to issue a duplicate permit. It would have to do. Somehow she and her sister would manage to travel separately, using the same permit, without getting caught.

Still Sara did not call. The Goodells had tried to console her, told her they were sure her sister's husband had returned and that everything was fine; she'd offered incense and prayed to the gods that it was true.

Two days before her flight, she'd been greatly undecided. What if they were right? Perhaps Rufino had returned and everything was settled. It was possible Sara was no longer in the village. Belize was a hundred and ninety miles long and seventy miles wide; a small country, but a huge space in which to find her young sister. Only the gods could arrange such a thing.

Then came a letter from Sara. The men had followed her, she had written, they knew about the call to Luisita. They accused her of calling her husband. They had beaten her and threatened her again. She had lied to them that Rufino was coming back for her in two weeks. She'd been too frightened to stay with the missionary, and a friend had helped her get to Mango Creek, where she was working at the Reyes Hotel for room and board. The letter had been written over two weeks ago.

The next morning Luisita had called Sara at the hotel. The young boy who answered had told her Sara was not there, that she had gone out. He'd agreed to give Sara a message to please call. But Sara had not.

For the next day and night she'd tried desperately not to believe her sister was missing, thought only of how to get her away from Mango Creek and away from the men who were threatening her life.

Running out of time, unwilling to take a chance that the Goodells would stop her, and horrified at her own audacity, Luisita had taken two hundred dollars from Mrs. Goodell's household account, salary that would not be due to her until the end of January, and sewed it and the money from her savings into the lining of a large, inexpensive handbag. Hating herself in her betrayal of the people who had been so kind to her, convinced the fates would extract punishment despite the note pledging to repay the money, she'd cried most of the night.

Yesterday she had called one last time and was told Sara had been gone for two weeks. The man did not know where. After a long debate with herself, she'd taken the gun the Goodells kept in their bedroom closet and a teddy bear from Danny's nursery. She'd ripped its seam and removed enough stuffing to make room for the pistol and sewed it inside. Then she'd waited until Sylvia Goodell retired for her afternoon nap, kissed the sleeping little boy, and hurried out of the house for the last time to catch a bus to the Miami airport.

The airline clerk had eventually accepted her sister's ticket in payment for the flight, and the next several hours had been a nightmare of waiting for the hand of the police to come down on her shoulder. Even seated on the plane, her fears had not relented. She had sighed in relief when the customs official at the Belize airport had not noticed the bear's unusual weight. The bullets were nestled in the huge jar of peanut butter.

At two A.M. the two boats carrying the weary volunteers slid silently into a small landing at Waler's Beach; the hotel, gray and ghostly in the moonlight, loomed safe and warm thirty feet away. The heat of the land descended as they disembarked onto the sand, where it was breathless once again.

The hotel was known locally as the Beached Whale, for its awkward size tail first to the ocean, and unpainted, gray wood construction. Veteran Woodie quickly stumped up the stairs and commandeered a corner room on the second floor.

Allison followed her inside. She looked silently around the room and sagged with fatigue. From the center of the ceiling hung an electric light bulb on a barren cord; aligned along opposing walls were two low wooden bunks with ancient mattresses and questionable pillows.

Her hair still tacky with seawater, she dumped her backpack at the foot of one of the bunks and extracted shampoo and a towel. Out the open window, on the moonlit sand, she saw several wooden picnic tables with benches under plastic tarpaulins. It slowly dawned on her tired mind that it was indeed an open window—no glass, no screens; nor were there mosquito nets over the bunks. Wooden hurricane shutters created a privacy of sorts but thwarted the anemic breeze. She gave Woodie a baleful look. "Tell me there are bathrooms," she said, desperately holding on to the shampoo.

"At the bottom of the front stairs."

"Thank you." She grabbed her towel, added a toothbrush and a robe, and started for the bath, wanting nothing more than the warmth of a welcome shower. At the bottom of the stairs, she found the hotel's concession to tourist sensibilities: a sparse set of duplicate washrooms with no gender designation. Fanciful cardboard signs suspended on string for each side were marked Free.

Tired beyond logic, she inspected the sign on the left door and found In Use on the back. She flipped it over then inched into the unlit room to discover that the metal stall lacked a shower curtain and the sink did not drain. She crossed to the opposite side; no shower curtain here, either.

Defeated, she undressed quickly and stepped into the stall to gasp out loud as cold water struck her in the face. After a futile attempt to find warmer water, she finally turned off the shower and lathered her hair, shivering in the cold. I hate this, I hate this, I hate this, she thought. She turned on the water to rinse.

Footsteps sounded behind her two seconds before cold water hit her in the face again. In bleary focus she saw Zachary Cross do a lazy about-face and mumble, "Sorry."

She yelped in dismay at her loss of privacy and the spray of cold water beating on her skin. Sorry? Sorry for the Scotch in the face. Sorry for the peek in the shower. Enough sorry already!

He retreated to double-check the sign, which indeed said Free. The second washroom was designated In Use, so he waited and pondered with due appreciation his split-second glimpse of full, perfect breasts and her sudsy embarrassment.

"Hey," he said when she stalked out, "I didn't mean to walk in on you. You didn't turn over the sign." He pointed out the Free sign hanging in the doorway, but the lady from Chicago glared at him, unamused, and stiffly climbed the stairs.

He flipped the sign to In Use and reentered the room to strip for his shower, which he, in turn, discovered to be colder than the ocean water. Damn! He wondered how she was going to handle two weeks of cold bathing in a semipublic bathhouse. What the hell was she doing here, anyway? Probably had a designer sleeping bag. Not that he cared.

He dozed until five A.M. Unable to sleep in daylight, restless to know his surroundings, he quietly left the room to take a look around in the pale-pink-and-golden wash of sunrise. The boat landing reached out into ocean water that was clear as glass. A medium-size, brick red starfish lolled in shallow, crystal water near the shore. Half a dozen mangrove cays dotted the seascape, not a cloud on the horizon—it would be hot today.

A few hundred feet down the beach was another small hotel. He counted seven wooden houses nestled among the trunks of tall, fluttering palms, each built atop pilings six to eight feet high. Small wooden outhouses teetered at the end of rickety walkways out over the water. He grinned at the efficiency of rural plumbing and wondered what the local people thought of the flush toilets at the hotels.

The only sounds were soft lap-lappings of water, complaints of gulls against frigate birds, a rooster reannouncing the thin, clear sunrise in a persistently scratchy *oo-o-roo-hoo* crow. He drank in the quiet. Littering the beach in the increasing golden light was a random assortment of fishing equipment due repair. Here and there were palm fronds, piles of conch shells—Pepto maws gaping empty, absent residents long since devoured by villagers. Coconut palms held smooth, green husked fruit tight in their fronds. He wondered how long it would be, if he gave it all up, before he got bored here.

A rustic seventy-gallon tank at the side of the hotel, fed by a rainspout from the metal roof, provided guests with rainwater for drinking; a giant rose-purple bougainvillea next to the tank paid its rent by providing a brilliant shade to cool the water. Frigate birds and seagulls wheeled and turned in circles at the shoreline.

The boatmen were back, one of them with three pinkly fresh fish laid out on a sturdy plank across the prow. Ankle deep in water, the boatman, Nathaniel, expertly gutted the largest fish and tossed the bloody offal to the waiting seabirds.

As he watched the birds steal the fishy prize from one another, Zachary had a sudden thought of his brother's smile. Jerry had taken great pride in his fishing skill. Somewhere in the sealed apartment was a ton of gear. . . .

"You eat what we catch," said Nathaniel, smiling. "Tonight will be this fish." Translucent scales flew, as he scraped the pliant body with his knife. "Catch him this morning." He flopped the fish over and began scaling the pink belly on the other side.

Zachary smiled also; it had been his first thought of Jerry without a blackened face. Grateful tears welled in his eyes, and he walked down the beach to allow the welcome grief.

Luisita was awake when the little boy tapped on her door. His name was Tonio. She asked him for tea, an American habit she enjoyed. While the boy was gone, she finished resewing the bear. The heavy pistol and a few extra bullets were safe in the bottom of her purse; her thoughts centered on her missing sister. What kind of men would attack and hurt a pregnant woman? Would such men be willing to kill her sister in an attempt to locate Rufino? Surely it was not possible. But why had her sister left the hotel? She was impatient until the boy returned with the tea. "Mrs. Reyes is in the kitchen," he informed her.

Luisita sipped the tea cooled with canned milk, gathering in warmed strength. A few minutes later she slipped into the hotel kitchen and approached the woman selecting fish from several small children.

"Mrs. Reyes? I am Luisita Chun, sister to Sara. The boy tells me Sara is not here. Can you tell me where I can find her?"

The woman paid the children for the fish and shooed them away, face impassive.

"Please, I know she's in trouble, and the baby is due very soon. Surely she told you about me. I am here to help her."

"The baby is here." Corla Reyes began the preparation of breakfast for her guests. "Fifteen, maybe sixteen days ago, she knock on my door to say her water is broken." She broke eggs into a large skillet, speared the yolks and stirred them about with a spatula. "She told me the baby was too soon, not due for another five weeks." Corla shrugged. "Three o'clock in the night the baby still would not come. So, I take her to the medical center at Maya Mopan."

With great effort, Luisita listened politely for the woman to finish the story.

"I stay with her as long as I can," Corla explained. "But my hotel is busy and I must be here. She was still in labor when I came home." The cooked eggs spilled into a large blue bowl. "I have not heard from her since then, and I have no one to help me in the kitchen," she said accusingly, shaking a huge, blackened skillet of bacon. "There were bruises on her face, and on her body."

Luisita fielded the woman's piercing gaze. "Some men are looking for her husband," she said simply. "They think she knows where he is hiding."

"I have not said where Sara has gone. There have been questions about her."

Clearly Corla wanted no trouble descending upon her house.

"Her husband has abandoned her," Luisita admitted. "Three months ago. These men say he stole money. It may be true, I don't know."

Corla seemed satisfied, carefully drained the bacon fat into a small container before transferring the fried meat onto a large oval platter.

"I am afraid for her. If these men find out where she is, it could be bad for her." Luisita's worry filled the space between them.

"No one knows but me," Corla assured her.

Her worry increased. They would have crossed the river to go to Maya Mopan. A birth in the middle of the night requiring a trip to the hospital would be worthy of gossip among the boatmen.

"You must call there," said Corla, proud that her hotel had a telephone. "The medical center has a telephone, too." She accepted payment for the call.

After three frustrating attempts, Luisita reached a clerk in the record office of the medical center. "I wish to know about a patient, Sara Copal." She spelled the name.

"One moment."

Rustling papers and the faint chatter of conversation filled the background. The voice returned. "We have no record of Sara Copal. Why was she here?"

"She was pregnant and in labor two weeks ago, maybe sixteen days." More rustling and an interminable wait.

"We have no record of this woman, or a baby, for this name."

"She was there! She was in labor for a long time—a young woman, brought in late at night!" Her fear transmitted itself through the phone. "The baby may have been premature. Surely someone will remember."

"Perhaps one of the doctors," said the young voice. "A premature child or the death of a child must be discussed with the doctor in charge. I cannot give you such information. Please, you must come to the center." The line was disconnected.

Luisita replaced the useless instrument in its cradle and sought Corla in the kitchen. "Please, I must go to the medical center." Her agitation made it difficult to think. "Is there a bus? It's been a long time since I was here."

"No bus. I have a car, and a driver can take you as soon as he returns," said Corla.

"How soon? I would like to go right away."

"Maybe soon. Who can tell?"

"Is there another way?"

"Cars are very scarce. He will come back soon. It is best

to wait. Did you eat breakfast?" Corla demanded.

"I was not hungry this morning."

"I will make you breakfast and you will sleep until the driver comes," Corla pronounced. "Then you can go to the medical center."

Luisita was suddenly too tired to argue. "I don't want anyone to know I am here," she said quietly.

"You are a Mayan woman, traveling alone, who stays at a hotel and not in a village," Corla said. "It has already been noticed. I do not have to tell anyone."

Six o'clock arrived. Allison swung her legs over the side of her bunk. Last night, still fuming from her unprivate shower, she had discovered there was no electrical outlet for her hair dryer. Past caring, she'd gone to sleep with wet hair. Now she stared grimly into her compact mirror—her hair was hopeless. She smoothed a dab of ointment across her shoulder, and the pulling skin eased appreciably.

Carefully facing Woodie, she changed into a fresh T-shirt, discarding the one she'd slept in. "Uhh, God," she groaned. "Let there be coffee!"

Two frail but mercifully hot cups of instant coffee later, she was seated at one of the picnic tables in the sandy yard, which served as a mess hall. The taste of stale coffee was unenhanced by the addition of canned milk, a flavor she hated. She smiled her thanks when Woodie passed a bowl of scrambled eggs, then eye-watering hot sauce. Coconut muffins, rock hard and aesthetically less than appealing, turned out to be savory, still warm from baking, even with what must have been margarine before it melted. The temperature was already in the high seventies.

Woodie's left eyebrow dipped slightly as she buttered a muffin, indicating her opinion of the discussion at the head table.

Eve was holding court in a skimpy tank top and a

wrapped skirt that showed off a deep, all-over tan, flirting with all three men. Allison was suddenly aware of her own pale skin and naked face. With her hair hidden under the straw hat, she recognized envy. Envy for the youth of the girl and her unlined face and browned body—most of all, her supreme and utter confidence. Envy for the time when she, too, had taken herself for granted.

The leaden weight of the knowledge of when and how it had ended sat in her brain, anything resembling carefree now beyond memory. She added another spoonful of instant in an attempt to strengthen her coffee and listened with one ear as Eve zeroed in on Zachary.

"So what do you do in Miami?" Eve stirred her coffee and licked the spoon with suggestive deliberation.

"Why? You planning to come see me?" He hadn't been hit on this openly in years. Certainly she was cute and sexy, but he didn't give up information out of habit, certainly without knowing what Eve planned to do with it.

"We didn't get a background sheet on you, and I need to know what kinds of skills and abilities I can call on. . . ." She smiled a lazy smile, ripe with invitation.

"Skills?"

"In the event of an emergency—CPR training, boating experience—whatever." Eve dismissed Harold and George, fully intrigued with the mysterious Mr. Cross.

He considered a moment; this was fair. "I'm an excellent swimmer, fair with boats . . . I've performed CPR."

"CPR? Training, or real life?" Eve's teasing blue eyes gazed into slightly bemused brown ones.

"Depends on what you consider 'real life.'"

"Okay . . . how many times have you used your training?" Eve was enjoying center stage.

"Three," he finally responded, then amended, "Four times." Once had been Stephanie Marie Cross. He'd come within inches of losing her. It had sealed the death of his marriage to Sue, and he didn't like to think about it.

"Four times?! That's . . . unusual." Eve's skepticism was not quite hidden.

After a long pause he enumerated, "An auto accident, two heart attacks, and a drowning." He was no longer amused.

"What on earth do you do?"

At her end of the table, Allison unconsciously waited for his answer.

"I'm a police detective. A cop."

Eve blinked, momentarily silenced. A police officer. From his face, she'd guessed blue collar. This was heavier action than she'd anticipated.

Then, in a voice laden with an irony only he understood, "If we run into any dope dealers, I'll be real handy."

Allison blanched at the word *cop*. The rest was lost in the familiar roar of nonsound in her ears, signaling withdrawal. A cop! She was going under. First the drinking and the cigarettes . . . He was a cop. She swallowed dryly, abandoned the coffee, walked quickly away from the table and up the stairs to her room.

Two minutes later Woodie came in and sat on the opposite bunk. "What is it, honey?"

"Oh, God, Woodie," she murmured, "I thought I could do it, but now I don't know."

"Thought you could do what?" Woodie busied herself relacing her special boot. "Get away from whatever it is by coming out here to the boonies?"

"Yes." She fought to slow down the withdrawal.

"Can't be done. I'm an old lady and I know a few things. And one is—you take your self wherever you go. If you ain't happy with it, you got to change it, not move it around like furniture."

Allison had to smile at this succinct summing up of life. Her center stabilized, finally, to the point where she could look into Woodie's crinkled face. "I lost my mother two years ago. She would have liked you."

A long silence.

"I've been sort of . . . out of the world for a while. I had an . . . emotional breakdown," she said haltingly. "This trip is . . . my first big trial for myself with people who don't know about me, you know?" The words were coming out in carefully leveled teaspoons.

Woodie listened quietly. This explained the too dark circles in the beautiful face.

"I used to travel all the time. I was a fashion model. Mostly magazines—some runway work. . . ."

She took in a deep sigh. She and her shrink had been through this a hundred times. Trust in someone. Let them know what's inside you; learn they'll accept you. It's the only way to know they won't hurt you.

"Then . . ." She let out the breath. "Then I was raped, three years ago, and . . ." Finally, she forced it out. "It was bad . . . he was a cop." And other cops didn't believe me, called me a liar, threatened me! She was losing control. Clenching her hands into fists, she forced her nails deep into the soft tissue behind her thumbs, a physical pain to focus on.

Woodie's face worked in sadness. Allison fought to control her rush of feelings and moved on, breathing in short, tight breaths. "He was sent to prison. My mother died during the trial—a heart attack. I couldn't . . . I went into a hospital. Couldn't stop crying." There. Enough was out. Her body was as taut as a kettledrum.

"That's a lot to handle, honey." Woodie placed a hand lightly on her rigid shoulder, looked down into her face, sending strength. "Don't sell yourself short," came her voice calmly, gently. "You got through all that. This'll be a piece of cake."

Allison's body slowly released some of the tension at Woodie's warm response. "I don't want anyone else . . ." she began, but Woodie shook her head.

"Honey, I figure if you want anyone to know, you'll tell 'em. It ain't my business." She stomped to the door. "You about ready?"

She smiled at Woodie's retreating back. "My shrink'd like you, too." She grabbed her backpack and followed the sprightly figure down the stairs. *If she can do it,* declared the little voice, *You can do it.*

◆ ◆ ◆

Zachary observed Allison's rapid departure from the breakfast table; a few minutes later he saw her follow Woodie out of the hotel and maneuver seating in the larger boat. Was it his cop's imagination, or had she waited until he'd settled into Nathaniel's smaller, faster craft?

So. The lady from Chicago didn't like cops. Not that unusual. Most people weren't comfortable around cops until they were in trouble. Then again, maybe she had something to hide. He'd made some crack about drugs just before she'd left the table. Someone that thin might be acquainted . . .

Still, he found himself annoyed. He hadn't intended to reveal himself as a police officer until he knew all the players. He followed that observation with the truth that a) he was on vacation, and b) he didn't have to know all the players, and c) he may as well know off the top if it was going to make a difference. For some women, it did. Cops were notoriously underpaid, and even without her makeup this morning, she had the high-maintenance look of an expensive woman.

He helped Nathaniel cast off. It wasn't the first time he'd been disappointed. The hell with her.

4

The volunteers were charged by breakfast and high on the anticipation of getting to the dig. As they sped through the water in the fishing boats, they got their first daylight look at the tangled clumps of mangrove and the lagoons that comprised the cays and separated the expedition from the Waler's Beach Hotel on the ocean from the scurvy station wagons waiting inland at Mango Creek.

At the crossing, Allison once again carefully managed seating in a car separate from him, confirming his suspicions, but he was soon caught up in studying the countryside as they drove up into the lower foothills of the Maya Mountains. From sea level, these hills had appeared as layered ridges of deep and gentle greens, blending into purple-indigo mountains; on the red dirt-gravel road, he saw the greens level out to scrub pine, then massive underbrush and tangles of vine-covered trees that obscured vision past a few feet off the berm. The treetops inched taller as land elevation slowly raised the vegetation away from the saltwater table under the marshy ground.

Passing few houses and fewer vehicles, negotiating potholes and washed-out sections of the road, the station wagons eventually turned onto a smaller dirt road and passed a sign proclaiming "Maya Mopan Village." They came to a stop in the small community, and two young men with machetes quickly climbed onto the roof of Allison's station wagon. Mayan women with babies and smaller dark-eyed children peeked from the neat thatched huts as the two-vehicle caravan lurched along the narrow track to a privately owned banana plantation.

After a stop at Earl Morgan's farmhouse to pick up equipment, it was another half hour back through a swampy access road to the site. They parked the cars and looked across a bog to a cleared area with a crude wooden table shaded by a light tarpaulin. The clearing was surrounded with what appeared to be small hills twenty to thirty feet high, covered with trees and vines.

Energized at being in this ancient place at last, Allison listened as Tom Rider instructed the group.

"We've walked the site and we know it's a Mayan ruin from the way the mounds are laid out and from the evidence of the worked stone that's visible. 'Worked' stone," he continued, "shows evidence of being squared. It has flat sides. You can see blocks sticking out of the overburden on some of the larger pyramids."

Fascinated, Allison realized the hills were mounds—and the mounds were pyramids!

"We carbon-dated some of the artifacts found here last year, and we know the top layer of the site is about four hundred years old, so don't look for the elaborate carvings of an older site. The first thing I'll want to do is complete a survey." Rider supervised Eve's unloading of equipment as he spoke. "We'll need three teams."

Each of the volunteers shouldered a shovel or pickax, carried trowels and machetes across the bog to the center of the clearing.

"The first team will work with me surveying the areas we've cleared over the past two weeks. The second will work with machetes cutting vines and underbrush. You'll finish clearing the large structure behind us. . . ." He gestured at the largest mound. "Put everything into piles for burning." He nodded toward the Mayas. "They'll show you how."

Zachary approached the men waiting quietly in the background, offering his hand. The first man introduced himself, "I am Emilio Chaya." Then, with pride, "Osari is my brother."

Shaking hands with Osari, Zachary was pierced by the thought that he would never again have an opportunity to introduce a brother. Christ, it didn't ever stop. He indicated the group of machetes. "You mind helping me pick out one of these?"

Emilio acknowledged his pleasure at the compliment by sorting through the knives, thumbing the edges, feeling their balance. Finally he handed over his choice. "Try this one."

Harold strolled over to join them while the professor proceeded to explain the duties.

"The third team will work with Eve removing matrix—uh, soil, from the top of the largest structure and work it through sifters with trowels. She'll show you what we're looking for."

As the volunteers sorted themselves out according to ability and work preference, Zachary smiled when he heard Rider suggest to Allison that she work with him surveying—and saw the move had not gone unnoticed by Eve. He'd bet the farm that Eve Kelsey and Professor Rider were back to a "professional relationship." Which, if true, put her heavy hitting into better perspective.

He gained enormous respect for the Mayas' ability over the next few hours, particularly when he learned each man was being paid eight Belize dollars—four dollars American—for the day's work.

"I figure Zachary and I, between us, are paying your boss somewhere in the neighborhood of fifty dollars a day for the privilege of learning machete work," Harold informed them with a wry grin.

"Akyantho," said Osari to his brother, and the two laughed at great length at the incredible foolishness of the foreigners. Paying to do machete work. Who could understand them?

The brothers were ageless: small by American standards —a little over five feet—they were reticent, wiry men, with broad faces, high cheekbones, and black, intelligent eyes; the heavy machetes came to their waists in length. Zachary immediately recognized their affinity with the forest, similar to his awareness of the pulse of Miami. It was apparent they felt, rather than studied, the thickness of the air and the depth of the jungle growth.

Emilio and Osari in turn found the towering Americans' notice of ordinary birds, insects, trees, and flowers as worthy of photographs, as well as their flamboyant and unusual attire, of great interest. They had not heard of Indiana Jones, thus did not properly appreciate Harold's costume, but they posed importantly for pictures with him, with wide smiles.

"Allison." Tom Rider was at her elbow. "As a fellow Chicagoan, would you like to help me complete the final survey?"

Working with the professor would keep her amply distant from Detective Cross. "Of course," she responded. She and another volunteer, Madeline Miller, followed Rider as he fought his way through underbrush around the largest pyramid to a cleared area in which three parallel mounds were quite discernible, denuded of trees and brush.

Rider gave Madeline a sighting stake attached to a line and directed her to the edge of the farthest mound, several yards away.

"We think these are house mounds for lesser priests," he said to Allison. "If you'll make the entries here on the diagram as I call them out." He handed her a pencil and a clipboard with a drawing of the entire site.

Madeline set the stake, and he took the sighting measurements, then directed her to a new position. While they waited he asked casually, "How long have you lived in Chicago?"

"Ten years," she replied. "Originally from a little town in Ohio. Springfield."

"Chicago born and bred," he said proudly. "So where is Mr. Shreve, or are you one of those independent career women?"

So the survey included her after all, with varying degrees of subtlety. Minimal to minute. "He's in Chicago." It was a technical truth. Mr. Shreve was her grandfather. Her father had disappeared into the bowels of the Broadway district in New York City when she was twelve, and she and her mother had moved to Chicago, where her grandfather had welcomed them into his huge old apartment.

"Your information sheet listed you as a photographer," he pursued. "Portraits, weddings, stuff like that?"

"Fashion."

From the blank look on his face, it was apparent that fashion was out of his realm, and she relaxed, knowing there was little chance he'd recognize her. In the distance, Zachary and Harold were cutting and pulling brush with the Mayas on the top of the pyramid. "How did you find the site?" she asked to change the subject. "Aerial photography?"

"Nothing so exotic," he said. "The uncle of one of my students owns the place. I made a financial arrangement with him, so anything I find belongs to me. The Belize government allows me to study it so long as it eventually comes back to their national museum."

Madeline, worried about snakes, proceeded to her next location with cautious deliberation. Eve approached to report on the progress of the other teams, and Rider glanced up to assess the sky with impatience. "I wish we'd had this weather ten days ago. We had a late rain and the first team lost a lot of time," he complained. "We're behind. We should have cleared that main structure by now. We can only get those four-wheels through so much muck and water. If it rains again, we're shut down. The Mayas disappear and everything comes to a halt until we locate new ones."

"New cars?" She didn't follow.

Rider moved off to get Madeline's attention, and Eve responded. "New machete workers. They don't like the work, and they have to be really desperate to take the job. They're not very reliable."

"Maybe they tire of helping people like us cart off their history." Although she smiled as she said it and managed not to put an emotional load on the statement, Allison didn't care for the young girl's offhand dismissal of a complex, ancient people as "unreliable." Eve gave her a withering glance, without response, and walked away.

After a few more minutes Allison managed to trade places with a grateful Madeline, and the survey was completed in time for lunch.

The second hour, Zachary sat for a moment, resting from the unusual exertion, and watched Harold exhaust himself. "Hey, Harold," he called. "I'm going to tell Rider you owe him more money. You're enjoying this too much."

Harold laughed. He was indeed having a grand time crashing and smashing through the jungle.

The Chaya brothers grinned also as they recognized Zachary's humor. "Akyantho," repeated Emilio, and Osari laughed out loud.

"What's Akianto?" he asked, stumbling over the unfamiliar language.

"Akyantho," corrected Emilio. "He's the god who protects white men. He also invented the machete." Squatting on the ground to drink, he looked up at Zachary, his eyes snapping with amusement. "Mayas learned to use the machete with great skill. We cut trails into the forests and make clearings for our crops. But the poor white men who lived in big cities had soft hands, and the machete raised painful blisters on his palms and fingers."

Zachary laughed and showed Emilio his blistering palm.

"See," said Emilio. "Akyantho took pity on the white man and invented *ta'k'in*— money. He gave them much *ta'k'in* so they would not have to use the machete and suffer the blisters."

Gesturing to himself and Harold, Zachary said wryly, "These two white men have been paying much *ta'k'in* for the privilege of raising blisters."

Emilio and Osari looked at each other with wide smiles.

"I'm going to tell Rider I want some of my *ta'k'in* back."

"You better say 'money.' *Ta'k'in* means 'shit of the sun,'" said the grinning Osari, and walked away to continue the sweaty work.

"Shit of the sun." Zachary laughed at the apt description of money. Pursuit of gold caused more shit than the world wanted to know about.

Thereafter, he kept pace with the brothers. Slashing slowly forward through the tangled undergrowth, he measured the lowering tension in his body. This was what he'd come to do—tire his body and ease his mind. It had been too long since he'd worked off enough anger to allow the world to slide by a bit. Peace was something *ta'k'in* couldn't buy.

Spying a furtive, squatty animal as it jumped from its burrow through the underbrush, Emilio paused for an instant, then deftly killed it with his machete. It had looked to Zachary like a huge rat, but on closer inspection he saw it was an armadillo. Emilio's grin of pride was unmistakable. It would be a meat dinner for his family that night.

The three worked two hours more, stopping occasionally to drink rainwater brought with them from the hotel. After lunch Rider pulled Zachary aside. "I've finished the survey and I'd like your help with what I think is a fallen stela."

Zachary read his excitement and was curious to see the stone. He knew little about Mayan culture but was aware that stelae were somewhat akin to ancient billboards. Large flat stones, placed upright like totem poles, they were usually carved, sometimes painted in stucco with information about a village.

Rider confirmed his knowledge. "No possibility of color after four hundred years, but a carving could give us a clue to the importance of this site. Mayan symbols and codes are understood now. Most of it was written to impress the peons, so it's pretty basic stuff. Dates and names, mostly."

With a tree branch acting as lever and a rock fulcrum, they managed to turn over the huge limestone slab to discover a small carving on the downed side.

The professor was excited. "This is terrific," he enthused. "It's been preserved from erosion and rain damage, and the image is quite clear. With this, I can get funding." He called Eve over to take an impression of the carving.

Several photographs and drawings later, the professor approached Eve and Zachary. "I'd prefer you not mention this to anyone else in the group. I'd like to keep the information as quiet as possible. News of a carving is an invitation to theft."

As a further precaution, with Eve's help they returned the stone to its original resting place, then Zachary rejoined Harold and the Chaya brothers on top of the pyramid and began firing the piles of leaves and felled vines and brush.

The survey completed, Allison joined Woodie and Colonel Sharp at one of the test sites on top of the central pyramid. Soon she stood in a low pit, passing up dirt and detritus with a long handled shovel so they could sort it through a square wooden frame covered with wire screen. As a team they had accumulated a dozen broken pieces of pottery when Eve came through to inspect their efforts.

"This looks like fill dirt that was brought in to shore up a house foundation or a stairway," she decreed, unimpressed at their trove, and moved them to another spot near the burnings. "Try here."

Within the next two hours they located nearly three dozen artifacts, including several pieces of a ceremonial plate and half a dozen flakes of obsidian. Each find, after being passed around the group for oohs and aahs, photographs, and inspection, was placed in a plastic bag with a small data card identifying their area of the dig and its exact location.

Eve collected the plastic bags for safekeeping and eventual evaluation by Rider. "It will be unusual to find anything whole," she told them. "Mayas apparently destroyed everything on a periodic basis in some kind of renewal ritual."

The three developed a working rhythm as Allison passed matrix onto the screen with her shovel, and the colonel and Woodie smooshed it through the wire. The rhythm was broken when a small scorpion rode in her shovel and landed in the sifter.

"Ya'll watch out for these heah monsters," drawled the colonel, using his trowel to fling the bony creature onto a nearby heap of sifted soil. "T'rantulas bite more often," he declared, "but some of these heah scorpions have venom that can kill ya." He tamped the brittle body into the pile of sifted earth with the trowel handle and covered it over. "That ought to give 'im something to do."

When she traded places with the colonel to give him a break from the sifting, she was thrilled she'd had the foresight to bring heavy leather gloves to protect against ugly creatures with four-plus legs and unhealthy manners.

A small distance away, Zachary found himself watching her with interest as he and George dragged underbrush into piles for burning. He noted the sensible leather gloves and admired her spirit as she handled the shovel with more and more efficiency, doing her full share, undeterred by scorpions or spiders. The lady he'd met on the plane surely hadn't looked the type.

He thought of her fragile appearance that morning at breakfast and remembered the feel of her too thin body and her fear on the boat ride last night. There had to be a pretty strong core under that soft exterior. By far the most interesting woman in the group. Maybe I ought to find out what she's got against cops, he mused.

In the late afternoon a serenity descended from the treetops onto the crown of the pyramid. Allison had the sense of a daily occurrence of this solitude in the four hundred or so years since the pyramids had been inhabited. A timeless event. The quiet moment when a day's oppressive heat gave over to the first cool movement of evening, the subtle change in light, and the brief silence of wild creatures, large and small.

For a few seconds aloneness descended, also. It had been happening lately. Her shrink had said it was good to feel it, but she wasn't so sure. It always came when something happened and then disappeared utterly: events she couldn't share, impossible to convey or describe to someone not there to feel it, that engulfed her in a terrible sense of isolation. It had happened just now. She wasn't alone, but she was lonely, just the same.

Sensing she was being watched, she looked up to catch Zachary's thoughtful gaze before he could look away. He held her glance a shade longer than necessary before smiling an acknowledgment at the shared moment, then turned to toss an errant vine into the fire. She realized she was a little thrown by the tiny encounter. She'd wanted sharing—well, here was sharing. And something else, long buried and difficult to assess, being thrust unwanted into her conscious mind. Uncomfortable. Physical.

Examining her confusion, she was resistant at first, then astonished to admit her interest in this thoroughly unlikely person. A surly, provoking man who smoked, who drank entirely too much and looked through her most of the time. The first man she'd had any remote attraction for . . . She forced herself to complete the thought: since that horrible weekend three years ago.

On the drive back to the toolsheds at the plantation, she was too late to ride with the professor and found herself in the same car with Zachary. He sat in front next to Eve. *This is some kind of mind game you're playing*, accused her silent self. *You've located someone who's completely safe because he's the opposite of anything you want.*

She stared in confusion at the back of his neck. A man who'd yelled at her on the plane, yet held her secure on the cold, wet boat ride. She studied his damp hairline and the sweat-stained workshirt across square shoulders.

He shifted his arm and placed it along the back of the seat, above Eve's shoulders. A man who flirts with young girls, she thought, "vacation romance" stamped all over him. She tried looking out the window, annoyed and ill at ease. Why did she care? If you thought he'd give you the time of day, you'd hide in an attic, she admonished herself. You're tired, that's all. It will all be gone tomorrow.

While Tom Rider made a courtesy call on the plantation owner, the volunteers stored their tools in sheds for the night. Woodie and the colonel asked Emilio to pose for pictures with the armadillo. He was proud to do so. Harold poked at the animal's body with his machete and jokingly posed with it, announcing he would henceforth answer to "Indiana" Harold. The cameras clicked away.

Eve joined the group and frowned in displeasure. "Why'd you kill it?"

"Eat him. He's good," he answered. "Cook him—like 'possum."

Her grim opinion of his answer was reflected in her face. Indiana Harold's face indicated he wasn't too sure about this, either.

Zachary's eyes crinkled in amusement, softening the hard line of his jaw. Of course he was going to eat it. In order to eat it, he'd had to kill it. No different from a Thanksgiving turkey.

"I wouldn't eat 'possum, either," Eve declared to no one in particular.

Zachary decided to enter the conversation. "Oh, I don't know," he said, never having eaten 'possum in his life, "it's pretty good." He gave the group a dead-sober stare. "A little stringy for my taste."

Sensing his amusement at her expense, Eve dropped the subject.

Allison added his support of Emilio to her assessment of this man who caused such emotional turmoil; it had been an effective reminder to Eve that she was a guest in Emilio's country, where hunger was a way of life.

They stopped in the Mayan village long enough to drop off Emilio and Osari. Half an hour later, about three hundred yards from the dock at Mango Creek, the cars swung to the side of the road in front of a rustic, rattletrap building designated Lisa's Cafe.

"Drinks all around," declared Tom Rider, "in honor of our first discoveries."

The volunteers, hot and tired from their first day as neoarchaeologists, duly proud of their finds, were in a proper mood to party. The savvy owner of Lisa's quickly pulled out his tape of local music and punched a new cassette into his sound system. He routinely made deals with tourists for their cassette tapes, and everyone within fifty miles knew where to come for the latest rock and roll. In seconds, Bruce Springsteen was rocking "Born in the USA" full-bore for the benefit of the Americans.

When Zachary helped Woodie from the backseat of the car, he noticed a young boy holding the hand of his young sister. He gave the little girl a grin, and she hid behind her brother's legs, as all shy little girls do.

Allison watched from inside the cafe as Zachary dug into his jacket pocket and came up with an opened package of Doublemint. He hunkered down slowly to reduce his imposing six feet to little-girl eye level. He held the gum just out of reach.

"What's your name, little one?" She was wrapped around the boy's legs like a vine. "You like chewing gum?"

She let go of a pant leg and held out one hand, clinging to safety with the other.

He waited. It was a big prize. She edged around to where he could see huge brown eyes and spiky lashes before he allowed a grubby hand to grasp the gum. He kept back one piece for the boy, who grinned his thanks. Then he tousled the girl's hair, undoubled his stiffening body, and took himself on into the cafe. Inside, he ordered a double rum and Coke, knowing it would hit him faster than the local beer. The little girl reminded him of his daughter at that age, and he didn't want to think about Steffie just now.

Allison moved quickly to the dance floor with her drink. The familiar cola flavor was warmed with rum and chilled with real ice. She drank thirstily for the cold.

"Allison!" Indiana pounced on her, one step ahead of George. "You want to dance?" Before she could reply, he triumphantly handed the balance of her drink to George and pulled her onto the dance floor.

As alcohol flowed into the tired and thirsty group, a party cranked into full gear. Caught up, Allison laughed out loud, suddenly free to enjoy being three thousand miles from home and dancing to good old American rock and roll in a funny little cafe in a river town in Central America. In the space of one day, life was less complicated, no one had recognized her, and two men wanted to dance with her. She hadn't danced in years and realized she had forgotten how good it was. She fell into the familiar steps with ease.

From a darkened corner of the floor, Zachary observed that Indiana Harold didn't quite hold his own with her more sophisticated style; and, that Allison, a natural dancer, was enjoying herself, hiking boots and all, as she subtly adapted to Harold's lesser ability. Trying to place her age, he studied her slender body. She moved with a simple, fluid grace that came only with practice and a feel for music. He'd guess late twenties—except for those lines in her face.

He settled on thirty-one. Younger when she smiled. It was the first time he'd seen her relaxed enough to have fun. She had a generous smile, he decided. Too bad she didn't use it more often.

He called up a memory of her profile just before she'd caught him watching her this afternoon. Something nagged just underneath his mind. In the quiet and the change in light, there had been a softness in her face, followed by sadness. Just for the hell of it, he decided to ask her to dance.

The colonel and Woodie joined the dancers in their own version of rock-swing as the song wound down. He finished his drink and was positioning himself near Allison when Eve took the glass out of his hand, put it on one of the tables, and pulled him onto the floor. George cut in on Indiana to dance with Allison to an old Lionel Richie ballad.

"So, how does this stack up against being a policeman?" asked Eve. "Must be pretty boring."

"No, I kind of enjoyed the change." She was a fair dancer, and he was getting into the music.

She lifted his left hand and inspected his ring finger. "No line from a wedding band—no wife?"

"Not anymore."

"How long ago?"

"Three years and change."

Openly happy with this answer, Eve settled her head on his shoulder.

The music left his mind and he moved on automatically. He and Sue had called it quits after the nightmare of Steffie's fifth birthday. He'd been on the phone at Aunt Opal's beach cottage. Sue was framed in the bay window—down the beach, as usual chatting up some guy.

About the time he realized there was no Steffie in her shiny new blue bathing suit, he saw Sue look around for her. Then she'd screamed and started running, the guy right behind.

It had been a lifetime in frantic slow-motion churning in loose sand down to the water, he and the guy finally finding his daughter, pulling her limp body out of the dead green Atlantic. Another lifetime when he couldn't get her to breathe, with Sue screaming at him, hysterical. A double lifetime as he willed himself not to panic, ordered the beach bum to call paramedics. Then he'd started the CPR rhythm. Breathing air into her tiny nose and mouth. Not too much. Not an adult. Pushing her little blue chest with short stiff bursts—counting to ten, breathing; counting to ten again, breathing. He'd cracked two of her ribs, but she was pink and her heart beating steadily when the ambulance arrived twenty minutes later. He broke into a cold sweat whenever he thought about it. He realized Eve was staring at him.

"From the look on your face, it must have been an unpleasant divorce."

Not true. It had been coldly polite. And permanent. He hadn't been able to forgive her, and Sue had never forgiven herself. They were even. And his daughter was wonderful, charming, and growing up a mile a minute. Missing her little eight-year-old face, he was testy. "That's none of your business."

"You're right. I'm sorry." Eve was hardly contrite. "But I'm glad there's no wife. And," she continued, "if there was a serious girlfriend . . . either she'd be here with you, or you wouldn't be here at all. So that makes you available." This time she was right. "So, do you investigate murders in Miami?"

"That's homicide," he answered. "I'm a vice detective." He'd seen too many dead bodies in Homicide; six years ago he'd transferred to Vice, where his rugged features made him a natural for victim detail and undercover work.

"Miami Vice? Like, uh, what's his name, Sonny Crockett?"

"Yeah." If he ever met Don Johnson, he'd probably punch him out.

"You ride around in a white Ferrari?"

So far he'd had this particular conversation forty-six times—dates, friends, friends of friends, friends of relatives, idle cocktail conversations. He was keeping count and mentally chalked up forty-seven. "Testerossa. Right." Green Ford sedan. The next question would be, How long have you been on the force? Over her shoulder he saw Tom Rider cut in on Indiana Harold to finish the dance with Allison.

"So, how long have you been a policeman?"

"So, how about I buy us a drink?"

"Sure." Eve was up for anything and led the way to the bar. He ordered two rum and Cokes, and they found a seat. "Really, how long have you been a police officer?"

"Sixteen years. Three in Ohio, thirteen in Miami." He decided to change the conversation. "So what's the story with you and the professor?"

Eve's startled blue eyes blinked at him in surprise. Then she smiled wryly. "Old news. Ancient history. And, none of your business." She took a long sip of the drink.

"It'll be my business if you're playing some kind of game I don't know about."

"No games. He's got a new wife back in Chicago."

"He forget to mention it?"

"I forgot to ask." She shrugged and picked up her drink. "I try not to make the same mistake twice. Let's dance."

At least she'd been honest. "Let's don't. I'd like to sit this one out." Eve finished her drink and sat fidgeting on the chair, at a loss for further conversation; he could see she wanted to dance. "Why don't you go ahead? I'll catch up," he told her.

"Right. See you later. . . ." She intercepted Indiana heading back toward Allison on the dance floor. Zachary finished his drink.

She was sipping ice from the bottom of her second rum and Coke when she felt his presence behind her. The music was an old Phil Collins ballad with a slow bass line. She couldn't remember the name of it and had a split focus on the lyrics.

"Dance?"

Her throat was suddenly too tight to answer. Determined not to be intimidated, she swallowed the balance of her drink and stood in response. She felt herself fully and confidently encircled by his arms as he moved her into the music, intimate and seductive; it complicated her concentration as she tried not to feel so much of his body.

Two drinks into mellow, Zachary was pleased at the feel of her, which confirmed his shower view. Despite her thin build she was softly full and pliant in front, her back firm to his touch. Surprisingly, very right. He was careful not to hold her intimately close, but in the contact of their bodies he felt her tension and was surprised. She'd seemed relaxed dancing with the others.

"So, is this what you expected?" he asked after a short pause.

She finally looked at him, guarded hazel eyes clearly

confused and unable to read his meaning, then looked away. So, the tension was a response to him. "When you came down here, I mean."

He tried again to break into her silence. "The country, the people . . ."

"I didn't expect the poverty," she answered. "I mean, I knew it was poor, but . . ." She didn't go on.

As the music flowed, he felt her relax enough to follow him smoothly and expertly. He led her into a few more complicated steps, and she stayed with him. "You sure know how to make a guy look good," he told her sincerely.

After a long, long silence, he heard a soft, "Thank you." He kept his close hold as the next song came up. She didn't stop dancing, but he felt a growing resistance to his touch.

With so many emotional reactions under way, Allison couldn't think. Lulled by the local rum, enticed by rich feelings at being in close contact with his body, somewhere in her head were also scraping, grinding, punishing sensations of a brutal male presence pushing their way into her mind—helpless, steeled feelings of confinement, an inability to get away. Part of her pulled desperately to stay in his arms, dance secure forever in the music; but fear was building, winning over.

She couldn't free her mind, and she was getting hopelessly lost. Unable to distinguish what was real from the fear, she was riding on the length of the song—except the song was over and new music had begun. She missed a step, and her body tightened further. Her throat closed.

Failure clouded Zachary's judgment. "Is it just me, or is it cops in general you don't like?" It came out more of a challenge than he'd intended.

She made an immediate move to free herself and stopped dancing. He loosened his arms to give her room, and she quickly drew away.

"Cops in general," she heard herself say. Anything safe had vanished; there was only panic. She was frozen in place, unable see him. How to get out? Now!

Eve materialized with a drink in each hand and offered one of the glasses to Zachary.

"Too bad," he said, accepting the drink. "You never know when you're going to need one."

Allison walked numbly through the bar out onto the patio and sat tightly on a low plastic chair, trying desperately to retrieve some part of the safe emotional ground that had just dissolved from under her. She and her shrink had talked about this. "The first time you allow good feelings about a man will be hard," he'd cautioned. "Don't expect to have good feelings without allowing bad ones, too. Your mind knows how badly you were hurt, but your body won't always react from conscious decision. Don't be surprised if physical attraction happens first."

Okay. So she hadn't expected the first time to be easy. But this hurt too much. She held back tears and shifted uncomfortably, her armpits tacky with perspiration. The end of the song, with its wailing saxophone solo and Springsteen's eerie vocalized train whistle leaving town, drifted from the cafe. Feelings . . . hurt. Damn it, everything hurt. She wished she were leaving, too. God, and this was just the first day. How was she going to get through the next ten?

Her heart rate slowly came back to normal, and she looked up to see a solemn face chewing gum and staring at her. She held tightly to a focus on the dark brown eyes. "Hi, cutie," she said to the little girl. "How old are you?"

The little girl didn't answer but after a moment pulled one hand up with the other and managed to hold up four chubby fingers.

"Four. Are you four?"

The little girl nodded uncertainly.

"Cat got your tongue?"

The little girl was sober, not understanding.

Allison reached out and picked her up, placing the child on her lap. "I know how you feel. The cat just got my tongue. It means you're shy with somebody and don't want to talk. Are you shy?"

The little girl nodded again.

"So am I, sweetheart. So am I."

Inside Lisa's, Tom Rider announced that the party would move on to the Beached Whale so he could release the boatmen for the night. The hungry group poured out onto the patio to mill around the station wagons. Zachary emerged with his arm around Eve in time to hear the shy little girl in Allison's lap announce that her name was Mella and point him out as the man who'd given her the chewing gum.

Allison looked up at him for a fractioned moment, then Tonio came forward to claim his sister, and the children disappeared around the back of Lisa's Cafe.

On the boat ride back to the Whale, Allison deliberately seated herself behind Zachary and Eve. One of the surest cures for interest in a man had always been imprinting him with another woman. Eve was unusually generous with concern, turned around often to ask how she was doing; handing back her parka, she moved under Zachary's arm to keep herself warm.

Not in the mood for sophomoric games, Allison accepted the parka with a thank-you that didn't come close to revealing her feelings. It had been forever since she'd had mixed drinks on an empty stomach, and she had a queasy feeling. When they arrived at the Whale, she got on solid ground none too soon.

She managed dinner, and afterward she paused at the doorway to the verandah, avoiding Zachary's appraising glance. Tom Rider motioned her in and made room on the sofa.

"The rumor's true," Tom confirmed. "We found a carved stela, and it's possible the site hasn't been looted." He continued, barely containing his glee, "If professionals had been in with power saws or heavy equipment, the stela wouldn't still be here." He handed her a pencil sketch of the carving. "The stone's been returned to its original position, so we don't have to worry about the locals."

Indiana passed Allison a warm can of beer and she sipped at it, thirsty after the salty conch at dinner. "With the poverty in this country, it's understandable that people take what they can find," she observed quietly.

Eve stepped onto the verandah in time to hear her remark. "It's criminal. They sell it for pennies—it disappears into the art market and winds up on some rich lady's mantelpiece." With faint but damning emphasis on "rich lady," Eve made evident her opinion of Allison and the conversation.

"Don't museums buy artifacts from art dealers?" Madeline was confused.

"It costs too much money, and it's too late to get accurate information because no one admits where it was found. When we find it, we place it in context with a site, do carbon dating, and add it to a scientific pool of information." Eve settled herself on the arm of Zachary's chair and defended their work fervently. "Suppose there's a burial chamber. If local people find it, they don't care about history or what could be learned, all they want is the money."

Allison was tempted to point out that for archaeologists, major finds usually translated into career, prestige, and money, not to mention occasional ownership of priceless items that managed to stray from lesser ethics. But she withdrew. It wasn't a crusade, just a point of view. She didn't feel that terrific; certainly not up to a philosophical confrontation with the nubile assistant to the professor.

Zachary watched Allison withdraw from the battle of opinion, declining to enter the fray. Shit of the sun, he thought. Mayas are gonna do what they're gonna do, and looters are gonna do what looters do, and Tom Rider and this group would continue rooting through the site. It was a first-come, first-served situation. Hassling about it wouldn't change anything.

"There's every possibility we'll find a burial chamber at our site—certainly a ball court." The professor was undeniably exhilarated. "Sometimes there's an offering placed beneath the center marker. Carbon dating on such an item would provide conclusive data about the original construction."

Allison's thoughts drifted from the discussion. Zachary and Eve had sat together at dinner, and here, opposite her on the verandah, Eve was perched on the arm of his chair and they appeared to be very much a couple. A stray melody wound its way into her thoughts. She felt his scrutiny and resolutely refused to meet his eyes.

She watched Eve slip off the arm, confidently seat herself at his feet; stretching out strong, tanned legs, she crossed her ankles and rested her head against his knees.

Good. Maybe now her inner voice would give it a rest. The night was breathless and she was hotly uncomfortable, skin sticking damply to her loose T-shirt. The refrain echoed again.

Half an hour later Zachary and Eve left the verandah.

Smoothly declining Tom Rider's invitation to sample the local nightlife, Allison, alone in her room, pulled off the stifling shirt. Rummaging for something cooler, she found Jake's gift and sat immersed in guilt for having forgotten it. Finally she carefully removed the beautiful foil in anticipation. Jake was known for his exquisite taste—and wicked heart.

Sure enough, she unwrapped a low-cut shirred-silk halter in a wonderful shimmering sea green, piped with emerald and turquoise ribbons, cut high in back and low in front. Very low. "You're an evil person, Jake Alston," she whispered, burying her face in the soft green fabric, suddenly teary and missing him desperately. "Rotten to the core." She read the card.

Hi Lovely.
I miss you already.
All my love,
JAKE

In order to wear it, she'd have to reverse it. The cut was entirely too provocative. Maybe in St. Tropez, but it was totally out of the question in this rural place among people she barely knew. If she reversed it, there was no fabric to conceal the scar. He'd know that, bless his wicked little heart. It was meant as a reminder of why she was here. To make sure she wasn't hiding.

His smoky-sweet cologne clung to the card and brought him close. She tried to imagine what he'd be doing tonight, but the thread of music nudged its way into her mind again, distracting her thoughts. She tried to identify it, but it wouldn't merge into conscious thought.

Chasing fragments of the song, locked into endless repetitions of it, she was restless and too keyed to sleep. She decided to take a walk along the beach to unwind. This was crazy. She should be exhausted—only four hours of sleep last night, the physical work all day, the alcohol . . . The music nagged and nagged. Unrecognizable. She got up abruptly and paced the narrow space between the bunks.

This was new behavior, confusing and nettling, something she couldn't get a handle on. Usually she slept too much, not too little. She'd hidden in sleep since she'd gotten out of the hospital. Now, suddenly, she couldn't sleep at all. The recognition came at last. The song from Lisa's Cafe . . . dancing with Zachary Cross . . .

"I will not be upset over Zachary Cross," she murmured, convincing herself as she slipped long legs into yellow linen walking shorts. "Or whether or not he has an interest in Eve Kelsey." She stepped into loose, strappy sandals and defiantly put on the tiny halter top from Jake, luxuriating in the soft feel of shirred silk against her skin. Maybe she would walk into the village after all.

She stared down her front at the uncomfortably broad expanse of curved flesh, feeling nude and on display. On a shoot she wouldn't have a second thought—business as usual with the photographer, advertising executives, any number of men and women looking on casually. But this wasn't business. This was here. Here, the extreme cut was out of place; it was "asking for it." Hurtful words, spitting out of the past, stopped her at the door.

Defeated, losing courage, she hurriedly reversed the top, wrenching the exquisite silk over her sticky skin to bring the high cut around to the front. "At least I can tell Jake I've worn it," she muttered in justification, and pulled on a huge, long-sleeved shirt—one of Jake's Irish lawn discards—to cover the scarring on her shoulder.

Walking quickly down the hall, she rolled up the too long sleeves and quietly descended the back stairs to the moonlit beach. A small breeze licked at her face, lifted tendrils of her hair, and lightly billowed out the loose thin shirt as she reached the water's edge.

This was better. Feeling a bit calmer in the cooler air, she saw them in the shadow of the purple bougainvillea, Eve on tiptoe, arms wound around his neck with her body tight against him, Zachary's hands at her waist. Hands that had held her own body a few hours ago, opening too many doors, causing too many feelings.

Deep in a kiss, they were too involved to notice her.

Tears scalded up from nowhere, for no reason she could think of. She turned instantly away and hurried blindly a few yards down the beach as raw feelings scraped into being—intense, desperate longings for something so normal, so innocent, to be able to kiss someone—without the fear.

It wasn't fair! None of it had been fair. Not their fault. If it was anyone's fault, it was hers. Oh, God, she wanted life back the way it used to be.

She leaned against a palm tree and carefully removed her sandals to keep their sandy crunch from announcing her presence. Holding them by the straps, eyes rigidly averted so as not to see again the lovers in the shadow of the bougainvillea, she returned to the hotel.

Avoiding the back steps, she made her way around the building; before she could climb upstairs to the safety of her room, swirling nausea exploded.

The unmistakable heat spread through her body, signaling the inevitable; it would be a matter of seconds. Dropping her sandals, she struggled across the yard to a wooden fence glowing white in the moonlight and grabbed on for support. The hot in her stomach built past tolerance and she doubled toward the stakes, holding on with both hands.

Into blackness came a hand supporting her forehead and rumbling, gentle commands. "Let go of the fence. Hold your hair out of the way."

She freed her hands to pull back her hair as bony ankles and sockless Reeboks came into focus on the moonlit sand. Him! He was pulling Jake's shirt from around her shoulders, trying to remove it.

"Take this off."

"No!" As spaced as she was, her mind rebelled; no way she would take off the shirt. He would see! In her haze she felt him tuck the shirttails into her shorts. Oh, God, what was he doing? She lost the beer and half of dinner. Her knees buckled, but his hand grabbed the waistband on the back of her shorts. More dinner hit the sand.

"Don't try to stop, let it all go," he ordered as she lost the rest of dinner and a couple of the rum and colas.

As if I could stop, she thought, angry and miserable, at the mercy of her body. Suddenly she gave over to grief, complete and overwhelming; silent tears cried in racking, soundless sobs, out of control and defeated. At last her exhausted stomach ceased its erratic heaving and her convulsions subsided.

He pulled out the bottom of her shirt and unbuttoned the two top buttons of her shorts before she could stop him, then seated her on a palm stump and disappeared while she cried on in broken, ragged breaths.

Slowly, the sobbing eased. Her nose and throat were raw and awful, and an evil bile taste lingered in her mouth. He returned with tissues and stood by quietly as she wiped her eyes and blew her nose. Seconds later he handed her a cool familiar can.

"Rinse your mouth with this. Don't drink it or you'll throw it up. It kills the taste of stomach acid. Old Cross remedy. Trust me."

She did as he directed. It was a can of Coca-Cola, and after a few rinses the worst of the taste was gone.

Picking up her sandals, he walked her unsteadily back to the beach and into shallow water up to her knees.

"I'll be all right." She was embarrassed at being sick in front of anyone, particularly him. "I'm sorry. . . ." Throat raw, her voice failed. Exhaustion was settling into her brain, and it was hard to think. He was taking care of her. Like Jake . . . not like Jake. Her mind wouldn't work.

"It's okay, Chicago, it's been a long day." He kicked his shoes in the shallow water to wash them off, then rerolled her sleeves and used cooling seawater to rinse her legs and hands, pouring it in handfuls across her wrists. "Stand still."

Her huge, tear-bright eyes reminded him for all the world of Steffie the night he'd told her he wouldn't be living with her and Mommy any longer. "You're not coming home?" The heartbreak in her eyes had torn at his guts.

She'd looked at him with pain too big for her pinched little face. "Ever?" The big tears had spilled over, strangling his heart, crushing the breath out of him so he couldn't answer right away. "Did I do something wrong, Daddy?" He had damned the world and every woman in it except his daughter in her misery, and sworn he loved her and held her and talked to her until she'd believed him, but the tears had nearly broken his will, almost sent him crawling back to Sue for one more try at their Humpty-Dumpty marriage. He might have done it had he not been convinced it would compound the damage to his child.

"Zach?" Eve's voice floated through the darkness. "Are you down here?"

Allison swayed in the water, and he steadied her with a hand to her waist. Dewy soft skin between the top of her shorts and some sort of silky green halter warmed at his touch; her slender body quivered with fatigue. Eve was standing at the top of the stairs holding a blanket.

"You sure you're all right?" he asked quietly. His concern was genuine, and he kept hold of her as he guided her back to the sand.

"Zach? Where are you?" Eve's voice was insistent.

He didn't reply, intent on Allison.

"I need to lie down. I'll be fine, now. Thank you."

He handed her the sandals and released his hold.

Confused by the silent sobbing, he watched her pass Eve in her escape up the stairs. Grief that deep and abiding had to have great cause. It wasn't related to her being ill, he was sure of it. She'd seemed pale earlier, on the verandah, and waiting for Eve in the shadow of the water tank, he'd observed her silent progress from the beach. His gut had told him something was wrong by the oddly careful way she was walking. When she deliberately avoided the back stairs, he'd followed her around the hotel.

"What was she doing here?" Eve wanted to know. "Why didn't you answer?"

"Apparently she was out for a walk."

"I wasn't gone that long, was I? I had a few things to do."

The smell of fresh perfume was overpowering as he absently accepted the proffered blanket. He was preoccupied with thoughts of his daughter and this new facet to be explored, and the situation with the girl reduced itself to something juvenile and unnecessary. Certainly his ego was flattered all to hell that she found his forty-year-old body attractive enough to chase, but given the competition—George and his Club Med hustle and Indiana Harold—he'd been too many times around the block to lose it for a cute little hard-body from Illinois.

Besides, it had been one hell of a day, and he no longer had an inclination to go one-on-one with a tireless university miss spreading her wings in Central America—hot-and-heavy kiss in the moonlight notwithstanding. He wrapped Eve in her blanket. "It's really a lovely idea," he told her, "but I don't think I'm up for playing in the sand. I'm going to call it a night."

When several attempts at gentle persuasion failed to change his mind, he was relieved to hear her demand a rain check to salve the bruise to her ego. Three minutes later, happily easing his sore body into his bunk, he briefly considered the more interesting woman across the hall. Well, she doesn't barf with class, he thought as he rolled over. But then, who does? For the first time in recent memory, he went immediately into a sound, dreamless sleep.

6

"Luisita." Corla Reyes spoke softly through the door. Luisita was instantly awake.

"The driver is here and can take you now."

The afternoon sun was bright through the open window. She'd slept more than four hours! She smoothed the dark plait of hair hanging heavily down her back, grabbed her heavy purse, and hurried out of the room.

It took half an hour in Corla Reyes' aging Land Rover to reach the Maya Mopan Clinic, a squat, ten-room cinder-block building. The clinic was new in the community, and even though she knew it represented the best medical care in the region, she could not help comparing it with the sleek Miami hospital where Danny Goodell had been born.

After much searching, the on-duty attendant was able to trace Sara's registration to her maiden name. "Baby Boy Chun, five pounds, fourteen ounces," announced the triumphant clerk, reading from the precious white form.

After an hour the young ladino doctor who had delivered the baby called her into his office. "Your sister had a difficult birth, in labor for nearly thirty hours. She hemorrhaged from a recent injury and lost much blood. It is most urgent that she return so I can examine her. Do you know where she is?"

"I am trying to find her," Luisita replied. "No one has seen her since the birth of the baby."

"She was here only two days." Familiar with Mayan birth ritual, he continued, "She received the placenta, perhaps you know where it's to be buried?" At her silent denial, he went on, "Her health is poor, and she will need care."

"What about the baby?" she asked apprehensively.

"A fine, healthy boy. He should be okay if her milk came in."

"She had no milk for the baby?" This was not good.

"Not when she left. I'm sure it's in by now, but in case it isn't . . ." He reached into a carton next to his desk and brought out two cans of infant formula and a baby's bottle and placed them in a battered paper bag. "Please give these to Sara when you find her."

He added two more cans and handed her the sack, then rose to signal the meeting was over. "Good luck to your sister and the baby. Try to convince her to come to see me."

"Doctor, I want to take my sister to the United States."

"I see."

"We will need the baby's birth certificate for the authorities. I don't know if she thought of it." She waited as he instructed an aide to obtain a duplicate birth record, then he left to attend his patients.

Luisita hesitated only a moment before asking the nurse on duty for an envelope. She returned to his office and placed it on his desk with thirty precious dollars sealed inside. Sara's life and the life of the baby might well have depended on this little clinic.

The certificate safely in her purse, the heavy cans straining the thin paper bag, Luisita found she did not know what to do next. She could only go back to Mango Creek and hope that Sara would return to the Reyes Hotel or try to reach her there.

She was halfway down the walk when the young aide called to her from the doorway, "You are Sara's sister?"

"Do you know where she is?"

The young girl glanced around to be sure no one watched. Doctors were supposed to talk with the patients, not nurse's aides. "I am Margita Martinez. I took care of your sister after the baby. She left with Rosa Chaya."

"How do you know this?" She grasped the girl's hands. "Who is Rosa Chaya?"

"Mrs. Chaya came late one night to see Sara and the baby. I helped take them to the car." The young girl was nervous. "Mrs. Chaya is a good lady. She brings food for the clinic. She and her husband live in my village."

"Which village?"

"Mopan."

"I know where it is. Thank you, Margita." She squeezed the young girl's hand. "Thank you. I am going there now. Thank you!" Her heart was full. Balum was guiding her to Sara, and she would not need the gun, a dead weight in her purse after all.

The driver knew well Maya Mopan Village. Half an hour later he showed her the home of Rosa Chaya and agreed, reluctantly, to wait with the car by the roadside. "I must be back in Mango Creek by six o'clock," he told her insistently.

She climbed the steep incline to the thatched hut, calling out politely, "I have come to see you."

"*Bay*." Rosa Chaya invited her inside.

A quick inspection of the traditional one-room structure revealed no evidence of Sara or the baby, and Luisita leveled a questioning look at the older woman.

"I've come for Sara and the baby. Where is she?"

"She is in Guatemala. My husband drove her to a small village there several days ago."

"Guatemala!" Luisita's heart dropped. Guatemala was dangerous.

"He sometimes drives *ts'ul* to the ruins there," Rosa said to her placatingly. "He will be home soon. Please stay and share our meal, and he can say."

Luisita struggled to regain her composure. "Is she all right?"

"She had a bad time with the birth and was very weak. And she was certain she was being watched. I could not convince her it was not true," Rosa confided. "No one has seen strangers in the village." Despite her assurances, Rosa was clearly concerned. "She would stay only two days and then she insisted to go to Guatemala. Her husband, Rufino, was born in San Ruiz and she was convinced he would be there, that he would take care them."

From outside came the sounds of noisy arrival of the Americans' station wagons; presently Emilio stepped inside the hut, carrying the slain armadillo casually across his shoulder. Rosa introduced him, her broad smile betraying great pride in her young husband as she bustled about, building up the fire, then cutting the animal from its bony shell to add its meat to their evening meal.

Emilio, tired from his day's work, first enjoyed his wife's pleasure, then politely gave Luisita his attention.

"I wish to go to the village where my sister and the baby are staying," she told him urgently. "If you will take me there tomorrow, I will be happy to pay more money than the *ts'ul*."

"I am sorry, but it's not possible. I must work until next week, when I have a day off."

"I have money, I will pay you. I cannot wait so long to see my sister. She's ill, and Guatemala is not safe," she pressed. There was no time for waiting.

"I would be very happy to do this for you, but money is scarce and the Americans will only be here for a few weeks. This is much money for us." Emilio tried to soothe her agitation, embarrassed by her behavior. "If your sister is still in the village, I assure you she is being well cared for. Maybe she has gone to San Ruiz by now."

She listened to him carefully, trying to calm herself.

"I have reserved the Land Rover from Mrs. Reyes to drive some Americans to the ruins on Tuesday. It is a large car and I can take you for no cost."

Tuesday was two days after tomorrow. "How much money to take me tomorrow?" she persisted.

Emilio, tired and hungry, upset by her insistent behavior, would not be swayed. Finally he told her firmly, "There is no car until Tuesday. I cannot take you until then." The matter was closed.

Defeated for the moment, Luisita was torn between the need to find her sister and the safety of discretion. Time on the travel papers was running quickly. Still, could she trust anyone to know she carried so much money—a fortune in Belize? T*a'k'in* did strange things, to honorable people, even. She had stolen money to come here; was she so different from these people? Emilio and his wife obviously were in great need to fear the loss of wages from the Americans. Rufino Copal had abandoned pregnant Sara for money; men had beaten her sister to get it back. She could not help Sara or the baby without *ta'k'in*. Her mind raced to find another way.

"The village is very poor," said Rosa. "You must buy in Mango Creek the things the baby needs. Then you will be ready for the trip."

"If I can arrange another driver," she asked, "will you give me directions to the village and the name of the people where Sara is staying?"

"Of course. The *t'o'ohil* is Jorgé K'ayum. He will know."

Luisita politely declined dinner, knowing that meat was dear, and waited while Emilio drew a crude but clear map, then thanked him and agreed to send word with Margita if she wished to go on Tuesday.

On the return drive, the driver verified the scarcity of cars in Mango Creek. "I would be happy to drive you when I return," he hinted. "Where did you wish to go? Perhaps I know someone who might drive you. . . ."

"I am not sure," she answered, suddenly distrusting. "I will know soon." She turned around often, watching carefully to be sure no one followed, but the road behind was filled only with dust from their passage in the filmy twilight. The driver deposited her at the Mango Creek crossing and sped away into the gathering darkness.

Inside the hotel, she immediately approached Corla Reyes about renting the car.

"I am happy to rent the Land Rover to you, Luisita, but it is promised already for the next several days," Corla said. "Do you wish me to see if someone else is willing to drive you?" Although Corla didn't ask her destination, Luisita realized Mrs. Reyes knew she'd located Sara.

Whom could she trust in Mango Creek? Corla Reyes? Who were the men who had threatened Sara? It could have been any man in Mango Creek. It was best to trust only the people who had helped her sister.

"No," she responded. "I have made arrangements to go next week. I would like to go sooner, that's all. I will wait until then."

That evening in her room, she rested and planned for the trip to Guatemala. According to Emilio, the road to the village was a shortcut used by local villagers to bypass the main highway. There would be no requirements for visas or passports. The Guatemalan government was worried about bigger problems than the comings and goings of undocumented peasants. Once she located Sara, she would pay Emilio anything he wanted to drive them to Belize City, where they could get a plane to America. This decided, she was able to sleep.

In the morning she summoned young Tonio. "You will take this money to buy milk." She showed him a can of formula. "Also diapers. You understand?"

The boy agreed and returned within the hour with several cans of formula, a box of Pampers, and two dozen cloth diapers. "This is all," he said. "The store has no more."

She picked up the repaired teddy bear. "You have brothers and sisters?" she asked, knowing an only child was unlikely in this country. Those willing to disobey the church were generally too poor for birth control.

"A sister."

"Take this for your sister," she said, and gave him two

quarters to insure his silence about the shopping. She packed the formula and diapers in her suitcase. Then she called the medical center; after several minutes Margita whispered into the telephone, "¿*Hola*?"

"Margita, this is Luisita Chun. Will you get a message to Emilio Chaya that I wish to take the trip with him on Tuesday?"

A nervous "*Bay*" came through the receiver into her ear. She replaced the receiver and returned to her room, and sat down to wait for Tuesday.

Zachary quietly waylaid a pallid Allison as she was leaving her place at the breakfast table. "How do you feel this morning?"

"I'm fine, thank you." She glanced briefly into his eyes but didn't hold the gaze. "Thank you again for helping me last night," she said awkwardly. "I'm not sure what happened . . . I don't usually drink, and . . . I hope you don't. . . ."

When Eve positioned herself protectively at his side with a bright, careless greeting, Allison excused herself to take a space in one of the fishing boats. Unable to talk with her further, Zachary couldn't decide whether she was upset at losing her dinner or embarrassed at losing control in front of him—probably both.

At the site, he watched her choose work space as far away from him as she could manage. Annoyed at her avoidance, he, in turn, made no move to approach her and devoted his time to perfecting his skill with the machete.

Jet lag arrived in force. Most of the group were slightly hung over, and for all the clearing and sifting, shoveling and burning, this day they went unrewarded; no new carvings, only unadorned fragments of pottery shards. The ball court was not where it should have been.

After work, at Lisa's Cafe, he noted that Allison turned down all offers to dance and gave her full attention to Woodie, Colonel Sharp, and bitten, sun-blistered George. Eventually she shared half a beer with a beaming Indiana Harold. Zachary contented himself with open pursuit by Ms. Eve Kelsey, who, undeterred as pursuer, danced intimately close. During the boat ride back to the Whale, he was bored and irritable and not quite sure why.

During dinner, he heard Allison tell Woodie that after braving the damnably cold shower, she'd happily paid two dollars American for permission to plug her hair dryer into an outlet in the laundry room for a blissful ten minutes. Her hair was clean and shining, and even in the garish lighting from the kitchen she looked soft and attractive. He left to take his turn in the shower.

She was halfway up the front stairway when he emerged from the washroom, toweling his wet hair. From his position at the bottom of the stairs, his view included a lengthy look at slender legs under a modest gold terry robe and an appreciation of the slight sway of firm, narrow hips. A consummate leg man, he pronounced hers long and firm, trim and fine. Christ, they went on for three days!

He called out, "Lookin' good, Chicago! I see you've managed creature comforts worthy of home." Startled, she looked down at him but didn't respond. When he got to the top of the stairs her door was firmly closed.

Still romancing those legs, he was busily incorporating them into a steamy inventory with the perfect, soapy breasts he'd witnessed when there was a tap on the door. For a wild moment he enjoyed a delicious fantasy that had those long legs waiting on the other side.

He opened the door to Eve in a bikini bottom and a cropped yellow T-shirt with a strategic rip in the center front. The shirt exposed strong swells of well-tanned flesh, openly declared no bra, and lacked any semblance of innocence. She handed him an opened can of beer, sweaty with condensation.

"How do you manage cold beer?" He took a long, welcome, icy swallow and felt the cold circle its way round his stomach.

Eve took it as her invitation in. She sipped her beer and the yellow shirt rode up, not quite exposing one of the pointy nipples. He wondered how many shirts she'd ripped before she got it right.

"Community fridge in the staff hotel." Eve closed the door and sat lightly on George's bunk. She pointed out a small wooden building three hundred feet away, and the yellow shirt rode up again.

The lower half of his body registered definite interest. He dismissed her full thighs and firm brown legs as not in the ballpark with those across the hall. But, he was also a breast man, and these were eights, and it had been a while . . . plus, Eve was here. Eve was willing, and the tantalizing hole in the shirt had his undivided attention. Between last night's major kiss in the moonlight and tonight's double feature, she was definitely pushing the proposition.

"We keep our own supply." She leaned across the space between the bunks to kiss him with an open mouth; he tasted cool and beer, in that order, while her free hand performed cold patterns on the bare skin of his chest. "There's more where that comes from," she said.

Then she stood in front of him and took another slow sip of beer; this time both nipples slid free of the yellow shirt with no tan line under the full breasts. She lifted a bare foot and slid it under his leg on the bunk, then leaned her hips in to him as she drained the can. The small, thin patch of fabric between her thighs was taut and full, and six inches from his eye level.

"More beer?" The salty, female smell of her kicked in a warming, primitive arousal.

"That, too," she replied. "Actually, what I had in mind was my rain check," she whispered. She removed her foot, then straddled his lap and deliberately brushed his lips with her breast before kissing him again.

He returned the kiss with deliberation and captured

both her nipples with his fingers, rolling and pinching them gently until she moaned into his mouth. Two could play at this game.

Eve ground her body against him, slid her tongue inside his mouth, and he was not greatly surprised to feel his arousal push against the confining Levi's. He stopped her hand in its decisive progress up the inside of his thigh. "Listen, girl," he said, "I have a roommate due here any minute."

"Room seven doesn't have a roommate." She moved exploring fingers against the front of him. Eyes bright with invitation, she applied additional pressure.

Why not? He kissed her in agreement and followed her out the door.

Sex with Eve brought no surprises; she kissed him once, then retreated to the bed to watch him undress, diaphragm case empty on the nightstand. Relieved to dismiss responsibility, he gave himself over to basic need and her no-nonsense approach. She quickly abandoned him for highly vocal, and immediate, satisfaction. Sometime later, sexual tension greatly lowered, glancing occasionally at the sleeping young girl, he stood at the window, smoking. Postsex was one of the few times he truly enjoyed a cigarette.

A silent lover, he'd never found a way to entirely turn off his mind and feel only sensation. Not in five years of faithful marriage, and not with any woman since. Dating Sue, he'd been good in bed, enjoyed pleasuring her, creating passion in her. In the three short months of marriage before Steffie had puffed out her stomach, things had changed. She'd become a taker, greedy for his attention, teasing and tempting him into functional erection as proof she was still desirable, demanding performance almost on command. After Steffie was born, her interest in sex with him had been only lightly rekindled, overwhelmed by a driving need to be attractive to other men.

At dawn he found Eve's well-used but reasonably functional razor and managed to scrape an unpleasant cold-water shave by the time she was awake, cuddly and sexy and more than ready for another go-round. In the bleak reality of the morning after, his level of interest had dropped to the bottom of the well.

Waiting out some unwritten social requirement while she dressed, he lit another cigarette and stared out the window at cobalt splotches in the turquoise ocean, contemplating how many years it had been since a relationship had mattered. There were a couple of women in his life since the divorce, he slept with one or the other on a mutually occasional basis, but there had been no one special for years.

If Sue hadn't gotten pregnant . . . He finished that thought the way he always finished it. There wouldn't be Steffie. He longed for the time in his life when sex had been more than satisfying a primal urge, for the bright, burning light of desire. Unlikely it would come again.

He paced the room, confined and caged in, and knew again why he didn't tomcat around much anymore—too old, too set in his ways. He'd been right the first time, sleeping with the girl was juvenile and unnecessary. And empty. At best, it had filled up a night without Jerry's face.

Finally she was ready, and they walked quickly to the Whale, the last to appear for breakfast. Scrambled eggs were rigid and cold, and he waited in irritation while water was reheated for instant coffee. When Eve made a point of greeting Allison, he smiled sardonically. She was wasting her time. The ice lady from Chicago wouldn't give a damn where he slept or with whom.

Still, under it all, he was pissed. He hated games. Across the table, Eve smiled a silly grin of possession. It was Lana's face, self-satisfied and arrogant. The kiss of death. He felt the prickly heat of anger and the sick-sweet stab of self-condemnation. He was smarter than this! He deliberately slid onto the bench next to Allison, who passed canned milk for his coffee with a brilliant smile and clear hazel eyes that looked directly into his and didn't see him.

◆ ◆ ◆

For reasons known only to herself—specifically, to avoid working next to Zachary Cross—Allison chose that morning to dig in a small hollow off to one side of the north end of the pyramid. There, behind several lines of smooth white stones she and George had uncovered yesterday that were vaguely reminiscent of ceremonial steps, she attacked the soft loamy ground with vengeance, locked in battle with unruly, disquieting memories.

All day yesterday she hadn't been able to get her mind past dancing with him, or the gentle, caring treatment he'd given her when she'd been ill in the yard. Finally she'd forced the thoughts from her mind by reconstructing his passionate kiss with Eve in the shadows and Eve's appearance with a blanket from his room for an all-too-obvious purpose. As far as his arrogant challenge about her not liking cops . . . no, she didn't like cops!

This morning her mind was taking her round and round on how he'd looked when he'd stepped out of the washroom last night—the tall length of him wrapped in that towel. How he'd stared up at her body, at her legs, called her "Chicago." She'd hidden in her room, unable to decide what to do, while the inner voice had nagged and hassled and finally cornered her with a confrontation.

Zachary's footsteps had scraped the stairs; after a pause, the door to his room had closed.

She'd removed her mother's ring and agreed with herself to open her door, and if he came out of his room, she'd invite him in and briefly explain about her fear of police. Not everything, but enough to make him understand that it wasn't . . . personal.

At that moment footsteps had stopped across the hall; the light tap on his door and Eve's voice had been clearly audible. A few minutes later she'd heard them leave together.

In the piercing light of a new day, and their late arrival together for breakfast, it was no longer important what

Zachary Cross did or did not know about her. She jabbed her shovel into the soft earth in frustration and struck red clay beneath the loam. Why this man? Why? And why couldn't she think of anything else?

The shovel jarred her attention as it hit something solid, and she scraped away red soil to uncover a row of rotted wooden poles lying parallel in the hollow. Dirt fell through the poles to reveal an empty space, and she gasped in disbelief.

Determined to isolate himself from Eve, Zachary took a break from machete work to chat with Woodie and the colonel at their sifting site. At Allison's cry, they turned in unison. From his vantage point he saw the ground sink in front of her. Scrambling down the slope, he shouted a warning, "Get out! Move!"

Allison looked up at his shout, dimly aware of the softened ground shifting and rolling under her feet; but she was trapped in slow motion, tangled in the fallen shovel, unable to move away. One foot broke through into space.

He got to her in time to grab an arm and yanked her to safety as a weakened pole gave way and fell with a deadened *thunk* into darkness. A second pole dropped away. He pulled her farther from the hole, tripped, and fell backward, taking her with him; they crashed, sprawling, to the ground.

"Are you all right?" He righted himself and watched, amazed, as she crawled on her knees back to the hole, peering into it with huge excitement.

The usually reticent colonel was shouting for Tom Rider to come quickly, and he and Woodie arrived at the caved-in area, beaming with anticipation. Seventy feet away, at the base of the structure, Rider called up to them not to touch anything until he could take a look and then began to scramble up the side of the pyramid, with George at his heels. Indiana Harold, the Millers, and Eve Kelsey all sprinted across the top from an excavation pit along the south wall.

"It's a chamber," Allison told them urgently. "I can see the bottom. It's got to be a burial chamber!"

Zachary could tell she was totally unconcerned that she might fall into the damned thing, and his apprehension grew as she leaned closer, trying to see into the dark interior of the hole.

"Watch it!" he warned.

More dirt gave way and crashed inside. He grabbed her belt to make sure she didn't take a header into the darkness. She jerked at his touch and then laughed, the excitement of the find lighting up her face. He had the split-second thought that somehow he knew her. It wasn't possible. No way he'd forget that face.

"It has to be. It's in the right place. It's a burial chamber!" Eyes sparkling, she grinned at Woodie and the colonel, including him in her joy without reservation, pulling his sleeve for emphasis. "I can't believe it, I really found it! Me!"

Caught up in her blithe exhilaration at finding lost and buried treasure, he dismissed everything else from his mind. Nothing was better than this! He watched her dance like a kid at Christmas, recklessly, at the edge of the pit, but he kept a careful eye on the ground.

"Hallelujah!" Tom Rider was in seventh heaven. "This is what we dream about!" He bustled about, sending Harold and Eve for flashlights and camera equipment and a tarpaulin to cover the site.

Barely containing their enthusiasm, the group chattered in excitement as they uncovered the remaining poles. Allison's face glowed as she and Woodie energetically scraped away dirt and the professor carefully judged the state of decomposition of the wood. Satisfied the poles would hold, he selected Zachary and Allison. "Help me record this."

Working with flashlights, the three lowered themselves on a rope anchored by a sixty-year-old ironwood tree, into a tiny room, slightly larger than a New York kitchen.

Zachary reached to catch Allison's waist as she let go of the rope, helped steady her balance on the uneven footing in the room. Debris and the small size of the musty chamber forced them into a close and humid proximity. Their lights played about, revealing evidence on one wall of faded paintings, heavily streaked with water damage and barely discernible.

She and Zachary, high on adrenaline and nervous hope, laughed and joked about the curse of buried treasure as they bumped awkwardly into each other in the narrow space, eventually coordinating their efforts to toss the fallen poles and some of the debris up through the entry.

Jubilant, thrilled at being a part of something so rare in a lifetime—the realization of a childhood dream—Allison felt pure joy flowing in her veins, untainted by the caution that otherwise dominated her life.

Zachary recognized an unaccountable pleasure in the close contact, innocent in its purpose, warm and comfortable in its experience. He was enjoying this. He hadn't thought it possible.

"There are several items here, but there's too much dirt and dust on them to be sure. . . ." Rider was doing his best to proceed with caution. He hadn't expected an important find and had minimum provisions for security. Armed theft was a problem on any unprotected site, and he would have to race the clock to identify the material, get it photographed and under wraps, with an untrained staff. "Where the hell is Eve with that camera?"

The immediate excitement of the find began to wear thin, and Zachary couldn't stifle a growing sense of confinement. He fought the drowning envelope of claustrophobia, but the deeper they moved into the tight chamber, the more he lost the battle. Aching to get out, he volunteered to check on Eve. As he moved to the entry more dirt fell, and he saw that the roofing poles would not hold indefinitely. "I'll get started on shoring this up." He pulled himself rapidly up the rope to the welcome surface and began to breathe again.

Eve arrived with the camera and various measurement devices. He helped her descend into the chamber, then located Emilio and Osari and explained the find. "We don't know what's in here yet, but we'll need ten or fifteen of these." He indicated one of the poles. "We need to secure the roof."

Osari nodded vigorously, he and Emilio craning their necks to stare with shared excitement and vast curiosity into the blackness of the burial room.

"It's too bad there's not a body. Probably looted years ago by locals," Rider called out, his voice hollowed by the chamber. "Looks like they didn't get everything." The Chaya brothers were strangely silent, and for a long moment Zachary felt the world was terribly upside down. Emilio and Osari moved away to select saplings to secure the roof.

Indiana and George unfolded a tarpaulin in preparation for covering the site for the night. After painstaking photographs and drawings to record their precise location and placements had been made, fourteen magnificent items were recovered and passed, one by one, up to the rest of the waiting volunteers. Priceless. Safe from a rich lady's mantel.

Along with known sacrificial items, three carved flint spearheads were found, each about twelve inches long and shaped like an elongated and peaked letter O. The outer surfaces had been delicately carved into seven separate profiles, presumably of the absent resident of the burial chamber, possibly gods.

Allison and Eve and Professor Rider returned to the surface. "The site is obviously much older than we'd anticipated—these are from a much earlier era. Look at the richness of design! The stela carving was from the 1500s, but this stuff could be eight or nine hundred years old! I've never seen anything quite like it!" Rider was clearly close to shock with the enormity of the find.

Joining the joyous group photographing the beautifully carved stones, Zachary was soon aware that Allison was perfectly at home displaying the priceless objects, showing them to their best advantage in her long, tapered fingers, while he and the others took their pictures.

The professor was so ecstatic that he, too, broke into dancing. Allison laughed at his enthusiasm and searched for Zachary's face to share the fun. She met his eyes for a brief second before Eve was there to throw her arms around him with a kiss that exceeded the bounds of celebration. Allison quickly switched her glance to the jigging professor. She had forgotten Eve. Some of the joy went out of her face, and she replaced it with a professional smile. The change was subtle. No one noticed.

Unprepared for Eve's proprietary move, Zachary had to acknowledge, with a supremely sour taste, that he'd brought it on himself for sleeping with her. Great. Terrific hindsight, Cross! He diplomatically extracted himself from Eve's exuberant embrace and moved casually to Allison's side. "How's your arm? I gave you a pretty good jerk earlier."

She looked up at him with the clear, unseeing gaze he remembered from breakfast. "I think it's fine. I'll know better tomorrow."

Emilio and Osari returned with a dozen precisely cut saplings and soon replaced the rotted poles. They gazed in awe at the unfamiliar items recovered from the grave. Zachary handed a stone spearhead to each of the brothers, who handled the ancient articles with reverence. He felt foreign and awkward and compelled to explain, "You have my word that these will be studied in a university. They will not be sold, they are not being stolen. They will remain a part of the history of this place. No one will take them."

Emilio looked at him steadily, his face unreadable. "They are already gone," he said simply. "They will not come back here." There was no judgment, only an acknowledgment of what was so. The brothers replaced the relics and retired to the center of the clearing to wait.

Tom Rider called for attention, motioning Allison to his side. "I want to formally thank you for the discovery of the burial chamber." He slipped his arm around her waist and gave her a resounding kiss on the cheek to cheers and applause from the rest of the group. "And, Zachary, where are you?" Spying him next to Eve, he added, "Thank you for keeping her from falling into it."

Allison flushed, embarrassed, and Zachary grinned at the unaccustomed attention.

Eve led the applause and laughter, then confidently slipped her arm through Zachary's and stood on tiptoe to pull his face level with her own. From the corner of his eye, he saw Allison turn away.

"This calls for a celebration," Eve murmured. "My place or yours?" Rider moved toward them through the group. Smiling conspiratorially, she removed her arm to stand a short distance nearby as Rider walked Zachary out of hearing of the rest of the group.

"I wish you hadn't shown the Mayas those spear-heads—it presents a problem."

"How?" He held his temper. "What problem?" He already knew the answer.

"It's an unusually valuable find." Tom tipped his head in the direction of Emilio and Osari. "Word on this'll get out. We'll have to protect the site from looting until we get back here tomorrow."

"You can't keep this secret—ten people know about it. Besides, there's nothing left but the wall. You're taking the small stuff." He gave in to his annoyance, half his concentration on Allison as she and Woodie started down the pyramid, carrying their tools. "By the way, what exactly happens to this stuff after you university boys finish with it?"

"It comes back to the national museum!" Rider was irritated. "What the hell do you think I do, keep artifacts?" His voice rose in anger.

"Just asking." The professor stared daggers but got the undeclared message: Zachary Cross would follow the progress of this material, and Tom Rider had better not come up short on the count. "Besides, what can happen overnight? They can't remove an entire wall without some pretty sophisticated equipment."

Deflected, Tom cooled his anger. "I think it's a fair possibility there's more," he said tersely. "We haven't reached the far wall because of the debris from the original break-in. We'll have to sift that tomorrow. I don't want to take a chance on losing anything. Normally I'd stay here, but this stuff's too valuable to let out of my sight."

Eve drifted closer to the conversation, but Rider did not ask his assistant to join him. Zachary said it for him. "Why don't a couple of us stay here tonight while you go back to the hotel and arrange something permanent."

Eve's face fell, as Rider accepted quickly. "Thanks. You being a police officer will sure come in handy."

Rider's emphasis on "police officer" was designed to remind him, in turn, of his public trust. Zachary returned a level stare, secure in his knowledge that robbing Mayan gravesites held no temptation for this particular officer.

Grasping Zachary's arm as soon as Rider strode away to supervise packing and transportation of the artifacts, Eve confronted him. "I really wanted to see you tonight." A solution brightened her petulant expression. "George and Indiana can stay here. That way we don't have to worry about your roommate, and we can—"

"Look," he interrupted. "Last night was last night, and this is today." He was running thin on good manners and didn't care. It had gone far enough. If he'd had his head on straight, it wouldn't have happened at all, and it damn sure wasn't about to happen again.

"Hey!" Eve was surprised, obviously thrown by his response. "I thought we had something special." When he didn't react, she moved from surprise to disappointment. "What's wrong? I really like you—"

He cut her short again. "You don't even know me." He tried one last time to soften his approach. "Nothing's wrong. You were terrific . . . but I'm not looking for vacation romance. I came here to find some answers in my personal life, and last night just wasn't part of the plan."

"But we're great together. You just said it was terrific . . ."

Zachary tightened with annoyance; freeing his arm, he shouldered the tools and grabbed the strap to his camera, avoiding her grasp. "Eve, they're waiting for us." He started along the rough path down the side of the pyramid toward the clearing and the waiting station wagons; she was forced to follow.

"You haven't answered me." Upset, she yanked at his sleeve. "Why?"

Jesus, was it possible she really didn't know? Surely she was smarter than that. Finally he stopped dead in the path. "You want an explanation," he said. "Okay. Here it is in braille. You came to my room with a peek-a-boo shirt, and the beer, and an invitation to your hotel room. I took you up on it. Your idea, not mine." He paused, forced by innate politeness to help her down the last, steepest part of the incline.

She grabbed his arm for support and held on. "You make it sound like you had nothing to do with it. You certainly didn't stop me, and last night I had the distinct impression you were enjoying yourself."

Her logic was maddening. With some truth in it. He had used her, no matter whose idea it had been.

Allison was retrieving her shovel from behind the lean-to in the clearing and could hear bits and pieces of their conversation as they moved along the path. Knowing it was Zachary and Eve, she specifically didn't want to hear what they were saying; she walked quickly into the open so they would see her.

His deep voice resonated across the clearing floor. "I enjoyed sleeping with you." Allison appeared in his peripheral vision; he realized she could not fail to hear. Immediately lowering his voice, he continued with intensity, "But any more chasing gets done, I do it. Clear?"

"Clear!" It was the first time in her life that she'd been nailed so totally, and Eve wasn't happy. She moved abruptly to Allison's side. "Were you looking for us?" she said sweetly.

"No." Allison's voice was carefully neutral. "I'm not looking for anyone."

At the plantation ranch house, downplaying his excitement, Rider obtained permission from Earl Morgan for a couple of volunteers to stay overnight at the site, explaining there had been a find of moderate significance. George passed, but Indiana leaped at the opportunity to spend the night in the Central American jungle. Morgan scrounged a couple of sleeping bags and while the rest of the group made its way back to the Whale, Indiana and Zachary were his guests for a lard-fried chicken dinner and baking-soda biscuits.

With the borrowed sleeping bags and a thermos for the morning, Morgan drove them, perched perilously on his vintage John Deere, back to the pyramid site. Jouncing through the muddy ruts to the clearing, he assured Indiana there was no reason to worry. "Biggest thing I seen on the place in ten years is a couple wild pigs, and that was several years back."

In the deepening purple twilight, Indiana and Zachary climbed to the top of the pyramid as the putt-putt-putt cadence of the old green tractor faded into the night. They settled in a few feet from the burial chamber with a tarpaulin staked securely in place over the opening. After flattening the small mound of earth from Woodie's sifting site, they built a campfire in its center. Knolls was a competent camper, and the two soon had the stump of a dead tree burning brightly and a supply of smaller wood to feed the fire throughout the night.

"I'm surprised you decided to spend the night out here," Indiana said jovially.

Occupied with his own thoughts, Zachary didn't respond.

"I kind of figured Eve might have something to say about it," Harold prodded.

"Uh, no."

Knolls, sensing accurately that it wouldn't be wise to press the issue, moved the conversation to what he considered safer ground. "What do you figure about the blond from Chicago? Allison."

Again Zachary declined response.

"She's sure some good-looking woman. You believe those legs?" Harold busied himself smoothing out his sleeping bag. "Nope, I sure don't understand a husband who'd let someone like her come down here alone. I tell you if she was mine, I sure wouldn't—and you can take that to the bank." Indiana plumped his weight down on the bag and prepared himself for a long conversation that was not forthcoming. "Betcha there's trouble in paradise." He poked at the fire and yawned involuntarily. "Yessir, there sure is a polecat in the woodwork somewhere."

Zachary finally addressed the commentary. "Well, whoever he is, looks like he's got money in the bank." He lit a cigarette and rolled out the second bag, dusty and decrepit.

Indiana climbed into his musty bag. "More'n I can afford," came the muffled reply. "Probably worth every dime, though. My first wife was a spender. Hell, I still miss her." He yawned again. "I may just take a run at her anyway. If you get 'em, you always know where you stand."

Knolls rolled over and was silent; Zachary stared into the fire and listened to the quiet. She sure was some good-looking woman. It was probably best she was married, because something about her hung about, stuck in his head with the irritation of a paper cut, irksome and annoying. It had been a long while since he'd been unable to get a woman off his mind. Something about the mystery of her . . . He frowned, dissatisfied with the taste of the cigarette.

He snapped the butt into the fire and sat quietly, listening to Indiana's slowed breathing; after a bit he began pushing a series of small green twigs into the flames, watching them resist, then smolder as their latent moisture sweat to the surface and boiled away in the relentless fire, then the final burst to flame. Gradually he became aware of a thickly pregnant silence, alive with movement in the night.

Working nights in the underbelly of Miami was hardwired and restless, a scream of hip-hop rap from open car windows, garbled, unintelligible rhyme in insistent preacher voices shouting down brassy, sassy salsa and golden-oldies Beach Boys. You didn't find women like her there, that's for sure. His was not the kind of life a woman generally understood. He got mugged, busted pimps, and scored dope in squalid alleys for a living. His life as a single cop had become nine at night to five in the A.M. in a human soup of losers and users; squalling taxi brakes, stinking bus engines, and the deep gravelly voices of souped-up, plain-wrap police vehicles melded with ground vibration from a sea of automobiles in any given day, quieting slightly at three A.M. but never entirely still.

The dichotomy between that world and this living silence seemed to call for measure in light-years. How soon would it be here? The bulldozers and tractor trailers and tourist buses and cement trucks and fast-food chains, traffic lights and lawyers and plastic wrap, and cops with guns to keep what passed for peace.

Inky darkness enveloped all but the tiny fire, and Indiana's breathing deepened to sound sleep. Zachary's mind reached into the quiet night, and he lay on his back in the dank sleeping bag, letting his eyes adjust from the firelight to the stars, drinking in pale cool moonlight and the silent flight of an owl. The expanse of starry constellations visible in the small cleared patch in the leafy canopy was mesmerizing and reduced his size in the darkness. He dozed as he listened to the haunting calls and sinister rustlings of night hunters; a light, diaphanous breeze swept away mosquitoes, and he soon joined Indiana in sound sleep.

He was not certain why he knew, but he felt himself abandon sleep and come alert. They were no longer alone. Without noise. Without warning. His first thought was their lack of weapons. Guards without guns. A foolish position. He opened his eyes to small slits; through his lashes he glimpsed two blurred figures opposite the campfire, staring at him, eyes reflecting firelight. Eyes without expression. Mayan eyes.

Emilio and Osari. He relaxed, opened his eyes, and smiled in appreciation. They had to be some kind of quiet to get this close to him without his knowing it. He chuckled at the irony. As guards, he and Indiana were seriously outclassed. These guys were good!

He climbed out of the sleeping bag and moved to the brothers, wondering how long they'd been watching him. His watch read 1:18 A.M. "What the hell are you doing here?" he challenged sleepily. "If I'd known you guys were going to guard the place, I'd have stayed at the hotel."

"It is not always safe at night," Osari said, mischievously.

"We came to guard you from the Xtabay," said Emilio, and both brothers broke into huge grins, teeth shining in their dark faces.

"Xtabay?" Zachary said suspiciously, suspecting correctly that they were laughing at him. "Right."

"Xtabay are beautiful women who live in the forests. Nymphs with long, flowing red hair—most beautiful."

"Their skin is red, and they have red nipples and red

pubises." Emilio grinned. Clearly an encounter would be a welcome thing.

Zachary chuckled at the unlikely prospect. "They pounce on unsuspecting campers, do they?"

"Ah, yes, they will come at night and call out to you—'Come, stay with me. Make love to me!' "

Osari was more serious. "But you must not stay too long with them without paying homage to Kanank'ax."

"The Keeper of the Forest," supplied Osari. "If you make love with Xtabay without lighting incense to the forest god, they will never be visible to you again."

"I'd be sure to pay respects to the forest god." Zachary was as serious as Osari.

"Only True People can see Xtabay," said Osari, staring past him at the dying fire. "Anyway, with so many *ts'ul* in the forests, Xtabay have gone into hiding."

In the expanded awareness of pleasant moonlight softening the full darkness, sitting on this old, old structure in the middle of the Central American jungle, Zachary wasn't entirely sure it wasn't possible. "Tell me, how have the Maya managed to survive all these centuries without being sucked into the white man's world?"

"It is happening," Emilio answered slowly. "Our father is *t'o'ohil* in our village." He fell suddenly silent.

"A *t'o'ohil*" —Zachary said the unfamiliar word slowly—"is what? A leader?"

"He is the wisest man in the village. He keeps the knowledge and teaches the stories and the traditions and passes them down through his family. It has been so since the time of the gods," said Osari.

"True People are Mayas?"

"Of course." Emilio laughed. "Our history is very long. Some say four thousand years. Americans are *ts'ul*, foreigners. Even in your own country. Except Indians, who are most probably True People of the United States.

"When the gods defeated Kisin, sacred maize was gathered and True People were made—their teeth were made from maize. See." Emilio pointed to his teeth as proof of this. "Maize is food—the blood of life."

"Kisin, I take it, is similar to the Devil in Christian religion?"

Osari nodded. "Hachäkyum caused an earthquake, and Kisin was swallowed up into the Underworld. We say this as Metlán. He is the Keeper of the Dead."

"In Yumeh—our father—says Hachäkyum no longer rules the earth, that the god of foreigners is in control now. Soon it will be Xu'tan," said Emilio.

"Xu'tan?" Zachary had a small premonition that he would not like the answer.

"We believe that when the last True Person dies, it will be Xu'tan. Then, once again the gods can try to make man perfect."

"Perhaps it is already time to try again," said Emilio.

"Perhaps." His brother stretched out on the ground and was instantly asleep.

Zachary yawned and nodded good night to Emilio, and crawled back into his sleeping bag. "Perhaps that's why there's a hole in the ozone," and he also slept.

When he woke they were gone; it was early, the group was not due for hours. He went back to sleep, dozing lightly in the cool predawn, and woke again, surprised to find it was after eight o'clock.

Indiana, too, was awake, and they relieved themselves off the top of the pyramid. "I wonder where the old priests pissed. It must have been a kick to pee off the top of one of these things onto the peons."

Zachary laughed. "Maybe that's why they were 'peons.'" The coffee in the ancient thermos was lukewarm and bitter. Even his hunger didn't add much zest to cold, greasy biscuits supplied by Morgan's cook. Last night's mystical stories seemed a century ago.

The work party arrived with Emilio and Osari—everyone excited with the find of the items in the burial chamber and eager to work. The brothers smiled a greeting to him and watched the group with serene eyes. Allison acknowledged him with a brief, polite greeting, then moved off to help Eve remove the tarp from the chamber site. Rider handed them a welcome breakfast of fried-egg sandwiches and hot coffee.

The rest of the day was concentrated labor. He worked out his stiffness from sleeping on the ground in the first few minutes of swinging his machete, and clearing progressed rapidly down the remaining slope of the pyramid. Rider and Allison worked to record the paintings inside the stifling chamber, combing the debris to find few additional artifacts, all of them in pieces. Ceremonial bowls that had once contained food, apparently broken at the time of the original entry to the tomb and discarded as having no sale value. The professor was delighted. The robbers had been amateurs.

That afternoon, Woodie, working with a trowel near Allison's "ceremonial" steps, uncovered a magnificent effigy figure of a woman, regally posed, wearing a brimmed and tasseled hat, holding a pet bird on one arm. Rider identified it as a fired-ceramic figurine ocarina. Priceless. He blew into it and produced an eerie note. "I've seen murals of musicians following funeral litters playing these," he marveled. "A few ceramic drums bases have survived, rattles and flutes. I can't tell you how rare it is to find one."

"I'd be obliged if you'd name her Ellen," said Woodie.

"Ellen it is," he decreed. After the official photographs were taken, the ocarina, too fragile for handling, was wrapped in layer after layer of cotton batting and whisked away for safekeeping.

Just after noon, when the growth obscuring two tumbled walls of a small ball court had been cleared away, Tom stopped work in the burial chamber long enough to clamber down the pyramid and survey the court. Finding the center, he scraped away soft loam and uncovered the crown of a large stone. "This is the ball court marker," he crowed to Zachary. "It's the most important stone in the structure. I'll want you and Eve to dig it up and see if there's an offering underneath."

Eve shrugged in annoyance, stonily silent.

"What kind of offering?" Zachary wasn't fond of the idea of working with Eve, but salvaging whatever might be under the stone appealed to him.

"It could be nothing—and it could be anything from jade beads to a carved statue." Rider was excited. "Let me know when you're ready to take it out." He made his way back up the slope.

Zachary labored carefully in the muggy heat with a mattock, prying up the stone flooring.

"So, did you enjoy your night out?" Eve said testily as she laid aside the paving stones in the pattern in which he removed them.

He paused and decided to deal with it. "Eve, let's clear the air. I enjoyed spending the night with you," he said honestly, and expanded the thought before she misunderstood again. "But I had to get a little distance, and I'm sorry I was so rough on you yesterday."

Eve's face mirrored her pleasure at this confession, and she smiled, confident she hadn't been mistaken.

He forged on, making a clean breast of it. "You were right. You weren't in this by yourself. I'm divorced, I'm twice your age, and I'm not sure why things went as far as they did. It isn't usually my style." He stopped for a drink of water, thirsty from heat and the labor.

"I don't care," she told him. "I just didn't want you to be mad at me."

"I'm not angry with you. But understand something." He waited until she drank and replaced the cap, determined to hold her attention. "I can't handle manipulating women. I was married to one . . . and someone I cared about just got buried by one." It wasn't working. She wasn't getting it.

"I don't know what you're talking about," she dodged, then offered a vacant smile of compromise, clearly intent on putting her own interpretation on his explanation. "I'm sorry I was so obvious. I promise not to do it again."

"And I promise not to play anymore." Giving up, he grabbed the mattock and spilled his frustration with her into expanding the hole.

When they had cleared a large enough space in the stone courtyard, he worked with a shovel to remove the surrounding earth from the designated stone. It was undoubtedly different from the flat paving stones that made up the court floor, shaped like a large tooth—or a kernel of corn—with the crown extending above the once level floor of the playing arena in the ball court.

While Zachary lashed the stone to two short wooden poles, Eve notified Rider that they were ready to move the marker; Rider insisted that Allison join him for luck. The volunteers abandoned their various activities and gathered around the ball court, cameras at the ready. Harold helped Zachary lift the heavy marker. It was all the two of them could manage to bully the stone from its ancient resting place.

As they heaved it aside, Eve peered into the hole. "There's something here," she cried. "It's jade!" She brushed away dirt sliding down the sides of the small crater. "It's an idol," she called out excitedly, scraping away the soil of hundreds of years. "It's about three inches high, fully carved."

The small green figure came free. She lifted it carefully from the hole to preserve the impression and examined the face. "It looks identical to the profiles on the spearheads."

Rider verified her description and joyously held it aloft for all to see.

Intoxicated with the exertion and the incredible find, Zachary returned Eve's hug, then sat on the marker to pose with her and the exquisite piece of jade. He called to George and pointed to his camera. "As roommate to the Official Jade Idol Locater and Excavation Official Extraordinaire, will you take the official portrait?"

George saluted at length. "Yes, O Great Official Official." He handed Allison his camera while he focused elaborately on the laughing couple.

"Wait a minute, wait a minute. Makeup!" Eve took dirt from the ball court floor and smeared it across Zachary's sweaty forehead and one cheek, and then her own. Then she held the idol next to his face and moved so they were cheek to cheek with the idol in the middle. George and the others snapped away. Allison, too, laughed and congratulated them on the find, and once again he had the fleeting thought that she looked oddly familiar.

Rider worked the group late into the afternoon. Zachary and George reset the heavy marker into its position in the ball court, while he and Eve and Allison completed sifting the last of the dirt and debris in the burial chamber, then resecured the tarpaulin over the opening with a light covering of brush. It wouldn't deter thieves, but perhaps nothing would fall into the open pit in the dark.

As the exhausted volunteers filed into the cars in the full twilight, the professor wrestled with the magnitude of his exciting, if unexpected, problems. The excavation team was overloaded with artifacts and information, and he knew he had to work quickly to safeguard the material before he could continue the less spectacular, but more important, scientific study of the site.

The carved blades and the idol were priceless. If word of the location leaked to professional thieves, the site could be overrun and destroyed overnight. Last night he'd slept with the carved spearheads wrapped in his pillow. Now there was the jade idol and the ocarina to consider, compounding his problem of security.

He couldn't chance it another day. There was no facility in the local area to protect something so valuable. He'd have to place the artifacts in a safe in one of the banks in Belize City.

A charter flight would be faster, but a car would be safer, and the drive would give him time to think how to disguise the location of the site until he could arrange financing and protect it properly with a permanent camp.

Authorities would have to be notified and official papers prepared; the bureaucratic nightmare would begin, and it would have to be dealt with. Word would leak there also. It would take all of two days, maybe three, and he would have to gamble that thieves would not deface the walls of the burial chamber in his absence. He made up his mind and called Emilio and Osari aside.

At dinner he rapped his coffee mug with a spoon for attention and made his announcement. "We won't be working at the site tomorrow." He waited as the group expressed their initial surprise, then quieted to listen.

"I know Tuesday is our normal day off, but I'm changing the schedule. The machete workers will work tomorrow and Tuesday to continue clearing the area while I catch up on the material at hand." He sipped his coffee. "I'm taking everything into Belize City for safekeeping. In honor of the success of this group, I'm giving you Monday as well as Tuesday—two days on your own while I'm gone."

The group's initial disappointment turned to interest at the possibilities of recreation, a not unwelcome thought for the tired volunteers.

"I know some of you had planned a drive to the ruins in Guatemala on Tuesday," he continued, "and you can still do that. However, for those of you who are diving enthusiasts, I've made arrangements with Nathaniel to take a boat trip out to the barrier reef tomorrow." Excitement rippled through the group.

"Everyone's invited to go scuba diving and camp overnight on Laughing Bird Caye—it's offshore about fifteen miles and offers some of the most beautiful diving in the world. We'll provide meals and transportation, so anyone who wants to go, sign up with Eve." He sat down to appreciative applause.

Later that evening Allison met with Woodie and the colonel on the verandah to discuss the change in schedule. Eve, seated across the way, was signing in names for the trip to the caye.

"The reef is marvelous," Woodie told Allison. "World famous. If you didn't bring diving equipment, you can rent it in town."

Allison turned most of her attention to Woodie as Zachary stepped onto the verandah and crossed to Eve, whose face brightened with animation as she entered his name on the sign-in sheet. Apparently the two were status quo. Not that she cared.

"I'm sure it is. However, I'm terrified of anything deeper than a bathtub. Unless planes land on it, there's no way I'm going to an island fifteen miles out in the ocean." Particularly if Eve Kelsey and Zachary Cross were on it. "What about you two?"

"Emilio was going to drive us to the ruins in Guatemala," answered Woodie, "but he has to work, so we talked to Mrs. Reyes and she's given us the car for tomorrow instead. Why don't you come with us?"

She considered a moment. "Are you sure? How far is it?"

"About seventy miles. On these roads that's two hours over and two back. We'll leave early tomorrow and spend as much time as we want at the ruins and be back in time for dinner. Mrs. Reyes said she could arrange a guide. It'll be fun." Woodie's eyes twinkled with pleasure. "It'll be a good chance to see Mayan ruins before looters and college professors go at 'em with shovels and machetes and bulldozers. How many times you planning to be down here?"

"Rovah seats six," said the colonel. "Plenty o' room."

Her imagination took flight. A step back in time. A bona fide, unqualified adventure. She nodded in eager agreement, fully committed. "I'd love to!"

Woodie patted her shoulder. "I'll tell Eve," she said.

In Woodie's absence, shy Colonel Sharp managed his longest conversation since his arrival.

"Ah've checked with Pr'fessah Ridah," he drawled. "He

sweahs it's wuth the trip. 'Cording to him, there's been no ev'dence of pr'fessional lootin' over theah yet. Been petition'n' the Guatemalan gov'ment to let him invest'gate—but him bein' an American an' all, they won't let him in."

Woodie returned to hear the tail end of this dissertation. "Zachary's invited us to go dancing at the local disco," she said. "Care to join us?"

Allison glanced at the detective and Eve deep in conversation on the divan. "I think I'll pack this evening, so I can sleep in a little tomorrow," she improvised, and escaped to her room.

Coward, tweaked the little voice.

"Oh, hush!" she said out loud, and pulled her backpack off its nail to begin packing.

9

Double-checking her pack, nervous at the change in schedule and the spur-of-the-moment excursion into another country, Allison neatened the rows of miniature supplies, trying to anticipate any possible emergency.

Woodie and the colonel had both left early from breakfast; at nine-thirty, when she got to the appointed meeting place by the landing dock, she learned both were suffering from a bad case of local water.

Worse, the remaining passenger was Zachary Cross, who seemed equally surprised to see her. Woodie hadn't mentioned him. Worried about the frail little woman, she dropped her things and walked with Woodie back to their room. "I'm not leaving you here alone," she declared. "Have you taken any medication?"

"If you're thinking about staying here and hovering about—you're wrong." Woodie was adamant as she pulled herself up the stairs. "You'll only keep me from getting my rest."

"If you and the colonel don't go, that leaves just him."

"So?"

"You know why I don't want to be around him. You didn't tell me he was going on this trip," she challenged.

Woodie calmly patted her arm and explained. "Colonel Sharp mentioned we were driving to the ruins and invited them to join us." She eased herself back onto her pillow, and Allison helped swing her feet onto the bunk.

"Them? Eve's coming, too?"

"No, Eve's going with the group to the reef. Tom made her responsible for the volunteers while he's in Belize City."

"Oh." So it was back to sharing the day with Zachary. No way.

"It was purely selfish on our part. He's such a capable young man, and for such a long drive—particularly into another country . . . besides," Woodie continued, "there is no earthly reason why you should back out of this trip. You'll be home this evening, and if you don't mind me minding your business, the less you let what happened govern your life, the faster you'll get past it."

"You don't understand . . ."

Woodie stopped her. "Yes, I do," she said distinctly with a leveled gaze.

She stared at Woodie in disbelief. "You?"

"Yes, my dear. Someone makes up the rest of the statistics, you know." It was said with the briefest sadness. Then, "Now, get down there. I know what I'm talking about."

Rocked by the confession, Allison sat in stunned silence. "Tell me," she wanted to plead. "Tell me how to make it okay. Tell me how to be normal again." The woman was ill, and she forced herself to hold the desperate questions inside. Woodie was living proof it could be done. But how?

Amid her confusion, Zachary appeared at the door to their room. "You ready to travel, Chicago, or do you have some additional packing to do?"

He ignored her glare. "If you're worried about me not taking the trip, forget it. I plan to roll in five minutes—with or without you. Hope you feel better, Woodie." He withdrew, and strong footsteps echoed down the hallway.

Furious at his attitude, with her psyche busy doing backsprings and double-digit accounting to find reasons why she shouldn't do it, Allison discovered herself accepting from the stubborn little woman that she would rest better without a fluttering roommate present and kissing her good-bye. "Five minutes with or without you," she mimicked to Woodie's amusement and wan smile of approval. He'd called her Chicago again.

Woodie closed her eyes. Allison recklessly waited a full ten minutes, pacing the room on tiptoe, thoughts racing and chaotic.

Woodie opened her eyes. "You still here?"

Galvanized by Woodie's disapproving gaze, she picked up the first thing she could find—her sleeping bag—added a bottle of Evian, and slowly made her way down to the boat, daring him to be gone.

Zachary stowed Allison's heavy backpack in the bottom of the boat, testy from Eve's jealous tantrum. He'd sought her out first thing this morning to tell her he'd decided against the trip. Two days on an island the size of a dime, as Nathaniel had described to him last night, was confining. He was a fair diver at best, but slightly claustrophobic from the gear; with rental equipment, a couple of hours would be all he could handle.

Woodie's description of the carved ruins in Guatemala had captured his imagination, and he genuinely liked the old lady and her friend the colonel. He hadn't known until a few minutes ago that Allison was involved in the trip.

Eve had taken it personally and accused him of lying, of having no intention of going on the trip, of leading her on when he was really planning to stay at the Whale and spend his time with Allison. He'd curbed the urge to spank her and walked away.

It was almost ten o'clock, and he wanted to get under way. Having had more than his fill of obstinate females this morning, he had every intention of dumping Allison's things on the dock and leaving without her. Women in general were a pain in the ass! He was prepared to wait another two minutes max, when she walked slowly down the back stairs, defiance in every step, carrying a sleeping bag. He was surprised she'd decided to go. And equally surprised when he realized he was pleased.

"You sure you want the sleeping bag, miss?" The boatman was puzzled; the man had said they would be back this evening.

Before she could answer, Zachary tossed it in the boat and said abruptly, "Let's go, we're late already."

Allison settled into the front of the boat, both dreading and excited by the fact that she was going at all, and the boatman pushed the skiff away from the landing. The engine chugged to life, and they were off. Guatemala. With Zachary Cross. She didn't believe it.

When they arrived at the dock in Mango Creek, she spotted the town's minuscule grocery store. While Zachary arranged rental of the Land Rover from Mrs. Reyes, she investigated its shelves of goods and wares, translating can labels into English, sorting through boxed soap and matches, tins of sardines, cans of applesauce and baked beans thick with dust, of questionable date.

Past sacks of rice, bins of shriveled potatoes with eyes grown well into fingerlings, she searched in vain for pretzels or biscuits, or potato chips, realizing at last that such items were far too expensive and frivolous for a community on the borderline of poverty.

Finally she purchased a hand of bananas and half a dozen bright red mangelos, a local fruit that looked to be a cross between oranges and tangerines, as well as a tin of crackers and three frozen cans of apple juice. They already had a basket of tuna sandwiches from their hotel.

At the side of the path to the dock, Allison passed a Maya ancient displaying thin, oblong, leaf-wrapped packages on a threadbare red blanket. Several townspeople were purchasing packets; she pointed to them, avidly curious. "What are these?"

Between the old man and his wife, they managed to describe the contents as Mayan incense made of resin from the copal tree in the way of his father and his father before him. He insisted she smell. The packets were richly aromatic with a heady, sweet woodsy-pine scent. Delighted with her find, she bought four packages.

Mayan incense. A fast disappearing folk item in this country. She would share with Woodie, she decided. At the boat, Nathaniel smiled in approval as she stashed the incense in her backpack. "Good for mosquitoes," he said. "Truly."

She smiled politely; she'd believe it when she saw it. Nothing deterred the bloodthirsty creatures, as far as she knew, except pesticides and smoke.

Waiting for Zachary's return, she tested her emotional balance and found it surprisingly stable. Encouraged that his mood had improved the minute they'd gotten under way, she found she was much more relaxed, also, and beginning to anticipate her adventure.

At the hotel, Corla handed Zachary a large metal can, battered and shiny from use, circa 1940. "Tonio will show you where to fill this. It is not always certain you can purchase gasoline when you need it," she warned. He walked with the boy another block to the local gasoline station, Mella tagging along at a distance, clutching her new teddy bear, watchful and silent. Tonio held the can while he worked the stubborn hand-cranked pump.

When he returned for the keys, Mrs. Reyes introduced Luisita. He recognized the petite Mayan woman from the airport. "Hello!" he said in surprise. "You're our guide?"

Luisita greeted the tall American with a happy smile. Hachäkyum had been listening after all. He was a good man—a *tsoy y-ol*. "Yes, mister." She smiled broadly. "I will take you to the ruins. I was born in Guatemala." Whereupon Corla, satisfied that the American was content, handed him the keys and slipped back into her kitchen.

He returned to the dock with Tonio manfully sharing the weight of the heavy can. Luisita followed with her suitcase several paces behind with the little girl.

When she spied Allison waiting in the boat, the little four-year-old ran ahead, proud to show her American friend her new companion.

"That's quite a bear." Allison examined the stuffed animal with its odd stitches. "What's his name?" But Zachary's arrival silenced the little girl, still shy around the huge man.

Tonio thunked the heavy can onto the dock, and while Zachary paid him for his labor, Mella gave Allison a moist kiss and whispered that the bear's name was "Señor Pico." She kissed the child's chubby cheek in return and gave her two packages of chewing gum. The little girl promptly ran to hand one to her brother.

Luisita stood quietly at the dock, watching. Allison looked up to recognize her and stared at the Mayan woman in surprise. "We were on the same flight from Miami."

"This is our guide, Luisita Chun," said Zachary.

"Yes, miss."

Luisita climbed agilely into the back of the boat, clutching her purse and the small, heavy suitcase, which she had refused to relinquish to Zachary. The boatman swung the skiff across the river.

"She's going to a village nearby the ruins. We'll drop her there and we ought to be back by, oh, six or so." Zachary addressed the boatman: "Can you pick us up then?"

"Can do," was the mellow reply. "If I am not here, I am at Lisa's Cafe."

The men in the gray sedan watched as the food and gasoline, backpacks and supplies, were transferred from the boat to the dock to the Land Rover. Information about the woman had been correct.

They had watched the hotel for three days and three nights, and at last she was leaving, traveling with two Americans. No matter. The men were interested only in where she would lead them. They were very patient, and soon the Land Rover swung out onto the gravel highway. The red dust had not yet settled when the sedan moved onto the road to follow.

The drive was indeed two hours, and it was noon when Luisita directed Zachary to turn from the main highway onto a smaller, sparsely graveled road. At the first opportunity he stopped the car at the roadside, keeping it in the shade.

Allison created a picnic for the three of them; he'd contributed warm beer, and he was pleased she'd thought to arrange enough food for Luisita. In addition to his camera equipment and some tequila, he had only a bag of trail mix and his cigarettes. "Are you sure this is the right road?" he asked Luisita. The lack of vehicle traffic was troublesome. He'd seen only one other car all morning. A dirty gray sedan had picked them up soon after they'd left the dock and tailed them all the way to the turnoff road; there hadn't been a gasoline station in the last fifty miles.

"I am sure," she answered. "Tourists do not come this way, only Guatemalans travel these roads."

"How much farther?" asked Allison.

"It is not far from here," Luisita assured them.

He noticed the pungent odor of raw gasoline and discovered the source in the luggage bay; the ancient metal can had tipped sideways and there was heavy seepage at the opening, the smell thick in the humid air. He lodged the can against the spare tire and tightened the cap. "How are you planning to get back to Mango Creek?" he asked, curious, wiping his hands on the roadside grass.

"I am looking for my sister and her baby." Luisita had no reason to distrust the American tourists. "If I can find them, I would very much like to return with you."

Reminded of the upcoming return drive alone with him, Allison responded too quickly. "Of course. We'll be happy to drive you." She turned to Zachary. "That is, if it's all right with you."

"Of course," he echoed; she seemed concerned for the Mayan woman, and he didn't care either way. "If we do, we ought to leave about five o'clock so at least half the drive will be in daylight." He addressed Luisita. "You think you'll be ready to go by then?" He didn't want to break down in this back country, particularly at night. He'd had enough experience with rental vehicles not to place abundant faith in their reliability, particularly if he had to do the repair work.

Luisita nodded firmly. She was certain.

They quickly gathered up the food and continued the drive. In the back, Luisita consulted her map. "Turn here," she directed. The turn took them off the small road and down a narrow, poorly kept dirt-and-gravel lane. The first road, although small, had been reasonably well maintained, but this was little more than a dirt track.

"We must be in Guatemala now," Allison said, nervously.

"You think so?" Christ, how could anyone tell? The jungle loomed from both sides of the skinny little trail stretched out straight and level in front of them. "We should have crossed some kind of border."

"Not this way," Luisita assured him. "This way is no customs, no procedures, no fees for poor people . . ." No searching of luggage, no demands for papers. No *mordida*.

There were no signs to indicate it was so, but he was convinced Allison was right—they were in Guatemala. He noticed Luisita grow silent and withdrawn. "If you'll give me good directions, we can take you to your village and then come back to the ruins," he offered.

She came alert. "It is best I stay with you until you know where you are. It is . . . complicated."

A few minutes later they reached another, smaller grass turnoff and a weatherbeaten sign in bleached-out

Spanish indicating ruins, one he would have missed had Luisita not pointed it out. Again he noticed the gray car, but when it did not follow them to the ruins, he dismissed it and held his full concentration on Luisita's directions through the confusing maze of ruts that served as a route through the ancient trees.

The track disappeared, and he stopped the Land Rover in front of a crude wooden arrow tacked to a giant ironwood. It pointed vaguely toward a faint footpath leading off to the right. "Looks like we've got the place to ourselves," he observed happily, with building excitement.

He and Allison quickly searched out cameras and equipment and followed Luisita up the trail in high anticipation. As they worked their way up the path, a rough stone stairway emerged; slowly the dense jungle gave way to a series of huge stoneworked structures.

Allison caught her breath. The ruins were indeed wondrous. Overgrown with trees and vines, moss and flowering grasses, the silent pyramids were tall and imposing, emanating austere mystery and an overwhelming sense of the massive power vested in the priests and kings who had dominated their construction. Huge, magnificently towering trees kept the clearings below relatively free of undergrowth, and they walked through delicate, waist-high ferns on the thick forest floor. A silent, timeless world. Ferns and lichen licked at fallen trees, and orchids trailed and vines swayed gently in the cool, moist air. A natural updraft was created in the shade.

She stopped in awed recognition. "This is a ceiba tree." She lifted her face to stare into its leafy canopy, hundreds of feet in the air. "They're sacred. No one is allowed to cut them down. Not even the government." She looked to Luisita for confirmation.

"We believe the trees hold up the sky. If you cut down any tree, you must ask permission of the Keeper of the Forest and you must ask permission from the Keeper of the Stars," Luisita said quietly. "The *t'o'ohil* in my village told me as a child."

Allison paused, fascinated with the thought. So. All things in life were connected. Every instant affected every other; everything was interlocked. What had been true through forty centuries was still being taught to Mayan children. Luisita was living proof. "I've read that if you're a good person, the gods allow you to spend your afterlife sleeping at the foot of this tree, with no work and no troubles."

"We think it is so," said Luisita, pleased that the American woman knew these things.

Zachary smiled also. "It's a beautiful idea."

Sunlight filtered occasionally through the thick leaves to light in brief patches on Allison's face and hair, and he felt, once again, that somehow he knew her. It unsettled him. Not possible he'd forget a face like that. With her permission, he stepped back a few paces and took a picture. As they wandered through the ruins, he began to lose himself in photographing this strange vacant place full of carved ghosts and mysterious history.

For a short time Luisita posed for him, also, then she shook her head against more photographs; however, when Allison didn't object, he included the beautiful woman in more and more of his shots. Christ, she's photogenic, he thought. No bad angles—the camera loves her.

Indeed, Allison was at home and fully comfortable with him now that he was behind a camera—the unaffected, wholesome joy that had once earned her three hundred dollars an hour and made her famous came shining through.

A certain smile, and he was flushed with warm, liquid surprise; recognition flooded his thoughts. He stared, dumbstruck, looking again to be certain. It was her! No wonder she looked so familiar! What the hell was she doing here? He was so astonished that he spoke before he thought. "I know you."

She knew instantly that he'd recognized her. For whatever reason, maybe the magic of this place, she decided not to deny it. She'd just have to convince him not to tell the others. Or, he would, and she'd deal with it. She was oddly unaffected.

"You're the Gallé Girl," he pursued. How could it have taken three days to recognize her? Jesus, Cross, you're slipping! Better not let the guys in the department know about this one. Something in his memory wouldn't fall into place, something about . . . his mind couldn't find it. "You're in magazines. Perfume ads . . ."

"Past tense," she said. His voice had revealed he didn't know the rest, she was still safe; his photographs would be purely amateur, and she'd never have to look at them. "That was a lifetime ago."

"Well, you sure look good in here," he said sincerely as he framed a second, closer shot. He'd had some of his better fantasies about her right after the divorce. "None of my business, but why'd you give it up?" His mind split focus, photographed that face but searched for the elusive strand of information about the Gallé Girl. Something a couple of years back. Maybe three. About the time his mother had died.

"Couldn't handle the close-ups," she said after an almost imperceptible pause. "Too many lines, here." She drew her index fingers down the lines on either side of her generous mouth.

"You're out of your mind. What lines?" Would lines kill that kind of career? The cop in him couldn't skip over the pause. He tried again. "You quit when you got married?" What the hell was it about her that wouldn't jell?

Allison had forgotten the wedding band. She smiled in slight embarrassment and regarded the ring, sad for the moment. "It's my mother's. I wear it . . . for lots of reasons."

So he'd been right—the ring was a cover. Not married! Somehow he'd known it. It was too large for her hand and too heavily worn. He grinned crookedly. Not married. . . . He loved it when he was right. "I'm surprised someone who looks like you is single. Those Chicago boys are losing my esteem."

The smile in her eyes was dazzling and genuine behind his compliment. The shot was priceless. A definite eight, working on nine. He began a small fantasy about making it with the Gallé Girl—his hand gliding up one of those ridiculously long, smooth legs, kissing that wide, full mouth. He thought back to the right feel of her when they were dancing, firm and pliant, and the thoughts put an emotional jolt through him a little lower than his stomach. As he rewound the film and found a fresh roll for the camera, he wondered again why she'd been so skittish. The Gallé Girl! Holy shit!

With Luisita trailing behind, she seemed relaxed and curious about the ruins, although she subtly moved off the subject of her career by pointing out the ceremonial ball court, an arena half the size of a football field filled with breathy, airy ferns. They walked over to explore it; the huge center marker appeared to be intact, and he found himself hoping irrationally that if there was indeed an offering under it, the stone would somehow be too heavy to move and the treasure would remain. It had been grand fun finding the idol with Eve, but there was a hollow feeling about it now, a vague sense of having disturbed something magical and, in a way, holy. The thought of Eve brought up a frustration of a different sort, and he dismissed it. Eve was history he'd have to live with.

He watched Allison's famous face as she ventured surprisingly knowledgeable facts about the structures and the people who might have lived there. He noticed Luisita's restlessness—it was probably old news listening to theories about the history of her people; plus, she wanted to see her sister, and he couldn't blame her. But how many times in his life would he be able to photograph the Gallé Girl? Soon, he decided. They'd leave soon.

After a series of wonderful shots of an exquisite moss-laden wall of carvings, he and Allison climbed to the top of one of the tallest pyramids and sat staring at the green of the jungle trees stretching into the distance; across the way was an opening on the top of a lesser structure. He was exhilarated. He, Zachary Cross, Miami cop, sitting in soft afternoon sunlight on top of a pyramid in Guatemala, chatting it up with a woman whose face was known by millions of people, whose picture used to drive him crazy.

"See that small hole that looks like a window?" she asked.

Her question drifted lightly into the top half of his mind. He focused and found the opening. "Yes. Uh, that would be what's left of a small priest's hut, right?"

"Current theories are they didn't live there. The cubicles are too small for permanent residence," she pointed out, content at last to meet his glance and not look away for safety, secure in herself and her knowledge about Mayan history, and glad of his interest so she could share this special place, even with him. "Priests probably made appearances in the rooms to receive tribute from members of the community who'd been allowed onto the grounds for ceremonial rituals. He probably assumed the persona of the temple god and received gifts and granted prayers, or whatever, then returned to his home elsewhere in the center."

"It makes sense," he said, having no interest whatever in what the priests had been up to. Carefully he kept his mind off her legs and on the conversation. "The only thing I know about Mayas is they built all this stuff without wheeled vehicles and no one knows why they abandoned it all to the jungle."

"They were a very intelligent people. They created the only true writing system developed in the Americas. And they invented the concept of zero to make ten—it was discovered in their calendars. I've wanted to come down here for years," she concluded, "to see for myself."

As they talked, Zachary went through another roll of film without one questionable shot, making occasional comments in the peace of the afternoon. He checked his watch, amazed to discover an hour had passed. Almost three o'clock. Then a cold, thudding realization that it had been some time since he'd seen Luisita. Too long.

Without alerting Allison, he looked about for the tiny little woman. A few minutes later it was apparent she had disappeared. He lost his concentration on the ruins and struggled to relive time, trying to determine how long she'd been gone. Every instinct that had gotten him through the nightmare of Laos and kept him alive working vice in Miami told him something was way out of kilter.

A sudden silence of chittering birds, a flight of parrots—too quiet and too noisy. He gathered his camera and equipment and remarked offhandedly, "Shall we go take a look at the village?"

Allison caught something in his tone and turned rigidly nervous when she realized Luisita was missing. "I didn't see her leave," she said. "How long has she been gone?"

"I don't know. At least an hour," he replied. They walked rapidly down the path to the car. He unlocked the car. "Her suitcase is gone."

Allison was baffled, upset. "It was heavy. It was all she could do to carry it."

"Yeah." He felt hackles tap dancing up the back of his neck. They had to get out of here. "Maybe she's started back for the road. We'll pick her up on the way out. Probably in a hurry to see her sister and didn't want to tell us." He unlocked her door and tossed his camera onto the front seat. "People down here don't like to say no, they don't like getting anyone unhappy." He shut the door and came around the front of the car to his side. Nervous. The heavy smell of gasoline danced in the heat.

She checked the backseat. "Nothing else is missing, as far as I can tell. I thought you locked the car."

"I did." Trying not to panic her further, he quickly started the Land Rover and turned it around, following their own wheel marks in the grass as rapidly as possible out the rough track. The useless shocks bounced them over ruts. "Either she unlocked one of the doors before we went up there, or she managed to get one open somehow and got her suitcase out."

The car had been locked when they came back. Why would she relock the car? Why did he have the distinct impression this was going south faster than he could figure it out?

They reached the narrow lane. "Which way?" he asked, giving her the choice. "Her village should be somewhere down there, and the other direction is home." He waited. Every instinct said home, and indecision was costing time.

"What if something's happened to her?" Allison's eyes were huge with apprehension. "We can't just leave her out here in the middle of nowhere." Her mind skipped for a split instant to mindless, running terror, and she knew she couldn't bring herself to turn her back on a woman alone in this wilderness.

"I think she left us," he pointed out, but he turned the car toward the village. "She can't have walked more than a couple of miles. If we find her, we'll take her on into her village. If not, we'll assume she knows more about this place than we do, and get the hell out of here."

Allison nodded in tight agreement.

Four miles down the thread of a road, the engine coughed and struggled, then ceased running. They drifted to a stop. The engine choked and sputtered when he turned the ignition, caught, then died a final time. The starter ground to a stubborn halt.

"What the hell!?" Zachary checked the fuel gauge. Empty. The gasoline can was no longer in the luggage bay, impossible to secure because the lock was jammed. A quick check under the chassis revealed a hole the size of a pencil—more likely a screwdriver—in the fuel tank. He was enraged. There was only one reason for this kind of vandalism. They were in danger.

At each discovery, Allison grew more and more silent. Then she opened her door and started jerking packs and supplies out of the backseat.

"What are you doing?" He could see she was rattled.

"Obviously we have to walk—I'm getting our things out of the car."

"Look. I don't want to make you crazy, but someone deliberately disabled this vehicle. That means somebody's planning to pay us a visit. Probably didn't expect us to make it this far."

"Well, you are making me crazy. If you're right, we . . . have to get away from here . . . the sooner the better." She was having trouble holding it together, struggling to get the heavy pack strap over her shoulders.

He took it away from her and handed her the sleeping bag and the cameras. "We have to get off the road. Who knows how far it is to the village and you can see down this road half a mile in either direction."

"Off the road," she echoed. "What are you talking about? You can't be serious."

He prepared himself for hysterics. "It's very possible that whoever did this is on their way right now. We're probably targeted for robbery." At this, she really went pale and he was concerned for a minute that she was going to pass out on him. If she did, she did; he was running out of explanation and short on charm.

He forced himself to talk to her quietly. "Listen, I don't have a clue what's going on here. We're on a back road in Guatemala with nothing between us and them but our good looks, sweetheart. Okay?" He watched her face as she processed this grim scenario, then was relieved to see her pull strength out of somewhere, stop fighting him, and prepare to deal with the situation.

"Okay." She could feel her mouth getting dry, and it was hard to swallow. Oh, God. What if he was right?

"We don't want to leave any tracks, so do exactly as I tell you." Her eyes widened, but she nodded in immediate understanding.

He broke off a stalk of dead weeds and directed her down the road. "Walk on the gravel. Try not to leave footprints." She carefully did as he indicated for a hundred feet, and he brushed away any tracks as they went.

Finally he chose a rocky incline and tossed their gear down the slope into a clump of bushes. They climbed down into the forest and he picked up both packs and gave her the sleeping bag.

"Now what?" she said breathlessly.

"Now we stay very quiet, listen for a car, and look for a place to spend the night."

"What!"

"Listen," he whispered as he moved forward through the tangled undergrowth, "it's nearly four o'clock. We can't walk around in the dark, and it'll be pitch black in two hours. Why do you think you're hassling a sleeping bag?"

She'd been too preoccupied to think about it.

"We'll find some water," he said, "and we'll spend the night. You do know how to camp, don't you?" He needed some time to figure out what was going on and he wished to hell he had his Magnum. To her credit, she followed quietly until a short time later when they were stopped in their progress by a small deep stream, some ten to fifteen feet wide, filled with huge boulders.

"We'll have to cross here."

She stared at him with huge eyes and shook her head firmly. "You cross. I can't swim. That's why I'm here." Her sudden giggle was bordering on hysteria.

He processed this with part of his mind as he checked for a way to cross. It explained her terror the night they'd crossed the lagoon. Another twenty minutes up the creek, he found a natural stone crossing for her and, on the other side, around a sharp bend a few hundred feet farther on, the rocky entrance to an ancient cave above a small waterfall, surrounded by wild cannabis in flower. The water flowing from the interior of the cave formed the creek.

In the twilight he carefully scanned the darkening sides of the canyon, noting damage to the trees and the high-water line along its sides several feet above their heads; the stream was apparently from an underground river system and had the distinct potential of becoming dangerous in the event of rainfall in the hills behind them. He was not too fond of the location, but he was running out of daylight and choices, in that order. On the plus side, from this vantage point he could see anyone approaching them.

While he assessed the possible danger from the water, she located a small flashlight in her backpack. They explored the cavern, discovering that it went quite a ways back into the riverbank.

It was also dank and cold, but huge ceilings, fifty feet high in some places, he estimated, made it large enough not to trigger his claustrophobia. In January the rainy season had presumably come to an end in Belize. Casting one last glance at the cloudless sky in the fading light, he decided to chance it. "Well, it ain't the Waldorf, but the price is right," he decreed, and dropped the backpacks on the sandy floor.

At his statement, Allison searched through a small compartment in her pack, found a small plastic vial, and took one of the pills. Her hands were shaking. "Valium," was all she said. Twenty minutes later, however, she was visibly calmer.

Full darkness descended with the finality of equatorial nights; the cave echoed their whispers as they discussed their situation, staring at the ring of light from the flashlight. "Bottom line, Mrs. Reyes won't know we're missing until we don't come back with the car tonight," he said carefully.

"She might assume we've had car trouble or decided to stay overnight."

"Let's say she does. Everyone in the group is on a two-day trip to Laughing Bird Caye, and Rider drove into Belize City." He calculated. "Worst case, they'll start checking on us when they get back from the caye and she tells them we're still gone."

"That could be at least thirty-six hours from now."

He racked his brain to determine what kind of danger they could be in. "Maybe Luisita set us up for a robbery. Christ, do they have phones in this end of the world?"

Allison disagreed. "I don't think Mrs. Reyes would risk her business with someone that dangerous. Besides, we'd have to have enough money to make robbery worth going to prison."

He didn't bother correcting her naive assumption. People were killed in Miami for less than his pocket change. Daily.

"Besides, I believe her about her sister. There were maternity things in her suitcase at the airport. And a teddy bear. . . ." She trailed off and then said slowly, "I'm sure it's the same bear that Mella was carrying at the dock."

He hadn't noticed the clothing but he distinctly remembered her telling the immigration officer she planned to be in Belize only a few days—she only had two weeks on her papers. What the hell was she doing in Guatemala? On a backroads route that bypassed Guatemalan authorities? His shoulder muscles tightened up a notch. "No procedures," she'd said. "Only Guatemalans use this road."

The gray car that had followed past the road to the ruins slipped through his mind. A random kidnapping? The mystery sedan that had not passed them when they'd stopped for lunch. He didn't like it. A lot. Not overtaken, just followed. Then their car disabled. What the hell did they want? Why hadn't they jumped us at lunch? Answer: There had been three of them then. Now, just two. On the other hand, it could be coincidental. Maybe they'd stopped for lunch, also.

They kept coming back to Luisita.

"Why would she carry a heavy suitcase from this remote place?"

He searched his mind to remember the contents of the package she'd brought from Miami. Nothing in it had been that heavy. Maybe the baby articles were a cover. "Why would she disable the car and take the gasoline? We were going to drive her to the village." It didn't make sense. None of it.

Eventually they gave up to hunger and tried to get comfortable for the night. He unrolled her sleeping bag while she held the flashlight, hyper and nervous, then seated himself next to her. He brushed her arm as he handed over the trail mix, and although she didn't move exactly, he felt her shrink from his touch. Her anxiety was palpable. The confident woman he'd photographed at the ruins, the lady he'd just mapped out the possibilities with, had disappeared. This woman was suddenly hard-wired for sound. Apparently Valium had its limits.

He lit a cigarette and saw her edginess increase. Sorry to offend Your Nonsmoking Highness, he thought, but this shit is making me nervous. Obviously her fear was directly related to being alone with him, but since he wasn't threatening her in any way, he couldn't decide what was wrong. She didn't know him, that was apparent, or she wouldn't entertain the fantasy that he'd take advantage of her, Gallé Girl or no, in the middle of a jungle with who knew what lurking in the underbrush. He soon discovered, after stubbing out the butt, that nothing he did eased her tension. Who could figure women. She'd been doing just fine until the subject of sleeping arrangements came up.

Restless, he searched through his pack and located the tequila. He sat cross-legged opposite the fire to take a drink and felt her tension level top out. He got up stiffly to put it back in his pack. Shit. If she'd seen what some of the women in Laos had endured . . . Jesus, who needed it. They had a hell of a lot bigger problems than her chastity.

Drawn by their body heat, mosquitoes arrived. Allison scrambled for her backpack and reseated herself on the blanket. Her emotional control was at the breaking point despite everything her head could do to talk herself out of it, and the high-pitched whine of tiny, bloodthirsty insects in her ears was the final straw. Rifling through the pack, she located the can of Off and took out the spray can to do combat. "I hate anything with more than four legs." She attempted a feeble smile. "Except butterflies."

When the air smelled violently of insecticide, she put aside the can and took out the plastic vial of Valium. *You don't need this*, said her inner voice. *It's just that it's dark. He's not going to hurt you. There's nothing wrong here. If it wasn't for him, you'd be out on that road with who knows what kind of prob-*

lems, and he's as nervous about this as you are. She put the tranquilizers back in her pack.

"You taking another pill?"

She flinched at his question. He probably thought she was a nut of some kind. "Not yet." She let out a jerky sigh. "I will if I can't sleep, but it's too early. I just needed one before. I guess I'm really scared."

He sprayed his arms with the aerosol. "Save the rest of it. Kills the ozone. Besides, we may need it tomorrow getting out of here. Now that every mosquito in Guatemala knows we're in this particular cave," he joked. "I don't know why I didn't think of it earlier." He busied himself scooping out a hole in the sandy floor of the cave. "What we need is a fire."

He disappeared into the darkness and returned a few minutes later with firewood and a small branch of cannabis. Soon he was stripping thin green leaves to brew "tea" in a tin of river water.

The prospect of a fire and light in the cave eased her anxieties appreciably. While he was gone, she took only half a Valium, then dug through her pack for the old Maya's incense; inside one of the packets she found neat rows of round golden brown briquettes, tacky with resin. She placed them liberally around various rocks and stones now visible in the gothic shadows of the cave, and she lit them, one by one, with a burning twig. Soon the glowing incense surrounded them with fragrant wisps of smoke that indeed drove away the mosquitoes.

Zachary was properly impressed. "Is there anything you don't have in that pack?"

"Gasoline," she answered, feeling better in the thin firelight.

"Damn. We could have been out of here."

The small fire did little to warm the dank dampness in the huge cave, but the black threat of total darkness receded to huge rocks and limestone walls, now jumpy but identifiable parameters in the firelight. The incense burned and flickered, winking eyes of blue-green flame and faint woodsmoke perfume. Allison pulled on Jake's jacket and a few minutes later propped the sleeping bag against her backpack and crawled into it for warmth.

She drank the proffered cup of tea quickly and returned the tin to him for his share.

Now that he knew the light from the tiny fire wasn't visible outside the cave, he concentrated on getting her to relax. He poured another cup of the hot and illicit brew for her. *It's a hell of a lot better than Valium, sweetheart,* he thought. *Illegal, but effective.* Out loud he said, "I've been meaning to tell you that I want to replace that jacket. Does it still smell like Scotch?"

She lifted her shoulder to sniff the crumpled calfskin, then smiled. The Valium was working wonders. "I think we're more than even since I dumped my dinner on your Reeboks." There was a wonderfully easy feeling curling its way down her backbone. "Scotch beats the smell of round-trip rum and cola every time."

He conceded a draw—and a sense of humor, when she wasn't looking. He brewed more "tea," generously donating the rest of the leaves to the fire and creating additional smoke that mixed gently with the fragrant, smoldering incense. His efforts succeeded in rousing more than a few disgruntled bats. He had two cups of the illegal brew and was careful to get only pleasantly buzzed, but she was flying higher than the bats. After a long silence in which he thought she might have gone to sleep, he heard giggles from the depths of the sleeping bag and crawled over to check on her.

"Hey," he whispered. "What's so funny?"

Definite giggles.

"I just had this great visual," she whispered back, shaking with silent laughter. "It's this married bat couple." She dissolved into more laughter as she came up out of the bag, pointing at the ceiling of the cave.

He got the picture and joined the fun. "Ethel . . ." and he was gone, shoulders heaving. "Ethel, you smell smoke?" He could get no further.

"Listen, Mel . . ." She took it up. "We got to do something about the new neighbors." Then she lost it, and he joined her. "I'm seriously . . ." More giggles. And she was gone again.

They said it together. "Well, there goes the neighborhood!"

She couldn't keep it in any longer and was laughing out loud, her tension forgotten. After a while the giggles passed, and she sank into seamless sleep.

He studied her face, innocent as she slept, feeling slightly guilty that he'd introduced her to an illegal drug. Obviously she'd never gotten high before. In this day and age that was a miracle in and of itself. Like twenty-year-old virgins.

He'd had some of the best grass in the world in Laos and learned early on from a haggard, dead-eyed sergeant never to let it control him, ever. Kids higher than kites had bought it along the Mekong, not giving a diddley-shit. A sure way to get a toe tag out.

He let the fire die down to coals and stationed himself for a while at the entrance, listening to the night sounds, just in case. A dumb, serious situation. His watch read 2:14 when he returned to the fire. He added a small rotten log and finally fell asleep with his face on the edge of her sleeping bag.

He was annoyed to wake late, nearly nine o'clock. White noise from the nearby falling water, the dim morning light filtering late into the darker reaches of the cavern, had combined with heavy tranquilizing effects of cannabis; his head was full of cotton, another penalty from the marijuana. He preferred the piercing clarity of a Scotch hangover and felt a hollow ache where the jolt of fresh-brewed, heavily caffeinated coffee would have been welcomed, even stale instant from the Beached Whale. Moving quietly to avoid waking her, he left the cave and stopped at a small eddy for a cool drink of the crystalline river water. Splashing his face to clear his head, he decided to check on the Land Rover.

When he returned she was drinking thirstily from the canteen, sleeping bag neatly rerolled, backpack at the ready. He marched stiffly across the space between them, aware of her intent gaze.

"You've been gone over half an hour," she said, a question in her voice.

"It's a damned good thing we didn't stay with the car last night," he interrupted. "It's gone." He was pissed. He truly hadn't expected it to be stolen. In the brilliant light of hindsight, he knew he should have watched the car, and probably would have, had he been alone.

"Gone!" she echoed.

He held up the ignition keys and supplied the answer. "Hot-wired. It's not that difficult on an old car." He threw them into his open pack in frustration.

She was shocked into silence, thirst forgotten. Gone. The implications of being without transportation staggered through her mind. They were in Guatemala! Belize would have been bad enough. "I guess we'd better start for that village," she said quietly.

Pleased that she hadn't come unglued, he nodded in agreement. She might turn out to be a ten by default. "We'll travel light," he directed with an enthusiasm he certainly did not feel. "Empty one pack of everything except first-aid items. We'll pick up the rest of the stuff when we get a car."

If they got a car. And if it was as big a problem as he had the feeling it was going to be, they weren't going to waste time coming back for anything. He pushed the canteen into the small stream and filled it while she emptied her pack.

"I have two of these." She held up a packet of instant soup. "We could have one now and save one for lunch. Just in case. . . ."

"Good idea. But it'll have to be cold—heating water will take too much time. It's late. We're pushing ten already." They shared the remaining crackers and drank soup, cold and scummy, and split the last can of apple juice before starting out, occupied with the seriousness of their situation.

He checked both packs. She'd shown surprisingly good judgment by abandoning the cameras. In a country this poor, they were too heavy to carry and of no monetary value. He emptied his of film and put the cartridge in with the medical supplies, but he made no other changes. He shouldered the lightened backpack, and she got to her feet.

"We're in this country illegally, aren't we?" she asked gravely.

They left the safety of the cave and worked their way down the riverbank to the crossing before he answered.

"Let's worry about our status in this country when we get to the village. We can tell them we didn't know we crossed the border. They may give us a hassle, but it's not our biggest problem at the moment." But it was a problem. Without a car it could turn into a big, hairy one.

She negotiated the stream carefully, jumping from one huge boulder across to the other, then the smaller ones as he steadied her progress.

"You have your passport with you?"

Her foot slid off a wet, mossy stone into the burbling water; he pulled her safely onto the bank. "It's in the pack."

"Good girl. It won't take brain surgery to straighten this out, just money and good old-fashioned common sense." That was one hurdle down. He had his also, plus his police identification. He paused. "How much money did you bring?" He had somewhere around twenty-five dollars.

"A little, maybe fifty dollars. And my Visa card." She had been certain it would be plenty. Now it sounded paltry, not much better than fifty cents.

"Fifty dollars!" Hallelujah. The Visa was useless out here in hicksville, but fifty dollars would guarantee a car and a driver, and with his money, barring a greedy official somewhere, they'd be okay. "All right, Chicago!"

He cleared the way for her progress.

She heard the genuine confidence transmitted in his voice and felt better; surveying the dense green growth as she followed him to the road, she gave a hollow laugh. "I was planning to buy souvenirs . . . have adventures . . . postcards to my friends . . ."

"So far, I think we've got 'adventure' covered." He joined her in ironic laughter. "Let's hope we find somewhere to mail a postcard."

At the roadway Zachary showed her two distinct sets of footprints in the soft soil and the broken glass from the car window. "There were at least two—maybe more, depending on how many stayed in the second vehicle. Broke the glass to get the door open."

Whoever it was had also walked up and down the roadway looking for tracks; she didn't notice, and he didn't point it out to her. As far as he could tell, the car had been driven away in the same direction they had been traveling: toward the village. Maybe the village wasn't such a hot idea.

She turned to face him in the roadway. "You think it was planned?"

"Hell, I don't know." He was feeling crawly, and her voice told him she was getting spooked again. "It sure looks that way. Let's get going."

They started for the village. Half an hour passed and they trudged into the escalating warmth with a minimum of conversation. "Adventure" was wearing thin.

"We know her village was near here," he justified, more for himself than for her. "You'd think we'd see someone by now." He stopped to look in the opposite direction, second-guessing their decision. "I don't know how far we'd have to walk if we'd gone back to the highway. Still, there might be more traffic."

"We drove for miles yesterday to get to the turnoff without passing a car, let alone a village," she offered. "I think this is our best bet."

He hoped she was right. The sun had long since burned

off the morning coolness, and except for her straw hat, they had no protection from its metal glare. A few minutes later they came to a grove of trees bookending a local bridge—thin, well-worn logs paralleled across a small ditch. He helped her down to the shallow stream, and she plunged her hands and wrists into the clear coolness of the water.

"How long do you suppose we'll have to walk?" she said, breathing heavily in the humid air.

"Could be an hour, hour and a half."

He watched as she deftly wound her hair into a heavy coil and pushed it into the crown of the hat. It was an unaffected act, a casual skill innate to long-haired women over centuries, heavily feminine, without wasted motion, and vaguely sensual to witness. Hair tucked in, she looked about nineteen. He stopped the drift of his thoughts.

"We can save the canteen." Cupping his hands, he scooped up water to drink deeply, then splashed his face and hair. She followed his example and drank also, running wet fingers over her face and the back of her neck. "Give me your kerchief." He doused it in the stream, pressed out most of the water, and retied it around her throat.

The coolness from evaporation was immediate. "That feels wonderful," she said gratefully, closing her eyes for a long moment. "Thank you."

Even without makeup, he could see why she'd been so successful as a model. His mind framed a picture he would take in the dappled shade, and he had the briefest flash of an urge to discover what it was like to kiss the Gallé Girl. He swiftly suppressed the idea and stooped to drink again. They were in quite enough trouble, thank you.

"What the hell is the Gallé Girl doing mucking around the jungle in Belize?" he asked so abruptly that she was startled. "I mean with the bugs and the accommodations. . . . this doesn't seem like the kind of vacation somebody like you would choose."

She looked at him, curious to know what he really thought of her, wary at the same time at his show of interest in her personal life. The day-old growth of beard darkened an unforgiving jawline. "What kind of vacation do you think 'somebody like me' would take?" She pushed herself against the rocky base of the bridge to stay in the shade.

Venturing into amply loaded territory, he proceeded with caution. Sort of. "Oh, I'd figure you for a yacht in the Greek islands, maybe a couple of weeks in Paris, French Riviera. Somewhere you get your hair done by some guy with one name, designer clothes, important champagne. Some place you don't worry about breaking a nail."

His scenario was tauntingly familiar. She'd seen the life-style for years—a lot of her friends were caught up in it. Jake reveled in it, though he'd given it up to help her since the trial. She'd tried it for a while in her mid-twenties. It had been as empty as it sounded when he said it.

Well, she'd asked, and he'd been honest; she'd be honest back. "I've been those places. They're places you go with someone . . ." She'd been about to say "with someone you love"; she shifted her thought, picking her way carefully through the admission.

". . . places most people share. Since I'm not . . . sharing my life right now, I came here. To think. Do something useful." She hadn't intended to say any of this, so she switched gears and smiled ruefully at her ruined manicure. "Why are you here?"

Not married, and no one in her life? Focused on this information, he didn't expect the return question so quickly. He decided to be equally open. "My brother died five weeks ago. I took it hard. My lieutenant decided I'd be a lot better use to the department if I took a few days off."

At the mention of the department and his lieutenant, he saw her body shift involuntarily and stiffen. He paused a moment to let her know he'd noticed the reaction; when she declined an explanation, he continued. "I didn't want someplace where I'd have time to think." He helped her to her feet, and they retraced their path back to the roadway. Nobody in her life. Too good to be true. And why the cool breeze when any mention of police came up?

The single-lane road stretched due east and west without a curve. He verified the cloudless sky. No shade would be forthcoming this day. They started out again, resuming a mutually private silence. A short distance later they passed an overgrown dirt track off to the left; parallel furrows of flattened green weeds and plants indicated recent vehicle activity. How long ago? They'd heard no cars. A farmer driving back to his fields? Or returning to the main road and long gone. He couldn't tell from the tracks if there had been one vehicle or two. Better not push their luck. With cars so few and far between, he decided they had a better chance on the larger road, so he said nothing.

Allison had been thinking. For once her silent voice was leaving her in peace on the matter, but she wasn't at ease. This man had been completely honorable in his treatment of her from the beginning of this frightening situation; it was time he had an explanation. She walked from the sunlight to the shelter of a small tree at the roadside and paused. "I'm sorry about your brother."

The cop's ear heard heartfelt understanding; he followed her into the welcome shade. "Thanks."

"I lost my mother," she started. "She had a heart attack two years ago." Trust someone. "I know how much it hurts when you lose someone you love." Trust someone. "I didn't handle it very well. I had an emotional breakdown. I didn't see her buried. . . ." She paused for the strength to tell him why she hadn't seen her mother buried, and about the trial and the reason for the trial and the reason for the fear.

Zachary listened carefully. So that's what had ended her career. A nervous breakdown. He'd been right in suspecting there was more. There was no joy in being right this time. Caught off guard, he was thoroughly unprepared to hear himself confess in a leaden voice, "The last time I saw my brother, I called him a son of a bitch." No one knew this. Why on earth was he telling her?

Suddenly his rage at himself came spitting out. He saw her flinch at his vehemence, but somehow in the middle of this stupid road in this stupid situation, he was compelled to tell her—to get it out of his gut to the Gallé Girl who wasn't the Gallé Girl anymore because she'd had a mental breakdown when her mother died.

"We were fighting. He wanted to drop out of college and I'm busting my ass for the money to keep him in, so he'll have a shot at being . . . having whatever he wants, you know? I called him a stupid son of a bitch, and I slammed a door in his face and walked out! I walked around for a couple of hours . . . and then I went to a movie. A goddamned movie!"

She was instinctively quiet, recognizing that something was terribly wrong.

"Somehow, I finally figure out it's his life. He's got a right to screw it up just like anybody else." There was raw acid in his heart, but he was going to say it just once, so—just maybe—it would stop going around in his head. "So I go back to see him, to tell him it's okay. That it's just him and me now, and whatever he wants is okay. Well, he screwed it up all right." A barrel of anger welled in his chest. "I get to his apartment and the landlady hears me pounding on the door and tells me the stereo's been going for hours and asks me if I'm the cops. I'm the cops, all right."

The scene in his mind was so real, it was yesterday. "So I kick the door in. I find Lana in the bedroom. She's still got the . . . the goddamned needle in her arm. Damn her to hell!"

He hadn't raised his voice, but his intensity was raging. She felt a chill of dread, not wanting to hear the rest but afraid to try to stop him.

"He made it to the bathroom. She gave it to him first and he made it to the bathroom." He turned away from her, eyes dull with the pain of it. "His face is all swollen and black where the blood's drained into it and his eyes are staring and his mouth is open like he's screaming—and his teeth are down on the floor in that goddamned bathroom. . . ." He leaned tiredly against the trunk of the tree and closed his eyes. "I wasn't even sure it was him at first . . ."

She closed her eyes against the hideous image that jumped into her mind.

"I'm a vice cop. I deal with junkies every day of my life," he said in a dead voice, "and I didn't pick it up that my brother's on a needle." Then he was quiet. It was all said, and he was drained. After a long moment of silence, his breathing eased and he gave her a small mirthless smile. "Sorry about that. I wasn't trying to upset you." He searched for a cigarette, then remembered her aversion and settled for a drink of water from the canteen. "I'm not handling it very well, either, I guess."

She tried to find something to say, knowing from bald experience that nothing would help. Truly, nothing. "He knows you didn't mean it," she said at last. "If it was the other way around, you'd know, wouldn't you?"

He looked down into clear hazel eyes, afraid to drink in relief. He searched her face for reasons it might not be true.

Any response he might have given was interrupted by the hard crack and the quick echo of a gunshot. Off to the left and very close by.

Reverting instantly to cop, Zachary pushed her into the trees. "That shot means somebody's here and maybe we can get a ride. Maybe." He thought for a moment, then shut down the hope in her eyes. "Anybody with a gun—I want to see him before he sees us. Stay very quiet and let's check this out. What we don't want is to get shot."

She nodded in nervous understanding, and he led the way cautiously through the jungle growth. In a few minutes they found the edge of a small clearing. The green wall of the jungle stopped quite suddenly, and he almost stepped into the open.

In the clearing two men with pistols were terrorizing an old man; one held his arm high up on his back, behind his thin body, and the other stood in front slapping him viciously in the face, asking questions in Spanish.

"Yo no sé, señor," the old man said. "*Nada.*" A dead goat, a lumpy brown belly with legs still twitching, was lying in the yard in front of the men. The missing Land Rover was parked behind the thatched hut centered in the clearing.

Allison heard the voices clearly, and her Spanish was sufficient to understand the men had killed the goat as a warning. She crawled closer to whisper the information to Zachary, but he motioned her to silence; he understood.

The men were clearly angry and close to losing control. The situation was worse than volatile, and the old man was likely to be killed. Without a weapon there wouldn't be a goddamned thing Zachary could do about it.

Allison took off her hat and peeked around Zachary's body to the violent scene in the clearing. A sharp intake of breath as she heard the men demand information about the "*mujer americana.*" As she watched, the second man turned his pistol away from the old man's stomach to shoot another animal. The hapless goat buckled instantly, hind feet jerking. Two more panicky goats strained and jerked at their tethers at the bark of the revolver. Chickens squawked alarm calls and paused at attention, peering nearsightedly this way and that. Horrified, she could not quite swallow her scream and collapsed back into shadow.

The men followed the sound, and Zachary reacted a beat too late. "Shit." He was seen. Maybe not her. Maybe. He stepped out of their line of sight and yanked her to her feet. "Follow me. Now!" He broke for the road and heard her close behind him, angry voices in their wake.

They moved quickly through the tangled trees. He heard the Land Rover's engine rev as they reached the roadway. She wouldn't be able to match his speed, and neither of them could outrun a car. It was hopeless.

He pulled her swiftly down an embankment into a small ravine and behind a heavy clump of bushes. A split-second look around confirmed no better place to hide, so he told her to stay put, did she understand? "Stay put!" She was terrified. He slapped her ungently in the face and told her again, "Don't move! I'll be back."

He threw down the pack and took her face in his hands and forced her to look at him. "Don't leave here or I won't be able to find you." She managed to focus, then nodded in understanding. He clawed his way up to the road and heard the Rover scrabbling on the dirt turnoff. Crossing to the other side, he sprinted down the road as hard as he could, checking behind him on its progress. It came boiling out of the small side road, spitting dust and gravel as it turned toward him on the roadway.

Pulling out the stops, he ran flat out for just a few more yards, then at the last instant jumped feet first off the opposite side of the road and scrambled farther down the embankment as the Rover slid sideways to a halt. He made an immediate hard left and ran parallel with the road back past the Rover, then stopped when the engine was switched off. He forced himself not to move and suppressed his breathing as his heart bucked furiously in his chest and his lungs demanded air.

The men were listening. Waiting. Hearing no sound, one of them descended cautiously into the underbrush. Zachary moved with the noise, quickly a few more feet down the slope, gulping air, his heartbeat a crashing pulse in his ears. At the bottom he discovered an overgrown pathway and followed it past a small cleared field bordered by a stream. He avoided tracking the soft ground by wading into the swift-moving water and, at the opposite end of the milpa, stepped from the stream directly into a head-high stand of dead ripe cannabis. He slid into the middle of the thick green mass and stooped down to his smallest size. Then he waited.

Two minutes passed. Silence. Pumped up on adrenaline, he was jumpy. What the hell had they stumbled into? Another minute dragged by. He stared at the plants. So the old man grew an illegal cash crop. So what? This couldn't be about dope. The men were dangerous bastards; shooting the old man's goats had been calculated and basic. These guys weren't mental giants, they were clearly pissed, and they had at least two guns. They were looking for a woman from the United States. It had to be Luisita. Christ, he hoped they didn't find her! Or them.

He wished a thousandth useless time for his Magnum—this uneven business was for shit. The minute hand crept from 11:14 to 11:34. He felt a cramp beginning in his calf, and he moved his leg a quarter of an inch to relieve the pressure. Forty was too old for this crap. Salty perspiration ran down his back and neck from the relentless sun. Pollen drifted onto his body, sticking to his sweaty skin, itching and irritating. No way he would move unless they found him, and they had less chance of spotting him if he remained absolutely still, a part of the earth and the air.

He hoped he'd thrown them off Allison by recrossing the road to jump. The car should have destroyed most of the tracks near her hiding place. Maybe they'd already found her. Maybe . . . His mind started a spin on the possibilities, and he could feel himself losing control. He called on something he'd learned in combat and fastened his mind onto a beetle resolutely crawling up a stalk of the bush in front of him. Nothing existed in time except the beetle and the sounds of the forest as a million billion ants and bugs and slugs and centipedes rustled about their business, and leaf pushed against leaf for space in the sky. He listened for something that did not belong.

The beetle was the size of his thumbnail, an exquisite blend of iridescent gold powder and burnt green; tiny, powerful forelimbs dusted with the same magic color pulled the heavy body skyward. Unhurried. Singularly purposed. His breathing slowed and concentration deepened; twenty minutes became an hour.

At noon, the sun directly overhead, it was ridiculously hot. The air refused to move. The beetle's weight swayed a leaf. Zachary denied thirst. He wouldn't think about her.

Finally the engine started. He tuned his concentration to the motor sound and listened as the car drove away, holding down his need to move, forcing himself to listen and wait. No sounds of struggle had flowed on the thick air. The beetle lifted its hard shell wing coverings and whirred across the open ground of the milpa.

Surely she'd had sense enough to stay where he'd left her. With luck, they hadn't been able to backtrack and find her.

Don't think about her, not yet. Wait. The oldest strategy of war. Wait. Wait some more.

Sure enough, a few minutes later the car returned from the other direction, then picked up speed and moved on. Finally he worked his way silently back to the road. This was really beginning to wear at his nerves. Too many similarities to Laos—those bastards would have left a man behind, all day if necessary.

As he came up to the roadway, he heard an approaching car. Mind-burned and edgy, he crawled closer to the berm. Jesus, to lose a ride would be foolish. The car slowed to a stop two hundred feet down the road, too close to where he'd left her. The Land Rover. He sagged in frustration. He couldn't do jack-shit from here if they'd found her.

He saw the boots and trousers of a man getting into the car. From his side of the road—not hers. That much of his ruse had worked. The Land Rover threw up another cloud of dirt and gravel and sped away.

Now he could think about Allison. Jesus, she must be terrified. Checking frequently behind him to be certain the men were gone, he ran back up the road, searching for the ravine. Things had happened so quickly, and now everything in the blasted jungle looked alike. He didn't dare risk calling out, they were too near the old man's hut. Furious that he was in this situation, and totally frustrated at not having the power to do anything about it, he nearly missed the ravine.

As he eased himself down into the shadows, he saw her staring at him, eyes wide with fright, rigid as a doe in a spotlight. She hadn't moved an inch, but she had the Swiss Army knife in her hand with an opened blade. He had a sudden surge of pride in her; that had taken guts. As he got closer he could see she was tranced out.

"You did damned good, Chicago!" he told her fervently. "Damned good!"

Nerves at the breaking point, adrenaline reacting, quivering, she could barely stand.

"I don't know who those bastards were, baby, but they were fucking serious, I can tell you that." He removed the knife from her rigid fingers and bent to massage the muscles in her calves. "I'd have been here sooner, but one of 'em waited back there for over an hour." He was glad she had been in the shade.

Jittery and in need of physical action, he tried to massage her shoulders, but she shied away and shrugged him off. He couldn't blame her for being jumpy. They shared the canteen, and he helped her drink, aware she was thirsty but had waited for him to return before she drank. Apparently, she literally hadn't moved except to get the knife. Christ, what made her tick? He was uncertainly impressed. "Can you walk?"

She nodded, and he sighed in relief. He'd been in worse places, but not lately. And not without hope of backup. He grabbed the pack and led the way back to the stream under the bridge, where he gratefully removed his shirt and washed away the itchy pollen. "It's after two o'clock and we still don't know how far it is into that village. The old man is a question mark. Could have been any number of situations going down." He paced the small bank. "I vote we start back for the cave. If a vehicle passes us in either direction, we ride. If not, we spend the night where we know it's safe and start out again tomorrow."

Shaky and emotionally wired, Allison could only nod agreement.

In the brutal heat it took nearly an hour to return to the cave. There had been no chance for a ride, and they were both drained from the heat and humidity, adrenaline exhaustion, and exertion.

Inside, Allison collapsed in the cool darkness, entirely too quiet. She hadn't said a word since he'd slapped her. He hoped to hell she wasn't having another breakdown. He dropped the backpack and welcomed the coolness of the dim cavern, watching her closely in his peripheral vision.

Suddenly her tensed whisper broke the silence. "I'm sorry I screamed." She began rocking in place, agitated and terse, in another place, another time. "It wouldn't have happened if I hadn't screamed." She seemed to return to the present. "They wouldn't have seen us. I'm sorry," she repeated.

Zachary was at a loss. She was right, of course. "Maybe you saved the old man's life," he responded. "Who knows. Sooner or later, they'd have run out of goats."

She looked at him and stopped the motion, sagging against a boulder to consider his words for a long while; then, quietly, "Thank you."

"At least we know who they are, and for sure they're bloody dangerous," he continued. "From now on, we can't be too careful."

Miraculously, the coals were still alive. He tossed on some twigs and quickly produced a small fire while she retrieved the dried soup from the pack; they took turns stirring the artificial soup until it was warm enough to drink.

"We can't stay here indefinitely, and it's obviously not safe to go wandering about without some sort of plan." Zachary was thinking out loud. "I didn't get a good look at either of those assholes. Straight black hair, they could be anyone. We'll just have to watch out for the car."

In the entire five hours they'd been on or near the road, the only other person had been the old man. He checked his watch again. Almost three o'clock. If he hustled, he could get to the old guy's hut and back by dark.

"I'm gonna pay a visit to the farmer. It didn't look to me like he was one of the boys, but it's hard to know for sure. Maybe they were having a lover's quarrel," he said sardonically.

She stared at him a moment and then stood up. He was going to leave her. "I don't think it's a good idea to separate," she said thinly.

"It's better if you stay here and get some rest. You model types got no fat on you, no reserve. If you pass out on me in this heat, I'll have to carry you." He was only partly kidding, and she could read his worry that she was losing it; he attempted to lighten the mood. "You're cute and all, Chicago, but I can travel much faster without you. If he's there, I'll have him take me into the nearest village and make arrangements for a car."

Plus, he could keep her whereabouts a secret until he had some measure of control back in their lives. "If it's dark, don't hit me with a rock or anything." He was finally rewarded with a pale smile.

He brought in wood and built up the small fire. The cave was wonderfully cool in the afternoon heat, but they both knew it would soon be cold and uncomfortable. He warned her again. "Stay inside. If you go out, anyone at the top of either side of this canyon could see you down here."

"I'll be careful." She handed him a flashlight. "You'll need this when it gets dark."

He didn't dare tell her flashlights made great targets at

night. "No, I won't—you keep it. I was just kidding about coming back after dark. I should be here by six on the outside."

She didn't know whether to believe him or not.

"You'll just have to take it on faith that I'll be back—hopefully with dinner." He shook the full canteen and tried again for humor. "You like roast goat?"

She made a face and shuddered, remembering the bloody sight of the collapsing animal. "I could eat goat hide at this stage." It was true. She was starving. The salty soup had awakened an appetite.

"Your job is to get yourself rested by the time I get back." She was still too quiet to suit him. As he readied himself for the trip, it occurred to him that he was too preoccupied with leaving her alone here. Not good. Why was it women always complicated things? Even women who held their own. On impulse, he gave her a quick hug and a brusque kiss on the cheek as he left the cave. He didn't like it that he was worried about her; it muddied his concentration.

Allison was surprised at the kiss, unsure how to read his actions. Unsure of anything. The last two hours had her reeling. Waiting for the men in the car to go away, she'd had all she could do to hold on to her reason; shock had set in after she'd managed the knife. She didn't remember much else until he'd given her a drink of water.

She watched him pick his way rapidly downstream. What if something happened and he didn't come back? Were they supposed to die for some reason? If someone killed them and buried their bodies out here, no one would ever . . . A tense black spider of fear crawled up her back, giving her a chill that made the hair stand up on her arms. She rubbed it away and retreated farther into the cave.

His absence was infinitely worse than his presence, and at first she was at a loss as to what to do. Then she took inventory of their meager supplies, repacking those to take when they left, checking out the cave opening every few minutes, pausing at every sound, making certain she was still alone.

The backpacks neatly stacked, she waited. As the seconds crawled into minutes, her anxiety built steadily to a steel-lined obsession about what to do if he didn't return at all and she had to figure this out on her own.

Her stomach began to spasm. She hadn't had that reaction since the really tough part of her therapy, since the phone call notifying her of her mother's death. And, before that . . . that weekend. She worked her head and shoulders to relieve the rigid muscles. Finally she took a Valium.

Waiting for the drug to calm her down, too jumpy to sit still, she took yet another tour of the cave to be certain she hadn't overlooked anything and discovered the tin of cold tea. She started to throw it out, then changed her mind and added some water, heated it on the fire, then slowly sipped the stronger, now bitter brew, searching for the relaxation she knew the herb would provide.

Ten minutes later, anxiety measurably reduced, life slowed down to seventy-eight, and her shoulder blades were sponge cake. No longer greatly concerned, she walked to the mouth of the cave and stared at the shimmering creek in the sweltering afternoon heat with a heightened awareness of grime. Forcing a comb through her hair, she was conscious of an itchy scalp and her bra sticking damply to the skin on her rib cage. Her mind followed the progress of perspiration formed at the base of her hairline as it trickled down her neck and under the loose T-shirt; in the hollow between her breasts, beads of water slid under the metal fastener and sideways down her stomach, a sticky tickle.

This must be the famous "Belizian water torture." She giggled at this profound identification, decided Zachary should hear it. She pulled Jake's shirt away from her body, flapping the bottom to create a cooling movement of air. "God, what I wouldn't give for one of those ghastly cold showers." Mobilized by the thought, she moved to the abandoned supplies and the small bar of soap stored in a plastic travel case. As she'd promised, she was extremely careful when she left the cave.

At a secluded eddy at the base of the falls, she removed her boots and socks, carefully placing them nearby, safe and dry. Slowly, deliciously, she lowered herself into the cooling shallow water, fascinated first with the air bubbles trapped under her wrinkled linen slacks as the water disappeared the creases, then with the progress of water up the shirt and T-shirt, altering the color from light to dark in its wake.

Bracing herself on her elbows, she leaned back luxuriously in the crisply cool, clear water. There's something about clean hair with women that men never understand, she philosophized silently, knowing Zachary would be furious at her improvised shampoo. She soaped her hands and worked the lather into her hair. It felt impossibly good. Men looked masculine and romantic with a two-day growth of beard, but women with dirty hair looked positively awful, and it was mysteriously important that she not look positively awful.

She tipped her soapy head backward into the water again, rinsed her hair, and confronted herself about Zachary Cross. I *do believe you have approximately normal feelings about this man*, said her silent voice. D*o you suppose it's possible*?

She stepped soggily out onto a small sandbank and finger-combed her wet hair into submission. Admit it. You had a great time at those pyramids . . . you were fine with him until Luisita disappeared.

And, you survived last night with a minimum of Valium. She smiled at the memory of sharing delightful, normal laughter with him. Something about bats. She fished the mushy soap out of the shallows to put it in its case. He was really hurting about his brother. She'd forgotten that men could hurt. She'd known that once, or believed it.

And he'd been smart enough to keep them safe in a situation that had gotten more and more dangerous. She felt secure enough with him that she'd been ready to give him a small measure of trust. *Until we saw those men kill that old man's goat, things were . . .* Her thoughts turned more and more to reality as she searched for a word. She waited for the water to stream out of her clothing, getting lost in the coolness of a tiny breeze. *Okay . . . not great, but okay.* She moved to her boots. *Definitely okay.*

A small sound. Like a cough. Or had she imagined it? She snapped to a crisp awareness. She'd been careless, standing in full view of anyone who might be looking down from the canyon rim. Zachary had demanded she be careful, and she'd been daydreaming. Fighting an overwhelming, paralyzing feeling that she was being watched, trying not to telegraph her fright to the watcher, she unconsciously held her breath as she covertly scanned the sides of the canyon.

Nothing.

And again.

Absolutely nothing. She relaxed a bit. It had been her imagination. She breathed again.

A definite cough, and louder. This time she froze and searched more carefully, lower down. She studied the rocks and shadows in the late afternoon light and, missing him once, came back with a jerk. It was a huge black jaguar, with implacable golden topaz eyes, perched high up in one of the trees a short distance downstream—safely, hooray and hallelujah, on the other side of the water. She saw its small ears pitch forward and the tail begin a restless twitch as the cat deepened its stare.

Luisita sat in silence in the old man's hut. Hard afternoon sunlight streamed in through the doorway, striking particles of dust drifting down. Jorgé K'ayum stood by in his white chiapa, grave with concern.

"Dead?" she repeated, stunned. How could Sara be dead? Perhaps she had not understood. The *t'o'ohil* and his son were Lacandon Maya, but she and Sara had not been in Guatemala since they were small children; their dialect was perhaps different enough. . . .

"Three days," said the little boy, not more than eight years old. The old man nodded his head in agreement, held his hands in the manner of carrying an infant. "There was a baby," said the boy.

She had not misunderstood. Sara was dead. Now they were telling her the baby, too. It was too much. She tried to find a place in her heart that did not hurt. The *t'o'ohil* motioned to the boy, who pulled her out into the harsh sunlight, led her past the prayer hut down a dirt path through a jumble of trees. The path ended abruptly at a site of many graves, each carefully aligned north and south, one newly covered. "Your sister is here," said the child. "Three days ago."

She stared at the broken ground, her throat dry and hot as the dirt on the mound, tears refusing to be born in her eyes. It was over. Such a tiny grave for Sara. Inside would be the small dog made of palm leaf to guide and protect her sister's soul in its long journey through the Underworld and a bone to toss to Kisin's vicious dogs so the soul could pass unharmed, a bowl of corn to eat during the journey. Sara's soul would have to travel many miles to find proof of her birth; the placenta had been buried in their old village many miles to the west. She shut her eyes in prayer.

Last night she had stayed with the family of the driver who'd picked her up on the road. They had confirmed that Jorgé K'ayum was *t'o'ohil* of the village, but they would not say whether a woman with a baby had arrived several days ago or if it was possible such a woman was staying with Jorgé. At dawn, after the morning meal of beans and tortillas, her host had dropped her in the village near the old man's hut. One of Jorgé K'ayum's neighbors told her he was across the lake at his milpa. The man would not answer questions about Sara and walked away, as was proper. The *t'o'ohil* was the authority in the village, the decision maker.

She had waited the entire day, confident that Sara and the baby were somewhere nearby and the *t'o'ohil* would tell her where to find them.

He had arrived with his small son a few minutes ago. Five feet tall, nearly eighty years old, Jorgé K'ayum stood arrow straight in his traditional, knee-length white shirt, long black hair framing his ancient face. He had not spoken, but somehow the young boy understood his thoughts. When she identified herself as Sara's sister, the old man's eyes told her Sara was dead before the boy could say the words.

Inside herself, Luisita felt hollow. Drained of purpose. "What about the baby?" she asked the boy. "Where is . . ."

"The baby is not here," he said solemnly. They returned

to the small village; past his father's hut, and three houses down he called out politely to the family inside.

"*Oken*," came the response. Inside the hut was a young Lacandon man of perhaps sixteen and his wife, and a small cradle. The young girl suckled a newborn.

"This is my sister, Nuk," said the young boy. "Bol is her husband. I am Little Bol."

She murmured a polite greeting, but her eyes sought the cradle. Another small baby lay inside. Hope surged through her heart.

"This is Sara's baby," Little Bol said proudly, pointing to the infant at Nuk's breast. Luisita's eyes filled with tears. She crossed the room to put her hand on the baby's face and assure herself that he was real. When the miniature hand, so perfect, wound firmly around her thumb, the knot in her stomach eased and she was able to smile at last. For her sister, who would rest safely in the Underworld, for the tiny little boy suckling his dinner, and for herself, Balum had been kind.

When the sated infant dropped into sleep, Nuk smiled and handed him over, then moved to prepare dinner for her family. Luisita cradled the tiny being in her arms and stepped outside. In the west, clouds drifted through the parrot's tail—the brilliant golds and yellows, reds and magentas, of a Guatemalan sunset.

Sara's baby. Now hers. Many things would have to be considered now. She felt the heavy pull of the money and the papers inside her purse. Time was running out.

Two years in the United States had changed many things but had created no doubt that she was other than a True Person. Would it be a good thing to take a male Mayan child to America? So many things could go wrong there. Small children died as an everyday occurrence in Central America, from diseases cured with ordinary pills. This she knew from newspapers in Miami. But, in Mayan villages, young boys learned to hear the thoughts of wise old men. Only Balum and Hachkäyum knew such things. She would have to seek the counsel of the *t'o'ohil* before she would decide. The boy's future in the village would depend on the *t'o'ohil*'s decisions.

The brilliant sunset faded abruptly and Luisita returned inside the hut to sit on Nuk's abandoned stool and study the sleeping baby. Nuk saw to her own child and bustled about building up the hearth fire as Bol moved to set up a hammock for Luisita.

Smelling ancient food smells from her childhood, half-cooked black beans and pure white rice, *k'oshosh*—fire-dried tortillas—made with red corn, Luisita embraced the life she had lived as a child. She smiled at Nuk and offered to help prepare the meal; placing her nephew in the cradle alongside Nuk's child, she considered: Sara was no more in this life. Perhaps she would send a message in a dream this night to help her know what to do.

As if answering her thoughts, Little Bol appeared in the doorway and beckoned her to follow. "My father wishes to see you." She felt the pull of the old man's mind.

Jorgé K'ayum stared briefly at Luisita. "The little one is Balum *onen*, hah?"

She nodded. "Also Kah—ladino, from his father."

The old man's eyes stared steadily into hers. The smoke from his homemade cigar drifted to the ceiling. "You wish to take him away?"

"I seek your guidance, in Yumeh—my father. What should I do?"

The old man looked to the ground. "You have lived two years with the *ts'ul* and you wish my decision?" He was pleased with her.

"Yes, in Yumeh."

After a long silence, Jorgé spoke. "This is not a good thing. Strangers will come here. . . ." He paused again, and she waited. "There is much cold," he said from a faraway place. "Too much cold and fear in the world. It dwells in the souls of all living things and has seeped into the hearts of the trees and the soil. Soon, food will not grow here. It is the punishment of Hachäkyum."

Finally he returned to the matter at hand. "The child will be safe if he stays here in the village, but he must watch the death of the forest, and the animals, one by one," he said with great sadness. Luisita shivered at the prophecy and did not reply. At last he looked up, and it was clear she was dismissed. "*Ki'iba' a wilik*—be careful what you see in your dreams," he said with a sigh.

She returned slowly to the hut with a heavy heart, to share the evening meal, lost in thought; Nuk and Bol ate quietly, politely asking no questions about her talk with the *t'o'ohil*. After dinner, Bol left to pay a visit to his brother and she helped Nuk wash red corn and set it on the hearth to steep in the lime and soften overnight. The baby slept quietly in the cradle next to Nuk's child, Jorgé's seventh grandchild.

"Where did my sister bury the proof of his birth?" she asked.

"Under the small tree, there." Nuk pointed to an ironwood sapling, healthy and green, several feet from the doorway to the hut.

She nodded in approval. "Your father has given me no choice for the baby. He says I must decide," she said finally.

Nuk nodded. She was not surprised. "My father has been sad since the government took the mahogany trees," she said matter-of-factly. "Sometimes sacred ceiba trees are taken also. Hachäkyum is angry at this. My father thinks soon will be Xu'tan. He says this will be a good thing. The gods will make a new world."

Luisita did not disagree. Nor had the old man's words surprised her. When she sought counsel from the *t'o'ohil* in her village before leaving for the United States, he'd told her much the same thing.

"This world is too old," he had said. "Too old, by many years." He, too, had not held a ceremony for the renewal of the god-pots. Everyone knew the incense burners, dedicated to individual gods, were to be renewed every seven or eight years, five cycles of Venus in the Mayan calendar. If they were not, the gods became angry, with dire consequences for the world and everyone in it. When questioned by the villagers, the *t'o'ohil* had replied, "It would only provide a little more time before Xu'tan."

She left the hut a few minutes later and walked in the twilight to Sara's grave. There she placed a small incense burner at its foot, lit the pom and sent her voice to Balum. "This is for you, Balum, to please you and make you happy. This is for you, Balum, to please you to keep Sara's infant safe and well. This is for you, Balum, to provide food for this village. This is for you, Balum, to let me know your wishes, to give me a sign and please you with my life."

The incense burned with an intense blue-green flame, and the ageless smoking perfume drifted up in a true straight line almost to her shoulders before curling and dispersing itself into the night air. After a while she followed the path back to the dirt road through the village, secure that she could now decide.

Behind her on the road she heard in the stillness the sound of an engine, harsh and foreign in the quiet of the village. She glanced around. It was the Land Rover approaching slowly, without headlights, and her heart leaped. Perhaps this was the sign. She was about to hail the car when something stilled her hand. The American man and woman were not in the car. She quickly lowered her face. As the car passed, she saw that a rat-faced man was driving, another man was turned away. Ladinos. She was disquieted. What had happened to the *tsoy y-ol* and the woman?

She hurried to Bol's hut. The baby was awake and hungry, and she opened a can of formula from the suitcase and prepared a bottle. She settled into the hammock and fed the child, rocking gently. "Adam," she decreed. "Your name shall be Adam."

The baby's eyes focused dimly on her face and stared solemnly unwinkingly, as he pulled on the nipple. Half the bottle and twenty minutes later, she quietly bid Nuk and Bol good night and curled in her hammock with the sleeping baby limp against her body. She sped another prayer to Balum for the safety of the Americans and tried to sleep.

In the unreal setting, a brilliantly backlit sky from a spectacular crimson-orange-and-yellow sunset lacing the treetops with golden edges, Allison stared at the huge cat, entranced. Faint black rosettes in the coal black hide were visible where sunlight bounced on the skin at certain angles; black on black—the rarest color of the breed. Here they were called panthers, an endangered species. From conversations with Emilio and Osari, she knew a sighting of this rare and magnificent animal was unusual and lucky.

None of that knowledge prepared her for the thrill of raw primal power staring down at her from the limb. "You're almost worth this nightmare," she said to him.

The jaguar froze at the sound of her voice.

"You just keep that gorgeous skin on your side of the river, and I'll stay on mine."

She wasn't exactly frightened by the cat, but she was intensely conscious of being alone. And very small. Aware, too, that there was no one to share this sight, that it would exist beyond this instant only in her memory; she tried to prolong time, imprint the essence of its being. The cat coolly received her stare for several long moments, then it jumped smoothly to the ground, hide glistening in a shaft of sunlight, and melted away into the long shadows of late afternoon as if it had never been.

Just as abruptly, the brilliant sunset began to fade into early twilight. Suddenly unsure it had happened at all, and highly aware of her visibility, Allison hurried up and across the rocks to the mouth of the cave.

Within the safety of the cavern, she felt clean and cool as the water evaporated from her wet clothing. Flashing back to the powerful image in the tree, she didn't see the scorpion, but she felt the shocking pain of its sting as it punctured the skin on the inside of her naked foot, below the bone of her ankle. Furious, she succeeded in pinning the dirt-brown little beast into the sandy floor of the cave with the heel of her hiking boot. The wriggling creature whipped its tail about, striking in vain at the leather. The pain in her instep escalated rapidly to the limit of her tolerance, and she realized she had to do something about the wound. Quickly.

Hobbling, numb with disbelief that it was happening, Allison instinctively sought the backpack, gulping in huge breaths of air. Her hands trembled with shock and the effort not to cry out as she located Band-Aids, the army knife, and a bottle of alcohol. Eyes blurring with tears from the pain, she managed to extract a blade.

The area around the puncture was white and rigid. She exhaled a gasp of new agony as she made a clumsy incision in thin, sensitive skin, then brought her foot to her mouth to manage an awkward and mostly ineffectual try at sucking out venom. She spit the blood onto the sand. Then she poured alcohol into the wound and cringed at the added assault to the pain level; finally she pasted Band-Aids across the cut with quivering fingers.

A few feet away, the scorpion was stubbornly working its way from under the boot. In a white rage, she went after it. It wasn't going to get away, and it wasn't going to sting anyone else. She grabbed the plastic soap case to capture it, but the soap was stuck inside, so she ground the tough little body into the softened bar of Dove, closed it up with the plastic lid, and put one of the rubber bands around it.

Now that she had it, she didn't know what to do with it. Feeling ridiculous, she gave in to pain and frustration and threw it aside in a fury. Huddled on the floor of the cave, she buried her face in her jacket to muffle the sounds of her misery.

After a few minutes the emotional outburst eased and she panted erratically as she pulled herself together. Crying didn't help. She'd learned that three years ago. "This solves nothing!" she scolded herself. "You've had worse, remember. At least . . . the damned thing . . . only stings once." A hollow bubble of laughter, bordering on hysteria, took up too much space in her chest.

Cold in the wet clothing, she put on her left sock and boot and hobbled to her pack, took out her journal, and located a ballpoint pen. "Get yourself together. You have to . . . stay calm and . . . rational . . . if you're going to get out of this. . . ." She sat again on the large stone, rocking back and forth to ease the pain. "Calm and rational," she repeated, "calm and rational . . . just until he gets back. Calm and rational . . ." She began a record of the injury:

Scorpion sting
About 4:00 immediate shock
extreme pain Incision Alcohol
4:30 lightheaded thirsty

She hopped again to her pack, keeping her foot off the ground. There was nothing in it for this kind of pain. Aspirin was useless. Her heart was thudding in its effort to deal with the shock to her system. She started to drink Zachary's tequila and remembered that alcohol would increase her heart rate and spread the poison faster through her bloodstream, put the bottle back in his pack, and came to the Valium. A relaxant. It wouldn't do much for the pain, but it might keep her calm. Taking the tablets with water, she hopped back to the stone to enter:

2 aspirin and Valium for pain at 4:35

"For Zachary," she repeated as she wrote, holding tight to the pen, fingers slippery with perspiration. "He'll need to know."

After half an hour her foot was swollen to the ankle and the ache was unceasing. She was shivering, her face wet and sweaty, and the rocking didn't help. Nothing helped. Driven to tears and the edge of endurance, she took another Valium.

She picked up the journal to make the entry when she remembered. Oh, God! What had Colonel Sharp said about scorpions down here? Some of them kill people. She fought for control. Do something! Don't just die here! Her mind began to function. It's still twilight. Go up to the road and flag down a car. Surely there are workers who go home at dark.

Moaning with pain, Allison jammed her swollen foot into a sock, forced it into the hiking boot, and tied the laces. At the confinement, the foot and ankle throbbed anew and tears from escalated pain blurred her vision. She jerkily gathered up her pack, then realized she'd forgotten Zachary. He'd be back soon. She had to leave some kind of explanation. She found a fresh page in the journal and made herself write:

Zachary—Scorpion sting/in case.
Bad reaction.
Jaguar nearby. Am going to
the road at . . .

She checked her watch. The dial was fuzzy; in her tears and the dimming light, it took a full minute to figure out.

. . . 5:15 to flag a car.
Will send someone for you.

She left the journal open at the written page and placed it on his pack. The book was balky, refusing to break and stay open. She looked around for a small rock and found the plastic case with the scorpion inside, slapped it on top of the journal. He couldn't fail to see it. She picked up her backpack and limped slowly out of the cave for the eternal journey to the crossing.

She came to the boulders and painfully made her way across. Her mind was numbed, and she was losing strength; her pack would not stay on her shoulder. Retrieving it, disoriented in the failing light, she could not remember if she was across the river. Dizzy from the poison and the drugs, her wounded ankle screaming in protest, she struggled to recross the stream and continued slowly along the stony bank above the river. The pack dropped to the ground.

A few yards farther on, she knew dimly she would not make it. She would have to go back. Weaving, she grabbed on to the roots of a fallen pine; the brittle wood snapped without warning and the weakened ankle buckled. Both hands lost their grip and she fell hard off the bank. Knocked breathless by the fall, she woke momentarily from the shock of cold water, then, losing consciousness, slid deeper into the slow-moving stream.

Inside the cave the journal buckled and slid with the soap case to the floor.

Zachary quietly circled the clearing before approaching the hut. "Hello. Anyone here?" Sweaty and breathing heavily, he stooped slightly to walk through the door, uncomfortable in the trespass. The hut was empty.

A marvel of efficiency, clean lines of cross beams showed beneath the thick thatch covering. A small shelf on one wall sagged with the weight of clay cooking pots with smoke-blackened bottoms. Sheaves of tobacco and assorted sizes of gourds hung from thongs tied in the rafters; a shock of corn leaned into a corner.

One of the slain goats had been gutted, skinned, and, suspended from a rafter, covered with burlap. Swarms of buzzing flies, drunk on the primal smell, looped and fought for space in a feeding frenzy at the pool of blood soaking into the dirt floor. The second animal was missing; the rest of the goats were in a small pen next to the hut.

Zachary examined a blackened three-stone triangle and the cold ashes of a hearth fire. Larger gourds and baskets and several rough woolen blankets were positioned in the slender rafters. The remaining furniture was a stout reed cot, a rolled-up hammock, and a wooden stool covered with animal hide. He had held no possibility of a telephone in this remote area, but the old man might know where to find one. As he sat on the rough wooden stool and battled flies thirsty for the sweat salt on his skin, he studied the goat carcass and waited for the farmer to return, his mind rolling over the events of the past twenty- four hours.

Somebody stealing their car was a pain in the ass, but this was getting complicated. These two guys had been more than willing to threaten people's lives to find this woman Luisita. As much as it pissed him off to let them get away with it, the whole thing was too dangerous to mess with. If the old man didn't come back tonight, he'd return to the cave and propose a new plan: this time they'd get up at dawn and go back the way they'd come. Screw the village—it could be miles down this dirtwater track, if it existed at all.

Still, the farmer had walked somewhere with the goat. There had to be a town, a village, another farmer living nearby. Wherever he'd gone, surely someone had a car or a horse or a something they could ride to get to a telephone. Who knew anything down here. He paced among the flies, deliberately unsettling them, frustrated to his socks. His watch told him he'd been gone an hour and eighteen minutes. He thought about her. Ex–Gallé Girl. She hadn't been in terrific shape when he left. An emotional breakdown, she'd said. It must have been some kind of breakdown to blow a career that big.

He reexamined their conversation before the crazies had started shooting the old man's goats. She'd been about to tell him something important to her, he was sure of it. But he'd lost it when she brought up her mother's funeral. God, that was weird. What the hell had he been thinking about? Something had triggered him to dump it all out about Jerry. He hadn't realized he was that wired about it. Jesus, Cross, he railed at himself. She tells you her mother died and gets buried while she's in a sanitarium or something, and you pile everything about Jerry on her.

His mind pulled him back to the healing part of their conversation, to hear her voice again: "He knows you didn't mean it." It had never occurred to him to turn it around. Of course, Jerry would know. "Just like I'd know if I'd been the one who bought it." The sound of his own voice startled him. He'd been drifting, and it wasn't like him. Don't think about her, he told himself. Think about how to get her out of here.

Twenty minutes later, in the middle of an incredible sunset, he judged it hopeless and decided to leave. He hadn't been serious about roast goat, but it was apparent that if they were going to eat tonight, he'd have to find a way to cut the damned thing or figure out how to kill one of the chickens.

He glanced around the rafters. Surely the old man had something sharp here, a machete or something. He for sure wasn't going to haul the whole damned goat to the cave. He could manage to kill a chicken if he found a machete—if he could catch the chicken. He had a sudden horrific thought of himself chasing chickens around a clearing in the middle of Guatemala. He was losing it.

No machete existed in the hut. He was almost relieved until he realized that if he caught one of the chickens, he'd have to strangle it. He deliberately made a fist and smacked it into the goat carcass, spinning it furiously on its rope, scattering the flies. They buzzed face and nose and ears. It was impossible to keep them at bay.

At a small sound he turned to find the farmer staring at him, thoroughly puzzled. Distracted by the flies and the prospect of murdering chickens, he hadn't heard the old man's approach. He offered his hand. "*Hola, señor,*" he said scrambling for Spanish. "*Hablo usted* English?"

The old man shook his head slowly, watching Zachary.

"American." Surely the old man would understand.

"*Sí, señor,*" The old man bobbed his head. "*Americano.*"

It took Zachary a few minutes to convey he meant no harm. Between his high school Spanish and Miami street pidgin, and the old man's equally halting English, he eventually learned that the man's name was Perez and the men were from San Ruiz; they had been looking for the woman with the Americans. So it had been Luisita after all. Something about a husband.

Apparently they'd stumbled into a local feud of some kind. The old man wasn't clear. They'd found the Land Rover out of gas a few miles down the road and were convinced he'd seen them or was hiding them.

"*Hombres malos, señor. Drogas. ¿Comprende?*"

"*Sí.* I *comprende,* okay." Zachary felt hatred run liquid through his stomach. *Drogas*—drugs. He should have known. Drug dealers. Iran supplied the heroin, Central and South America exported cocaine. Between them they kept America's junkies flying. And crashing onto tile floors in bathrooms. Bastards. And dangerous. "*¿Dónde está un teléfono?*"

"*Sí, señor, teléfono.*" Perez screwed up his face in his effort to communicate outside his language.

Eventually Zachary gleaned that the nearest phone was several miles away, at a town farther west on the gravel road, deeper into Guatemala. San Ruiz. Home of the bad guys.

"*¿Dónde está un pueblo? ¿Con un*"—what the hell was the

word for automobile—"*carro*? *¿Cuántas horas*?"

"*Dos horas, señor.*" The old man pointed vaguely off to the west, the direction of Luisita's village. "*¿Un carro*?" He shrugged and gestured with his hands that he wasn't sure."*Pero no teléfono.*" The nearest village was two hours, and there was no telephone—possibly a car.

Zachary told Perez that the Mayan woman had disappeared. He lied that the American woman was missing also. That it was urgent that someone call the authorities. He emptied his pockets and gave Perez a couple of tens and several single dollars. The old man had no paper but located a stub of a pencil.

Zachary wrote his name and the name of the hotel on one of the ten-dollar bills. "Call collect. Tell this man, Rider, where I am and that I need help—assistance—and to send the *policía*." He tapped his shield. "*¿Comprende policía*?" The word was universal.

The frightened man took the money and told him it would take a full day's time to make the calls. "*Teléfono, uh, no serve, señor,*" he mumbled.

Zachary tapped the money. "You make sure it *serves*!" he said firmly. "I need food." He motioned to his mouth and made chewing motions.

Perez lifted down one of the gourds hanging from the ceiling, took out several eggs, and then broke off two ears of field corn from the shock in the corner.

Zachary carefully put the eggs into various pockets in the jacket. He declined the corn and pointed at the goat. The old man shook his head in despair. "Not the whole thing." Zachary indicated with his hands. "*Poquito.*"

Perez produced a knife and cut a chunk off the carcass, and Zachary stuffed the bloody meat into another pocket. "I'll be back *mañana*, uh, *noche*," he repeated to the old man. "*Mañana noche.*"

"*¡Mañana, no*!" the old man said strongly. "*No tiempo.*" No time.

"Okay. Two days. *Dos mañanas.*" Zachary held up two fingers.

"Sí." The old man held up two fingers also. He understood two days. Zachary would be back tomorrow night; Allison couldn't handle *dos mañanas*. One of the chickens would buy it *mañana* if he had to drown it.

He stopped on his way out of the hut and returned to the corner to pull one of the blankets down from the rafters. Now he could sleep somewhere other than next to the fire. "*Dos mañanas*," he said again, and pointed at the blanket.

He repeated his requests a final time, and Perez nodded in silent agreement.

Pushing himself down the track in the early twilight, Zachary considered the evening ahead. It would be black in an hour, and he was worried about her. He'd see what kind of shape she was in, and maybe they'd spend the night with Perez. She'd probably feel a whole lot safer in the hut than she did alone with him in a cave in the middle of the jungle. For sure they'd stay in the old man's hut tomorrow and watch the road for vehicles to get them the hell out of Guatemala. *Teléfono* call or no *teléfono* call.

Tired, wanting nothing more than to put the meat on a spit and crash for an hour, Zachary quietly entered the cave. If she was already sleeping, he didn't want to wake her. He dropped the blanket and his eyes adjusted gradually to the low light. Her sleeping bag was rolled and stacked next to his backpack by the remains of the fire, but she was gone. He didn't want to believe it. Why on earth would she leave? He couldn't possibly have passed her outside. She was just gone. And her backpack was gone.

"Damn it to hell!" He examined the empty cave. Jesus, maybe she'd freaked being by herself for so long. People did crazy things when they panicked. She hadn't doused the fire, the coals were still hot. He must have just missed her. But if she'd gone to the road, he'd have seen her, unless she'd gotten a ride. He'd have heard a car. . . . His stomach twisted. She wasn't the careless type. Had someone come in on foot? One of the bastards that had chased them? Someone else? She hadn't taken her hat or the sleeping bag, but her backpack was gone. What the goddamn hell was she thinking about? He called out in frustration into the fading twilight, "Hey, Chicago! Where are you?" If she hadn't made it to the road . . . maybe she was lost out there somewhere. "Answer me!" Damn! Damn it to hell!

He had no way of guessing how long she'd been gone; it was nearly dark, and he was furious. Why the hell couldn't she just do as she was told! He should have taken her with him. She'd been scared when he left and he had known it, but she'd have slowed him down. Guilt made him even angrier. He should have taken her.

He played the flashlight along the floor of the cave. It was too sandy for clear prints, but there appeared to be no sign of struggle. It would be pitch black in twenty minutes. "Why would she leave!" he raged, damning all independent women anywhere. Now he had no idea where to look for her, and even if the old farmer made the call, anyone looking for them would have the same problem he had trying to find her.

Furious, he tossed small pieces of wood onto the coals as he sifted through possible actions. In order to leave, she'd have had to cross the river. It was now close on to full darkness and getting dangerous. He didn't know much about Guatemala, but any jungle was full of predators, including snakes, that went on the hunt at night. Stay here and wait, go out and look. Look where! He dug the half-empty pack of cigarettes out of his backpack and lit one in defiance. Damn her anyway! When was he going to learn not to trust women? And this one had had a mental breakdown. Jesus, what a mess!

The jaguar, measurably bolder, had carefully followed the woman's progress along the bank of his river. Shallow eyes had watched without conscience, coldly fascinated by her fall into the water. He had been waiting. From time to time, when there was no movement, he cautiously crept forward, belly hugging the damp earth next to the water. The sunlight faded and still he waited, inching closer, nervous at the pungent human smell. Finally he gathered to charge. At the last moment the wind shifted and the cat caught another human scent; midstride, his attention wavered at movement on the other side of the creek.

Across the water Zachary caught his breath when he saw the great cat retreat into the underbrush. "Christ on green crutches!" His breath exploded. "I wouldn't want to argue with that one." The double rush of fear and excitement hit his adrenaline system like a great shot of raw whiskey. If it hadn't moved, he would have missed the dangerous animal in the darkness.

The huge black cat had been stalking something. Or someone. Oh, Jesus, a kill. He willed it not to be so as he waded, thigh deep, across the slow-moving stream, splashing and posturing, hoping like crazy that jaguars were either cowards or assumed humans were too dangerous to go after. He grabbed a small branch of driftwood from the river and snorted at the thought of bashing a cat that size with something so absurd, hoping against hope that what he wouldn't find was her bloody body.

His adrenaline jumped another notch when he found her pack, then he saw her half-submerged in the creek. She'd fallen on her back and water licked at her neck, under her chin, bright hair streaming in the black water. "Oh, please, no," he pleaded with whatever power might be listening. He pulled her dead weight across his shoulder, quickly splashed back across the stream. If the goddamned jaguar was going to come at them, he wanted the water to slow it down.

All the way back to the cave he struggled to throw off the feeling that the cat was tracking them, fought being spooked at every sound. Inside, winded, he shook out the old man's blanket and put her on it.

He checked her pulse and examined her for signs of

injury. Nothing obvious. No broken bones, no blood. Christ, if he'd been thirty seconds later, that cat would have been at her. What the hell had happened? She must have fallen in trying to cross the river. He shivered again at the thought of the massive cat, trying to throw off the bogies. Her breathing was shallow and her heart rate too slow, skin ice cold from loss of body heat in the cool water—hypothermia. He slapped her chin gently. "Allison! Hey!" He wondered how long she'd been in the water.

She responded by moving her head only slightly. "No," she said weakly, semiconscious.

"Hey. What happened?"

She couldn't or wouldn't answer. Locating what was left of his tequila, he forced her to drink some of it. She choked on the raw alcohol, but some of it went down. Not the best of remedies if she had a weak heart, but the best he could think of under the circumstances.

He took off his jacket to cover her and found three of the eggs had not survived the strenuous journey. The chunk of meat was gone—somewhere on the dark trail between them and the jaguar. The egg in the pocket with his cigarettes was miraculously whole. So much for natural packaging. He placed the cigarettes on a nearby rock and put the egg in the water tin and set it among the coals. It was going to be a long night.

When he built up the fire, nervous bats flipped and dodged their way out into the night. He was well aware that he was creating too much light and smoke if someone was searching for them, but it was more important to get her warm, and for sure it would keep that bloody cat out of the cave. Let him eat the goddamned goat meat.

He unrolled her sleeping bag and confronted a new reality. Her wet clothing would soak the bag and make it twice as hard to get her warm. Shocky and incoherent, in and out of delirium, she fought him with incredible strength as he attempted to remove her jacket, striking at him with her fists. From her unfocused, glassy look, he knew she wasn't seeing him; clearly she was locked in a terrified battle against something or someone else.

"No," she ground out through firmly clenched teeth, and nearly succeeded in getting away from him by crawling across the floor of the cave. She staggered to her feet and faced him, weaving. Nothing he could say to her came even close to calming her down. Whenever he tried to touch her, she eeled out of his grasp, repeating like a looped recording, "No . . . no . . . no," and shaking her head.

It wasn't a fair contest. Tired as he was, he soon succeeded in pinning her arms firmly against her body. "No. No. No!" she repeated, a litany building in hysteria.

"It's okay. I'm not going to hurt you," he told her, trying to soothe her escalating panic. "I'm not going to hurt you." He held her immobilized until she gave up and went limp. When he removed the sodden jacket, she began a piteous plea.

"Please. Please. Please." He relaxed his hold for an instant to sit her down, and she came at him swinging. Their struggle resumed; each time he thought she had given up, he'd release his hold and she'd start again. Finally, hating himself, he hit her to try to knock her out. At the blow, she quit and was quiet.

"I'll sure give you stubborn, girl," he said, panting, not without guilt. He carried her to the blanket, pulled off the hiking boots. Talking quietly all the while, he unzipped her slacks and, feeling slightly voyeuristic, rolled them down around her hips and carefully held pale pink bikini panties firmly in place as he pulled the soaked linen down legs every bit as gorgeous as he remembered. "All I want to do is get you warm," he justified. "You gotta stop fighting me, sweetheart. It's been a real long day and both of us could use a rest." It was obvious she had tuned him out.

He worked soggy sleeves down each arm and removed the thin cotton shirt. He peeked under her khaki T-shirt to see if she was wearing anything else; relieved to see a ridiculously feminine bra, he pulled her into a sitting position in front of him. "I hope this isn't one of your favorites," he went on conversationally.

Taking the bottom of the T-shirt in his fists, he ripped it neatly up the back. As he peeled the shirt over her arms, he was quite truly shocked at what he saw. "Jesus Christ," he said flatly. One by one, pieces began falling into place.

A large, rectangled area of skin beginning on her left shoulder and stretching across the middle of her back was mottled and pink, like peeled sunburn. He stared dumbly at the neat pattern of small, perfectly symmetrical scars etched inside the patch of new skin. Measuring an inch and a half high, three dots up, three across, the patterns made no sense. At first. Then it dawned, and he drew in his breath. Cigarette burns.

The dots were scars from cigarette burns. Some bastard had methodically and with a great deal of precision burned the letters WHOR across her shoulders. For some reason there was no final E. The skin across his own shoulders crawled and rippled in a chill, and he felt a rolling in the pit of his stomach. His mouth was woodenly dry. "Jesus Christ, baby."

Hell, no wonder she couldn't tolerate cigarettes. "What kind of crazy son of a bitch . . ." Another piece fell into his memory. It had been a rape case three years ago. Not Chicago—New York City. A high-fashion model claimed she'd been kidnapped and raped by a New York cop. It had been her? The Gallé Girl? He couldn't believe it had taken him this long to put it together.

He racked his memory. Three years ago—the summer Steffie had nearly drowned. Right, and after that his mother's sudden illness and funeral, followed by the divorce from Sue and the loss of his daughter. He and Jerry had struggled with their grief and the thousand and one details of the insurance claim and the estate; he'd been caught up in the hassle of the divorce—learning to come home to a deadly silent, furnished single life. It had been one hell of a year—for both of them, apparently.

He juggled his thoughts. He didn't remember associating her with the trial. Faint images danced in his mind—press photos, murky shots in the backseats of taxis, of blond hair and dark glasses. A vague memory that it had taken forever to get to trial built slowly into a stronger recall: sequestered jury, a gag order on the press.

The boys at the Miami precinct, irritated at the bad publicity and anticop sentiment, had smelled a rat—a cover-up for the cover girl. Cops didn't rape high-fashion models. High-fashion models were all for publicity, so why all the secrecy? They'd all been pissed as hell that the case had gone to court. Then the cop had drawn an eight-year sentence; when he didn't appeal, the case had dropped out of general conversation. The son of a bitch should rot! Christ, no wonder she didn't like cops.

He stared down at the violated skin. What it had cost her, he could not imagine. He hoped she hadn't been awake for it, but he knew she had. At least some of it. "No. No. No. No." The frantic pleading assaulted his mind. This was one asshole he was going to look up when he got back to Miami.

Anger constricted his throat as he carefully removed the ruined shirt, then he leaned back and pulled off his own T-shirt and quickly brought it, huge on her thin body and still warm, over her torso, gently moving her arms through the sleeves.

Shaky, he moved her carefully onto the sleeping bag, removed a sock, and covered her leg. So that was what the fight had been about. "Please. Please. Please." The desperation in her voice echoed in his brain. In removing the last wet sock, he discovered her swollen foot with the incision.

"Oh, baby," he said sadly. "What's this?" Finally something that made sense but gave him a chill at the same time. He pulled aside the soaked Band-Aids. The wound, washed clean in the water, was open, oozing a thin clear liquid. "A cut shouldn't swell like this. Looks like you stepped on a snake, baby. Is that what happened?"

He tucked the sleeping bag around the rest of her body and continued to talk to her as he examined the wound. "What'd you cut it with, the army knife?" He didn't like the look of this. Not at all.

"What the hell were you doing walking around in bare feet?" He kept himself busy, trying not to think about it. He rinsed his mouth with the tequila and sucked at the cut until he could spit red blood. "I wish to hell you hadn't cut it, sweetheart. I'm not sure you helped." Wounds in this climate took forever to heal.

Out of tequila, he looked through his pack for something to put on the wound and found the journal on the floor of the cave. He located alcohol in her pack, Band-Aids, and a tube of prescriptive salve. After treating the wound, he poked more wood into the coals to brighten the fire and tiredly opened the journal. He found her entries immediately.

"Scorpion?" he said in surprise and great relief. Not a snake. How in the hell had she managed to let a scorpion in her boot unless she'd had them off while he was gone? Washing her socks or something. Jesus, women! He closed the journal and deliberated. She was shivering. He put Perez's blanket on top of the sleeping bag and sat down to think. What the hell did you do for a scorpion sting? The soaking in the river had probably slowed the venom's progress, certainly her slow heartbeat hadn't hurt. What else? Fever.

She was definitely feverish. He found several aspirin and dissolved them in a small amount of water while he finished reading her notes in the journal. The information was clear, concise, and rational. He tried to remember what he knew about scorpions. Some were deadly, most were seriously painful to adults and severely dangerous only to small children. He had no idea what the Valium had done to her but guessed that it wouldn't hurt to add the aspirin.

It had happened about four o'clock, and it was now nearly seven. Unless she was allergic to the venom, which he could do nothing about, she'd probably be all right. If it had been one of the deadly variety, she'd be history by now. He reread the journal, then, purely by chance, found the sprawling, frantic note to him on a later page: "Scorpion sting/in case." What the hell did that mean?

He saw the soap case on the floor and carefully edged it over with his boot; he saw the scorpion firmly embedded inside. He fought the urge to crush it and kicked it away. Wet soap and boots off. She'd probably taken a goddamned bath! Washed her hair, no doubt. "Bad reaction." Bad enough to drive her out of the cave on a foot that must have been hurting like hell. "Jaguar nearby." It had to be the same cat he'd seen going for her at the river. She'd either seen it or heard it and had started out into the darkness anyway.

"Will send someone for you." The words scalded as he read them again. He could tell from the erratic scrawl she'd already been in trouble, probably scared out of her mind. She'd been going through hell, alone, and gutsy enough to worry about him. "Will send someone for you."

He turned to look at her, his throat tight with feeling. It had been a long time since he'd held genuine admiration for a woman. But this lady was clearly someone special. He felt hope turn over slowly inside his heart. Hope that somehow he could do it right. That somehow he would know how to do or say whatever it had to be to stay in her life.

He had a rush of caring he hadn't felt since his daughter was born. He'd loved Steffie the moment he saw her, and he'd accepted all six pounds six ounces of her, slippery pasty gray and wrinkled, unquestionably as his own flesh from that moment. Nothing reserved, nothing held back.

He stared in wonder at this unusual woman, her face wet with perspiration, dark hollows under her eyes, amazed at the new feelings she generated in him. A woman who'd taken out a knife to defend herself against two men with guns, who'd had more than her share of terror. He leaned forward and kissed her softly on the bruise beginning to form on her chin. "When we get out of this mess, baby, I'm gonna start over and do it right."

After she drifted into sleep, he brought in a large dead branch and spread her wet clothes on it next to the fire before he fished the cooked egg out of the cup and absently peeled away the shell. She needed food, and a hard-boiled egg wasn't going to do it. He ate the egg, washing it down with river water.

Spying the cigarettes, he retrieved the pack and furiously spilled them into the flames, crumpled the box, and tossed it after. Then he sat, watching her sleep, gauging her even breathing. She needed food, and he needed to get her out of here; jaguar or no jaguar, he was going to have to make another trip to the old man's hut.

Ninety minutes. He pushed the butt of a small dead log onto the fire, adding large sticks of dry wood to create enough flame to discourage the jaguar and keep the cave well lit during his absence. He'd be gone ninety minutes. It had to be now. If she got worse during the night, he wouldn't dare leave her. And if she got really bad, he'd have to try to get her to help—carry her if he had to, cat or no cat. Forty over, forty back. Ten minutes at the hut. She'd be okay for ninety minutes. He checked her pulse, which seemed normal, maybe a little fast, but the shivering had stopped and she was breathing evenly, deep in sleep.

Ninety minutes. He grabbed the knife and the flashlight and held his breath as he made his way once more into the blackness across the river and skittered through the trees, expecting death to land on him at any moment. Earlier on the same path, he'd been fine. Just knowing the goddamned jaguar was in the area made every shadow swell with danger. It took forever to reach the roadway.

Thirty breathless minutes later, he slipped inside the empty hut and checked the hearth ashes, cold and undisturbed from the afternoon. The old man had been gone a long time.

He snapped on the flashlight in the gloom; the goat carcass was still hanging in its burlap wrapping; all but a few die-hard flies had disappeared into the night. Wasting no time, he poked the thin beam into the rafters, seeking the gourd and the eggs the old man kept there. Two luckless young pullets, disturbed and nervous, peered down from their roost, blinking in the light. He smiled in satisfaction. Hello, dinner.

He opened the largest knife blade and punched it into the door frame. Still breathing heavily, he reached up and grabbed the legs of the nearest bird and pulled it, squawking and flapping, off its perch. Holding it clumsily with one hand, he reached for the knife and dispatched the bird. "Sorry, pal," he mumbled, "this time you lose." He managed the second chicken with somewhat more finesse and much less noise.

He pulled the gourd from the rafters to find two eggs remaining. Damn. He dug into his pocket for the money from her pack, peeled off ten dollars, surely enough to repay the old man for the things he intended to take, then put the chickens and both eggs into the smallest cooking pot and placed it by the door. He was reaching in the rafters for another blanket when a man with the face of a ferret stepped through the door, dull moonlight glinting off the blue metal of his revolver, a huge .357 Magnum—an older Smith & Wesson, from the look of it. Even with the short barrel, it was ninety percent effective in one-shot stops. It had nailed hundred and thirty pound goats with great permanence yesterday afternoon.

"*Hola, señor,*" came the terse greeting. "*Cómo está*?"

Zachary, supremely aware of the target area his bare belly presented to the gun, slowly lowered his arm from the rafters and turned to recognize one of the men from yesterday's fiasco. "Uh, I don't speak, uh, *no hablo español,*" he stalled, irate with himself.

Six feet tall, the guy couldn't weigh more than a hundred and twenty pounds wringing wet—heavy use and abuse of the product was Zachary's best guess. Yesterday's clothes and yesterday's gun. The damned thing made a hole like a watermelon exploding out the back of your chest. Son of a bitch, this was getting old!

"Is okay. I speak English." The Magnum was pointed unsteadily at Zachary's bare stomach. "I knew you would come back. I say to Paulo, there is nothing to eat out there." The man glanced at the dead chickens in the pot by his foot and smiled broadly with rat teeth. "This for her?"

"No. It's for me." Zachary forced himself to relax and concentrate, then ran his best game. "Look, the old man said you guys are looking for this woman, Luisita. She ran out on me at the ruins. I don't know where she is, and to tell you the truth, I don't give shit one."

"I don' believe you." Rat-face wasn't buying it.

Zachary did his best to personify an outraged American tourist. "It's true. She punched a hole in my gas tank and stranded me. Why would I lie to you? I hope to hell you find her!"

The man grinned tightly, rat teeth protruding. "Nah, we did that. Stole your car, too." He broadened the obscene smile. "Where is she? You can tell me."

"I'm telling you, I don't know. I don't!" Zachary backed up that truth with a lie. "I don't even know where the other one is. They're both gone."

The rat-man's smile faded; his eyes, hard and bleak, narrowed to slits. Zachary tried again. "Okay, I came back here for food. I knew the old man had chickens and I'm hungry." He estimated the distance between his stomach and the gun. Murderously close, and not close enough. Deliberately speaking rapidly, he tried another tack, agitating his way closer to the gunman. "Look, I got money. I'll pay whatever you want if you get somebody to drive me back to Belize. Or get me to a bus stop. I don't give a shit, anything!"

"Shut up!" The gunman's English was less than fluent, and he was laboriously processing Zachary's speech into Spanish.

In his concentration, he unconsciously lowered the heavy pistol, and Zachary moved. He spun the flashlight into the rat-man's face and cracked the heel of his hand down across the skinny wrist. The Magnum slammed to the floor.

In the darkness, anger came flooding out as he smashed his fists into the rat-man's gut with emphasis: "Listen, you son of a bitch! I'm fucking tired of guns in my face, and I don't give a shit what your problems are. You got it?" The skinny man crumpled heavily to the floor and gasped noisily for air.

Zachary retrieved the flashlight and picked up the gun exultantly. At last, the welcome feel of power! Life force flowed into his body, clear and clean as ice water. He checked the chambers: three bullets. Three bullets! Disbelieving, he searched the man's pockets to find only a few pesos. How in the hell did someone have only three bullets for a fucking Magnum! The lazy son of a bitch hadn't bothered to reload after shooting the goats. He hauled him outside, unbuckled the man's belt and jerked it furiously from around his body.

"Now. Get this the first time, asshole, I don't know where the woman is!" Speaking tersely, Zachary shoved him prone with the ball of his foot. "On your face," he demanded. "I don't know who she is, and I don't know where she is!" The man resisted slightly as Zachary fastened the belt first around his ankles, then trussed his arms behind his back, pulling the end tightly through the buckle. "What's your name?" When the man didn't answer he prodded him with the Magnum. "Hey! Shit for brains—your name!"

"Alberto," the man wheezed, guts obviously hurting.

"Say it, Alberto!"

"You don' know where she is."

"Right! Believe it!" He put the revolver to the side of the man's head. "Where's the car?"

Alberto was stubbornly silent.

"Don't play fucking games with me. If I have to go look for it, I'll come in here and blow your brains out, just to make myself feel better!"

"I don' have no car. I walked from the road."

"Bullshit!" Zachary kicked the man's chest in annoyance, calculated to get the truth. "You lie to me and I'll kick your face in!"

"It's true! Paulo took the car to San Ruiz; he comes back tomorrow."

He looked at his watch. Christ, he'd been gone over an hour. He didn't dare leave her any longer. He had few choices. He could beat the truth out of Alberto, which would probably take a while; he could kill the bastard, which wasn't a choice; or he could leave him and hope the asshole got the message. The belt would hold him ten minutes on the outside. He chose the latter. "Alberto. You tell your friend, Paulo, if I see either one of you again, I'll kill you. ¿*Comprende*?"

The man looked at him, eyes glittering in hatred, and said nothing. Zachary fixed the gun under his belt. At the roadway, he checked for a vehicle. He hadn't heard an engine, but he was approaching exhaustion and had been distracted killing the chickens. There was no sign of a car. If there was one, most likely it was hidden somewhere relatively close by, but looking for a side road in the darkness could take forever. He hadn't found keys in his search of the gunman—maybe the bastard had been telling the truth.

He had to get back to her. He tucked the awkward cooking pot under his arm and moved down the road as fast as he could, part of his mind exultant that at last he had a weapon. Some of the god-awful helpless feeling lifted. Three bullets didn't alter the balance of power in the Western world, but it was a hell of a lot more weight than he'd had yesterday crouching in the weeds. Pacing himself to a fast walk, he listened to the cacophony of frogs and crickets in the night. "Hang tight, baby. Just be okay till I get there," he said, and pushed his pace up a notch.

The closer he got to the cave, the more worried he became. If something had happened again while he was gone, he wasn't sure he could handle it. "Two more minutes, baby." Holding the heavy gun at the ready, he felt better as he worked his way to the river, though he wasn't sure it would stop a cat that big if it decided to make a run at him. It would have to be a very close shot, well placed.

From the cave entrance he saw her stumbling aimlessly near the fire in her bare feet. He felt a surge of relief that she was strong enough to stand—a good sign, but he was surprised she was walking on her injured foot.

He carefully placed the chickens and the blanket on the floor of the cave and spoke gently. "Hey, Chicago . . ."

At the sound of his voice, she whirled around, nearly losing her balance. It felt good just looking at her. "I'm glad you're awake," he continued quietly, jabbed with guilt at the sight of her damaged face, the bruise on her chin now fully black and blue.

She stared at him, eyes huge with tears. "You were gone," she accused. "I tried to find you and you were gone."

Hallelujah, she was lucid. He casually draped his jacket around her shoulders, led her back to the sleeping bag, sat her down to check her foot. "How're you feeling?"

"It hurts," she said as he examined the wound. The swelling had eased somewhat, but the cut was open and bleeding slightly.

"How long have you been awake?" He poured water over the proud flesh and rinsed it with alcohol. The log had rolled out of the flames, and the fire was little more than smoking coals. Her skin was cold again, clammy to his touch, and she was trembling. The cool air in the cave crept into his own bare skin. He tucked the edges of the sleeping bag close around her and added the second blanket, his jacket on top.

"I tried to find you," she repeated, and closed her eyes. "I didn't think you were coming back," she said, so quietly he had to lean very close to hear.

"I had to get food," he explained. "Now go back to sleep while I fix us something to eat. I'll wake you when it's ready. I promise."

Shivering, eyes closed, she didn't answer him. He busied himself building up the fire. She was going to be fine. His relief released enough energy to concentrate on food.

He found three medium-size rocks in the rubble at the front of the cave and pushed them into the coals in the manner of the old man's hearth. As soon as the fire was burning brightly, he rinsed out the cooking pot, filled it with water, and balanced it over the rocks.

Sighing, he balefully addressed one of the stiffening chickens, grabbed a handful of feathers and vowed never again to take for granted the pristine packages of neatly wrapped, eviscerated fowl in the supermarket. The feathers stubbornly refused to come off the bird and he glanced up to find her watching him.

"That's a chicken," she said vacantly.

"I know what it is, sweetheart."

She stared at him stupidly. "What are you doing with a chicken?" Her eyes were glazing over.

"We're going to eat it if I can figure out how to get rid of the feathers."

She looked at the pathetic bird. "You have to scald it," she said vaguely.

"What?"

"Scald it. Dip it in boiling water. Then the f-feathers come off." She shivered again.

He stared at the scruffy chicken. "What's your next choice?"

She looked away from him. "I tried to find you and you were gone." He was losing her, and she was still cold. He dispensed with tradition and skinned both birds, cutting off heads, wings and feet, gutting them like fish. After tossing the entrails into the water outside the cave, he rinsed their scrawny bodies in the stream, pushed the carcasses into the pot, and added the two eggs. So much for Julia Child.

After a moment's hesitation, he opened the sleeping bag and slid inside next to her. He was cold, and it was taking forever for the water to boil. Tiredness pulled at his mind, and his body protested the hard ground under the sleeping bag. "I ain't much for backwoods medicine, sweetheart," he whispered, clasping his arms firmly around her, unhappy with the icy skin he felt against his chest through the thin shirt. She seemed terribly small next to him, but he had the welcome sense of finally being able to do something to protect her.

The bulk of the gun was reassuring at his back, and it was bliss just to lie down and rest the weight of his mind for a few minutes—just five minutes. After a bit he loosed his hold so she could turn and spoon her backside against his bare stomach, like a little girl. As she warmed from his body heat, the trembling ceased and she fell into sleep. It was heaven to relax next to her innocent warmth, to not think about anything except being next to the Gallé Girl from the perfume ads—hell he didn't believe it. Just five minutes, he promised himself, and, grateful for the luxury of closing his eyes, he went out.

He woke hours later.

After a moment of disorientation, he gave himself over to twilight sleep next to her wonderfully warm and distinctly feminine body. The softness of her turned his skin electric, every humming nerve ending exquisitely connected with some delicious and interesting part of her.

He trailed his fingers gently along the swell of her thigh, absorbed in the hot-silk feel of her; he encountered on her hip the tiniest space of thin lace he knew to be pale pink, then the plunge of soft, downy skin into the sudden hollow of her waist, abdomen smoothly taut under the tips of his fingers. He wanted her, wanted to make love to her. Slowly. Exquisitely. Wanted her to want him to do it.

He'd never taken advantage of a woman and for sure didn't want to start now; he put his arm around her ribs instead. There he encountered the undersides of her breasts, soft and warm through the shirt. He ached to slide his hand up under the fabric and feel the soft-firm roundness of her, possess the tantalizing peach-brown nipples he'd glimpsed in the shower, knead and caress them. He allowed endless, delicious seconds, enjoying this first, genuine desire for a woman in recent memory.

A few minutes later he forced his stiff, reluctant body to move away from her, out of the cozy sleeping bag into the chilly cave.

Reflexively he checked for the gun, found it safely in place. The fire was nearly out, and it was after four A.M. The chicken was tepid, but fully cooked. Awed at the feelings she created in him, he found himself studying her face, peaceful in sleep, as he wolfed down pieces of chicken and fed small sticks of wood to save the fire. When it was safely ablaze, he found more wood in the predawn light and stacked it nearby.

"Hey." He shook her just enough to bring her conscious and gave her a cup of broth, wondering that even the gossamer touch of her hair against his hands made him feel alive with an awareness he hadn't felt in years. He was at once taller, stronger, younger. "Drink this," he told her quietly, and she did.

When he was satisfied all was well, and she slept once again, he slid back under the blankets, high as a schoolboy, delighting in the touch of her skin. Gathering her close against his bare chest, willing his hands to remain in reasonably neutral places, he felt her melt against him and he pressed his mouth briefly against the brutal scars on her shoulder before he slept.

A thin gray dawn crept through an overcast sky. With the light came a fine mist of rain, gathering on the leaves of the foliage in the canyon, spilling quietly onto the ground and splashing onto rocks at the entrance to the cave, wearing at the boulders in the process of centuries. High up on the side of the canyon, the coal-black jaguar stared down with yellow eyes at the entrance, watching for the intruders that had invaded his cave.

It was a delicious kiss, long and slow and deep and wet and timeless. The world had ended. When it began again, there was only the taste of his mouth and the feel of his body, safe and strong, smooth and long, against her. She wanted to see his face, but her eyes wouldn't see him, she felt only languorous kisses that made nothing else possible. How could she feel his arms holding her breathless, hands caressing her skin, making magic things happen inside her body—warm and full and exquisite feelings—and not see his face? She wanted to see him. It wasn't fair. She ran to the stone bridge and looked into the water, but he wasn't there. Then she saw him, eyes glowing golden, poised on the limb, exchanging stare for stare. She smiled and stretched and turned over in the sunshine and enjoyed the warm.

"Morning."

She opened her eyes, confused. Barely daylight, dank and gloomy, her sunlight became the heat from a cook fire and two rough, woolen blankets that covered her sleeping bag. It had been a very strange dream. Important and unusual. . . . He was back! A clay cooking pot was balanced on stones over the fire.

"I really hated to wake you," he said. "You were smiling."

The fire crackled brightly. He sat a few feet away, sipping from the tin cup, shirtless under his jacket.

"You ready for breakfast?"

From the safety of her blankets, she did a quick mental check. Her body felt clean and strong and restored. Good feelings lingered from the dream, but something else—strange and odd.

What had he said? She stared at his worn face and tried to piece together coherent memory. "Yeah," she croaked. Her jaw was inexplicably sore. She cleared her throat and tried again. "Yes. I am hungry."

In truth she was ravenous. Struggling to sit up, she pressed her injured foot against resisting blankets. "Owww!" Her jaw hurt again. The sting in her foot brought a flood of recognition and a spate of blank spaces.

The dream forgotten, she examined her injury and discovered she was wearing very little below her T-shirt. She gasped and jerked her leg back under the blankets and winced again at the drag on her skin. Bewildered, she pulled away as he knelt beside her to uncover her foot.

"Let me have a look." The cut was beginning to heal over, and from what he could tell, there appeared to be no infection. He poured a small amount of alcohol on the wound and covered it with a couple of Band-Aids. God, she was gorgeous. "I think you're going to be lucky this time," he said conversationally, tucking her foot back inside. "You want to tell me why you were running around without your boots?"

She thought for a minute. "No."

He held out the tin cup, steaming in the chilly air. "It's chicken broth. No salt, no pepper, no guarantees. Watch it, it's hot."

She took the cup and, after discovering one side of her mouth didn't hurt, gratefully sipped the warming broth. Her mind raced, trying to fill in the blanks. Everything seemed aeons ago. "I stepped on a scorpion," she said, gingerly moving her sore mouth around the words.

"I know. I found your notebook."

Notebook? She blinked in incomprehension. What had happened to her mouth? And something was different. Something was definitely different. In the way he was looking at her, in his voice. Something was changed. God, the soup was good. "I made notes in case . . ." The blank space about the journal filled itself in. "Is there any more?"

She handed him the cup; he dipped it in the pot and returned it to her filled with chicken and broth. Ambrosia.

"There's a boiled egg, if you want."

"I hate boiled eggs." It had to have happened last night, it had gotten dark . . . why hadn't he waked her until now? There was a huge gap in her thinking.

"Good. I'll eat it."

She watched blankly as he cracked the egg. Using her fingers to scoop pieces of chicken out of the cup, she searched her mind for solid ground. Some point of reference. Everything was out of kilter. What was different? How had she hurt her mouth?

He ached for her as he watched the mental struggle, and came to her rescue. "You were pretty out of it when I got back last night. You probably won't remember too much. I fished you out of the water about fifty feet below the crossing."

She looked at him, major disbelief written on her face. "What!"

Zachary suppressed his discomfort at the memory and kept his manner light. "You were giving a big black cat one hell of a dilemma. He couldn't decide whether or not to take you out."

Her eyes widened and she had the nightmarish feeling that he was telling the truth. "There was a jaguar. Down by the river. It was in a tree down there. It's all black with . . . yellow eyes. You saw it, too?"

"Honey, we were that close to getting engaged." His fingers indicated a half-inch gap.

She put down the tin and moved deeper into the blankets as the reality of her situation expanded. None of this made any sense. "I was in the water?" The T-shirt she had on was white. Hers was khaki. The one on her body wasn't hers. Her clothing was gone. From a far-off distance, she heard his answer.

"Apparently you fell in trying to cross to the road."

Her legs were bare! He'd undressed her! As the knowledge cut through her, she could feel reaction building. He'd undressed her! And she didn't remember. Her mind was rattled, and too many feelings were rushing in. He'd handled her! Her breath was coming in too short, not enough oxygen. She stared at him, dry-mouthed. What else had he done? Nonsound began to build in her ears, and she closed her eyes and dug her nails into clenched fists, willing her mind not to go away. Not this time. She felt him next to her and flinched when he put his hand on her arm.

"I undressed you because you were wet and freezing," he said gently. "Do you remember being cold last night?"

A small part of her mind knew it was truth and latched on to it—a small thin line against the terror; her breathing labored on.

He changed to a matter-of-fact tone of voice. "It was the fastest way to get you warm. You've got my shirt on because nothing else was dry."

The tiny ray of truth attached itself to a small particle of logic. She began to stabilize. If she'd been in the river, of course she'd been wet. She stopped sinking and tried to listen.

"You'd been in the water a long time and you were unconscious when I found you." He decided to skip over the part about hitting her. "Your clothes are dry and I'll leave you alone to get dressed now. The boots are still wet, so just put on the socks. Can you do that?"

His voice was calm and rational, and she was able to open her eyes, but she couldn't look at him. "Yes," she managed. She watched him walk to the mouth of the cave and stare into the mist. After a few moments he disappeared outside. Lying on top of the blankets her clothes were soiled and wrinkled, but damp dry and folded neatly. She pushed the blankets aside and awkwardly pulled on her slacks, paused at the ruined T-shirt, ripped up the back.

Tears slid from her eyes. So. He knew. She removed his T-shirt and put hers on, turning it back to front, using safety pins from her pack to fasten the torn ends together. Then she buttoned Jake's thin shirt over it. In a terrible way, she was relieved. Now he'd know why she was afraid.

Zachary stared through the mist into the myriad greens of the jungle, unhappily aware of the weather, barely conscious of the morning chill. It wasn't supposed to rain; Central America's rainy season was normally over by now. It seemed she was taking forever to get dressed. Finally he heard her behind him and turned to watch her progress as she limped across the rubble at the mouth of the cave. She had on one hiking boot with her injured foot covered by a cotton sock and wrapped in a plastic bag from her pack. He smiled at her ingenuity.

"Pretty fancy packaging, Chicago," he sallied, trying to gauge her mood.

She did not respond to the compliment. "It was dumb to take off my boots," she said from a small distance. "I'm sorry." She held out his T-shirt. "It's cold. You'll need this."

He shed his jacket and gratefully pulled the T-shirt over his head and down over the gun at his back. Even the thin cotton made an immediate difference; he hadn't realized he was so cold. It smelled of her, a faint aroma he couldn't identify; his skin tingled with the warmth lingering from her body. As he donned his jacket, he saw a safety pin at her throat where she'd fastened the ripped T-shirt. Fielding his glance, she turned away.

"I'm sorry about ruining your shirt," he said tentatively, painfully aware of her discomfort.

The wall of mist outside the entrance was a muffled quiet; but inside the hollow cavern silence roared and grew into a huge sleeping bear between them. He knew he should be facing the monumental problem of getting them the hell away from here, but, watching her profile, his mind was filled with unwanted thoughts of the rape. Some bastard brutalizing and defiling the slender body he'd held in his arms last night.

Knowledge of the terrible scarring created a push-pull battle of need to know versus not ever wanting to hear about it. Questions gnawed at him, and he knew they were written in his face. Without warning she turned and moved carefully back inside. He followed soon after and waited until she settled a safe distance away from him, the fire dying between their feet. A long minute passed, then another. When she didn't open the subject, he knew he was going to wake the bear.

"I saw your back," he said uncomfortably, and watched his statement jerk through her body in the murky light. "It made the papers in Miami, so I have some idea of what happened, and . . ." And what? Tell me about it? Is it what I think? Who was he? Why did he do it? Unexpectedly there were too many things in his head.

He wanted to tell her he was sorry, to convince her that somehow he could help, make it easier, make it go away. He had no idea how, just that he wanted to try. And when he got back to the States, nothing on God's green earth was going to prevent him from making the sick son of a bitch sorry he was ever born! "I don't know what to say. I just . . . I'm sorry," he finished lamely.

She held her breath while he spoke, barely hearing his words, caught in some terrible place between dread and relief with no avenue of escape. Nowhere to get away. Would it be in his eyes from now on? Or would he stop looking at her, the way some people did when they knew? Would he think about it? Of course he'd think about it.

Would he see her the way she had been? Naked and terrified and helpless?

In her ensuing silence, the tension in the space between them filled up the cave and continued its climb to a point of no return. She began an unconscious rocking motion. He felt her withdrawal, sensed he dared not let it build. "They're cigarette burns, aren't they?" he pushed. "Will you tell me . . . how it happened? I mean, how he managed to . . ."

She interrupted his labored questioning and resigned herself to answer. Anything to ease the painful tension in the air between them. "We met on a plane," she said tersely. "He invited me to dinner. He was . . . charming and persistent." A dead smile. "He managed to put a drug of some kind into my food at a restaurant. I woke up in a farmhouse." Undressed and helpless. Full of more terror than she knew could exist in the world. She drifted away as her mind searched for a place to hide, somewhere not to allow the chunk of pain forcing its way into her stomach, congealing, deadening her feelings and her ability to think.

He decided not to wait her out, to force her to talk to him. "Is he still in prison?"

She came back to earth. "Yes." It wasn't supposed to still be like this. It wasn't supposed to still hurt this much. "Six more years." A whisper: "Unless he's paroled."

Zachary's gut hurt. He pushed the question at her. "How come he only got eight years? He didn't use a weapon?" It was the only explanation he could muster.

Anger began to break over the wall, into the sea of pain. "He said we were using drugs, that it was my idea and he went along with it." She stared hard at him, daring a reaction to her words. "He was taking drugs. I don't take drugs. I don't take drugs!" Her voice took on a raw edge, grating with the rage of unavenged hurt and humiliation. "A pickup. It's what he called me at the trial. From the plane . . . and I told him I liked to party. He said I brought the drugs, and he'd never done anything like that before. Things had . . . gotten out of hand." She drifted out and back.

"I couldn't prove it wasn't true. He said he didn't remember doing it. . . . He was a police officer with a clean record, and I couldn't prove it wasn't true!" Her voice was climbing. "He said the burns were my idea—that I was a mind case. And someone on the jury . . . believed him." She got up suddenly, knocking a chunk of wood into the fire; a halo of sparks went spiraling toward the top of the cavern. "And I wound up in a hospital—just like he said." With a vast sadness, "He said I would, and I did."

She retreated to her seat, her eyes welling tears, glittering brightly in the firelight as they traced tiny shining ribbons down her cheeks to drop onto her shirt. "He killed my mother with his lies."

Zachary had the uneasy sense that time had stopped and that he had to get it started again. "You lost it when your mother died?"

She closed her eyes and swayed. He started to move across the space between them, but she heard him move in her direction. "Don't." The command was soft but final. "Please, don't."

He moved instead to the fire, stomach raging, hurting for her. Poking at the fire, pushing in small remnants of charred wood to create new flames, he studied her face in the firelight. "I'd say you had a pretty good case to hate cops." He was hot with shame for the rotten bastard who had defiled the uniform, and he burned for retribution.

"You've been afraid of me, haven't you?" He read the answer in her silence. "You're afraid of me right now." God damn the son of a bitch!

After a moment, a tiny, "Yes." Oh, the relief to admit it at last. And some part of her realized that by saying it, telling it out loud to him, she was gaining ground, calming down, putting aside some of the fear.

"I swear to God I wouldn't hurt you." Guilt for her bruised face screamed at him. He'd already hurt her.

"I know—but that's separate. I can't explain it. It's like I don't think you'll hurt me, but I don't know it. I don't trust it."

Except she did know it. She could feel a return to the small corner of herself that was determined to leave the nightmare behind.

"It is different—now that I know you. But I still have the fear." This was also true. Confused at the warring emotions, she brushed at the tears and left a trail of dust across her cheek.

"Why'd he burn you?" Now that he'd started this, he wanted to know it all. He didn't want her to ever have to talk to him about it again, and he for goddamn sure didn't want to hear it more than once.

She exhaled a very long sigh. Her shoulder was stiff and aching, and her stomach began to spasm again. She shifted uncomfortably against the stone. Why wouldn't he let it alone? "He said I was a w-whore." The word came out ragged. It was the first time she'd been able to say it to anyone except her shrink. "He said everyone should know about me—that I should be punished because I made money with my body . . . I let men take pictures of me without clothes . . . for money."

She could feel it, she was going to tell him. The pain was hard-edged and violent, tearing. Rocking began again. "He was going to mark me so everybody would know." Then, past the pain and into nonfeeling in order to be able to say it at all. "If he couldn't . . . then nobody else . . . He did it to hurt me, to make me beg." She stared at him, unseeing. "I did beg." Her voice was dead. "I crawled on the floor . . . I begged like an animal. . . ."

Zachary's nerve failed. He couldn't listen to any more. He didn't want to hear what she'd already said. He wanted to stuff the words and the knowledge and the pain in her voice back inside Pandora's box, let his mind create its own scenario where she hadn't hurt, hadn't screamed, hadn't been forced to beg the sick bastard. He crashed into the circle. "He marked you up because he was impotent." It was common among sadists, and extremely dangerous. Jesus, she was lucky to be alive.

"Yes, he was impotent!" she flared suddenly. "He'd try

. . . and when he couldn't, he'd get drunk and . . . I don't want to talk to you about this!" she said violently. "He was going to kill me!"

He'd pushed her to the brink, and she was holding on to the outside edge.

"You're absolutely right," he told her. "I don't think there's any doubt he intended to kill you." He deliberately changed the subject to the present. "How many treatments have you had?"

"What?" The shift was too quick for her.

"You've had skin treatments. How many?"

Finally the rocking slowed down. "Just one. The doctor says maybe three more."

"The burns are too deep to cover with makeup?" he asked without thinking. The treatments had to be painful, and he was determined to lead her somewhere it was safe to talk about.

"I need it gone," she said tersely.

Jesus Christ, Cross, of course she needed it removed. Jerk! He knew suddenly what had happened to her career. "That's when you quit."

"When my mother died, it didn't matter." She shuddered at the memory of the pressure from the secrecy. And the trial, the hideous mail, the stress on her mother. Everywhere she'd turned there'd been lurid speculation, suspicion. Preventing public knowledge had been one of the few things she'd been able to control. "Jake put me in a hospital. I was released five months ago."

"Jake?" He had a sudden pang of envy. Not envy. Jealousy. Nowhere in the book was he prepared for jealousy. It whipped through his mind. She'd said she wasn't married, but obviously there were men in her life. At least one. "Who's Jake?" He tried to keep the question casual and marked it down as an icy cold realization.

"Jake's . . ." There was no explaining Jake. At that time, and since, Jake was life. At his mention, she realized she hadn't thought of him for several days. How could she have forgotten Jake! She got up and hobbled to her pack.

"I'm not going to discuss this any longer," she said in defiance. "I've answered all the questions I'm going to answer." It was final.

He believed her and was pleased. Her voice held strength, and she had taken a stand from a position of control. Good for her! He'd find out about Jake later, right now his gut told him she was in good enough shape that he could tell her about last night. "Listen, Chicago, we have something else to catch up on." He braced himself against one of the rocks as she reluctantly gave him her attention. "You remember the assholes who chased us?"

She looked at him askance. Was he kidding?

"I met one of them at the old farmer's place last night." He carelessly brought the Magnum from its hiding place at his back and stopped abruptly at the frightened look in her face. He shook his head, hastening to reassure her. "No. I just tied him up with his belt and left him there. I did give him a couple of bruises for the old man, though."

"I don't care what you did to him," she said, her voice remote. Then, after a moment, "What about the old man?"

"He's fine. He told me it's a two-hour walk to the local village, and San Ruiz, which is even farther, is the closest phone."

She'd been fighting all morning to stay upright as one avalanche after another of emotional upheaval came cresting over her defenses, breakers in a hurricane—the scorpion, a near drowning she didn't remember, waking up undressed, talking about the scars, the endless questions about the rape. Now a new wave of information to be processed. He'd seen one of the gunmen, fought with him, had the man's gun. Was there a way out? A phone . . . Would he leave her alone again? Oh, God! Things were spinning out of control. Then slowly they centered, and she waited until she could speak calmly. "I can't walk that far. You'll have to come back for me."

Her voice was flat but steady, the same voice she'd used yesterday when he'd left her alone—scared and determined not to let him know it.

"New rules," he said firmly, fighting the urge to ignore her fear of him, aching to gather her up and hold her close, convince her he would take care of her, protect her, keep her safe. He restrained his impulses, knowing that anything against her will, however innocent, might tip her over. "We don't go anywhere unless we go together."

She looked at him with guarded eyes, trying to believe in him. In an instant everything was the same, and everything was different. Maybe there would be an end to chaos. If he didn't leave her, maybe life could return to logic and reason.

"Hey. I promise." Looking into those huge eyes, he'd never meant anything so totally in his life.

Precarious on an emotional tightrope, she struggled within herself and succeeded in giving over a fragile trust. As she did, she felt the weight of a thousand demons lift away from her shoulders.

Zachary watched her do battle and gave a silent shout of jubilation when he won. Trust anywhere was rare and precious, but here, from this woman, it was a gift from the gods. A bond and a beginning. He radiated a huge, grateful, lopsided grin. Goddamn, he was doing it right! After a pure moment of dizzy pleasure, he continued with care. "I talked with the old man. His name is Perez, and I gave him some money to call Rider to send someone to get us. I couldn't tell you last night." He paused when a crack of hope showed itself in her face for a brief second.

"When? Are they coming here? I mean, do they know about the cave? Did you tell him—"

He stopped her. "I didn't tell Perez about the cave. I told him I didn't know where you were." He paused. "I'm pretty sure he's a decent guy, but what he doesn't know, he can't tell anyone."

She shifted her gaze to the floor in comprehension.

Uneasy at the unpleasant rationale, he hurried on, speaking his thoughts. "This is Wednesday. Assuming nothing's changed from when we left, Rider got back from Belize City sometime late last night. They're only about seventy miles from here. There shouldn't be any question now that we've had trouble."

Restless, he moved around the cave. "If I were him, I'd put someone on the road this morning to track us down." He checked his watch. "Assuming they started out at six o'clock, and the roads are passable in this weather, the earliest they could probably get to the ruins is in another hour." He tossed a few errant twigs into the fire. "They won't take a car back on that mud track, but they might walk back there to look for us."

He didn't like the answer that was coming at him. She couldn't walk that far, and there was no way he was going to leave her alone to wait for a car that might not arrive. He changed the subject.

"In the meantime, we have the food problem solved." Using a small stick, he stirred the chicken, long reduced to a bony soup. "This will last us the rest of the day, but if they don't show up until tomorrow, we're going to be hungry." It wouldn't hurt his waistline to miss a meal or two; she would get the lion's share of the contents of the clay pot.

In the pale gray, rainy morning, Bol walked down the road toward his milpa. It would be a good day for the hot work of clearing brush for burning. He smiled as he thought proudly of his new young son asleep in the cradle. Nuk was a good wife. Men grew beans and corn, but women cooked the beans and ground the corn into tortillas that kept a man warm inside on such days. He heard the sound of a car from the direction of San Ruiz and paused to allow the sedan to come alongside.

The driver leaned out and smiled anxiously. "I am looking for Sara Copal. She is staying in this village, can you tell me where I can find her?"

Bol hesitated. It was the duty of the *t'o'ohil* to tell this man that Sara was dead.

"I am worried for her and the baby," the man said harshly. "Her husband should be with her."

Bol heaved a sigh. The *t'o'ohil* was not here to guide him, and the man would have to be told. "I am unhappy to tell you that your wife is dead," he said with great sadness.

"Dead? Are you certain? Sara Copal?" The man slumped against the steering wheel and hit his fist against the dashboard in distress.

"Sí, *señor,* four days ago we have buried her." Bol shifted in discomfort. "The baby is fine. My wife has been taking good care of him."

At this the man searched his face, seeking truth. "Where is he? I must see him. Can you take me there?"

At last, something he could do to help. "Sí, *señor.*" Bol got into the car, and the car's wheels spun on the muddy road.

Inside Bol's hut, Och was hungry, wailing for his breakfast. His protests stirred Adam into an equally insistent wail. Luisita poured milk into a bottle and attached a nipple even as Och was satisfied at his mother's breast; she changed Adam's diaper while the bottle heated in the cooking pot, and the baby quieted, certain that food was not far behind.

As she fed the child, she pondered her decision. All night she'd dreamed bad things: a strong wind sweeping through the forest, red dust everywhere, blinding and choking her. The wind identified strangers—the two ladinos who were driving the Americans' car; red was a portent of blood, danger. It was undoubtedly a message from Balum and confirmed her decision. When he was old enough, Adam could return to the village, but until then . . .

"I'm going to take the baby to America," she said to Nuk. "I will leave as soon as possible."

"The *t'o'ohil* will understand," Nuk said, and sighed. "For a long time now, my father is very sad. He no longer makes the pilgrimage to Palenque. Many *ts'ul* go there now, many tourists. It is no longer possible for him to talk with the gods in Palenque."

"What about Yaxchilán?" Yaxchilán was the center of the earth, where the gods had created True People.

"He will make one more trip to Yaxchilán. When the government builds the dams on the Usumacinta River, this too will be gone," Nuk said sadly. "It will be Xu'tan."

Adam, full and sleepy, was returned to the cradle, and Luisita set about preparing to leave. As she rearranged the baby's things in the suitcase, she removed most of the clothing purchased for Sara and gave it to the smiling young mother.

"How far to San Ruiz?" From there she could hire a car.

"Not far. Around the lake is fastest." Nuk stored the American clothing on a small shelf and took down a bright red cotton shawl and presented it to Luisita as a gift in return.

A car approached as Luisita thanked the young girl for the gift, and she peered quickly out the door. Not the Land Rover, thank the gods, but a muddy sedan with a young ladino driving and Bol a passenger. It skidded to a halt on the slippery road, and the men labored up the incline toward the hut. She waited until Bol stepped inside, followed by the driver, a young man in his twenties.

He stared hard at her for a moment, then eyed the cradle. "Is this him?"

Luisita positioned herself in front of the baby.

"He is the baby's father," explained Bol.

"Rufino?" A mixture of rage and grief flowed through her body. Now, after all these months, Rufino had returned?

"Who asks about Rufino?" The insolent voice rattled through the single room of the hut.

"Sara was my sister," Luisita said, containing her anger. If Rufino had returned, surely it was the sign she had prayed for. She was furious that he had abandoned Sara, but perhaps he could explain. "Sara is dead," she said in a tight voice. "She was waiting for you."

"The boy told me," he said abruptly. "Four days ago. I am sorry I was not here." He looked around the hut warily and saw the opened suitcase. "It's very dangerous for me, and I don't have time to talk. We have to go. I'll explain in the car."

"Dangerous?" Her heart twisted. The dream hadn't lied. "How? What's wrong?"

"I have no time for this," he said. "I am here for my son. If you wish to come with me, we have to leave. Now."

He made a move toward the child, but she stopped

him. "Not until you tell me what's wrong." She was adamant.

"Two men are after me," he told her. "I've done nothing, but if they catch me, it will be very bad. It's too long to explain." He moved again toward the baby. "I came for Sara. If Sara is dead, I want the boy."

The mention of the two men decided her. "I will carry the child." She moved swiftly, tying the red shawl around her body. "You will tell your father?" she said to Nuk, who nodded in confused concern.

Things were happening too fast for the young girl; still, she quickly wrapped the morning's tortillas in a small cloth and put them inside the suitcase. "You will be hungry soon," she said nervously. Things should not be decided so quickly. Her father, the *t'o'ohil*, would not be happy that he had not been told of this.

Luisita was soon ready to leave. When she placed the sleeping baby inside the shawl, he woke for a moment, then relaxed against her, safe in his miniature hammock. She grabbed her purse and walked to the car, steadied by Bol, who carried the suitcase and put it into the back of the sedan. Nuk's anxious face looked down at her from the doorway of the hut. The engine started as she waved an American farewell and got into the car with the baby. Bol shut the door and the sedan shot forward, fishtailing in the mud-slick roadway.

A few minutes down the road he leaned across to push down the door lock; Luisita knew at that instant that she had made a terrible mistake. Too frightened to move, she clutched her purse close to her body, shielding the infant. "Don't drive so fast," she demanded, unnerved. "It's dangerous for the baby."

He shrugged and slowed the sedan slightly and looked over at her. "What's your name?"

"Luisita." It confirmed for her that this was not Rufino. Rufino, husband to Sara, would know her name. She struggled not to panic. "Where are we going?" she asked.

"Not far. I am meeting a friend, then we will talk." She

nodded and her mind raced to think what to do. Resting against her stomach was the heavy weight of the gun in the bottom of her purse. It would be a matter of time until he found it. And the money. Then all would be lost. She sat, blindly rigid, swallowed in panic.

A few minutes later Paulo slowed the car to ease across a washed-out section of the road. Fifty yards farther on she saw the Americans' Land Rover idling at the side of the road, and her heart sank when the rat-faced man stepped out into the roadway. Paulo allowed the sedan to drift to a stop and unlocked the door. "This is my friend," he said. "Get out."

Clutching her purse, she climbed carefully out of the car with the baby.

Alberto brushed past to reach into the sedan and lift out the suitcase; he tossed it into the back of the Land Rover. "We're taking this car from here," he directed. "That one will get bogged in the mud."

Desperate, she slipped her hand inside the shawl and shook the baby awake; Adam whimpered. She shook him again, and he began to cry the thin, high squall of an unhappy child.

Alberto looked up sharply at the baby's cry. "A kid? What the hell we doing with a kid, Paulo?"

"I'll tell you in a minute." Paulo jerked her arm. "What's the matter?" he muttered, already furious that she'd challenged him over the baby.

"He is hungry," she said meekly, thanking her gods she could speak at all. "There is milk in the suitcase."

"So, feed him." Paulo was uninterested.

She placed the baby on the front seat of the Rover. The engine idled roughly with no key in the ignition. She pulled the heavy suitcase into the front seat as Alberto continued to rage about the baby.

"What the hell we doin' with a kid?" He was livid, his yellowed rat teeth protruding in his frustration. "You supposed to get the woman, not a kid!"

"Keep your voice down!" hissed Paulo. "His wife is dead.

What was I supposed to do, dig her up? Listen, she told me the kid's mother was waiting for Rufino. So he's here somewhere. All we gotta do is go back and tell the Indians to give him a message." Paulo was derisive. "When he shows up, he finds out we got the kid, maybe it will persuade your friend to give back the money. Who knows?"

Alberto thought this over. He still didn't like it, but he didn't have a better idea. "We can' stand here all day. The lake road's washin' out. Leave your car here. We'll drive the Lan' Rover to San Ruiz, take care of this, pick it up in a coupla days!"

Paulo realized that for once the ugly man was right. He stomped ominously around the sedan, locking the doors. "Somebody steals it, then what? I got no car," he grumbled.

Luisita was no longer listening. "Take care of this" meant her and the baby. Galvanized to action, she upended the case against the floor of the car, creating a barrier between the baby and the dashboard. Why was there no key? The engine was running, would the car go without the key? She held tightly to the purse, needing strength for what she was about to do.

Praying one last time to Hachäkyum, she scrabbled in her purse for the pistol. Little Adam was screeching and the men were coming toward the car. At last she felt the barrel and her fingers found the handle. Desperation flowed into her body, giving her strength.

"I told you to shut that kid up!" Paulo was irritated.

Both men halted in astonishment when she pulled the pistol out of the purse. Holding it in both hands, she backed them around the car. "Give me the keys," she demanded.

Alberto, cunning as the rat whose face he had been given, grabbed the sedan's keys from Paulo and dangled them in his outstretched hand. "You don't want to shoot me," he bluffed. "We weren't gonna hurt you, honest."

The two men began to separate, drifting slowly apart. "We just want to find Rufino, that's all," Paulo placated.

"Yeah, that's all," echoed Alberto. "Son of a whore ran out on us. Set us up and ran out on us." He moved sideways. "We gotta find him or it's our ass."

"Shut up, Alberto. We're not going to hurt anyone. We're not going to hurt you, we're not going to hurt the baby," soothed Paulo. "We just want to talk, that's all." He took a step away from Alberto, then another.

She saw it was going wrong and chose Paulo, the liar, the man who pretended sorrow for her sister's death, and pulled hard on the trigger. The gun bucked in her hand, and both men jumped at the exploding sound; the bullet plowed a furrow in the mud between Paulo's boots, spattering his pant legs.

The echo died in the drizzle, now dissolving rapidly into light rainfall. This time they moved back as she indicated, allowed her space to move cautiously around the car to the driver's door. At the crack of the gun, the baby screamed in fright, wailing and thrashing on the seat. But she forced herself to concentrate on the men. "The keys!" she demanded again.

Alberto held them out. "Sure, here they are. You want 'em, you got 'em."

"Throw them to me," she directed. "Throw them!" She pointed the gun at Alberto, and he immediately tossed the keys into the air. She watched helplessly as they landed in the ditch behind the men. Panicked, she knew she would have to get out of here quickly. "Turn around," she demanded, and brandished the gun. "Do it!"

Both men swore but wheeled slowly in their tracks.

She climbed into the Land Rover. Inside, the car was different from the sedan and she stared in horror at the controls. As she struggled with the gearshift, the baby increased his wail to a shrill, red-faced screech. Her nerves beginning to shred, she pushed at the gas pedal. The engine roared heavily, but the car did not move.

She could see the men gathering their courage to rush the car. Frantic, she tried the other pedal and forced the gearshift forward. The Rover lurched into reverse, and the men dove headlong into the muddy ditch. She dropped the gun to the floor and managed to step on the brake. The baby had rolled against the suitcase but, other than being shaken, was fine.

After an eternity of grinding gears and frantic pushing on pedals, she managed to pull the gearshift down, and this time the car moved smoothly forward. She steered it onto the slippery roadway and with more sheer luck than judgment managed to straighten it out and drive away.

"Bitch!" Paulo spat in the mud, furious at the muck on his face and clothes from the dive into the ditch and unable to believe what had just happened. "You didn't search the purse? You idiot!" he bellowed.

"Me? You're the one that shoulda searched her! You drove her all the way here and didn' know she's got a gun?" Alberto fumed. "She coulda killed us! Shit!" He slid in the mud on the steep sides of the ditch, scratching through the muck and weeds for the keys. "I woulda searched her first thing, you can bet on that," he muttered furiously.

"Shut up! Just find the keys and shut up! She gets to the highway, we'll never catch her" Who knew she had a gun! Shit!

"Yeah, well, we don' find Rufino, we better leave the country." Alberto searched wildly through rocks and mud. "Miguelo trusted him because we say he was okay. We got to give him Rufino or the money, one."

"You said he was okay; I never said he was okay," Paulo snarled, appalled at their sudden turn in fortune. "I didn't know the son of a bitch, you said he was okay! You said he wouldn't take the money. You said he wouldn't leave his wife. What you don't know is gonna get us killed!"

Five minutes ago there had been a good possibility of finding the bastard and taking him back to Miguelo. By delivering Rufino, he could have proved to Miguelo that he, Paulo, could be trusted again and life could go on as before. He could have worked it out and gotten rid of this stupid rat-faced jackass in the process.

Shit! Who would figure she had a gun! Now Miguelo wouldn't trust him again, and small-time, rat-bastard Rufino was living it up somewhere on thirty thousand American dollars. His life wasn't worth shit because Rufino delivered a suitcase thirty thousand short. If Miguelo decided he and Alberto were in on it, he'd kill them, too. Slowly. The thought was enough to keep Paulo in the ditch on his hands and knees, searching for keys to his sedan.

"Yeah, well, we find Rufino an' we get the money, I'm gonna kill him anyway for gettin' us into this mess." Alberto was scared. "She can' get too far. She ain' got no key and she don' drive so good. She stops the car, she'll kill the motor and we catch her in five minutes."

Paulo wiped his muddy hands on his pant legs and leaped across to search the other side of the ditch. "Yeah, we ain't catching nobody if we don't find the goddamned keys!" Idiot, rat-faced asshole!

Luisita's hands were sweating and slippery, in a death grip on the steering wheel. She guided the jouncing Land Rover through the rain and mud. Boggled at her audacity in shooting at the men, she had only one thought: Get away! Thank the gods, the road was straight and there had been only one area washed out from water. The heavy car had moved through the mudhole with ease, but she was afraid to stop even to check on the baby. After a few minutes he'd ceased his angry wail and, lulled by the motion of the car, settled into silence.

It began to rain harder and Luisita struggled to see through the windshield. She knew there should be wipers, but she couldn't locate the control mechanism; the dirty glass turned the road into a nightmarish confusion of wiggling reddish brown images. She put her head out the open window, but the rain smashed her in the face, blinding her.

The gauges on the dashboard were a mass of useless dials until she finally recognized the speedometer, registering between fifteen and twenty no matter how hard she pushed the gas pedal; the engine vibrated and screamed in harsh complaint, but the car would would go no faster.

She shook her head and tried to think. It rained harder. The baby began a small whimpering sound, and she glanced at him. When she looked up, in the murk the road was barely visible and there was suddenly a mass of green in front of the car—a tree had fallen or something. She couldn't see! Whatever it was, she was going to hit it head on! The baby!

She stabbed frantically with both feet for the brakes; the car went skating sideways, out of control. Letting go of the steering wheel, she threw herself across to the baby, holding him close as the car shuddered into a lazy slide backward off the road into the ditch, pitching and rolling, nearly turning over, then righting itself as the engine stalled out.

Shaken, unhurt, she looked instantly to the baby. Adam calmly, greedily nuzzled her breast, seeking lunch. She cried in relief. Surely the gods were toying with her today. She struggled in the canted seat and placed him inside her shawl, held him close while she tried to think. The rain pounded a din on the roof, drowning her thoughts. They would find her and maybe kill her if she stayed with the car. If she left the car and went to the road, they would still find her—and she could not keep the baby warm and dry.

Then it was too late to decide. Through the streaky windshield, she saw the man with a gun slide down the ditch toward the car. She scrambled for the pistol, no longer at her feet. It was over.

He jerked open the door of the car and aimed the Magnum at the back of her head. "Okay, asshole, out of the—" Zachary stopped midsentence at Luisita's terrorized face. "What the hell are you doing here?" He checked the gun and slipped it into his pocket.

It took a moment for her to recognize him and overcome her fear. "Oh, please. Help me," she pleaded.

From the front of her shawl came the unmistakable wail of an unhappy baby. He stared in surprise, at a total loss. A baby?

The barricade had been Allison's idea. She'd sat through his dissertation about potential rescue efforts from Rider. Then, out of her silence had come a quiet query. "What if we put up some kind of . . . roadblock?"

The simplicity of the solution had been blinding. Of course, a roadblock. Something to block the path of Rider's rescue car. Better than that. A barrier to stop anything that moved up or down the road until they could hail it. A sure way to get the hell out of here. "You're fabulous, you know that?" he'd shouted, his admiration ringing through the cavern. He'd started to hug her and changed his mind when she backed away. "Gorgeous and fabulous!"

The impetus of rescue propelled him into the muggy morning, energized and determined to create the barrier all the quicker so he could return, like a moth, to the light of her. In the last five minutes things had rivaled the best five minutes in his life, and he wanted more.

Relatively dry under her poncho, he worked feverishly, uprooting a last few bushes from the soft stream bank, adding them to branches from low trees and undergrowth, then carting it all up to the roadside. He spread the brush across the road, creating a large green barrier, one that any sane driver would slow down to investigate, rain or no. He was intent on returning to the cave when the complaining roar of an overworked motor came over the sound of the downpour.

Determined, he positioned himself halfway up the ditch near the barricade. When he recognized the Land Rover, he decided that when it stopped for the roadblock, he'd use the gun. He was through playing games in Guatemala, and one way or another he was going to get the goddamned car back! He readied himself with the Magnum.

The car was a few yards away and still coming strong when he realized it wasn't going to stop. He watched in disbelief as the driver braked furiously at the last moment and the Rover skidded off the road. "What the hell . . ."

He'd scrambled up the ditch and across, down to the car—only to find Luisita! And a baby! Christ, what next?

Luisita was frantic with relief. The *tsoy y-ol* would help. "They will follow me! We must get away—quickly!" She struggled to get free of the tilted car, pulling at the suitcase; at the open door the baby yelled in protest when rainwater splashed in his face.

Zachary tried to slow her down. "Is your baby all right?"

"Yes, yes, he's fine," she cried. "Please! They'll be here soon!" She was frenzied to get out.

"Luisita!" He shook her. "There's nowhere to go! I'm as stuck out here as you are!" He pushed her inside to examine the infant. "What's going on? Who's chasing you?"

He took the tiny baby out of her arms and satisfied himself it was unhurt. "Are you talking about a little rat-faced bast . . . jerk and some guy named Paulo?"

"Yes. They'll kill me if I don't tell them about Rufino, and I don't know!"

"How the hell did you get the car?" he said incredulously. It didn't make sense that she could have managed to take it away from those two with a baby wrapped around her middle, but, Christ, nothing had made sense for three days. Who the hell was Rufino?

"I have a gun," she said breathlessly. "Somewhere on the floor." They were trapped. The gods would now decide.

His fingers found the gun. A cheap .22-caliber pistol, the kind homeowners keep around the house—too small to be effective against someone really determined to kill you and big enough to be dangerous around children. He checked the chamber, knowing the smaller-caliber bullets would be useless in the Magnum. Full. Minus one. Recently fired. "Did you shoot this?" He was impressed.

She nodded. "I wanted the keys to the other car, but he threw them in a ditch before I could stop him."

He thought rapidly. They'd have to find keys or hot-wire another car. Either way, it bought time. "We're going to be fine, little lady," he assured her. The baby began a stronger protest, and he handed her the infant, then pocketed the second gun. Between the Magnum and this pistol, he felt a hell of a lot more equal to Paulo and the rat-faced boy.

At the baby's cry, she began to function. "He is hungry. There is food." She indicated the suitcase.

He climbed out of the car and quickly assessed the damage; his boots squished in three inches of mud on the hillside. Even bone dry, it would be tough to get sufficient traction to free the car, but at the moment it was impossible. The rain continued in torrents as he sped through his options. It would have been so simple if she had managed to keep the damned thing on the road. Nothing in this bloody country was simple!

No percentage in staying with the car. Sooner or later, if those jerks were following her, which was likely, they'd come down this road and spot it. He'd have to take her to the cave until he could figure out something else. "Come on," he ordered. "Let's get out of here."

She wrapped the baby inside her shawl, and he pulled her out of the car, trying to shield the infant from the pouring rain. He grabbed the handle of the suitcase and passed her the heavy purse. "We can't go anywhere unless I can get this crate out of the ditch, and I can't do that until it stops raining." He helped her up the incline onto the roadway and handed her the suitcase. Minutes later he had covered most of the car with the brush from the barricade. Then he took back the soaked and crying child, lifted the poncho, and zippered it inside his jacket, then led the way down the other side of the road toward the cave.

When he first left the cave to work on blocking the road, Allison had stayed at the fire. She knew someone would be coming. They'd be out of here soon. Away from crazy men shooting goats and threatening people. Away from places where people nearly drowned. He was going to see to it.

Unable to switch off her energy, she picked up one of the old man's blankets. Simply woven in coarse red-and-black dyed wool, it was scratchy and irritating to her hands and gave off a fetid, oily smell. Something about its rough texture focused her senses. He must have covered her with it last night. She distinctly had a sense that she'd been safe, and warm, and something else . . .

She suddenly knew. Not something—someone. She pressed her hands against the blanket and was absolutely certain the memory was accurate. Heat from his body last night had warmed her, kept her safe. His arms had held her, secured her, hidden her away. He'd slept with her under Perez's red-and-black blankets. The knowing unsettled her for a moment, and she looked to the mouth of the cave where she'd last seen him.

Then something new and fantastic, clear and welcome, and she felt the realization as a physical reaction—a sense of peace and elation at the same time. Her mind wasn't shutting down at the intimate thought of his body. No familiar roar of panic. No need to hide.

In fact, she felt ridiculously high, and another bit of information locked into place—an extraordinary thought: reliving the feelings, the pain and rage and humiliation, from this morning's conversation had somehow unlocked the euphoria exploding in her now. It all made sense in an absurdly simple manner. In order to feel good, she'd had to feel horrible.

No. She'd had to allow feelings. All this time shutting out bad feelings had also shut out good ones. Something central had changed.

The jaguar streaked through her thoughts once again, and she identified what about the morning's dream had been different. In her dream she'd been feeling good. Again, feelings. But more than that, there hadn't been terror. For the first time in the three years since the rape, she had dreamed a normal dream. A dream without fear.

She circled the fire, holding the blanket, astonished at this new ability to put it all together. It had started with him—at Lisa's. She'd wanted to dance with him, had enjoyed dancing with him. All along she'd been attracted to him despite her fear of him, had gone against her fear to take this trip with him. And she'd been more than envious of Eve. She'd been jealous. Jealous that he'd kissed her, that they'd spent the night together.

Feelings. Normal, ordinary woman's feelings! All of them.

Then he'd been standing, quietly framed in the cavern opening, watching her, and time had entered slow motion.

"It's still raining pretty steady, and I'm going up to the road now." He'd walked back to see her. "Just thought I'd check with you before I go."

In the half-light, for the first time since they'd met, she truly saw him, as he was, without a barrier of fear. A thin scar was visible on his temple, parting one of his brows.

She lifted her foot for his gentle inspection, proud to feel no hesitation and, magically, unsurprised. She was no longer afraid of him. No need to stay on guard, no refusal to feel his touch as he examined the cut on her ankle.

Apparently satisfied that the healing process was undisturbed, he replaced the cotton sock and grinned at her. "I'll have the road blocked in twenty minutes. I'll be back then. Do you want anything, water?

"Water." She wasn't thirsty, but she didn't want him to leave just yet. It felt too good to feel good, even if she could not explain that somehow her life had just begun again.

He brought the water. This time, when she took the cup, her skin met his with a life of its own, tingling and electric. Testing herself, she traced the faint scar with her fingers. "How did you get this?"

He looked at her, surprised at her willingness to touch him. He hadn't thought about the scar in years. "John Tullis got me with an ice skate in the sixth grade. Ten stitches."

"Your jaw is sore because I hit you," he continued, relieved to confess it. "You . . . you were giving me a pretty good fight." A desire to kiss her flowed from every pore in his body. "So this might hurt." Slowly, inexorably, he leaned in to her, seeking permission. Then, without touching her in any other way, he closed his eyes and kissed her.

A kiss that in another time might certainly have led somewhere wanton. He ended it as he began, gently, careful not to scrape her face with his bristly chin. "I just kissed the Gallé Girl," he teased as reality came back from suspension. "I want a real date when we get out of here."

Not the intimate, mutually confident kiss in her dream, but a softly caring, exploring-this-moment kiss and a gentle invitation to join with him in open possibility. She smiled with shy pleasure, savoring the sensations shivering in her body, drinking in his battered face, the unruly brows with the tiny scar, his tight, hard mouth that held a kiss of slow surprise, surrounded by the scruffy three-day beard. "If you promise to . . . shave," she managed to banter, shaky, high on feelings she did not yet trust.

"Done." He almost kissed her a second time, wanting desperately to lose himself in kissing her again, but he changed his mind and walked back out into the rain.

She basked in the memory of the feel of his mouth in that perfect kiss and was tense with anticipation for his return. He'd been gone far longer than twenty minutes. Through the drumming downpour came an odd cry, and her thoughts of him scattered. A bird or an animal, she decided.

When she heard the cry a second time, she was driven to the mouth of the cave. She stepped into the open and spied him through the gray-green downpour, dripping in her borrowed poncho.

Feelings of relief faltered a bit when she saw someone following him. Luisita! Where on earth had he found her? She watched their progress as he helped the young woman rapidly toward the cave.

She started to call out, but he motioned her not to speak, so she waited in silence until they stepped inside the lee, out of the rain. Her joy became apprehension. Something was wrong. She could feel it. Luisita quickly sought the fire; he took off the poncho and unzipped his jacket to reveal an infant, who greeted her with a lusty wail. The cries had been this baby!

Zachary saw the stunned look on her face. "Don't ask."

"He is hungry." Luisita hurriedly opened the wet suitcase to set out a bottle and a can of formula; then she unwound her soaked shawl from around the baby and began to remove its damp clothing. The naked infant squalled, thoroughly out of patience.

Zachary grabbed the can of formula and patted his pockets for the army knife, located a blade, held it briefly in the fire, then deftly punctured the top. "I'll explain in a minute," he said. "Right now we need to get him quiet. Fill this about half-full."

Allison picked up the empty bottle and poured several ounces of milk into it. "Isn't this supposed to be warm?" She had no idea about babies, and this one was extremely upset, red-faced and howling.

He took one look at the furious infant, now changed and wrapped neatly in a maternity dress from the suitcase, and offered the bottle. "I think room temperature is adequate under the circumstances."

The hungry baby sucked lustily at the rubber nipple, and order returned to the cavern. Luisita moved a small distance away to feed him.

He took off his jacket and spread it and the shawl and the baby's clothing on a branch next to the fire. "I've got good news and bad news," he said as he peeled off his T-shirt and wrung it out. He put it back on to dry from body heat. "The good news is the roadblock worked."

Allison watched him re-dress, antennae tuned. On some remote plane she was quietly curious about the body she'd slept next to last night and acutely aware for the first time of the graceful proportion of his spare torso, hard-muscled and lean. On a conscious level she waited cautiously for the reason he was no longer exuberant and why he'd brought Luisita and a tiny baby into the cave. Something ominous was waiting outside in the rain.

He looked into clear, intelligent and, at last, unguarded eyes, hating what he was about to say. "The bad news is, she drove the car off the road and I'm not sure I can get it out without help." May as well lay it all out, he decided. Time was getting short. "The positively rotten news—" He took a breath and prayed inwardly she could handle it. "She says the two guys that shot Perez's goats are following her."

Allison blinked and stared at him, her recent victory of confidence and stability thrown into a spin as she processed the dangerous situation. A small rope of fear circled its way around her stomach.

"Apparently, she managed to take the Land Rover away from them with this," he continued with a wry smile, and laid Luisita's pistol, pointed at the wall, on the rock between them. He put the Magnum next to it.

"They have a car," came Luisita's voice from a black shadow. "They threw away the keys in the ditch, but they will find them and come after me."

"Off the road? Could we push it out?" Allison balled her hands into fists and dug in her nails.

"Not in this rain," he answered. "I covered it with brush from the roadblock. I don't think they'll see it if the rain keeps up." He glanced out to the downpour. "How far back did you lose them?" he asked Luisita.

She thought for a moment and replied carefully. "I am not sure. It seemed like a long time, but the car would not drive very fast. Maybe ten minutes, I think."

"What's wrong with the car?" he asked cautiously.

"I don't know. I don't know about cars," she replied. "I didn't drive one before." The *tsoy y-ol* would take care of things. Hachäkyum would see to it.

Luisita calmly put the tiny baby over her shoulder and patted its back as Allison stared at her in blank surprise. With a baby she had driven an automobile for the first time? People do what they have to do. And she would do what she had to do. After a few pats, the unconcerned infant obligingly burped up an allotment of air and resumed emptying the bottle.

Zachary turned to stare at Luisita. Hell, no wonder she'd driven off the road. He realized now what the laboring sound of the engine had indicated. She'd been driving in too low a gear—probably in first. Top speed in first gear couldn't be more than ten or fifteen miles an hour. From the sound of the motor, she'd had it floored. It was a minor miracle that she and the baby hadn't been injured. Ten minutes at fifteen miles an hour wasn't very far. He tried to calculate. Ten minutes equaled one-sixth of an hour; fifteen miles divided by six?

Something under three. A whole lot under. Damn! Assuming it took these assholes at least three minutes to find the keys to the other car, if they were following her, they could be cruising through here any second. With any luck they wouldn't see the car in the rain. He prayed fervently for a downpour for another ten minutes.

The baby, now full, sagged into sleep, and Luisita pulled one of the blankets off the rock to make a small bed for him. Allison limped to her side and inspected the ground around the rock. "Be sure it's safe," she said. "I was stung by a scorpion in here yesterday."

Luisita handed her the quiet infant and shook out the blanket to satisfy herself that no scorpion had taken up residence.

Luisita examined the blanket, Allison examined the baby.

Supremely safe in his sleep, the little boy lay limp in her arms. His eyes were firmly closed, and his pale rosebud mouth moved in a slight sucking motion in a tiny square face with huge cheekbones and spiky lashes framed by a full head of straight black hair. His skin was flawless, the color of pale coffee, and unbelievably soft.

Zachary watched with split concentration from across the fire, enjoying a small flashback of the supreme thrill it had been to kiss her. Finally. And the feel of heated-satin skin of her breasts next to him in the night, soft as the baby's. His body warmed involuntarily at the memory. God, she was beautiful, and it was obvious she was taken with the infant.

The other three-quarters of his mind was occupied with how the hell to get the Land Rover out of that ditch. He knew in his heart that the ground was too soft from the rain. Maybe he could get enough traction by putting the brush from the roadblock under the wheels. Even with the guns, he didn't want the bastards to catch him trying to move the car. He listened in silence to the women's subdued conversation as they watched over the child.

"How old is he?" asked Allison, rocking the sleeping infant while Luisita refolded and arranged one of the blankets on the dirt near the fire, then rolled a second one lengthwise.

"He is three weeks tomorrow," came the soft reply.

"Your sister's child?"

"Yes," Luisita answered simply. "She died four days ago."

Allison was unprepared for the tears that sprang to her eyes. "I'm so sorry," she said. "How terrible for you."

Luisita's face was impassive, as was proper, showing no trace of the deep sadness in her heart, but she was grateful for the American woman's concern. She stopped to fuss with the dress that had been purchased for Sara, now wrapped around Sara's child. "She will sleep at the foot of a sacred ceiba tree as it holds up the sky," she said softly. "Kisin cannot send her more troubles."

Allison hoped fervently that it was true for the mother of the little boy. "He's a beautiful baby," she said. "You must be very proud. What's his name?"

The Mayan woman coiled the rolled blanket around the edge of the folded one, creating three walls of a makeshift cradle. "He is the first child in this family. His American name will be Adam." She grew quiet.

"You have no children?"

"No. There was only my sister. Now there is Adam, and me. I want to take him back with me to the United States, but I am afraid."

"Afraid of what?" came Zachary's voice, causing them both to start. The baby in Allison's arms reacted to her sudden movement, then settled down.

"The police," Luisita answered, timidly. "When my sister called, I didn't have enough money. Sara was in trouble." She paused, mortified at her confession. "I stole money from the people I was working for."

Allison glanced from the the peaceful child in her arms to Zachary, aware that theft was no small problem. His face was a frown of concentration.

"Is that why these guys are looking for you?"

"No!" Luisita became agitated. "They don't know I have the money. They're looking for Rufino. He's the baby's father." She told, haltingly, of the call from Sara. "They thought my sister came here to meet him and knew where he was hiding." In her distress she stood rigid, explaining earnestly. "I saw them follow me to the ruins—that's why I ran away. I didn't think they would hurt *americanos*. . . ." Her voice trailed away.

"Do you know where this guy is?"

"No!" Luisita was emphatic. "I did not talk to my sister before she died. I have never seen Rufino. They know this now because one of them lied to me that he was Rufino. He tried to take the baby," she explained. "When I wouldn't let him take the child, he took me, too."

"Why?" asked Zachary. It still didn't add up.

"One of them said he would use the baby to convince Rufino to give back the money," she answered apprehensively.

An appalled silence followed her words. Allison saw that Zachary shared her shock at this information. None of them doubted the men were dangerous enough to blackmail with the baby's life. He got up abruptly, then picked up Luisita's pistol and moved to the mouth of the cave to check outside.

"Were you going to give them the money?" Allison handed the baby back to Luisita, who placed him cautiously on the nest of blankets before she answered.

"It was for plane fare . . . for my sister." She seated herself on the sandy floor next to the baby. "The last time I talked to Sara, she had not had the baby and she wanted to come to America." She swallowed the lump of grief the memory brought to her throat.

Allison studied the plastic wrapping around her injured foot. "Was it a lot of money?"

"Yes. Two hundred dollars. I will pay it back. I swear."

"I believe you." Looking down at the beautiful sleeping child, Allison had the wrenching realization that when she got back to Chicago, two hundred dollars would mean less than a day's work. For the baby's mother, three weeks ago, two hundred dollars had literally been the difference between life and death. For this woman, stealing that much money might mean going to jail. The abyss between her world and Luisita's was so vast, she could scarcely believe it.

The solution was maddeningly simple. "When we get back to Belize, I'll arrange the baby's fare, then you can return the money," she insisted. "I'm sure when you tell these people about your sister's death, they'll understand. If it will help, I'll talk to them and I'm sure he will speak for you, too."

Luisita was too grateful to remain politely quiet, her heart too full of gratitude. She would offer many prayers for this good fortune. "If you will do this, I will repay it. I swear I will work for nothing until this debt is repaid. I just wanted my sister and her baby to be safe. Surely they will understand if I can give it back."

"If we get out of here, you won't owe me a thing," Allison said fervently. "Let's worry about it later. I promise we'll help you, but let's get out of here first."

Outside, in the pouring rain, the jaguar moved, powerful shoulders easing his body across the rugged terrain, belly to the ground, stalking his cave. The salty odor of humans was disturbing and dangerous.

The big cat was hungry. Last night's hunt had not been successful, and he'd been chased by men with dogs from the nearby village. The sound of the crying child drew him closer to investigate, heavy black fur matted with mud and water, tail twitching with interest at the wailing cries from inside the cave.

Now it was silent. He approached the cave and flattened into the wet earth. Nostrils flared, he sniffed the air, gauging the information it brought about the humans inside.

A man appeared in the mouth of the cave to stand guard. The cat watched and waited, then, stopped by the presence of the man, got to his feet with deliberation, changed his course, and moved to higher ground, gliding smoothly from shadow to shadow undetected, undisturbed by the pounding rain. There was another way.

18

Deeply conscious that Zachary was keeping watch at the mouth of the cave, Allison left Luisita with the baby and worked her way quietly to his side. She stared with him out at the steadily pouring rain; the ominous guns were in a crevice in the wall next to him.

Some of the earlier magic layered itself over her worry. "What do you think?" she said quietly.

"I think she's telling the truth. I think she was caught in one hell of a mess and she did the best she could."

And I think you're beautiful.

"What about the stolen money? She says she'll give it back. Do you think she'll be arrested?"

"Depends on how determined her ex-employers are to make her pay for it—who knows? Probably not. I'll see what I can do." Wanting to touch her, needing to feel her skin against him, he moved slightly and succeeded in brushing his bare arm against her. Instead of satisfying him, the electric softness merely opened a thousand doors of need; still, it was sinfully good, heating his blood and starting the wicked imp of lust dancing among his senses.

She stood her ground and allowed liquid feelings from

contact with his body to flow into her soul. After a moment she ventured, "If she'll come to Chicago, I can help her get work."

He turned his head to look at her with renewed appreciation. "If she gets that kid into the States," he pledged. "I'll bring them to Chicago."

The pact was real and complete; they would see each other again. The warmth of feeling grew, and he closed the space between; with infinite care not to hurt her bruised chin, he placed his hands on either side of her face and bent to kiss her. Lost in the taste of her, he experienced again the floating absence of space and time.

She did not kiss him back, but she was fully there and he felt her allow him in. Her lips barely parted, silky soft and pliant under his mouth, and he drifted with his fantasy for an eternity of seconds. His breath and heart and mind were filled with her—the smell of her, the feel of her. Then he pulled away. Don't tip her over. Do it right. "You're something else, you know that?" he said huskily. He dropped his hands and stepped back a pace, sexual energy a trip-hammer in his chest.

He wanted to do incredible things, to bury his hands in that bright, wonderful hair, to hold her close and kiss her forever, insist on the response he sensed was there, real and possible for him. But, goddamn, she made him dizzy, and he couldn't afford to get more distracted. Do it right!

He forcibly brought himself back to the reality of here and now and changed the subject. "It's been raining hard for nearly an hour. If it doesn't let up, we're going to have trouble getting to the road."

He pointed to the water flowing from the murky depths of the cave, spilling onto broken rocks and giant boulders at the base of the waterfall, half a dozen feet below. "So far, the water's still clear. Help me keep an eye on it. If it gets muddy or starts flowing heavier, we'll only have minutes to get out of here and across to the road."

When he switched his concentration to the danger from the rain, she reluctantly abandoned delightful, resonating, shimmering feelings and made herself listen, then nod in understanding. The water was a danger that had not occurred to her. As she listened, a free-fall of feelings washed through her, testing to see if she was still whole. There was no fear. And a fresh delight in the joy of being free. The situation was impossible, but if he kissed her again like that, nothing on earth could prevent her from kissing him back in kind. She struggled to stay on track.

"What about the men?" she asked. "What if they followed her and they're out there?"

"I don't know. Let's avoid the road for another twenty minutes, then go up and start working on getting the Rover out of the ditch."

She looked at her watch; it was almost eleven. "Maybe we should eat now."

He tucked the pistol in his belt and dropped the Magnum in his jacket pocket, then walked her back to the fire. Being in her presence made him ravenous. "We're going to eat and leave here in about fifteen minutes," he said to Luisita.

Luisita got up, retrieved her purse, and brought it and Nuk's wrapped tortillas to the fire. Reaching into the bottom, she brought out a fistful of .22-caliber bullets.

His eyes widened in appreciation at the sight of the ammunition. It wouldn't fit the Magnum, but it gave him extended firepower for the pistol.

She thrust the shells into his hand. "It is not my gun," she said, eyes downcast.

"Stolen? The people you worked for?"

She nodded. "I was afraid."

"You'd better let me keep it, then. I'm a police officer. I'll see it gets back to its owners when I get to Miami."

"*Bay*. Yes," she repeated, then quickly bent to warm Nuk's tortillas in the flames. Soon Allison and Zachary were seated side by side, deliciously rubbing elbows as Luisita showed them how to bend the wholesome, pliable corn-flour bread and use it to retrieve cooked chicken from the clay pot in the fire.

"Heaven," pronounced a hungry Allison, senses tuned to being next to him, everything fresh and real and exquisite. Refusing to think about even a minute from now, she was living every second fully and completely, high on sensations long buried, now unsealed—still brand new, and free.

"Heaven," echoed a contented Zachary, filled to the brim with having kissed her—twice. He watched as she ate and shared food with him, taking in the incredible change from the withdrawn, frightened stranger on the plane to this delicate, intriguing woman by his side, able to tip his world sideways.

If it went no further than this cave and the trip back to the real world, he was alive inside himself for the first time in years, in a way he had never hoped to be, had forgotten he could be. She made time expand for him, and he was doing it right. Maybe, just maybe . . .

Close outside the cave came an animal cry, a screeching, yowling wail, haunting and primitive. Luisita looked up, startled, then smiled. Light came into her eyes. "Balum. He is the baby's *onen*. It is a good sign," she said cheerfully. "It is a very good sign." She moved quickly toward the mouth of the cave.

Zachary rose to follow her, and the sound came again, raising the hair on the back of his neck. Allison's eyes widened in the dim light and she shivered, unnerved by the primal threat in the scream.

Watching her eyes, irises huge in the dimming firelight, he mentally rechecked the heavy Magnum tucked under the belt at his back, reassured by the pressure against his spine.

"It shouldn't be a problem. It won't come in here because of the fire. And if it does, I have a weapon this time."

"I don't want you to shoot it. They're endangered, and black ones are extremely rare." Allison was serious.

"I don't want to shoot it, either, but endangered species get just as hungry as anybody else." He laughed grimly, knowing full well he'd kill it in a second if it threatened her in any way. He'd empty both guns doing it. "He stays out there, he's safe in the gene pool. But if he comes in here, all deals are off."

She glanced at the sleeping baby. "If it comes in here, I'll shoot it myself."

"What's she talking about, *onen*?" he asked.

Allison busied herself removing the plastic wrapping from her foot, and he moved to her side, unbidden, to check on the wound.

"*Onen* translates as something akin to lineage, but it's more complicated," she explained. "Maya are born into clans which have *onen*. There are several—Jaguar is one, Monkey, Deer—various animals and birds. Then there's a personal *onen*, which you come to know during your life."

His presence next to her made it hard to concentrate. "I'm not sure I can explain it to you, but it also has to do with decisions relative to approval for marriage. Apparently Luisita and the baby are Jaguar *onen*. Sometimes *onen* appear in dreams to foretell events or give signs. Maya accept dreams as actuality, not different from real events." She recalled fleetingly the kiss in her dream, and the jaguar. Both had become real within hours, she realized suddenly; a tiny thrill made its way up her back. "I had a dream last night . . . about a jaguar."

As he listened Zachary carefully inspected the cut on her ankle, happy to touch her. If he were Maya and dreams were real, he'd already made love to her.

He removed the Band-Aids with care. The cut was healing nicely, but it would not tolerate heavy activity without breaking open; the flesh was taut and pink, no sign of infection. He pressed the skin firmly, and she reacted with an ordinary response. He was pleased. "I think you can wear the boot now." He swabbed the area with alcohol and fixed the last of the Band-Aids in place. "Make sure you lace it up pretty tight so the sock doesn't move around too much."

He looked at her firelit face, extraordinarily beautiful.

He wanted more than dreams. He wanted hours of her, acres of time, aeons.

"Yes, doctor," she teased, dismissing the coincidence, warmed with the pleasure of his attention. Glancing down, she encountered two black eyes, blinking blindly in the firelight. Too young to focus more than a few inches away, the baby was yawning and moving gently in his makeshift cradle, staring at the fire. She nodded toward the tiny face. "He's awake."

"Uh-oh. We'd better get another bottle ready. I'll tell Luisita." He got to his feet and moved off.

At the entrance to the cave, Luisita searched both sides of the ravine for sight of the jaguar. For an instant she saw him high on the side of the hill, slipping into an opening in the rock, and her heart sang. This was very good indeed. If the jaguar was here, he would allow no harm to the baby. Perhaps he had already influenced the American woman's promise to help get Adam to the United States. She whispered a prayer of thanks to the giant cat and wished fervently for *posol*—a food offering—to entreat his continued care.

She smiled. It was evident the *tsoy y-ol* was besotted with the beautiful woman. They would make a good couple; many fine children would come of this. She turned to watch them by the fire, the woman's bright hair flowing in the light, his face turned up to her as she smiled. The sound of their low voices drifted across the cavern, and she heard Allison explain the importance of *onen* and dreams. She had not met Americans who were familiar with the Maya way of life. Truly the American woman was *tsoy y-ol*, also. A proper match for him.

She turned again to the outside and watched as the rain abated dramatically; within minutes patches of blue sky appeared between the whitening clouds. Shafts of sunlight lit raindrops resting on the sea of leaves in the rugged ravine, turning the valley into an ocean of light, winking and sparkling. Zachary joined her, and together they watched the grease-gray rain clouds scudding toward the eastern horizon.

"Old Mensäbäk's servants are through for today," she told him, eyes dancing with pleasure for his good fortune at being in love.

"Well, let's hope they're through for the season," he said. "The baby's awake and we need to get the hell out of here. We'll need another bottle soon."

"I will get it." She left to retrieve the bottle and filled it with formula from the opened can. The nipple slipped from her fingers and spun in a lazy circle on the dirt. The baby began to fuss.

Allison finished lacing her boot and joined Luisita. "May I pick him up?" Luisita nodded, and with infinite care, one hand under the delicate head, Allison scooped him up and smiled with great joy as he quieted under her touch. He couldn't weigh more than six or seven pounds. She was entranced with him. "Shall I hold him, or do you want me to rinse the nipple?"

"I have another," said Luisita, opening the suitcase and taking the nipple off a second bottle. "It is too soon for him to be hungry," she said. "He may not want this."

Allison beamed with pleasure and carefully arranged the baby in her arms, aching with unexpected joy at the feel of the tiny little body next to her stomach. Until today she hadn't been aware of a maternal bone in her body. This was a whole new range of feelings to be explored. She laughed with delight as the baby took the bottle.

Across the way, Zachary paused in his inventory of what to take and what to leave in order to pocket the keys to the Land Rover. He put the cameras and film in his pack, her journal, some of their dwindling supplies. She was framed in the firelight, feeding the baby, laughing out loud. A man anywhere on the planet couldn't help a surge of pride at this sight.

He watched the demanding child suck mightily on the bottle and exhaled with relief that it was a healthy baby. The importance of keeping them safe welled in his mind. Perez's blankets might end up under the wheels, but they were damned sure getting out of here as soon as he could manage it. He stacked the blankets by the mouth of the cave and returned for the backpacks. The jaguar could inherit the bones abandoned in the bottom of the cooking pot.

Luisita rinsed the dusty nipple in the burbling stream of the cave, then approached the American. "How can I help?"

"You can take your suitcase down to the rocks where we crossed the water," he instructed. "Then help me with backpacks and blankets. We'll be leaving as soon as we get everything at the crossing." He looked back toward Allison and the infant. "She shouldn't carry anything until we get across the water. Maybe not then. I'll have to see how her foot handles the activity."

She nodded and picked up her suitcase and took up his backpack. "Should I take this now?"

"Fine." She walked out the entrance, and he dropped the second pack and crossed to Allison, still feeding the baby. Cautiously, he held out the plastic case with the scorpion pinned inside. "Remember this guy? I found him in the back."

When she saw what it was, she instinctively moved the baby aside and studied the case. "Is it still alive?"

He pulled the lid away; the scorpion waved an exhausted leg in hopeless defiance.

She looked with distress at the hapless creature she'd forgotten. "I don't want to leave it like that," she said. "I'm the intruder here. It didn't walk into my world, I stepped into its. Can you get it out of the soap?"

His compassion didn't extend to the ugly creature. "Are you sure?" He poked at the scorpion with a small stick and pried its crunchy body out of the sticky mass. Dropped onto the cavern floor, it crawled weakly in circles, hampered and vulnerable, legs mired in a coating of white soap mixed with dirt. He saw in her face that she was upset at the thought of leaving it helpless, so he took mercy on the sorry sight and cleared the plastic box of soap.

Filling it with water, he immersed the soapy creature and shook it fiercely in revenge. Finally he dumped it out, free and clean again, if more than a little dizzy. All appendages once again operational, it scuttled slowly under a boulder, and he pushed a pile of sand against the rock with his foot, pinning it inside. He grinned sideways at her. "Satisfied?"

"I know you probably think I'm crazy. . . ."

"Only slightly deranged," he teased.

The baby refused more of the bottle and began to whimper. "What's wrong?" She was alarmed.

"Too much air. You know how to burp him?"

"I saw Luisita do it," she said, suddenly unsure.

"Just prop him over your shoulder and pat his back," he instructed.

She put the baby up to her shoulder, and the whimpering ceased as she gently bumped his body.

Adam gave a healthy belch, and she couldn't have been more pleased. Babies weren't totally mysterious after all. Milk and air go in, air comes out, milk stays in. I can do this, she thought with unaccustomed pride.

"I remember my little girl. When she was born, I thought I'd be scared to death of her. Turns out they don't break and they're people size before you know it." He could not keep the longing out of his voice. God, it would be good to see Steffie again and toss her up in the air, make her giggle and squeal.

She heard the note of longing and was surprised. He hadn't said anything about being married.

He realized suddenly how much he had yet to tell her. "I'm divorced." He hastened to change a subject that could not be explained in hours, let alone minutes. "We're ready to leave when he is."

Zachary scraped more sand against the boulder and gathered up her sleeping bag. Jerk. He'd picked a great time to tell her he'd been married. What was done was done. He concentrated on the problem of the car. The bedroll would probably wind up under the tires also. With it and the blankets and the brush from the roadblock, one way or another they were getting out of here today.

High on the side of the canyon, the jaguar moved restlessly, grooming the last of his damp fur into place in the warmth of new, bright sunlight. From the interior of the cavern, drifting up through the narrow fissure behind him, he heard the sounds of their activity. Odors peculiar to humans moved with the dry cavern air seeping up through the maze of ancient limestone passageways.

The sound of a whimpering child mixed with the smells, exciting the great cat, agitating his interest. He was hungry, and the path to the food was safe and clear. His toilet complete, the jaguar paused a moment, eyes glowing with cold black points in the midday sun. He turned to begin his search, huge, powerful shoulders working his way slowly down familiar tunnels, seeking the food smell, creating no sound in the dark.

At the river crossing, Luisita jumped the space between the boulders, splashed through the shallows, and placed the pack well up on the bank, then returned for her suitcase. From the river she could see almost to the mouth of the cavern. No sign of *tsoy y-ol*. He was probably talking to the woman. She smiled; she had not missed the enviable kiss that had passed between the two earlier this morning. Something had changed mightily since their drive to the ruins; there had been no such companionship then. Soon they would lie together and make many fine children, as it should be.

She looked again to the side of the canyon where she'd last seen the jaguar, but it was not there. She uttered another fervent prayer of thanks; the trees in the ravine swayed, creaked softly in the slight breeze, scattered their load of raindrops to the soft forest soil. The baby would be safe today, Balum and the *tsoy y-ol* would see to it. She picked up her suitcase and carried it quickly across the creek, putting it next to his pack, then froze.

Fifteen feet away stood Paulo, and Alberto, with his rat face grinning in delight. The men jumped forward, and she turned and charged through the shallows to the stone crossing, icy terror closing her throat. The baby! Leaping recklessly across the boulders, she stumbled through the stones and gravel at the other side, cutting her knees and scraping her fingers as she fell against the bank.

Alberto grasped at her ankle, and she went sprawling again. Twisting, she kicked him away with all her strength. Scrambling and writhing on the gravel, she got to her feet and sprinted toward the cave, Paulo right behind.

Inside the cave, Zachary held the baby, keeping pace with Allison as she threaded a cautious path toward the entrance, favoring her injured foot. He saw Luisita running pell-mell along the bank with two men, one of them Alberto, close behind her.

"Damn it to hell! They're here." He gave her the child, then searched quickly through the pack for the flashlight and thrust it into her hand. "Take this and get as far back as you can," he said tersely. He stripped off his jacket and threw it around her shoulders, then grabbed Luisita's purse and slipped the Magnum inside. "I don't have a clue how this'll go down, but I'll keep them out of here." He tucked the purse and one of the blankets under her arm.

She was blank with fear; Luisita screamed outside in the ravine. Then it was quiet. She looked out to see the girl in a heap on the riverbank, with the two muddied men standing over her. She felt a surging leap of rage at their brutal treatment.

Drawing courage from a last look at Zachary's angry face, she turned and instinctively sought the darkest shadows. Holding the sleeping baby close to her body, she inched her way through the rocks into the deepest recesses of the cavern. Her mind whirled with fury and concern for the infant. These men had threatened the baby in her arms. She'd kill them before she gave him up!

In the harsh light of the flashlight, she could see that the cavern hooked sharply to the right to form a bubble of limestone, slick with the seepage of water. The room was half-full of wet sand, and the head of a giant boulder protruded from the center of the floor, like a bald island. The dome of the bubble was a little higher than her head, and she had the vague impression of an igloo. At the extreme bottom right of the bubble was an indentation—the base of a thin shaft that appeared to lead upward into the side of the canyon. She felt the updraft of air being drawn smoothly into the blackness of the hole.

She crouched behind the boulder on the blanket while her heartbeat thumped furiously in her temples and racketed in her chest. Light from the flashlight disappeared into the opening in the earth, hardly more than a crawl space. She decided she would go into that grim hole only if it became absolutely necessary. Her mind wouldn't define "absolutely necessary," except that she would know.

Carefully searching the wet floor for living creatures, she placed the baby on the blanket long enough to put her arms through the sleeves of Zachary's huge jacket. She engaged the zipper and moved the fastener up three or four inches, then took the revolver out of Luisita's purse and worked it around to fill up the space at the back of the jacket.

Then she cautiously placed the sleepy child inside in the front of the jacket as Zachary had done. She snapped off the flashlight and held on to the gun in the inky darkness, listening past her heartbeat, straining in the silence to hear what was going on outside.

Zachary rechecked Luisita's stolen pistol and fingered the seven extra bullets, mentally lighting candles that it wouldn't go down dirty. If there was anything written in stone, it was "Don't trust junkies—ever." Any rube cop in any city in America could cite you that one. Don't trust anyone who threatens kids, either.

Twenty yards down the ravine he saw Alberto yank Luisita to her feet and push her toward the entrance to the cave. Then ten. Fighting and kicking and enduring his abuse for her stubborn refusal, she was being manhandled slowly toward the opening.

They were taking no precautions, and his gut told him they didn't know he was in the cave. Studying the men, he felt his adrenaline shoot up like a rocket. The second bastard had a semiautomatic Uzi pistol, with at least forty rounds in the magazine. A vicious weapon, and he had it pressed to her side. No wonder they were coming openly, brazenly, to the cavern. Christ, he could knock down fifteen men with the damned thing.

His only chance with the twenty-two was to wait until they were near enough to pick one of them off and hope to hell Luisita was smart enough to hit the ground and give him a shot at the other one.

But the gunman stayed too close to her for him to get off a clean shot, and he was forced to wait as they climbed up the rocky entrance above the falls. Then they were twenty feet away, and he was out of choices. He slid the smooth leather case of his detective's shield out of his hip pocket. Here went everything.

Flashing the metal in the brilliant sunlight, he stepped outside the cavern, keeping part of his body behind a boulder.

Aiming the pistol carefully at the second man's head, "Police officer," he announced. "That's far enough."

Alberto's eyes flared with hatred, and he stopped abruptly. "You!" he spat in recognition. He twisted Luisita's arm, holding her firmly in front of him. She struggled, determined to get free, and he cuffed her into submission. She was caught, panting, angry and crying with pain and rage.

Paulo recognized the tall American and stared at the badge. What the hell was a cop doing in a cave in the middle of Guatemala? Shit!

He hesitated and shifted the Uzi to the woman's head. He had superior firepower, but it was no good killing an American cop. If he did, Alberto was too stupid to keep his mouth shut, and he'd have to kill him, too. And the woman. The baby. Too much killing. Miguelo would never stand for it. Shit, he was dead for sure. What the hell to do now?

Alberto was infuriated. "I'm gonna kill you, asshole! I wan' my gun, you rat-bastard son'f a bitch."

Zachary recognized the thin line in the man's screeching rage and decided to do his best not to cross it. "There's no reason for anybody to get killed here, Alberto. You want your gun back, I want my car back. Let's work it out."

"What's he talking about?" Paulo was rattled. "How the fuck he's got your gun? What happened?"

"Jumped me from behind the other night," Alberto lied. "So what?"

"So what? You didn't tell me, that's what! You know this guy's around and you don' tell me! A fuckin' cop?"

"How the hell I know he's a cop! He's not wearin' a fuckin' sign!" Alberto's rage was running away with him. Tied up with his own belt! Half an hour rolling around in goat shit to get loose! He should have killed the American asshole cop when he had the chance.

Zachary couldn't hear enough of the exchange to translate, but he read Paulo's fury and the surprise in his face. Alberto hadn't told Paulo about the other night; he hoped the younger man had enough brains to be reasoned with. Paulo. His name was Paulo. "What's the matter, Paulo—he forget to tell you? Hey, you got some partner, Paulo."

"Shaddup, asshole! So you don't know where she is, hah?" Alberto, frothing, shoved Luisita forward for emphasis, then yanked her back. "So what's she doin' here, hah? Where's the kid?"

Zachary ignored the rat-man's question and continued working on Paulo. Something had prevented him from opening up with the Uzi; maybe he was smart enough not to kill a cop unless he had to. He hoped to hell he was calling it right. "Why don't you pull the plug on this, Paulo. Before it gets stupid and our friend Alberto gets somebody killed."

Paulo subtly positioned himself behind Alberto's body. Zachary shifted the pistol to Alberto's stomach and saw the man's eyes register the danger. "There's nothing for anybody to win here, Paulo. We don't know this guy you're looking for, and that's all there is to it."

Paulo was sweating. It was getting messy. He'd have to deal with Rufino another day. Sooner or later the asshole would come up for air. So far the cop had nothing. "Where's the baby?" he said sullenly, buying time, too aware that the cop knew both their names. Damn Alberto, the talk-too-much son of a bitch!

Luisita jerked her head up and stared at Zachary.

"The baby's not a part of this."

The *tsoy y-ol*'s voice was feathered steel, and she sagged in relief.

In the ravine, the sun ground down on the three men and the struggling woman; the air shimmered and quivered, sultry and close, alive with birdcalls and the hum of busy insects.

Then it got deathly quiet.

In the sudden silence, rivulets of moisture gathered in the hollow of Zachary's back, trickled down his spine; his hand was slick with perspiration on the butt of the small pistol. Even the ground thrummed with a dull vibration as everything took on an additional dimension.

He waited, senses tuned, priming himself. Mentally he chose Paulo's head as his target for the first shot if it started going south. He hoped to hell the pistol was reasonably true, and that he'd kill at least one of them before they had a chance to hurt the woman.

"I'm a cop," he said again to break the eerie silence.

"Now, Alberto here is dumb enough to think he can get away with killing a cop," he continued quietly, "but you and I know different, don't we, Paulo."

Inside the cave, Allison could hear bits and pieces of the conversation between Zachary and the men. "I'm a cop," came floating back to her clearly, and she strained to hear what would follow. Bracing herself for a crash of gunfire in the pitch black of her hiding place, she rocked with tension, the world outside lost to her, their confrontation reduced to murmurs and a distorted garble of male voices. The flashlight in her left hand, the blunt butt of the heavy revolver clenched in her right fist, she closed her eyes and concentrated on holding her breath and not making a sound in order to hear.

Suddenly drops of cold water fell on her head. They scared her to death as they trickled down her scalp until she remembered the formation had been water slick when she'd found it. She shivered in misery and moved forward. If it fell on her back, she could keep the baby dry.

Then she froze in terror. Over the top of the boulder, she saw something blacker than black at the other end of the chamber. Something inside the cavern, creeping toward her, less than ten feet away. Something huge.

She pointed the flashlight, snapped on the beam, and gasped in shock as the circle of light illuminated two startled yellow eyes. The huge cat stopped midstride in the sudden light to utter a taut, snarling growl. A warning.

The walls and floor of the cave thrummed and vibrated with tension as the great cat stared at her, unblinking in the round white light of the flashlight; nervous and distracted, its tail whipped from side to side. Water from the ceiling increased from drops to thin, steady streams, and a drumming, ominous sound filled the cavern.

The jaguar's cry rose from a deep, resonant growl to an irate, screeching wail of defiance. Terrified, Allison kept the light in its face. Then, raising the gun, she closed her eyes and doubled tight to protect the baby with her body before she pulled the trigger. The gun bucked in her hand as she fired; three explosions filled the cavern, blasting her ears until the gun clicked empty. The cat jumped over the boulder, brushing the top of her head, and disappeared toward the front of the cave as she collapsed onto the blanket and soothed the terrified child.

The drumming sound was suddenly deafening. Vibration filled the interior of the cavern, and the baby was frightened into stillness.

On the western edge of a second range of mountains twenty-two miles away, rain from the storm had long since poured down the slopes and through the hills to streams and rivulets that joined to form the magical Suscinta River. Ten miles away the Suscinta raged into flood. Then, eight miles to the west, the riotous river suddenly disappeared in a thousand places; pouring down through fissures and sinkholes and caverns and secret waterways, it snaked its way under the ground. Rejoining in hundreds of tunnels, rushing together through porous limestone, building in force and deadly purpose, it roared through the belly of the mountain, seeking the mouth of the sacred cave, known to Mayan priests for centuries as the place where water gushed forth from the Underworld. The cave of the jaguar.

"There's no point to this," Zachary repeated. "If you kill her, you gotta kill me."

From inside the cavern came a bizarre, curdling scream, then three dull, muffled blasts of gunshots. Jesus, Mary, and Joseph, what the hell had happened! Before he could move, a blur of black fur came shooting by him so close that he felt the heat from the animal's body.

At the shots, Luisita jerked free from Alberto's grasp and ran for the cave as the snarling cat came spitting past Zachary out the entrance; it stopped short at the sight of the two men and the running woman, then gathered to charge.

Nerves stretched too tight, Paulo pulled the trigger of the Uzi, mindlessly firing two dozen rounds at the jaguar, missing the animal in his haste.

Bullets zinged and ricocheted and spat against the rocks in front of the cave. Had it not been for the boulder, Zachary would have been cut in half at the knees. He fired at Paulo. The first two shots missed. He corrected, and the third clipped Paulo's ear as the huge cat charged and the panicked man fell sideways with the gun.

Paulo shot another burst, and Zachary dived for cover behind the boulder; this time Luisita dropped to the ground in front of the cat. The frantic animal cleared her body and leaped into Paulo's face; the Uzi went flying as the jaguar rode his body onto the jumbled pile of rocks and boulders at the bottom of the falls. The solid *thwack* of breaking bone was clearly audible as Paulo's skull made solid contact with a granite boulder.

The agile cat scrambled across the rocks and jumped into the pool of water, swimming steadily across to the opposite bank.

Alberto, too, had flung himself prone on the ground when the jaguar charged; now he got to his feet and stared blankly down at his still partner, then raised his hands under Zachary's pistol.

Zachary's mind spun in confusion. "Allison!" She'd used the gun to shoot at the cat. "Answer me!" His heart stopped when there was no answer. Noise was screaming from the mouth of the cave.

"Goddammit, answer me!" He crashed his fist into the rat-man's face and knocked him down. "You move, and I'll kill you!" He started into the cave and met a wall of sound as he watched her run frantically across the floor to him. What the hell was happening? Earthquake? Sweet Jesus, the water!

An inch of water came foaming over the floor of the cave at them, then two. "Where's the baby?" He started past her.

"No! No! We have to get out of here!" She dropped the empty gun and struggled to close the zipper in his jacket. He saw the baby tucked inside. Quickly he freed the fabric, helped her get it closed and move past him; the water was four inches deep and spilling across the full width of the waterfall.

He felt the booming roar as it boiled out of the back of the cave, spouting into the air when it hit rock and boulder obstacles, black and angry and roiling. They didn't have minutes—they had seconds. He scrambled to follow, found her kneeling by Luisita, pulling at her body. Alberto had taken to his heels and was halfway to the crossing, slipping and struggling along the muddy bank.

"I'll get her! You go! *Go!*" He helped her down the rocky slope now under six inches of cascading, muddy water and dashed back to pick up Luisita.

He knew instantly it was hopeless. At least four bullets had entered her back, and the exit wounds in her stomach were brutal and ragged; blood gushed in huge arterial spurts, staining the water. He stuffed her dripping shawl into the bloody holes. "Hold on, sweetheart," he said helplessly; there was no time to attempt a tourniquet. He slung her slight body over his shoulder and splashed down the rocks after Allison.

Her ankle forgotten, ears ringing, deafened from the crash of the gunfire in the cave, Allison thought of nothing but the child and the relentless river, brown and dangerous, rising faster than she could move down the bank toward the crossing. Thirty feet. Just thirty feet and she'd be there. The rat-faced man had stopped at the edge of the water. Why didn't he cross? What was wrong?

She slid and caught herself, knowing that to fall might harm the tiny being she held next to her body. Behind her, Zachary was carrying Luisita over his shoulder, loose as a rag doll. She reached Alberto, staring at the foaming water, eyes blank, mouth gaping in fear. The huge boulders of the crossing were vague shapes under a foot of opaque, muddy water. She paused, unsure she could continue.

"Can you get across?" Zachary kept his voice calm and steadying as he laid Luisita's body on the ground next to Alberto. "Take off your shirt." Alberto didn't move, didn't seem to hear; buttons flew as Zachary ripped it off his body.

"We'll have to cross now, or wait until it goes back down." He stuffed more of Luisita's shawl into the bloody gaping holes in her belly."She's not gonna make it if we don't get her somewhere fast." He knotted the shirt around her body and came back to Alberto, searching his clothes. He found car keys, shoved them in his pocket. The rat-faced man stood in dismay.

With a roar, the mouth of the cave filled with a surge of booming, spurting water, shooting ten feet straight over the falls, roaring and thundering and crashing into the creek. Huge boulders were no longer visible in the stream. Zachary knew it was now or never. He grabbed a fallen branch and pushed the butt into the soft ground and jerked Alberto into position to help him hold it over the crossing.

"Hold on to this," he shouted to Allison."If you lose your footing, for Christ's sake don't let go and we'll haul you back!"

Wordless, she did as he directed and inched her way across the first boulder, angry water tearing at her knees as she readied herself to jump the space between.

Alberto panicked and abandoned his hold to scramble out of the raging creek; the heavy limb sagged, nearly pulling her off balance. Letting go of the branch, she flung herself forward and landed on the hidden rock, yelling in pain as her weight came down full force on the injured foot. Lifting the jacket to keep the baby out of the water, she propelled herself toward the bank, thigh deep in the dragging water, willing herself to reach the safety of the trees.

Zachary swore at Alberto, then held his breath and watched, helpless, as she stepped off into the water, nearly losing her balance and righting herself at the last instant. He thanked every god in the universe when she reached the other side.

The branch thrashed away in the rabid river. He grabbed Luisita's body and leaned into rushing water that sucked at his thighs, battered his feet and legs, determined to drag him under.

A two-foot wave of water crested down the stream.

Allison saw the wave barreling at him and braced herself at the edge of the water, holding out her hand. The water smashed her feet and ankles, clawed sand and gravel from beneath her boots as it boiled down the ravine, nearly toppling Zachary.

He jumped with its momentum toward her, Luisita limp across his shoulders, and managed to grasp her outstretched hand. She pulled as hard as she could, and they both reached solid ground. Across the creek Alberto was crawling up the steep side of the canyon.

A few feet away water licked at the suitcase and his backpack. The baby's food was in the suitcase. Allison hobbled on her fiery foot to retrieve them.

As she followed him toward the road, holding on to saplings and brambles, her hearing returned to pound her skull with a dull ache. She saw only the horrible red bloodstains streaking the leaves and grass as she passed. Luisita's blood. How could she lose so much blood and live?

She had watched in shock when Zachary tied Alberto's shirt around the jagged holes, horrified at the mass of blood and the terrible sight of the insides of Luisita's body. She'd never seen a bullet wound, had no idea it could be so hideous. Stunned by the sight of the wound, she barely remembered crossing the water. You do what you have to do, she thought in some remote corner of her mind, and followed the bloody trail. You do what you have to do.

When they found the path to the road, the going was easier, but the stains were a darker, blacker red.

After an eternity, they reached the road.

He lowered Luisita to the ground and checked for a pulse. Incredibly, the tough little woman was still alive. He opened the suitcase and grabbed cloth diapers, stuffed them in with the shawl to pack the wound.

The upper part of his body was drenched with blood—how the hell was she still living! "Is there a car?" he panted over his shoulder.

Allison saw the gray sedan. "Yes. Over there." The sight of his bloody torso closed her throat. Maybe he'd been shot, too. There were—thank God!—no hideous, ragged holes.

He saw the sedan, and it occurred to him that the river would rip out at least half the wooden bridges they'd crossed getting here. He'd have to turn it around and pray there was medical help in the village. Nothing short of Bethesda was going to save the Mayan woman. With wounds this bad, she should have been dead already.

"Hold this here and try to keep her calm if she comes to." He positioned Allison's hand on the sticky red diapers and forced himself not to get distracted with her welfare. She seemed a little shocky, but functional. He pushed aside his exhaustion to sprint toward the car.

On her knees, alone with her horrible duty, Allison stared at Luisita's pallid face and reeled at the insanity that had put this woman on her back on a muddy road in Guatemala to bleed her life away. The baby moved, and she thought to unzip the jacket and reached her hand inside. Two little black buttons stared back at her solemnly, wide-eyed and huge in the tiny face; she stroked his cheek and patted his chest.

Luisita stirred and opened her eyes, pupils wide with shock. "Miss . . ." Her voice was little more than a ragged whisper.

"I'm here, Luisita. The baby's here." Allison tipped her body forward so the little face was visible to the dying woman. "We'll have a car in a minute. You just hang on."

"Miss . . ." Balum had provided this *tsoy y-ol* woman. She lifted her gaze from the baby to Allison's face with great effort. "You will . . . take care of him?"

Allison refused to understand. "Of course. You're going to be all right. We're getting you to a hospital and you'll be fine."

"You will take care of him." It had been decided by the gods. The American would take care of Allison, who would care for the child. "There is no one else. . . ." She closed her eyes. "Tell . . . the *t'o'ohil*," she said faintly.

Allison's eyes filled with tears, and a crushing weight pressed her heart. Sobbing, she took Luisita's limp hand and placed it inside her jacket on the baby's chest, then covered it with her own. "If you die, I give you my . . . my word of honor that I will . . . take care of him," she promised, brokenly. "I swear it. . . . Oh, God . . . are you sure? Is this truly your wish?"

"It is. . . ."

The death sigh left Luisita's body, filled her nose and mouth with blood that spilled through her teeth to run down the sides of her face and mix with the red soil of the road. Her hand slid slowly away from the baby, out of the opened jacket, and flopped to her side, without life.

The baby stared, unwinking, at Allison. In the distance she heard the sound of the sedan's motor and looked up to see a gray blur moving toward her on the road. She bowed her head, and her tears fell on the baby's quiet face.

He knew from Allison's face that Luisita was dead; he checked for a pulse anyway, found none. He couldn't imagine how she'd lived to cross the river but gave selfish thanks that she had. Otherwise he'd never have considered crossing the water.

He pulled off his gory shirt, used the back to wipe the blood from Allison's hands as best he could, then covered Luisita's face and placed her small body across the backseat of the sedan. He settled Allison and the baby inside, tossed in the suitcase and the pack, and got in, exhausted, too drained to face the drive or think what kinds of complications they would face as foreigners bringing a dead woman to a rural village.

Allison collapsed against him, lost in grief, and he held her close, crying his own tears until Adam, warm inside the jacket, began to fuss. Slowly she shed the jacket and removed the dress once destined for Sara that Luisita had so carefully wrapped around his little body. Zachary took them from her to cover Luisita as best he could, then resolutely started the car.

The baby went to sleep as they crept along the washed-out track toward the village. At the sight of thatched huts, he stopped the car. A collection of barefoot children, drawn by a car with *ts'ul* driving, gathered a few feet away. He called out the window, "Does anyone speak English? ¿*Hablo inglés*?"

The youngsters giggled and bumped against each other, too shy and excited to speak with foreigners. Finally a small boy, seven or eight years old, joined the group and steadfastly examined Zachary's face. Tilting his head, he looked at Allison with equal contemplation before he spoke. "I am speaking English. I am Little Bol."

Relieved, Zachary got out of the car to prevent them from seeing Luisita's body. "Little Bol, we'd like to see the village elder."

"My father is he," replied the boy, staring up at him, totally unconcerned at the shirtless American's size and bloody clothing. "He is *t'o'ohil*."

"Can you show me?" He gave silent thanks for the boy's English.

"*Bay*." Little Bol pointed to a small hut some distance away. "My father is here." He walked toward the hut without a backward glance.

The gaggle of children fell in behind the car and quietly followed its progress along the village road. By the time the procession reached the hut, Little Bol had gone inside. Zachary waited by the car until the boy reappeared at the door with an ageless man clad in leather sandals and a simple long white shirt.

He marked the weathered face and dark rheumy eyes that saw directly through to his soul and did not question this man's absolute authority. It was apparent in his bearing, his hawkish gaze, and the respect emanating from curious villagers gathering nearby. Zachary placed his age somewhere between sixty-five and ninety—surely he was the boy's grandfather.

"Sir, there's been an accident, and the children should not see."

The old man approached the car with surprising agility, and the children melted away to huts and hidden mothers while the men of the village watched and waited. Zachary's antennae could not get a fix: there didn't seem to be danger in the normal sense of the word, but there was definitely something eerie about the old man, who did not seem surprised to see Luisita's body.

Glancing briefly inside the car at Allison and the baby, the elder uttered a single word. "Come." Clearly she was not invited.

Zachary stood by the car with no intention of moving. "I don't wish to leave this lady," he said to the old man's departing back.

At the doorway to his hut, the ancient said a few words to someone inside and a young girl came scuttling out, hiding her face from Zachary's sight to approach the car.

"*Por favor,*" she whispered to Allison.

"It's okay. I'll go with her. You talk with the *t'o'ohil.*" Allison gathered Adam and got stiffly out of the car.

"I'm not too sure about this," he said.

"I'll be fine. Just give me the suitcase—the baby's food," she said tiredly.

He handed the case to the young girl and touched Allison's shoulder. "Anything goes sour, you scream your head off, you got it?"

"I'll be fine," she assured him.

He let go of her reluctantly and watched until she and the young girl entered a hut three houses away. She didn't appear to be limping too badly, but he was worried about the damage to the cut; he should have taken the time to check it.

He was worried about her, period; and he didn't like being away from her, particularly now. Annoyed, tired to the bone, he walked to the elder's hut.

The old man sat inside, waiting for him, calmly smoking a dense, homemade cigar. A small barefoot woman, middle-aged, maternal, looked at Zachary with open curiosity as she placed a wooden stool, obviously for his use, next to her husband. Then, with great dignity, she walked into another room in the hut, separated by a light curtain.

"I have some concern about the young woman. We've been stranded for the past three days and she's been injured," he began.

The old man cut him off. "I am Jorgé K'ayum," he said firmly in English. "What is your name?"

Zachary swore inwardly at the fatigue that had spawned his lapse in manners. He quickly introduced himself, dug out his identification and shield. "I'm a policeman from the United States down here on vacation."

Jorgé examined the badge and identification briefly, handed it back without comment. He studied the young, bedraggled man, shirtless, with streaks of blood saturating his muddy clothing, read his exhaustion. "The woman is with my daughter and her husband, Bol. Tell me about Luisita."

Zachary nodded in wary relief. "She was shot by a man named Paulo, who's also dead. That's all I know about him. Except his body will probably wash up somewhere along a river a few miles east of here."

"Will Paulo's body also have a bullet hole?" the old man asked with a piercing gaze.

Zachary realized his appearance was against him and that he could do little to allay the old man's suspicions.

"He died from a broken neck. He and a big jaguar got into an argument, and he lost." He saw the elder's interest quicken at the mention of the cat. "Look, I'll be very happy to explain everything that's happened, but can we do this with the local authorities to save time? I really need to get her out of here."

Eighty-year-old Jorgé K'ayum smoked his cigar, eyes brightly alert, in no hurry whatsoever. "Authorities will have many questions." He let the comment hang in the thick white coil of smoke circling and dancing above his head in the hut and waited for an answer from the foreigner.

Allison entered the thatched hut. When she saw Nuk's baby asleep in the wooden cradle, she sagged in relief. The girl would understand her needs for Adam. Wordless, she held out her hands with Luisita's blood, caked and horrible, drying on her fingers. The girl found a cloth and brought a clay bowl of water. Allison scrubbed the red from her fingers and wiped it gently off the baby's stomach with the cloth.

While her midwestern self cringed at the youth of the young mother, she knew that families were started in Mayan culture not much later than puberty. Young men were quite often married to much older women, young girls occasionally married old men, and marriage in general was sometimes a multiple affair—a loose arrangement of decision and consent between the parties, age notwithstanding, and appalling to missionaries who stormed the practice with dire threats of a vengeful, disapproving God.

Adam stirred in discontent. He was due to eat again, and a fresh diaper was imminently desirable. Allison opened the damp suitcase and rescued seven dry Pampers, two cans of milk, and the remaining bottle, nipple intact. She managed a diaper with reasonable success and, tired as she was, figured out the sticky tabs. Nuk watched in silent fascination.

She exhibited the cans to the young girl. "Is there a place to get baby's milk?" she asked. The girl didn't answer, simply shook her head. Allison tried again in halting Spanish. Her head did not want to work. "*¿Dónde está . . . la leche?*"

Nuk giggled and shook her head again.

Adam increased his demand to a lusty wail, and she dreaded the thought of going back to the car and facing Luisita's still body yet again; the knife to open one of the precious cans was in Zachary's pack. She began to quiver with shock and fatigue. There were only two cans. They were never going to make it without more milk.

Nuk picked up Adam before Allison could stop her and pushed his angry face under her blouse. The wailing ceased. Allison laughed weakly at her own ignorance. Of course Nuk would have milk. She sat on the low wooden cot with a raw giggle at the young mother. "*Gracias,*" she managed. "*¡Gracias!*"

As she watched Nuk nurse the baby, she felt the iron weight of tiredness creep through her body. The ache in her back and arms from the unaccustomed weight of a child, even a small one such as this, added to her emotional exhaustion. Her mind sought anything, any diversion, to avoid replaying the narrow escape from the men and the river, to shut her thoughts against Luisita's death.

She surveyed her muddy boots and generally scruffy appearance with dismay and took off Jake's shirt, no longer caring to conceal the pinned-together T-shirt. She could smell her own body for the first time in memory, and a bath was out of the question. The dull throb of the wound in her foot pulsed with her heartbeat, sapped her remaining strength, and sent her into drowsy lethargy in the afternoon heat.

She didn't want to think about anything now. They were in a village, Zachary was talking with the elder, surely she didn't have to think about anything now. . . . Twenty minutes later she shook herself awake, and Nuk handed her an equally sleepy Adam and a white cotton blouse, a duplicate of her own.

She carefully bumped the baby's bare little back, then, satisfied no air lurked inside, she found a newborn's cotton shirt in Luisita's case and and fit him into it, tying the tiny strings. Then she shed the torn T-shirt, washed briefly with the water before changing gratefully into the clean white blouse. At last she was able to curl up on the cot with Adam's quiet little body next to her and sink into blessed sleep.

Two hours later Nuk touched her shoulder. Allison roused herself with great effort to find Little Bol standing by the cot. "The *t'o'ohil* wishes to see you," he told her. "I will take you." She gathered up the sleeping child. "You can leave the baby with Nuk," said the young boy.

Instinctively she resisted. "I'll take him with me. Where is my friend? Where is Mr. Cross?"

"The *Americano* is not here," answered the boy.

"Where is he?" she demanded thickly, head pounding with the need for sleep and escape.

"He has gone with the others to get the car."

Her heart rate returned to normal, and she cradled the sleeping child, prepared to follow the boy. If Zachary was getting the car, things were okay. Outside on the road, the sedan was gone. Somewhere in the village Luisita's body was being prepared for burial. She collected her thoughts to be ready to talk with the elder. It seemed odd that he would spend time talking with a woman, but if he'd sent for her, she had little choice but to see him.

She followed Little Bol to the elder's hut and nodded as she entered to a quiet, dignified woman sitting at the rear of the dwelling. The old man was seated with his back to her. Purely on instinct, she waited quietly for him to acknowledge her presence.

After a suitable time had elapsed, Jorgé turned around and smiled in approval. The woman was polite. He nodded to the wooden stool that the American *ts'ul* had recently vacated, and she sat, holding the child that was the subject of his interest.

"I'm Allison Shreve," she said as calmly as she could manage. "I'm very pleased to meet you. I hope you don't mind that I brought the baby. He's been through quite a lot today."

"It is Sara's baby."

She could not hide her surprise that he knew about the child, and he watched as she collected herself. "Yes—Sara was Luisita's sister." Her chin trembled as she said the name.

"He is a Lacandon child." His eyes were testing, unrelenting, and he sought the truth in her bruised face.

"Yes. Jaguar *onen*."

It was his turn to blink in surprise.

"She told me before she died. She gave me this child with her dying breath, and I swore I would take care of him." Every particle of her being began to sense danger; best to let him know where she stood.

"He is Lacandon," he repeated, unmoved as stone.

She scrambled for anything that would convince this man of her strength. "A jaguar could not take this child from me," she said, head pounding. "He came into a cave where I was hiding and screeched and howled at me and passed by so close I touched his fur. But he did not take this child from me." She stared directly into the old man's hard eyes. "The river could not take this child. As you can see, it tried." She pushed out muddied boots and still-damp pant legs. "Nothing on earth can take this child from me while I live," she said with finality. "I gave my word of honor to Luisita."

The old man smiled with infuriating patience and said nothing for a long time. Sounds of the village were amplified in her brain, and blood pounded in her temples while she waited him out.

"This child is Lacandon," he said again. "If you take away this child, will he be Lacandon?" Again he watched for truth.

The heated air in the hut imploded. She did not know how to answer his question. Of course he'll be Lacandon, she wanted to scream. But would he? He'd be raised in the United States, she realized suddenly—he'd grow up among American children, eat pizza and hot dogs, ride bikes, and watch TV, speak English and drink orange juice, wear blue jeans and sneakers. Pledge allegiance to an American flag. Did she have the right to take him away from his land, his people, his heritage?

None of this had occurred to her until the old man's question forced it into her mind. During the slow, terrible drive to the village, she had considered the changes it would bring to her own life, but not to his. "I swear . . ." She stumbled. "I swear I'll raise him well. I swear that I'll bring him back to this place, that he'll know his heritage."

She paused to ask herself if these things were indeed truth. She found no doubts, so she continued, the strength of belief in her tone. "I will let him decide when he is old enough if he wishes to return here to live. I swear on the jaguar. I swear on my life." She kept her voice quietly under control, challenging his authority no more than was necessary.

"I will consider these things," he said stiffly. She had answered well. Still, he was unconvinced and wished time to think.

She paused at the door. "Will you . . . I would like to know when Luisita is to be buried," she said with difficulty. "I should be there."

"*Ts'ul* cannot attend," he said shortly, and walked through a curtain into an adjoining room. The quiet woman in the corner looked at Allison, shook her head briefly, then looked down at the floor. There would be no appeal.

Outside the hut, Little Bol once again escorted her to Nuk's home, and she walked in thoughtful silence, her courage fading with the sunlight into the oncoming dusk. Where was Zachary? She needed to see his face, hear his voice, feed from his strength.

Inside Nuk's hut, she gazed at the peaceful infant in her arms and saw that Zachary's pack had been placed next to the suitcase. She put the baby on the cot and limped to the pack. She found the ointment and removed her boots. The cut had opened and bled; her flesh was stuck to the sock, but there was no indication of infection.

She worked ointment into the cut, and Nuk appeared with thin strips of cotton to wrap around her foot. "*Gracias*," she said to the girl. "*Muchas gracias*." She smoothed more of the ointment on her shoulder, then lay down on the cot to doze and wait for Zachary with the baby asleep on her belly.

She woke to the sound of approaching cars and held her breath. This would be the police.

Zachary peeked into the hut, relieved at the sight of her. She was lying on the cot, but her boots were off, and she'd obviously tended her foot. He knelt next to her and saw she was waiting for him.

"You were asleep when I left," he explained huskily. "I didn't want to wake you. We got the Rover out of the ditch—pulled it out with the sedan. How's the baby?"

"I think he's okay." Her relief at seeing him was overwhelming and made it difficult to think. "What happened? Are the police here?"

"No. The old man decided to go ahead and bury her. Says it's not necessary to involve the Guatemalan authorities. I hope he's right." He watched her carefully as he spoke. "If they see the body, they'll know she was shot in the back—the next thing you know they'll start asking questions and we could be here for weeks." His heart went out to her exhaustion; her bruised chin, faded to purple and yellow, still caused a guilty stir in his conscience.

"Besides, there's no possibility Paulo survived. If he didn't break his neck when the cat jumped him, he drowned. We couldn't have gotten him out. That water came too fast."

He could see her mind was elsewhere. She'd withstood the shock of Luisita's death, but she couldn't take much more. He didn't need the hassle of an investigation, either. The sound of chanting voices drifted in the door with the cool evening air.

"That must be part of the burial ceremony." She moved the sleeping baby to sit up on the cot and swung her feet to the floor. "We're not allowed to attend. The elder told me."

"You saw him while I was gone?"

"He wanted to know about the baby." Her anxiety was building.

"What about the baby?" He hadn't thought about what would happen to the little boy.

"Luisita gave him to me. But he's not going to let me take him."

He looked his astonishment. "Wait a minute! What are you telling me? She was unconscious, how could she—"

"No. She died talking to me." It was imperative that he understand. The old man meant to keep the child. Her voice rose, insistent. "I promised her I would take care of him." She put her hand on the sleeping baby's chest. "He's going to try to keep Adam here."

Zachary's mind whirled with this new information, reviewing his talk with the old man. What had been said about the child? There had been so much to explain. Bits and pieces reassembled themselves as he spoke. "I told him what she told us—that the bastard that killed her wanted the kid for some kind of blackmail." He ran his hands through his hair in frustration. "I had no idea she gave him to you. Are you positive?"

Fatigue and strain finally took their toll, and she exploded in fury. "Yes! Why would I lie about it?" How could he question her about Luisita? About something so important?

"I meant about the baby. Are you sure that's what you want to do?"

"Yes," she said emphatically. "I don't know if I meant it when she died . . . or if I was trying to give her some peace of mind. But it's all I've been able to think about. It's what I want to do."

Soothed by the baby's even breathing, she looked at him once again, trying to explain. "Something happened. I don't know how to explain it, but he's mine. She gave him to me, and I accepted him, and he's mine." It was hopeless to try to convey that a change of some kind—not physical, but basic and maternal, total and absolute—had taken place inside her body, inside her psyche. It was an altered state that had no explanation, but she'd been aware of it the instant it happened. "He's mine. I can't explain it, but I will not leave here without this child." It was final.

"Well . . ." Zachary sat back on his heels, heaving a sigh. "We're sure going to do some fancy footwork to get him out of here. The old man's word is law around here, and if he says no, things could get difficult." That was the understatement of the year. No way in hell the old man would allow it. Christ on a green crutch!

Nuk came into the hut to pick up the suitcase and backpack. She paused at the door, indicating they were to follow, and waited while Allison stepped into her boots. She led them in darkness to a small hut some distance away. It had been prepared with a hearth fire and a cradle. Beans were heating in a cooking pot over the fire, cooked tortillas covered with a cloth were stacked in a small gourd nearby, and a second pot of heated water sat with one side banking the hearth.

The single cot boasted two red-and-black blankets. A hammock strung by the fire was draped with their clothes, now washed clean of Luisita's blood.

Zachary laid the baby in the cradle. Outside the hut, chanting voices droned on. Inside, sounds of the hearth fire, hissing and crackling, filled the dwelling. Nuk left them alone.

Allison moved to the hammock and took up Jake's shirt. "This is dry," she said distractedly. "Why don't you wear it until yours is ready."

He fingered the thin shirt, and the label on the collar caught his eye: Made in Ireland for Jake Alston. So, his last name was Alston. He slipped it on, perversely refusing to enjoy its soft, linen smoothness against his skin; he'd never owned a shirt like this in his life. Whoever Jake was, he had expensive taste and, apparently, the money to indulge it. He was also big; the shirt was ample across his shoulders. He wondered again how Jake Alston fit into her life.

They sat to eat, grimly aware of the chanting voices of the villagers. Allison fed Adam half a can of formula and put him back in the cradle. "He'll be out of milk tomorrow," she said absently. She limped to the doorway to look out into the night, thoughts of Luisita full in her mind.

He moved to her side, listening to the cadenced voices drifting with the smell of smoky incense from the god-pots. "We'll drive to San Ruiz in the morning and get everything we need. Right now, you should get off that foot, and we both need about three days' sleep." He walked her to the cot and tucked her in, wanting desperately to lie down beside her and sleep dreamless sleep. Perhaps in a while. Right now he needed to see Jorgé K'ayum.

As soon as she closed her eyes, he returned to the elder's home, psyching himself. Strength had to be met with equal strength. Inside the hut, he had the distinct impression the old man was expecting him, had even sent for him somehow. Brushing the feeling aside as ridiculous, he stared into Jorgé K'ayum's coal black eyes. "We're planning to leave in the morning," he said. "I understand there's some question about the child."

The old man waved him to the waiting stool. "You did not say to me about the child," came the papery steel voice. "He is Lacandon."

Zachary's mind darted into a dozen corners, trying to hide from the piercing gaze, seeking the manner in which to respond. The old man hadn't gotten to be village elder solely because of age; getting caught in a lie could be the kiss of death. He'd accepted the account of Luisita's death, but he could decide in a second to change his mind, something Zachary dearly did not want.

But he found that he was unable to lie to the old man —the eyes would not permit it. He crossed his fingers and settled for the truth. "I didn't tell you because I didn't know. She was dying when I left to get the car. Allison says they talked and Luisita entrusted her with the welfare of the baby, and I believe her," he said stoutly.

"You did not hear these words pass between them." Jorgé's eyes did not waver as he pronounced this statement.

"No. But she wouldn't lie about it." Conviction rang in his words.

Jorgé K'ayum withdrew into himself. "We will speak tomorrow." The interview was over. The old man rose slowly and walked through his doorway and down the path. Zachary watched him cross the road and enter the god house, where the villagers chanted prayers for Luisita.

When he got back to the hut, he saw she'd moved the baby from the cradle to her side on the cot. Drowsy, she looked up at him in question. He shrugged. "I haven't a clue. He said he'd let us know in the morning. Let's get some sleep." He pulled off Jake's Made in Ireland shirt, and his heavy boots, and bent down to brush his lips against the top of her head. His body was demanding rest; he eased his weight onto the hammock and stayed awake long enough to wish her good night.

Despite the delicious feeling of the baby, small and precious next to her, the warmth of him oozing smoothly into the sore muscles of her body, Allison's mind was riddled with the old man's unspoken threat. She could not escape the old Maya's words. "If you take away this child, will he be Lacandon?"

She tugged the baby closer and tried to melt into sleep. But she could not. Fear she was so certain she'd conquered licked once again at the edges of her mind.

Adam could be taken from her if she slept.

Early in the morning it was cool enough to warrant the blanket. She covered Zachary with his jacket as he slept soundly in the hammock, then woke Adam to give him a bottle. For a while she sat quietly on the cot with the baby in her arms. Sometime in the night the chanting had stopped, and the silence was total. Finally she decided what she must do.

She brought Zachary's pack to her side and searched through it to find what she needed. Carrying the baby wrapped in a blanket, she left the hut.

Consciousness filtered up slowly from the depths of exhausted sleep, brain signaling something amiss. Zachary fought his way through layers of hazed-over reality, finally registering predawn and unfamiliar surroundings. Nothing made sense for three or four seconds, then he saw the empty cot and cradle. Adrenaline pumped energy into his system.

He padded in stockinged feet to the cot. Enough of Allison's body heat lingered in the blanket to indicate she had not been gone long. He pulled on his T-shirt, now fully dry from the fire, pushed his feet into stiffly reluctant boots, and hopped to the doorway in time to see her, a dozen yards away, carrying the baby toward the prayer hut. He threw on his jacket and grabbed the pistol, just in case.

Walking well behind, on silent cat feet in the foggy morning, he followed as she left the prayer hut and walked along a dirt path for some distance, away from the village. Finally she reached an opening in the jungle, surrounded by huge black trees silhouetted against a dull blue-gold eastern sky.

He realized what she'd found; the village graveyard, where Luisita had been buried. He watched her locate a newly covered mound well to the far side of the clearing and kneel at the freshly turned earth. He heard the sound of a scraped match and, after a few moments, smelled smoky-sweet incense as it burned on a small flat stone at the foot of the grave.

She moved to the grave adjacent to Luisita's and knelt again; the fragrance became stronger as incense smoldering in a small burner sent out woodsy-pine scent to blend with the first. He walked quietly to her side and draped his jacket around her shoulders.

Together they watched green-blue flames wink and flicker in the ground fog shrouding the graveyard. The two spirals of smoke lifted, joined together to form a single column, shoulder high, then danced toward them in thin interlacing patterns to faintly encircle their faces.

Allison spoke fervently into the silent dawn. "This is a prayer for Balum. We ask that Luisita and Sara go safely into the Underworld. Please allow them to sleep under the sacred ceiba tree." She took a deep breath. "I promise I will raise Sara's son to be strong and brave and to know that you are his *onen*." The incense burned to a pale ashy powder, then puffed and disappeared in a stray breeze.

"Amen," he said softly.

She shifted the sleeping baby and looked up at him. "I had to do this—I tried not to wake you."

"You did a good job," he said, then took her elbow. "Let's go. The old man might get wired if he finds out we've been here." They hurried along the path and approached their hut. He pulled her behind him when a shadow moved inside the dwelling.

Jorgé K'ayum peered up at the tall American. "I have been waiting for you," he said calmly.

Allison followed Zachary into the hut. "We've been to her grave," she said. "I took the baby there."

Zachary waited tensely for the old man's response and was relieved when he showed only mild irritation.

"I know this," Jorgé responded tartly.

The elder's eyes shifted to the baby in her arms, and Allison was instantly on guard. She readied herself to do battle for the child.

"You said we couldn't attend the burial, but you didn't say we couldn't pay our respects. Luisita was our friend. We needed to say good-bye." Zachary tried to appease the old man.

Jorgé K'ayum ignored him as if he hadn't spoken and looked to Allison, his manner stern. "I have given the matter of this child much thought, and I have come to a decision." His voice was no longer neutral.

Silence welled in the hut, and Allison felt her skin crawl; she met the old man's lethal gaze with trepidation but refused to look away.

Jorgé K'ayum was equally unbending. "You have truly suffered many tragedies. I am sorry for this. However, you know the reason for my wishes." Stony eyes burned their way deep into her heart. "This child is Lacandon Maya, Balum *onen*. He is to remain a Lacandon Maya child."

The old man's voice thundered in Allison's ears. "There is to be no question of his heritage, no matter what *ts'ul* law may say."

Jorgé moved to the doorway. "You may keep this child as Luisita wished, and care for him. But you must promise from your heart that you will allow him to choose freely when he has ten years if he wishes to return to this village. If you do not, Hachkäyum will punish you and cause terrible things to happen in your life."

Allison was shattered. In the space of an instant she suddenly understood that he was giving in; he was allowing her to keep Adam! She nodded in a rush of burning tears. "Yes. Yes! I promise."

The old man looked to Zachary for his response, clearly holding him equally responsible.

He answered without missing a beat, "I agree."

The old man left without a word and did not pause in his march to his hut.

Allison breathed heavily in disbelief. Adam was hers! The tiny, black-eyed bundle in her arms was now her sole and total responsibility. All her intentions of fighting for the child were washed over with thoughts of how little she knew about babies and how on earth to be a good enough mother to take care of him. Excitement filled her body and she grinned hugely, with nowhere to put her energy. She placed the baby in the cradle and spun in indecision—what to do first?

He watched her walk in circles, laughing in spite of himself at her dizzy joy. The thing of the moment was to scoop her up in his arms and gave her a giant, bone-crushing hug. "Congratulations," he told her with vast enthusiasm. "You did it. I don't goddamn believe it, but you did."

She untangled herself from his arms and rushed to the cradle and picked up the baby one more time to assure herself it had really happened. "I don't believe it, either. I was ready to fight him."

She stopped in the middle of the room, surprised at herself. "I was going to knock him down and make a run for it." She giggled with mild hysteria. "I really was." The baby woke and yawned widely, then popped open bright, inquisitive eyes and stared in fixation at her face. "I'm your new mommy," she crooned.

"Well, new mommy, we'd better get a hustle on before anything else gets in the way."

"Hello," came a shout from outside the hut. Zachary stuck out his head to find Little Bol. "My father says you will please come with me," said the boy. "You have a visitor."

"A visitor?" Who the hell could that be? He handed her the keys to the Land Rover. "This could be the police, anything. I'll have to find out. If I'm not back in ten minutes, you take the kid and get out of here."

"I don't think we're in trouble," she said. "He's given his word. He wouldn't go back on it."

"You're probably right. Chances are it's nothing. You pack, and as soon as I get back, we're on our way."

"We'll be ready." She smiled, then returned her gaze to the baby's face.

Outside the elder's hut, Zachary checked on the pistol

pressing his spine, then stepped inside, prepared for whoever might be waiting.

"*Hola, señor.*" A wrinkled face greeted his tight glance. "Perez!"

Behind the little farmer, Jorgé K'ayum smiled slyly. The wily *t'o'ohil* could have directed the boy to identify Perez as Zachary's visitor but had chosen instead to see what he would do.

"*Hola, señor,*" repeated the wiry old man, jumping to his feet. "*No teléfono, señor.*" He dug into his pockets. "*Lo siento.*"

Speaking too rapidly for Zachary to follow, Perez chattered at length in Maya and Spanish. At Jorgé's nod, Little Bol translated. "The storm took down the telephone and he did not place the calls you requested, so he gives you back the money." Perez held out two damp and wadded ten-dollar bills and several single dollars.

Zachary was chagrined, then insistent. "No. Please tell him to keep the money. I took many things from his home. Ask him if it is enough. If he wishes more, I will arrange to send it to him."

Perez listened to Little Bol's explanation and sat for a long moment, calculating the cost of the things he had found missing in his hut, taking into consideration the payment left in the hollow gourd. Then he gravely held out a ten.

"*Muchas gracias, señor,*" Zachary said gratefully. He took the old man's hand, pressed the money in it, and shook it vigorously. Ten dollars couldn't begin to repay the pleasure he'd enjoyed under those particular blankets. "*Muchas gracias!*"

"*De nada, señor,*" Perez said with a quizzical gratitude, his failure to make the phone calls forgotten in his pleasure at having been well paid for items he could now replace.

"How did he get here from San Ruiz?" asked Zachary. "Is the road past the ruins passable, or did he come another way?"

Again Little Bol translated both question and answer, and Zachary learned that two bridges had washed away, but one had already been repaired. The crew from the village had told Perez about the Americans and he had come to see them, but now he must return to work on the second bridge.

Zachary turned to Jorgé K'ayum. He held out the keys to the gray sedan. "The owner of this car is dead. I hereby grant his car to this village, to do with as you wish." He placed the keys in Jorgé's outstretched hand.

The old man's eyes warmed and he smiled at the tall American. He was *tsoy y-ol*. The baby was in good hands.

Inside the hut, Allison gingerly took Luisita's purse out of the suitcase. Zachary swung through the door, smiling and energized, to join her. "I squared our account with Perez," he informed her. "I have forty dollars left from your backpack, but we're going to need it all for gas. Too bad we lost your credit card. I doubt if we could use it anyway." He produced the money from his hip pocket along with their passports and his shield. "It was fifty until I bought a couple of chickens."

"You got a bargain." She laughed, savoring the memory of yesterday morning, a light-year ago. With the purse in her hands, her laughter quickly died. Luisita had been alive yesterday morning. "He needs formula. Maybe there's money in here."

He took the purse and emptied it on the cot. There was precious little: Luisita's identification, a letter in Maya from Sara Chun postmarked three weeks ago in Belize, and a coin purse. Two paper documents.

He inspected one of the documents, a record of the baby's birth, and handed it to her. The father was listed as Rufino Copal. The other paper was a travel permit. "Issued in care of Mr. and Mrs. Paul Goodell, Miami address. I'll keep it so I can contact them when we get back." He opened the coin purse and found a small wad of money. They counted fifty-five American dollars and twenty-two Belize.

"She told me she took two hundred dollars from the

Goodells, but it's not here." She returned the purse to the suitcase.

"We can get home without it, now." He handed over her soggy passport. "Unless we do something major wrong, we'll be home this afternoon. Are you ready to leave?"

"Yesterday!" she said emphatically.

They quickly moved the backpack and the suitcase into the Land Rover. Jorgé K'ayum, followed by Perez, the silent wife, Nuk with her baby, Bol, and finally Little Bol, approached the car to see them off. Village families gathered on either side.

Nuk stepped forward to hand Allison a damp red shawl. It had been Luisita's. "*Para el niño*," she said softly.

Allison understood: it was to be kept for Adam. She took the shawl with great care and placed it over the sleeping baby in her arms. A round of good-byes and American handshakes propelled them to the car. Allison managed a kiss of gratitude on the cheek of a furiously blushing Perez and renewed her promise to Jorgé K'ayum in a wordless glance.

Settling her inside, with Adam securely in her lap, Zachary slid onto the driver's seat at last and put the car in motion, tooting the horn to the delight of the children and finally earning a smile from somber Little Bol.

The thatched huts of Jorgé's village slowly disappeared and the jungle closed in on both sides of the sticky little road. The roar of the motor was satisfyingly strong; silence descended as Zachary took great care in guiding the Land Rover over precarious bridges and washed-out sections of the muddy lane.

Forty-five minutes later small wooden houses and livestock began making regular appearances by the roadside. Within minutes they entered San Ruiz, a collection of ramshackle houses and cement buildings with muddy streets from the recent rains, a marketplace with street vendors, mongrel dogs, and barefoot children, slightly larger than the Mango Creek community.

They were soon directed to the gasoline station. There

Zachary filled the tank three-quarters full and satisfied himself that the repair to the puncture in the tank would serve until they got back to the coast. He also learned from the station owner that the town indeed had a functional telephone at the local hotel.

Allison got out of the car with the baby to examine the wares of a street vendor, whose baskets were strung on thongs from low branches of a flowering tree next to the station. The toothless man sat on a sagging plastic chair, patiently working thin strips of sturdy grass around the base of a new basket in alternate rows of light and dark. His wife displayed half a dozen shawls and several finely cross-stitched blouses.

Zachary ambled over to join her as she pointed to the largest basket—an oval, picnic-style hamper with sturdy strap handles and an intricate pattern on its lid. "*Muy bonita. Cuántos dólares, señor*?" she asked.

"*Quince*," came the old man's reply. She examined the basket with a critical eye.

"Souvenir?" Zachary teased. Normal behavior. A great sign.

"It'll be a souvenir if I can get it to Chicago." She laughed. "Otherwise it's a bassinet. What do you think?"

"I think it's a damn fine idea. Point for your side." He picked up a small, delicately woven rose shawl. "You think an eight-year-old would like this?"

"She'll love it." Allison chose another in a pale blue cotton and lined the "bassinet." Bargains were struck with the basket maker and his wife, and they returned to the car with their treasures. Minutes later Zachary gifted an astonished Allison with the largest room the local San Ruiz Hotel had to offer.

She put Adam on the bed in his new bassinet and glanced around the grubby room with a mixture of gratitude and concern. There was a minimum of privacy—a thin cloth curtain separated the bath from the bedroom with its ancient double bed—and a maximum of mattress, sagging and questionably clean.

"We'll wash up here, have lunch, and then leave for Belize. You want to flip to see who goes first in the shower?" Zachary teased, and bent to kiss her lightly. She froze instantly at his touch, and he realized the kiss was a mistake. Jesus, Cross, he told himself, take your time, keep your distance. Don't give her the wrong idea. He crossed to the bath, pulled aside the curtain, and eyed the old-fashioned tub standing on clawed feet. "Well, this hasn't seen Mr. Clean recently, but it'll have to do. He swore they had hot water."

He handed her the room key. "I'm going to need a razor and the baby needs formula and diapers, and probably several hundred dollars' worth of equipment—none of which will be available in beautiful downtown San Ruiz." He grinned at her. "You do whatever it is gorgeous ladies do in baths and I'll see what the local grocery store has to offer. An hour be enough?"

"Yes." She nodded gratefully; embarrassed at her reaction to the kiss, unable to express herself, and confused at her sudden lapse into uncertainty, she wanted desperately a few minutes alone to collect her thoughts. His eyes were seeing through her. More than anything on earth she wanted to be alone and away from the bed, and to be clean. Then things would return to normal. "Yes," she said again. "Thank you. An hour will be fine."

"Lock the door," he said, and stepped into the hall. She heard him wait until she'd turned the lock, then his footsteps faded down the hallway. Desperate to do something to keep her thoughts at bay, she grabbed a washcloth and unwrapped a miniature bar of soap and sudsed down the tub and the sink, rinsed away the grime, and plugged both drains with crumbling rubber stoppers.

She turned the hot water on full force in both, undressed to her skin, wrapped herself in a towel, and dropped her underwear into the sink to soak; then she eased onto the bed next to the sleeping baby. Listening to the water rush into the tub, she assessed. Some kind of shock response; an overreaction to the last four days.

There was absolutely no reason to be afraid of a bedroom just because Zachary Cross was in it. She stopped short at light footsteps and a knock on the door.

"Who is it?" she said tersely, keeping her voice down not to wake Adam.

Zachary's voice came from the hall.

Heart pounding uneasily, she eased herself off the bed and talked softly through the door. "I'm not dressed. What is it?"

"I found a few basics in a little store next door—sort of a CARE package."

Feeling absurd and vulnerable, she screwed up her courage. "Wait a minute." She unlocked the door and peered at him.

He handed in three extra towels and a small paper bag. "I didn't think you'd be in the tub yet, and these should come in handy. See you later." He pulled the door closed and waited again until she locked it before he walked away. Inside the bag were two toothbrushes, a hairbrush, a bottle of shampoo, and a razor. This time she would have kissed him.

The baby was sleeping soundly and the tub had filled with the promised hot water. She poured an outrageous amount of shampoo into the water and watched it foam with great anticipation. Then she rinsed her bra and panties. After rolling them in a towel, she stood with her good foot on one end and twisted the other until the cloth buckled then pulled up on it with all her might. When she unrolled the towel, the lingerie was damp dry; she switched on the bed lamp and draped them on the peeling shade.

At last she stepped gratefully into her first proper bath in a week and luxuriated in the feel of steaming, foamy bathwater washing her skin and cleansing her soul, and generously lathered shampoo into her hair for the next five minutes.

Adam woke without ceremony as she rinsed her hair. He was uninterested in whether or not she was wet or dry and unwilling to compromise. She grabbed a towel and wrapped it around herself, another for her hair, and managed to locate the bottle with the last of the formula. The bottle emptied and the dissatisfied Adam was demanding more with a lusty cry when she heard welcome footsteps outside the door. Sighing with relief, she let Zachary in, embarrassed at being undressed but more concerned with the baby. Wordlessly she handed him the empty bottle.

He held himself in check at the sight of her, disheveled and barely wrapped; he opened a can in record time to silence Adam's complaints. "Give him to me," he said, studiously avoiding her skimpy outfit. "You still have ten minutes. I came back early, just in case." He sat on the bed and fed the baby, bending his huge body to accommodate the tiny being. "We're under control here. Carry on."

She grabbed her clothes and fled past the curtain into the bathroom. Inside, she tried to settle down. Why did he always seem to have things under control while she was barely hanging on to kite strings? She toweled her hair and tried to think calmly. It wasn't a disaster, the baby had merely gotten hungry before he'd gotten back with food.

So she'd been caught unprepared. So she was naked under the towel. He'd already seen her naked, in a shower at the Whale. Why was this so different? She wasn't afraid of him, so why did she feel so exposed? She fluffed her hair and searched through her things to realize her underwear was currently decorating the lamp shade.

There was a light tap on the bedroom wall. Before she could say anything, pink lace bikini panties and matching bra, dangling from his huge hand, came delicately around the curtain. She took the items without comment and closed her eyes with a small grin of defeat. It wasn't as if there was much she owned that he hadn't already seen.

22

With the baby pulling on a renewed bottle of milk, Zachary walked the room. How could any woman look so consistently good under any kind of situation? Grubby, sopping wet, tired, worn out, wrapped in cheap hotel towels—she was purely, bloody beautiful! He stopped to inspect two lacy additions to the lamp shade.

She'd be upset if she had to come and get her things in front of him, so he retrieved the wispy pink articles. He stroked the lace with his thumb and forefinger and let his mind wander to the night under Perez's blankets when these thin silken items had been the sole obstacles between his exploring fingers and tempting, soft, forbidden skin. He delivered the feminine articles safely into the bathroom to a silent Allison.

The realist in him doubted there was genuine hope of keeping her in his life. Two many strikes against it. She'd come down here wearing Jake Alston's clothes. Jake Alston, whoever he was, was way ahead of him. But that didn't mean he intended to toss in the towel. He perched the baby against his shoulder and thumped him gently on the back. "No sir, kid. Your new mommy gets the old college try," he pledged to the obliging child.

He finished feeding the baby and propped himself against the tired headboard, contemplating the independent infant lifting its head to stare at him from the safety of his chest. He'd wondered a thousand times about having a son, a male child to love and teach and learn from and watch grow, the way he had Steffie. It had to be the same and somehow different from a girl child. His dad had hinted about a "stemwinder," a grandson. Instead he'd fallen hopelessly in love with his granddaughter for the first two years of her life. He'd died just as Zachary and Sue had gotten into serious trouble in their marriage, and no stemwinders had been forthcoming.

Armed with her clothing and determined to regroup, Allison came out of the bath to face the two of them, the baby alertly awake on Zachary's stomach. "It's your turn," she said.

He stared up at her appreciatively. Jake's shirt had disappeared, and she wore the chaste white peasant blouse Nuk had given her, loose and comfortable. "You look terrific. Can I still have a date?" Keep it light, Cross. No more sudden moves. "How about I take you to lunch?"

She blushed. "Lunch sounds terrific."

"Good." He answered her with a grin and gestured at his purchases, stacked on a rickety table. "We have formula—ten whole cans—and a can opener, we have two dozen diapers, we have alcohol and bandages, we have baby powder, we have Band-Aids, and we have money left over for lunch. Oh, and I called Rider."

She stared at him. All this while she'd accomplished a bath?

"He was at the site, but I talked to Eve." He pushed himself past the pause in which he wished fervently that he hadn't brought Eve's name into the conversation. "Rider notified the Guatemalan authorities Tuesday night that we were missing. The storm prevented anyone from sending a search party yesterday. The phone lines were down until this morning."

She was looking at him, but he couldn't see inside her

eyes. "Woodie was there and I talked to her for a while. She's been pretty worried about you, but I told her you were in better shape than I am." At mention of Woodie she returned, and he wondered how in the hell she could turn herself off and on like that.

"She's not still ill?"

"She seemed fine. Said the colonel sprained an ankle climbing out of a fishing boat, so she's looking after him." He handed her Adam and pushed himself off the bed to take his turn in the tub.

"What did you tell them about the baby?" she called belatedly through the curtain.

He popped his head out for a moment. "I didn't mention the baby. Which, by the way, could use a bath and a new diaper." He paused and shrugged. "I figured it was something you'd want to handle."

He disappeared and she studied the baby's face, focused on hers with wide black eyes, the unmistakable smell of a well-filled diaper wafting upward. "Yes, indeed, you need a bath, my man," she whispered into his face. "We'll figure out how to explain you when the time comes."

To distract herself from any curiosity about the squishy tub sounds coming from the bathroom, she propped the baby over her shoulder and set about transferring the food and diapers from the paper bags into Luisita's suitcase, setting aside the alcohol and Band-Aids to re-dress her foot. When she'd examined it in the bath, the healing process had seemed well underway.

She changed the baby with the last of the Pampers. Eyeing the wicked-looking safety pins, she promised herself that self-sticking diapers would be the first item of purchase when she got home. That and two tons of formula.

He opened the curtain, barefoot, clean shaven, clad in wet Levi's. "It's his turn," he said, reaching out his hands. "Let's go, kid."

She drew the baby back. "He's too little to put in a tub."

"Yeah, but he'll fit in the sink just fine."

She approached the bathroom cautiously. There was barely enough room for one person, let alone two and a baby. Two inches of water filled the sink. Zachary calmly unstuck the tabs on the disposable diaper and placed it to one side. "You want to do it or learn from an expert?" He took a naked Adam out of her hands and gingerly put the baby's feet into the tepid water, then lowered him slowly into the makeshift bath. Adam's eyes were wide with wonder. "No soap on a youngster this small," he said. "Do we still have the drinking cup?"

She retrieved it from the pack and wedged herself between the tub and the sink to hand it to him. He used it to carefully pour small quantities of water on the baby's shoulders and back, then tipped him back to pour more water over the crown of his head. "I christen thee Adam Zachary Chun," he said kiddingly, and poured another cup. The baby blinked but lay confident in his large hands.

"Towel," he ordered, and she handed him the last dry bath towel. "No rubbing, just patting. Here, you get this part." He handed her the baby, towel and all. "Keep him warm, even in this heat he can chill from evaporation."

She took Adam to the bed and patted him down with the towel as Zachary finished dressing. She puffed some powder into the diaper and refastened it around the baby's bottom. Adam Zachary Chun gave a gigantic yawn and began to nod off. "That seems simple enough." She laughed. "I think I can handle it."

The light in her eyes opened the door to his heart. He studied her bright face. "I think you can handle anything," he said sincerely, wanting very much to share everything in his life with her, everything he knew or would know and everything he could think of. "Last one out the door pays for lunch."

They found a small cafe and put the hamper with the sleeping baby next to her in the wooden booth. The waiter took their order, and Zachary glanced at the baby. "Any second thoughts yet?"

"About him? No. I don't know why, but there's something very right about this. I was taking too long to start my life again. Now I have a reason. . . ." The waiter arrived with lunch, a feast of scrambled eggs with rich, orange-yellow yolks and crispy bacon, and hash browns, toast and jelly with real butter, and cups of delicious Guatemalan coffee with canned milk.

He sat back contented to watch her stuff in the last of her hash browns and sipped his coffee. "How about dessert?"

"I'd pop." She smiled. "When I was working, I used to dream about eating like this. Then I'd have half a grapefruit and fourteen carrot sticks and a cup of black coffee."

"You must not be planning to go back to work."

"Oh, yes, I am," she said quickly. "One of the reasons for this trip was to gain weight so I'd be camera ready." She thought back to the last several days of erratic meals and laughed out loud. "I came down here to practice making decisions and get a tan—and gain five pounds." She looked down at her browned arm resting next to the baby and sobered. "Well, I've certainly made decisions, and I'm a darker shade of pale—two out of three isn't bad. Now that I have the baby to think about . . ." She trailed off.

Reality was staring at her in the form of his lean, clean shaven face with the hairline scar through his eyebrow and clear brown eyes that ignored her defenses. Another decision was due, a huge one about Zachary Cross and her feelings about him. Decisions about human beings required commitment and purpose. They amounted to promises; promises demanded trust.

Was she capable of trust? She'd already made an enormous commitment to being responsible for a tiny child. Could she add to that a relationship with a man who lived hundreds of miles away in Miami? The weight was growing with every breath.

"You going to have room for anyone else?" He tried very

hard to keep the question casual, but it came out with an intensity he could not deny. He took a deep breath and plunged ahead. "I've never said this to anyone in my life. Hell, I didn't even feel this way about my wife. But I really don't want to lose out here." He could feel himself going south and forced his mind back on track. This was no way to convince her to let him stay in her life. He started again. "I'll come to Chicago, whatever you want . . ."

She stared into her coffee, searching for answers in the muddy liquid, answers that stubbornly would not come. All she could see was the color of the river. . . . She struggled for honesty. "You know what happened to me in New York. You should also know that I'm still in therapy. I probably will be for a very long time."

"I don't care." It was true.

"I have terrible problems with trust." She paused, tried to find the right words to explain herself. "Not just other people. I don't trust me. I'm not sure I'm capable of . . . committing, of staying involved."

He listened carefully to every word, absorbing and extracting every ounce of possible meaning. Was she trying to tell him no? His eyes held her face, willing her to explain.

"Even before New York happened to me, there was only one valid relationship in my life, one person I've . . ." She searched for an adequate explanation. And there really wasn't one.

"Jake." Damn Jake Alston all to hell and back.

"Yes."

"Why haven't you married him?"

She looked up at him, unable to say. She didn't know him well enough to discuss Jake. "That's what my mom wanted to know," she responded lightly, sliding around the subject. "Why did you marry . . . your wife?"

"Sue." He provided the name. "That's what *my* mom wanted to know," he laughed wryly. Then, baring his soul, he answered honestly. "I married her because I thought the baby was mine. She said it was and I believed her."

It was none of her business, but she was compelled to ask anyway. "Is that why you're divorced?"

"No." He looked down at the sleeping infant next to her, then into her eyes. "I love my daughter. She's my kid with or without my blood or chromosomes, or whatever it is they measure these days. I'll never have the tests . . . she's mine. Nothing changes that."

Then he went on. "I divorced my wife because she didn't love me enough to keep other men out of her life. So, I do understand about trust and commitment. When you give it, you give it all the way. When it gets broken, you can't fix it. But you and I haven't broken a trust—we're just now starting to build one." He reached for her hand and took the slender fingers gently into his own. "I'll take a chance that we don't break it, if you will."

She looked into his earnest face and wanted with all her might to tell him yes, but at the last instant she could not say the words. "I need some time to think about it," she said finally. "A week ago I didn't even know you, and you have to agree things have been pretty crazy the last few days. There hasn't been any . . . ordinary time for us."

And there's something I haven't told you.

It wasn't a no. His smile leaped across the table at her. "You want ordinary? Are we talking boring ordinary here, regulation ordinary? I like the Twins and the Mets, depending on who's winning, I hate washing dishes. I'm, uh, forty, I drive a Chevy Camaro and pretend it's a Porsche—which I cannot afford because I make thirty-two five a year, I live in an apartment . . ."

He paused to take a breath. "I'll have child support for the next ten years and college after that, I eat hot dogs with mustard, I drink beer, I like rock and roll, I give out Tootsie Rolls on Halloween, I can't barbecue for shit, am I in the ballpark?" He grinned. She was laughing at last.

"You want more ordinary?" he continued, leering at her. "How about I hate matching socks when I do the laundry, I always wash at least one green washcloth with my underwear, I eat ketchup on scrambled eggs, I watch TV—I don't get Vanna White—I play the lottery, I adore lacy pink underwear . . . and I love watching you laugh." He kissed the inside of her palm.

The waiter approached with the check. Zachary counted out several extra dollars and waited for an answer. The light was back in her eyes.

"Yes," she began. Of course it was a yes. There was no other answer.

"I'll take it," he interrupted. "Anything that starts with a yes, I'll take. We'll work out details later. Right now we need to get started for Belize. We still have to figure out how we're going to explain him to the outside world." A crooked grin lit up his face.

"Really, I—"

"No," he stopped her. "You gave me a yes, that's it. Let's get out of here." He picked up the hamper cum bassinet and prepared to leave the cafe. She laughed and stood up to join him.

At the edge of San Ruiz, a stone structure and wooden gate defined the Guatemala-Belize border. A uniformed official stepped smartly out of the guardhouse and approached the car. The graying, suspicious little man with vigilant eyes stared without quarter into his face.

"*Señor, identificación, por favor,*" said the unpleasant little man with ceremony, tilting his head to look in the window at Allison. "*Señora.*"

"*Sí, señor. Turistas,*" Zachary oozed jovially, and produced their passports.

The official ponderously inspected the wet documents, closely comparing the photographs with each of their faces. "*Momento.*" He walked away with the passports back to the building. Allison tightened up as they watched him place the opened documents on the top of the desk to leaf through a notebook, then pick up the telephone.

"Hang on. Probably routine," he warned her. "Don't panic on me."

"¿*Americanos*?" questioned a young guard suddenly on her side of the car, drowning out the conversation inside the office and preventing her response.

"*Estados Unidos*," she answered, with deliberate difficulty in pronunciation to discourage further conversation.

A fly came in the window and batted erratically against the inside of the windshield with an incessant *bzzzz* as the guard inside the building talked on. Every sense on alert, Allison heard the baby stir in the hamper. The fly buzzed her face and landed briefly on the basket, and she shooed it away to watch it bump stupidly again and again into the glass of the windshield before it finally flew out the window. Perspiration gathered under her blouse, and she steeled herself to be discovered. This was crazy. The baby was hers. Why did she feel like a criminal?

The senior guard replaced the telephone receiver and walked briskly back to the car. "Señor Cross, we have a report that you are lost," he said severely, "but I am happy to see that it is not so."

Zachary gave a hearty laugh as relief tore through his body. "Nope, we're just fine," he said affably. "Just caught in the storm."

"Sometimes we lose tourists in the rain." The man gave his version of a smile at his small joke and handed back their passports; he waved them forward.

Zachary eased the big car through the gate and drove on slowly until the border station was a dot in the rearview mirror. "One down." He exhaled a huge sigh, trying to quiet the adrenaline rush. "Rider nearly nailed us with that missing persons report. There wouldn't be anything about a child in it."

"That was scary," Allison admitted. "Even with the baby's birth certificate, that was scary. I had no idea. . . ."

"You'll probably have to identify him at the Belize City airport, and for sure at U.S. Immigration in Miami. I don't know what they're gonna ask for, but I doubt if a birth certificate will be all that's required." The car bounced over a washboard section in the road, and he glanced at her scared face. "I've got some friends I can call. We'll get it managed."

She relaxed a little. She would do what she had to do. The baby shifted in complaint, and she moved the hamper onto the seat and fanned him with the lid. The day was sticky and warm, as usual, and his hair was wet with moisture. Yes, she would do what she had to do. For the baby, and for Zachary.

When they passed the turnoff road to Guatemala and the ruins, she felt a spasm shudder its way through her stomach at the thought of Luisita, who had died on that road, who had received her promise that she would care for the child on the seat next to her.

All things were connected. All things. She looked over at Zachary's face as he concentrated on driving on the smoothest parts of the rural highway and knew she wanted him in her life.

All things. If she wanted him in her life, there was another thing she would have to tell.

This time she would have trust him.

Zachary found a shaded area to stop the car and held the fussy Adam while Allison prepared his lunch. Something was upsetting her greatly. He could see it building in her face and the way she held her body. He kept his peace and gave her time to work it out, waiting quietly while she fed the little boy and burped him carefully.

She moved the sated Adam out of her lap and into the basket before she finally spoke. "There's something I have to tell you," she said heavily. The closer they got to the hotel, the more the inevitable turmoil their return would cause pressed her into a corner. Time to decide was running out. All she could think about was whether or not to tell him, to start with a clean slate, to know where things were going to stand. If she was going to tell him, it should be now, before he moved further, deeper, into her life.

"Something I don't want you to know." She moved away from the car, unsure she could continue.

Alerted, he braced himself for what would come. The pain in her was an agony, and he knew for sure he wasn't going to like it.

"It's very unpleasant." She moved about restlessly. "It took me almost a year to tell my therapist." She bit her lip and forced herself to concentrate, unable to look in his direction. "I didn't tell the jury—I wasn't sure they'd believe me."

The whole truth. "And I didn't want my mother to know. But I have to tell you . . . because it's in my mind between us, and if we . . ." She didn't finish. If she told him, they might not have a future. If she didn't, it would be a future without trust. Without trust, there was no hope.

She shifted her arms uncomfortably and began before she could find a reason to stop. "Everything I told you about the . . . rape was true. I woke up and it was dark. He'd taken off my clothes." She cringed at the memory.

In her effort to revisit memories filled with terror and pain, her voice was painfully halting, labored. "He was . . . in bed with me, trying to . . . have sex with me. But he was drunk, and he couldn't. I tried to lie still . . . but he knew I was awake. He tied me to the bed frame with some kind of twine."

She stared into thick, shimmering air, unseeing. "He kept trying, and every time he . . . failed, he'd turn on me and hit me. Tell me it was my fault. I wasn't turning him on. He tried to give me some kind of drug. Mixed it in a drink. I was terrified of him. I even tried to drink some of it. He said I spilled it on purpose and hit me. When I screamed, he . . . it excited him. So he kept hitting me and hurting me to get . . . capable. But, not long enough to do it."

Zachary held himself rigid, not wanting to hear, not about this.

"When someone hits you long enough, you get numb . . . I pretended to pass out." She began to pace. "It went on for hours, him drinking and hitting me. I'd be 'unconscious' whenever I could. Eventually, he got too drunk to do anything and went to sleep. I tried to untie the twine, but it was too tight. I couldn't get it off. He couldn't untie it, either, he had to cut it off. . . .

"The next morning it got really bad. He started drinking at daylight. He was . . . naked and he put this wooden chair in the middle of the room and sat on it, staring at me—like he hated me. He kept putting drops of this liquid in his drink and smoking cigarettes, one after another. He started calling me . . . his whore."

Her voice trembled and dropped to little more than a whisper. "And he told me how good he was with whores, how they loved being with him and . . . how they earned money with their bodies, and since I made money with my body, he was going to make me his whore. Then he decided to . . . mark me so everyone would know what I was."

He felt the skin tighten across the back of his neck while rage built in his throat, choking him.

"He started burning me with his cigarettes. Nothing I said . . . I begged him . . . I promised him things I don't remember. All he wanted was to hear me scream, so he could get excited. I really did pass out. So I don't—I don't know what he did while I was . . . Whenever I woke up, he'd start again. . . ."

She forced herself to turn to him. She had to see, to know if it was going to change the way he looked at her, and she hurried on to get it out, to get it said. "Eventually, even that didn't work for him. I knew I couldn't stand any more, so . . ."

She watched his eyes for change. "So I kissed him. And I thanked him. I called him 'lover'—other things. I told him he was right—I was a whore and I wanted to make love to him. I begged him to let me prove it—to please let me make love to him any way he wanted."

"And I was good—I was very good. I made sure he enjoyed it. Even after he cut me loose, I made sure he wanted more."

Too late.

She saw the change in his face.

Too late to stop. Too late to take it back. Too late. . . .

She turned away, unable to stop the tears. "He left me alone to go somewhere. Into the kitchen. I ran. I don't know how I got out. I remember running. Through trees. I remember trees. It was fall. I remember leaves were falling and I was stepping on all these beautiful colors while he was screaming at me, calling me his whore. I got to a lake. There were some people in a rowboat. They said I was naked. I don't remember. I woke up in a hospital. Jake's the only one who knows. . . ."

The shame in her voice killed him, but he willed himself to remain silent. To let her finish. And to hear about Jake.

"He said I had to do it," stumbled her broken voice. "He said . . . Jake said he would have killed me. I don't know. I don't know. I just know I made love to him. And I don't know if I . . ." She turned to look at him, tears streaming down her face. "So you see, it's me. I don't know. . . ."

"Jake was right," he said harshly, forcing his throat to work, cutting her off. Jesus Christ, she felt guilty! "Jake was right. The guy was a maniac, and you were smart enough to give him what he wanted and get out of it alive. That's what you did. You didn't make love to him." The dead look in her eyes clawed at him. "He was going to kill you, for Christ's sake! Surely you know that. You don't make love with somebody you're afraid of. You make sex. You make survival."

He came at her slowly, hands wide apart in gentle appeal, and tried in his fury to speak softly, to convince her what he knew to be true. "He'd taken it too far. The bastard was a cop! I don't care what you did for him, baby, I don't care how good you were. Sooner or later he was going to figure out a hundred ways you could track him down. Sooner or later he was going to kill you. You're just goddamned lucky you got out of there before he did."

She backed away a step. She wasn't making it clear. He wasn't understanding her. "I know. I tell myself every day. But, it gets lost. It gets mixed up with the dreams, and I keep seeing myself smiling at him. I see myself . . . making love to him. Telling myself it was just sex doesn't make it . . . It's not the way it was," she said helplessly. "And I can't get back to the way it was. The way I used to be. I'm this other person. I don't want to be someone who can do what I did."

She wasn't making it clear that it wasn't about then, it was about now. "I'm terrified that if I try to . . . I don't want it to be like that. I want to be me, again. . . ." She gave up, weeping, swiping at the tears. Why couldn't she make him understand?

"I do know," he said.

She glared at him through her tears, furious with him for being the reason she now had open wounds, furious that he still wasn't getting it. "Don't tell me you know! You never did what I had to do. You don't know!"

How could he know about a dead zone in your mind that allowed nothing, felt nothing—because to feel at all opened the door to an ocean of fear and humiliation.

But he had some idea. And because he knew his own pain, he tried again. "I can't know what kind of hurt you feel. But I know about losing a part of yourself—when something in you ceases to exist." His voice carried the weight of unalterable, ungodly experience.

He knew all right. He'd been a kid in Laos two fucking hours when it had happened to him. A minuscule squeeze on a trigger and the body of a thirteen-year-old sniper had dropped out of a tree. That killing, and the others that followed, had turned his head inside out, changed him into someone he didn't want to be. Capable of killing. And absolutely unable to go back to being the person who had never taken the life of another human being.

"I know this. Life doesn't give you a chance to do it over," he said, determined to reach her. "Once in a while you get a second shot at something. You make a choice. Even if, later, you decide it's a wrong choice, you don't ever get to know what it might have been if you'd gone the other way."

He offered his hand. "Your choice takes on its own life, and the best you can do is ride it out. Eventually, you get past it and figure out how to live with who you are. If you do it right, and you get very lucky, you become a better person and make better choices."

She heard the truth in his voice and decided he had a

genuine understanding; she raised her hand to meet his. "You sound like my shrink." She looked at him with a quivery sigh and allowed him to grasp her fingers. Her eyes were seeing him again. "I guess I'm stuck with it, huh?"

"Looks like I am, too." He grinned and wiped her tears with gentle fingers. "I don't care what you did with the demented son of a bitch. I just care that you got out of it alive and you're here for me to find. . . ."

He brought her closer, searching smoky hazel eyes for her response. "I'm very serious. I don't want you to leave my life. I'll probably make mistakes and do wrong things, but I promise you. I'll try to get it right and be whatever I have to be—and I want to kiss you more than anything in the world right now."

And the kiss sent them spinning. The tentative, careful joining rolled over into a slow, delicious meltdown in the pit of his stomach. Heat went spiraling from the core of his being to crash off the scale into the base of his brain. He worked his hands in her hair and gently held her face to his as one kiss melted into another, even better and endless.

A blinding rush of feelings she hadn't felt in her lifetime since Jake, followed by a deeper, bone-searing drive as she felt his body give inward and fit warmly against hers, holding her safe, sending her hands exploring around his neck. Time stopped, but her feelings went reeling onward; nothing existed except him and the way he made her feel.

An old farm truck rattled toward them on the road, crashing into their perfect world. As it hurtled past, catcalls and whistles of encouragement from half a dozen young men in the truck bed shattered the calm afternoon. They came to earth and broke apart.

"Damn," he said thickly, the ache of wanting her surging everywhere in his body. He hated letting her go, hated the high-spirited young boys whose coarse shouts had halted the perfection of kissing her. He held her close to him, folding her in his arms and taking care not to crush her as he kissed the top of her head.

Allison's mind spun. Was this possible? She had responded to his kiss this time with a well of caring that shocked and astonished her. Feelings, except fear and pain, were still new and raw and foreign, not easily trusted. In spilling out her torment from three years ago, she realized that being afraid of him had not returned. Was this then truly something special between them?

Exhilaration and a quiet peace continued to rush through her. That much, at least, was real. Her pulse now raced with exciting and utterly dangerous feelings. Perhaps her body could be trusted to respond after all. Maybe the gray wall of nameless fear, now reduced to a faint, thin mist, was equally groundless.

He released his hold and turned her face up to him. "Tell me yes," he demanded heavily. "Say it."

"Yes." It came out involuntarily, without thought. "Yes," she repeated slowly, eyes shining clear and trusting. A definite yes.

He kissed her again, with reason and purpose, and proved to himself that she meant it. Yes. A few breathless seconds later he reluctantly saw her to the car and they checked again on the sleeping Adam. Somewhere in the universe the planets were moving into alignment. He was doing it right.

Corla Reyes was speechless. Tonio found her, breathless, at the local market and told her the Americans were in the hotel. She quickly thanked her gods and prayed in the next breath that her car was safe. She flew rapidly through her kitchen and found Zachary Cross waiting impatiently in the lobby with a beautiful woman.

Pleased he was willing to pay rental for the extra days, she ushered him into her office while the woman waited outside. She sent the boy to locate a boatman to ferry them back to the Whale and collect payment for the car.

Tonio's bare feet pounded out the door on his mission. After a few minutes they returned to the lobby, and Corla assured him she would see to the repair of the gas tank. She thought to ask about Luisita, but Zachary interrupted her efforts with questions about arranging a flight to the airport in Belize City.

"Cesar Cotura runs a charter service," she told him. The flight from here has gone for today. There's one in the morning from Waler's Beach."

"It's just as well," he said to the woman. "We're too tired to travel today, anyway. It'll give us time to check on the flight to Miami."

The woman nodded but didn't reply. Tonio and the boatman arrived, and the woman rose to leave. In the basket at the woman's side Corla glimpsed the dark skin of an infant sleeping quietly and contained with great effort her curiosity about the baby as she said good-bye to the American couple.

They walked to the dock with Mella chattering and capering around them. Señor Pico was introduced to Adam, each thoroughly unenchanted with the other, but Zachary's inspection of the stitches in the big, saggy teddy bear confirmed his suspicion that it had indeed provided a hiding place for Luisita's stolen gun. His interest in the bear paid off in a sticky good-bye kiss from Mella.

Tonio earned a hug from Allison, a handshake from Zachary for his speedy work in finding the boatman and helping to carry Luisita's small, red-stained suitcase to the dock. He and the little girl grinned wide smiles of farewell.

Half an hour later Zachary helped pull the skiff onto the sandy landing at the Whale and steadied Allison and the sleeping baby onto the dock. He grabbed his pack and sprinted to his room for money for Corla Reyes, plus the boatman's fee.

Woodie came stumping down the hotel stairs. "I thought I heard you two down here." She beamed delightedly, then stopped short as she recognized the unmistakable passenger in Allison's basket as a baby. "Ye gods and little fishes!" she exclaimed. "What have you two been up to?"

She craned her head to examine the sleeping infant. "Well, whoever it is, it's a good traveler." She peered closely at Zachary's smiling face, then at Allison, who looked up confidently in return. "I'm glad you're back," she said, full of relief, eyes snapping. "Looks like things are in pretty good shape, but you certainly had me up nights for a while."

"Things are fine, Woodie." She gathered up the baby for Woodie's closer inspection. "This is Adam."

Woodie, not missing a beat, and fully cognizant of a new and obvious connection between Allison and the tall policeman, said with a pointedly raised eyebrow, "Looks like things are more than fine to me. Now, give me that child, you must be exhausted."

She took the baby from Allison's reluctant arms. "I'm a grandmother seven times," she scolded, walking carefully up the stairs with a running commentary. "I've carried more babies up more stairs than you can count. You just get yourself up here and tell me all about this. Right offhand, I'd say this child needs a diaper. You got any?" She disappeared down the corridor.

Zachary laughed and handed Allison the suitcase. She started up the stairs after Woodie, but he stopped her, drawing her face down to his and giving her a reasonably chaste kiss. "I'm going to go check on the charter and make sure we're on it tomorrow. I'll be back soon." He kissed her again. "Don't leave home without me."

She kissed him back for his answer and watched him stride down the beach before turning to follow Woodie to the safety of her room, with the sudden exhaustion of arrival at a safe haven.

Woodie was delighted to bide her time baby-sitting until Allison braved an energizing shower, luxuriated in having a hair dryer once again, and changed into welcome clean slacks and a silk shirt. "I know it ain't my business," she crackled, "but my patience is thinner'n a whisker. You going to tell me what happened, or am I gonna die like a cat?"

Allison laughed weakly. "It would take a week. I'm still reeling from two baths in one day," she joked. She moved comfortably around the room, fixing a bottle for the baby, and told the story of what had happened to them during the last four days. Hesitantly reliving Luisita's death brought a fresh round of tears, but she was proud to find in the telling a new, stronger core of strength.

When she'd completed the story, Woodie gave her a huge hug and sighed in relief. "I'm so sorry, child. Her death must have been a terrible shock."

"If her husband stole drug money, Zachary says it's only a matter of time until someone kills him. It could take months to find him, if he's still alive. I couldn't leave a baby in a situation like that."

She caught herself listening for the sound of his footsteps.

"Well, don't you worry. Raising a baby's instinctive. Comes natural. Once you learn a few basics, you'll be a fine mother. Anything you want to know, you just ask me." Woodie's bright eyes sparkled. "No wonder you and Zachary Cross are . . . friendlier," she hinted.

Her face glowed under the older woman's scrutiny. "I guess it shows?"

"Honey, right now we'd use your face in a lighthouse back in Maine." Woodie paused expectantly. "Ain't my business, of course, but are you sure there's not a little more to your story?"

"You're right." She smiled, blushing generously. "He's been wonderful. He knows about the rape. We've talked about it, and it doesn't make any difference to him."

"Well, I should say not." Woodie was indignant. "Any man worth his salt don't hold it against a woman. My husband, rest his soul, never spent a day he didn't look after me. Made me forget it ever happened at all." She paused. "Been dead seven years and I miss him every day. But life don't wait for you to get over things. It just keeps pushing you along, and you got to move with it or get run over."

Slow footsteps came down the hallway. They were not his. Allison discounted them and smiled. "He wants to see me when . . . after we get home."

"You gonna do it?" Woodie's eyebrows and dancing eyes signaled her vast approval when Allison's smile widened into a self-conscious grin.

The footsteps stopped outside their door. "Ellen?" The soft drawl came through the door, followed by a light rap. "You in theah?"

"Yes, Bill." Woodie's eyes snapped with pleasure.

"'Bill'?" mouthed Allison, grinning at her. "'Bill?' I'm not the only one with a story," she whispered teasingly.

The sprightly little woman had the grace to blush as she hopped up to open the door. "Come on in, but prepare yourself for a little surprise."

Bill Sharp limped into the room and dipped his head in greeting. When he saw the baby asleep in the hamper, his mouth dropped open a bit. "Well, I guess!" he said, brought up short. "That's some surprise. Can't be more'n a few weeks." He sat down next to Woodie and peered into the hamper. "Do I take it he's your'n?"

"He is now," Allison said, still happy with her discovery that Woodie and the colonel—Ellen and Bill—were an item. "This is Adam Zachary Chun, three weeks today," she said proudly.

Woodie's eyebrows did another waggle when she heard the baby's middle name. "My, my, somebody musta done something right," she teased back, and Allison broke into laughter. "What you going to tell the folks about the baby?"

She looked down at the rousing infant, realizing she was still uncertain how to explain his presence. Settled into serious thought, she wished Zachary were here to help. "I don't know." She sighed. "Actually, it's very hard for me to talk about . . . maybe I'll just say I found him."

Bill Sharp said nothing, taking his cue from Woodie, certain she would share with him the entire story at a later, private time. "Well, Ellen, I reckon it's about time I got back to ma room." He stood up and limped to the door. "Y'all let me know if theah's a thing I can do, y'heah?"

Woodie limped to join him. "Ain't we a pair," she cracked. "He sprained his left leg and I'm short on the left. Sure keeps us in step. Otherwise, we bump into each other."

Allison dissolved in laughter and fell back on the bunk as she listened to the two of them limp down the hall. Still bubbly, she bent to feed the hungry baby.

"Hi."

In a simple gold shirt, pale yellow slacks, shining hair catching a thousand glints of light, she looked elegant and smashing. The sight of her took his breath and increased his heart rate. There were freckles on her nose.

This afternoon, he realized, was the first time he'd been away from her in nearly three days. There had been an odd, hollow feeling in his heart, as though part of him were missing. He'd tortured himself, wondering if things would change now that they were back in a relatively normal situation, if his feelings would alter or diminish.

But with just one look at her, the empty place was full again. You're in serious trouble, Cross, he told himself. She came into his arms, and he fought the urge to bar the door and kiss her with a passion that would drive him to make love to her on the bunk, on the floor, anywhere.

Instead he kissed her lightly, and her response had an honesty that drove him crazy. He pressed his open mouth against her neck, tasted tantalizing perfume on her throat with his tongue. He kissed her again, demanding of himself that he keep his need for her under control, and searched her face. "God, you are gorgeous!" She blushed and pulled herself away, and he allowed her to sit on the bunk next to the basket with the sleeping baby. "Everything under control here? What have we told the outside world?"

"Woodie knows everything and she's probably told the colonel by now, but no one else," she said, dizzy with the kiss and relief that he was here, that her feelings for him were still real. She relaxed into a relative security that somehow the two of them would know what to do. "He's been perfect, but it's only a matter of time until we have to say something," she chattered nervously. "What about the flight?"

"Seven-thirty tomorrow morning. I got the last two seats. It's only an hour hop. Eastern to Miami goes out at ten-thirty, so we'll have plenty of time to figure out exit problems with the baby." He kissed her nose. "Have you thought about Miami? Are you gonna stay a couple of days? Buy some things for Adam? See how a couple of ordinary days work out for us?"

Mysterious hazel eyes with smoky irises looked into his, and she didn't answer right away.

"Or, I can get another week out of my lieutenant, I'm sure, and come to Chicago for a couple days. . . . What do you think?" He studied the emotions chasing their way across her face.

"I think Miami sounds fine," she said slowly, blinking back sudden tears. "I think Miami sounds . . . good." She was rewarded with a wide, lopsided grin and a brief kiss.

"We have to make a couple of quick decisions, and then I'm going to have to find a shower. These jeans are gonna need their own ticket home." He resigned himself to be serious when what he really wanted to do was find out if she was ticklish and tumble her back on the bed. "I'll go along with whatever you want to say about the baby."

"It's been driving me crazy. There's been so much to deal with since . . . Luisita died. And explaining him means talking about her. I don't want to lie, but I really don't know how many times I can do it." She dreaded the endless rounds of explanation. "If I thought we could get away with it, I wouldn't tell them anything, but there's no way I could lie about him, I know it."

He hadn't considered it, either. One way or another in the last few days, they'd bypassed police procedure in at least three countries. Getting out of Guatemala had been his sole focus this morning, and they'd been unbelievably lucky at it; walking on tightropes was getting contagious. "I say we gamble we can keep him quiet long enough for us to turn in early. Worst case, he's discovered and the rest of the story comes out tomorrow morning."

"We'll be on the charter at seven-thirty," she supplied, hopeful.

"We go to dinner—that keeps people out of your room, and we make it simple. They're only gonna want to know about the cave and the village, anyway. I'll handle the tricky questions and you just look pale and bewildered." He laughed at the now incongruous description of the woman he knew her to be and kissed her again.

She smiled in relief at the decision. "I think Woodie's

still with Colonel Sharp. If she agrees—it's her room, too—it's what we'll do." She slipped out the door and was back in a few minutes. "They understand. They haven't told anyone."

He got up to swing open the wooden shutter and looked down into the yard, thick with shadows in the tropical night. "We can leave the baby right here, I've got mosquito netting we can put over the hamper. We'll sit at this end of the table so we can hear him if he wakes up."

Twenty minutes later, the baby safely asleep, he collected her with a kiss, and they walked down the stairs to face the avid curiosity of their peers.

At first everyone listened expectantly as he talked. Carefully modulating his voice to subdue his energy, he noticed with satisfaction the gradual onset of politeness from his audience as they transferred the bulk of their attention to their evening meal.

Speculation and, except for George Edley, lurid interest in what might have passed between the two of them during the past three days waned from their collective imagination.

Allison, feeling alive and vital for the first time in recent memory, watched his performance with senses keenly tuned for the slightest sound from sleeping Adam. She did her best to appear listless and tired.

Woodie and Bill Sharp kept conspicuously silent, Woodie's mobile brows captive in a poker face as she, too, listened for sounds from the baby.

George, however, was unable to contain his envy. "I'm here to tell you that I'd have traded places with you in a second," he said to Zachary with intended gallantry. "Anybody that gets to spend three days in the jungle with this lovely lady can count himself pretty lucky, I'll tell you."

Allison gave him a wan smile.

Zachary ignored the remark while Eve stared a hole in Allison's forehead. What was so dangerous about a stolen car and a walk through the jungle in Guatemala? No question about it, Allison Shreve looked entirely too happy to have suffered very much from walking a couple of miles. This was no longer the aloof, rich bitch who'd arrived from Chicago last week. The woman settled next to Zachary at the end of the table was confident and secure.

She'd been to the San Ruiz ruins. Even on foot it wouldn't take three days to get to the Mayan village there. Allison and Zachary were hiding something. Clearly the two of them were lying. They'd shared more than a friendship. Two to one their car hadn't been stolen at all. They'd probably checked into the San Ruiz Hotel for three days and had a gay old time. Her face ached with the effort of appearing unconcerned, and her stomach churned with the double sting of rejection and betrayal.

Indiana was darkly disappointed. "I'd have thought it would be more difficult on foot out there. The jungle can be pretty dangerous. Snakes, all kinds of things. I don't know how these flimsy huts survive the kind of storm that came through here yesterday. We had trouble getting out of the site today—old man Morgan had to pull us out with his tractor."

Eve watched Allison's uneasy reaction to the comment with interest and noticed her involuntary look toward the window of her room with its open shutter. Her opinion was reinforced. Something had happened they weren't owning up to.

"How are things at the site, Tom?" Zachary was pleased to turn the conversation away from further questioning.

Tom Rider had waited politely with his own agenda. From the moment Eve had informed him they'd called from San Ruiz, he had dismissed the two to concentrate on salvaging what was left of his plans for the dig. "Indiana's right, it's too muddy to work out there now, so I'm shifting to a site on one of the cays about halfway out to Laughing Bird. We've located a house mound on it, and I've been meaning to have a look, so we'll spend the next two days working out there."

"That's a shame," Zachary said smoothly, fully aware he'd be gone. "I was looking forward to doing more machete work with Osari and Emilio." Pleased at his success in diverting the attention of the group, he found himself enjoying a small charade. It was the first time he'd allowed himself to play in years. He looked quizzically at the woman who'd come into his life a short week ago and knew she was the basis for the change in him. He read in her eyes amusement before she quickly looked away to prevent a smile in conspiracy.

Eve, who did not miss the exchange, allowed her feelings of resentment toward the lovers to expand and deepen. The whole thing was a farce!

Tom Rider, intent on his new plan, didn't register Zachary's put-on. "The rest of the work on the original site will be exacting and primarily technical in nature. I want to make the announcement that, thanks to your hard work and our extreme good fortune, the Belize government has advanced funding to provide security until we're certain there are no more major discoveries to be made. This is a most unusual step for this country, and we can be very proud."

The group as a whole broke into appreciative applause, and Zachary signaled Allison with a look. They excused themselves and escaped up the stairs to her room to check on the baby.

Eve's sullen eyes followed their exit. After a moment she saw him reach out the window of Allison's room and pull the shutter closed. Feeling publicly rejected and humiliated, ignoring a hopeful look from George, she got up from the table with a burning face and left the yard.

Relieving tension, the conspirators giggled quietly together as they satisfied themselves that Adam had slept soundly through their performance. "I'd trade places with you in a second," he mimicked George. "Anybody that gets to spend three days in the jungle with this lovely lady . . ." He kissed her laughing mouth. "He'd have been all over you like a cheap suit. I can see you in the jungle, trying to beat him off with a stick."

Despite their best intentions, their subdued laughter

roused the baby. Zachary fed him while she quickly changed the diaper. He watched in silent approval of her newly acquired maternal skill. "You're getting pretty good at this," he said as she deftly fastened the safety pin. Her eyes shone with the pleasure of his approval.

Adam, willing co-conspirator, made no sound as he placidly consumed his dinner and stared first into the face surrounded with a bright halo of light, then one framed with a circle of dark. The bright and dark heads drew together without words, incorporating the three of them into a single unit, and shared the silence until Adam, sleepy, glutted, and secure, was put down once again in the hamper.

Zachary turned her face up to his and bent to kiss her throat. "We'll be on a plane all day tomorrow," he said, his voice muffled against her skin. "I'll call Miami from the airport and get someone working on immigration requirements. Whatever it is can be handled." He held her close, breathing in the sensual perfume.

"I'll do whatever you want when we get there. I'll get you a room—or you can stay with me," he said, proceeding cautiously. He felt her stiffen ever so slightly. "I'll sleep in Steffie's room," he hastened to add, "until we see how things go." He buried his face in her hair. "I want to make love to you. I've never wanted anything so much in my life." Leaning back to look into her eyes, to see what was written there, he read the struggle as she sought to maintain her trust. This time he lost.

It wasn't just the baby, she realized. Certainly Adam had changed things in a way she hadn't considered, and his well-being was her priority, but faced with committing to an intimate sexual situation with Zachary, even under the best of circumstances . . . She crumbled. Maybe when some of the problems were resolved. "If it was just you and me . . ." she began.

He shifted gears immediately. The baby had taken precedence, as it should be. Tomorrow would bring what tomorrow would bring, and he would have to bide his time. But he could kiss her and hold her this night. "No pressure, I swear. I'm just trying to make sure you know I'll be there. We'll get through this." He kissed her lightly, reassuringly, and her resistance melted into an honest, responsive kiss in return. Into their intimate quiet came a light rap at the door.

"That's probably Woodie," she whispered, teasing. "Should we let her in?"

"No," he joked grumpily. The opened door revealed Tom Rider, his face fixed in a small professional smile, accompanied by a uniformed policeman.

"Sorry to disturb you, I know you're pretty tired," Rider said formally. "This is Captain Tomason. He's stopped in to check on things, make sure everything's all right."

"Captain." Zachary nodded an acknowledgment and reached out to shake hands. "Zachary Cross. I work Vice in Miami. Glad to know you." Hackles stiffened on the back of his neck. Damn! He was forced to introduce her. "This is Allison Shreve."

"Captain," said Allison, offering her hand. Without thinking, she stood to obscure his view of the baby asleep behind her in the hamper.

Tom Rider excused himself. "I'll see you two bright and early tomorrow morning," he told them. "Good night."

"Do you mind if we talk in my room, Captain? As you can see, the lady's exhausted and should be in bed. I was just saying good night."

Captain Tomason would not be diverted. He was in a hurry and had no mind to be shifted about by Americans down here sifting through temple sites and taking materials that belonged to Belize. "This will only take a moment, I'm sure, and I'll get right to the point, if you don't mind." His mellow Creole voice was as polite as he was immovable. "I am told you left Mango Creek with a young woman and that you came back without her."

"That's true," said Zachary, antennae humming. "Luisita Chun. She was our guide to Guatemala."

"Is she still in Guatemala?"

"Can I ask the reason for your questions, Captain?" As

he sidestepped the question, Zachary tried to detect the tension, born of suspicion, that normally accompanied an investigating officer. There was none. Why was he here?

"We have a report this woman is missing. She left with you, did she not?"

"Yes." Someone wanted information badly enough to send the police to ask about Luisita. "Who's looking for her?"

"A friend. Do you know if she found her sister?" Tomason persisted, his curiosity piqued with their resistance.

Until this moment he'd had no real interest in the matter. It was as a favor that he'd agreed to talk to the Americans at all. Corla Reyes had called him, insisting something had gone bad with a young Mayan woman who'd driven with these people to the San Ruiz ruins. Something about a baby. His shift ended, he'd been on his way this evening to meet the girl he intended to marry, sweet sixteen-year-old Nicola, who lived to dance at the local disco, and his sole interest had been dancing into the night next to her tempting body. Nicola Reyes was still too young to bed. His visit had not been official, but purely to please his prospective mother-in-law.

"No, her sister was dead." Zachary waited to see what the man would tell him with his questions.

"Dead. I see. So, this woman—Luisita, stayed in the village?" This was not good. Captain Tomason took out his notepad and began making notes.

"Yes. Her sister is buried there."

"I take it," Tomason consulted his notes, "Luisita Chun was in good health when you left her."

They'd reached the crossroads. He could no longer evade without withholding information about a crime from a fellow officer. He looked at Allison, sending the message.

The baby stirred in his bassinet, and she put her hand on Zachary's shoulder. All things were connected. All things. It would have to play as Luisita's gods intended. She nodded her head in agreement to tell the young policeman.

"No. She was killed," Zachary said tightly. Here came the worms out of the can. Mice and men were about to make new plans.

Captain Tomason came alert. Two deaths. This was not good at all. "Killed, Mr. Cross? How did such a thing happen?"

Zachary faced inquisitive dark brown eyes squarely and answered as concisely as possible. "Two men followed us to the ruins and stole our vehicle, apparently drug runners, we don't know. One of them shot her, I don't think he intended to kill her, but he did. She died at the scene. We took the body to her sister's village for burial."

"Shot her? When was this?" Captain Tomason was disturbed. This was most unpleasant. "Where did you report this?"

"It happened yesterday morning near San Ruiz. She was a citizen of Guatemala. It was handled there. She was buried last night." He tried desperately to keep it simple. He could see his answers were upsetting Allison.

"In Guatemala? I see." Guatemala was another matter, clearly a superior would now have to be involved. Matters with foreigners were always difficult and complicated. He turned to the woman. "I'm told you have a small child with you, a baby."

"That's right."

So. Someone had reported the child. Corla Reyes, the boatman, someone. They should have expected it. Zachary was annoyed.

"The child is from Guatemala and the mother is dead?"

"Yes. A week ago. Complications from childbirth." She could feel the net closing in, helpless to stop it.

"So bad. I am sorry. But how is it that you have the baby?"

She took a deep breath. "Luisita was the baby's guardian." She kept her voice firm and strong. "Before she died, she gave the baby to me to take care of. I agreed to do it."

"Gave you the child?" He looked around her body to

Adam, sound asleep in the makeshift bassinet. "Is this the baby?"

"Yes." She waited, uneasy, anticipating. What would happen now?

Zachary stood by quietly, waiting to see which way it would go. If she handled this, she could handle anything U.S. Immigration would throw at her.

"It is a Mayan child." An orphan. Another problem. Tomason's pencil flew over the notepad.

"Yes. Luisita and Sara were Maya." She was unable to keep irritation out of her voice. What difference did it make if Adam came from the moon?

"And what are the plans for this baby?" Captain Tomason was very unhappy. Two deaths, a baby, a missing father. Most difficult. There would be no dancing tonight.

"I'm going to adopt him." Jorgé K'ayum's warning rang in her ears: *He is Lacandon Maya, no matter what ts'ul law may say*! "I'm sure there are legal questions to be answered, but I'm prepared for that."

"I do not doubt you, miss. However, you must know that children are very precious," he said circumspectly. "It will be necessary for someone to look into this."

Allison blanched. They could not leave tomorrow after all. "How long will that take?"

"We will speak with the authorities in Guatemala. Please do not worry. I am certain it will all be perfectly fine."

She began to tremble. She hadn't considered that the legal nightmare would begin here. At the airport, perhaps. She sent a pleading look to Zachary for help.

"How quickly can we accomplish this, Captain? As you probably know, we're down here as tourists and we're due to leave shortly to go back to the United States. She's telling you the truth. I was with her when these events occurred. I'll give you a sworn statement. It can also be confirmed by Jorgé K'ayum, the elder in the Mayan village. I'll be happy to drive there with you this evening and we can straighten this out."

"I am sorry, that is impossible." Captain Tomason was deeply disturbed with the situation he had uncovered. Dancing with Nicola was not only out of the question, he would spend the evening talking with his superior and beginning an investigation. He wrote down the name, Jorgé K'ayum. "Someone will surely look into this," he soothed the agitated American woman. "If the elder can confirm this story, I am sure this will be most satisfactory."

"Fine." Zachary shook hands with the young captain, guiding him to the door. "The lady and the baby need some rest. If there's anything else you need to know, I'll be happy to cooperate if you'll step into my room."

"That won't be necessary tonight, Mr. Cross. I'll take a full statement from you tomorrow at the station. Good night, miss," said Captain Tomason from the doorway. "Not to worry."

They were alone.

"How long do you think we'll have to stay here?"

"I don't know, a couple of days, at least. Could be longer."

She paced the room. "I'll have to find a doctor for him tomorrow morning. I want to make certain he's in good health. I was going to wait until Miami, but . . ."

"He's fine."

"But he sleeps so much."

"They're supposed to sleep at this age. Sleep and eat and use up diapers. That's all they do at three weeks. Trust me, sleeping is normal. Sleeping is good. Sleeping is what we should be doing. Take it from a father." He kissed her forehead. "You get some sleep, there's nothing to worry about here. We'll give them the statement about what happened, they'll check it out, and we'll be free to leave in a couple of days. I'll see you tomorrow morning. Early."

He opened the door to find Woodie about to knock and leaned down to kiss her on the cheek. "Anything she needs, I'm across the hall."

"Well, that answers my question," Woodie whispered,

peering into the hamper at the baby. "I was going to check to see if you wanted me to find sleeping quarters elsewhere tonight. Do you?"

Allison blushed and whispered back, "It's not like that."

"I'm a fine baby-sitter if you want to, uh . . ."

She threw a sock at her roommate.

That night, her sleep was restless and she dreamed of the jaguar. It jumped once again over her body, pursued by dogs, only to be trapped on a ledge in the cave with black water lapping at its paws.

Friday morning dawned clear and golden. Zachary rose early and jogged along the white sandy beach behind the hotel, second-guessing his decision about Luisita's death. Had it happened in the United States, or even in Belize, the course of action would have been clear: report it to the police and cooperate while investigations ran their course. He and Allison were guilty of nothing more than being in the wrong place at the wrong time.

Luisita was dead. Paulo was dead. Filing a report with the police in Guatemala, or Belize, or the United States, would have led to the conclusion that he and Jorgé K'ayum had reached in the privacy of the old man's hut. If they'd dealt with the authorities and the inevitable red tape and bureaucratic bullshit set up to clear the matter properly, they'd be sitting somewhere in Guatemala with a three-week-old baby, probably in custody.

Still, the shortcut was wrong, and he knew it. In the back of his head he'd known all along it was wrong, and now it was going to bite them in the ass.

He was hot from the run and the shower threw stinging needles against his skin. Damn it to hell, anyway. The good news was he'd have more time with her before the inevitable decision arrived, maybe in Miami, whether or not she would stay with him—or go home to Jake. Why wouldn't she tell him about Jake? He'd feel a hell of a lot better about the guy if he had a clearer understanding of their relationship. He second-guessed himself again. Maybe he wouldn't at that.

He dressed and settled at the hotel end of the breakfast table to wait, glancing toward her window now and again when he heard murmurs of conversation. His fertile imagination warmed at thoughts of her moving around, getting dressed.

Conferring in quiet tones, Allison and Woodie fed and changed Adam, anticipating the six A.M. breakfast call. All was quiet on the eastern front when Allison heard Zachary's voice drift through the window into the room.

"Good morning, Captain."

"Mr. Cross. I am glad you are awake this early."

She recognized the gliding Creole lilt of Captain Tomason's voice and put her knee on the bunk to open the shutter, peeked out the window to the yard below. She saw Tomason seat himself across from Zachary at the breakfast table. The cook, annoyed at having his routine disrupted, disapprovingly plunked down a kettle of hot water before the two men.

"There is a problem I must discuss with you and Miss Shreve this morning." Tomason's eyes were unreadable.

Zachary sighed and began spooning instant coffee. "What can I do for you, Captain?" He reached warily for the canned milk.

"I have discussed this distressing matter with my superior, and last evening we placed a call to the authorities in San Ruiz."

His heart sank. He'd hoped to inform Tomason before it was discovered. "And there's no report of the death of Luisita Chun."

The captain nodded once in acknowledgment and continued. "I see you know this. You can understand, then, why one of my deputies was dispatched to the village to speak with Jorgé K'ayum. We had hoped he could verify these matters, particularly where this child is concerned."

Allison held her breath and motioned Woodie to listen also.

Zachary's graveled voice carried clearly in the thin morning air as he looked up in surprise.

"K'ayum's the village chief. He said he had the authority to handle it. What did he tell you?" he asked suspiciously. Christ, had the old man lied? Denied his decision?

"Jorgé K'ayum was not in the village. My deputy has called this morning. The elder is gone with his son on a pilgrimage to Yaxchilán. His family does not know what arrangement he made with Miss Shreve concerning the baby. And they do not know when he will return. I regret to inform you it is my duty this morning to take custody of this baby until we speak with the elder and the matter can be fully investigated. I hope I shall have your cooperation."

"Surely other people in the village can verify his decision. Everyone knew we left with the baby, and the old man agreed to it. What the hell is this? What's going on?" His gut was on fire. There had to be more to this than Tomason was letting on. Custody! She'd never agree to it. Never. He glanced again at the window. Open. She'd be down any second. He'd have no opportunity to prepare her. He shifted in frustration.

Captain Tomason raised his polite voice in warning. "A body has been found—a man with a broken neck and a gunshot wound to his head. It was found yesterday in the river by men from K'ayum's village."

"He's the one that killed Luisita. I was there, I saw it happen—"

Tomason cut him off. "This man is said to be the baby's father. As you can see, the matter is very grave."

"His father?" Confusion and surprise forced him into silence.

Frozen at the window, Allison fought for breath. The

voices receded into formless haze. Custody. Luisita's bleeding face welled through her mind. *You will take care of him. There is no one else.* Custody. No one to prove he was hers. What if she couldn't prove it? She had sworn to Luisita on her word of honor.

Fear took over, shattered reason, propelled her to action. Police. Police would take the baby. No! If the baby wasn't here, he couldn't be taken into custody. First was to get the baby away. Somewhere safe. She forced herself away from the window, demanding a cold, clear plan of action from her mind. Time. She needed time. Time to bargain, time to plead her case. Men could not be trusted to bargain fairly, to hear pleading.

She would take the baby into the village, find a lawyer, contact Zachary later and decide what to do. She needed time. With icy calm, she moved about the room, found her backpack, and dumped it on the bunk. Opening the bloodstained suitcase, she quickly removed the remaining cans of milk, the diapers, Luisita's purse, Adam's bottle, and began stuffing them into her pack.

Woodie watched her, concerned. "What are you doing, child?"

"Just until I get a lawyer. Someone who can convince them to let me keep him," she pleaded. "They won't listen to me." She threw in a skirt, Luisita's shawl, a blouse, the sandals, whatever came to hand. She grabbed her purse and checked for money and wished fervently for the credit card somewhere in the river in Guatemala.

Woodie put out her hand and forced Allison to look at her. "This ain't my business, but I doubt if there's a lawyer in a hundred miles. Certainly not in Waler's Beach. It's not much more'n a crossroads."

"They won't believe me," she said desperately. "They'll think I'm lying. I can't prove he's mine—Luisita's dead!" The reality of her precarious position where the child was concerned spurred her on. "Once they have the baby, I can't do anything. I just need time. Please, Woodie," she begged.

"Think it over real careful before you leave." Woodie moved to the door. "'Course, I'm not here, so I don't know what you're doing. I'm already down to breakfast. Good luck, honey." She let herself out.

Allison collapsed on the bunk and looked again out the window as Woodie clumped heavily down the stairs.

"Morning, Zachary. Young man." Woodie plumped herself down next to the young policeman. "Mind if I have some of that hot water?" she said pleasantly.

Tomason returned her greeting and pushed the kettle within her reach, then returned his attention to Zachary. "It is all very well to tell me that you can explain, but three people, Mr. Cross. The mother, the father, and the guardian of the child. . . surely you see why we wish to verify that the baby is in safe hands."

"He's not the father—he was trying to find the baby's father. With an Uzi. Something to do with drug money. He was driving a gray sedan. I left it in the village. If your deputy's still in San Ruiz, ask him to find out who owns it. The baby's father is some guy named Rufino. We've got the birth certificate to prove it."

Captain Tomason listened closely and made a few notes. "I will be happy to take a complete statement as soon as Miss Shreve is ready," he said quietly.

The smiling cook, back on schedule, ended further discussion with a hoarse shout of "Breakfast!" promptly at six o'clock, thumping bowls of hot scrambled eggs and platters of bacon onto the tables. George and Indiana, the Millers, and Colonel Sharp appeared from various locations, hungry and vociferous, showing little interest in the presence of the police officer, politely keeping conversation among themselves. After an exchange of greeting and a jealously good-natured dig from George, they got to the serious business of brewing instant coffee and appeasing their well-earned hunger.

Woodie, studiously preparing her eggs, avoided Zachary's questioning eyes. "Won't you join us for breakfast, Captain?" She sweetly handed Tomason the plate and utensils from Allison's vacant space next to her at the table and passed him a platter of bacon.

Zachary's antennae went up; something was amiss. Acerbic Woodie was clearly humoring the young officer. The hotel had contracted with Tom Rider for meals for himself, Eve Kelsey, and eight volunteers. Ten plates. No more, no less. Woodie had given the policeman Allison's breakfast plate. He glanced up at the window. The shutter was closed tight. Unless he was entering never-never land, Woodie had signaled that Allison wasn't coming down for breakfast.

He automatically scraped scrambled eggs onto his plate and passed the bowl to the captain, watched him fix another cup of coffee, douse it liberally with canned milk, and spoon in great quantities of sugar. What was she doing? Why wouldn't she come down to breakfast? He'd heard no sounds from the baby. Maybe he was awake and she couldn't leave him. Had she heard the captain's declaration about taking custody? He forced himself to smile across the table at Woodie and ask jovially, "Didn't see you two out jogging this morning." Where is she?

"We were up early, but not that early," she replied amiably.

"Trouble sleeping?"

"I guess I was just thinking that it's only two more days before we have to . . . leave here."

She had placed just the slightest emphasis on "leave." Oh, shit! If he wasn't imagining the whole secondary conversation, Woodie had just told him Allison was planning to leave, which meant she knew the captain intended to take custody of the baby.

His mind raced to cover all the possibilities. Leaving was a double-edged sword. Legally she hadn't been advised that she must give up the child, but it made her look guilty as sin. Damn! Where the hell could she go that they couldn't find her? It wasn't as if she could hail a taxi. A white woman in a brown country, particularly as beautiful as she was, would go unnoticed exactly nowhere.

Should he try to stop her and see if he could make her listen to reason? And do what? Convince her to let Tomason take the baby into custody and wait out the old man's trip—which could be weeks, maybe months? Trust that Jorgé K'ayum would confirm his decision? Trust the Belize authorities to take the word of an old Guatemalan Indian who lived in a dirt hut in the middle of no-bloody-where that he had the right and authority to give an American woman an orphaned child?

No way she'd have that kind of trust, and, in fairness, he wasn't sure he would, either. Interfering in her life was dangerous. If she lost the child, she'd hold him responsible. If he helped her get away, he became an accessory. Get away where? He kept coming back to the futility of her action. There was no way she could get out of this little junction, let alone out of Belize with the baby. Surely she knew that.

He calmed down. He was entertaining an overactive imagination this morning. She was probably tending the baby. He looked at Woodie, who was watching him intently.

Eve Kelsey walked down the stairs and joined the waiting group, cheeks brightly defiant. She seated herself next to Zachary. Captain Tomason finished his coffee. "I should like to see Miss Allison Shreve now," he said politely.

Woodie's look changed to one of resignation, and she bit her lip in concern.

Eve glanced quickly up and down the tables, scanning the faces. "Where is she?" she said, looking from Zachary to Woodie and back again. "Sleeping in?" Her remark fell heavily on the silent trio.

Tomason stood and Zachary moved to join him as Tom Rider, ashen, came rushing to the table, nearly speechless with agitation. "Everyone will please remain seated," he addressed the volunteers, struggling for composure. "Captain Tomason." He grasped the man's arm. "I need to speak with you immediately. You, too, Cross."

The group sat in a shocked silence to see unflappable Tom Rider so upset; something was gravely wrong. Small pockets of whispered speculation began to buzz along the table.

Seconds later, in a small storage room converted to a field laboratory, Rider struggled to remain calm as he showed them a sturdy, cotton-lined cardboard box, now empty. "The ocarina," he agonized. "It's priceless. It was here until a few minutes ago, and now it's gone. I don't believe it!" His hurt was palpable. "Whoever took it can't be very far. It was here ten minutes ago, I swear it. I washed it last night and let it dry overnight in my room. No one knows I had it. No one!"

Zachary watched him move hastily among the work-tables, searching fruitlessly as he talked, desperate to convince himself that the artifact was there, merely overlooked in his distraction. "I want you to search the hotel, all the rooms, the luggage, everything. I haven't been more than twenty feet from it all morning. There were people in here this morning, but I made sure no one saw it. It was in a box. I keep it hidden here."

"Who?" Zachary prompted without sympathy. Rider was an idiot to have the thing with him. He didn't know much about Central American artifacts, but the ocarina was a beautifully crafted item and had to be worth at least five figures in the art market. There were half a dozen boxes of the same size stacked on the counter against the wall. He opened each of them as he waited for an answer. They were empty.

"Who? I don't remember who. . . ." Rider paused to concentrate. "The Miller woman, Edley, and Colonel Sharp. Eve, the cook—he brought me a cup of coffee earlier. We've got to find it!"

Zachary was furious. "I thought you took the stuff to Belize City? What the hell were you doing with it, anyway? Jesus Christ, Tom, a three-year-old could break in here."

"I told you, no one knew I had it. I was doing work on it. It's too fragile to let anyone else touch. It doesn't goddamned matter!" Rider yelled back. "I had it, it's gone!"

"Gentlemen!" Captain Tomason's quiet voice cracked through the room. "This is getting nowhere. Since I am here, I will look around. Perhaps it has been misplaced. Perhaps not. But I can do nothing until I know what it is I am looking for."

Rider reacted immediately. "There's a sketch. Eve made a drawing." He scrambled to a file and began searching through a drawer of manila folders.

Tomason turned to him. "Is there anyone besides Miss Shreve who has not come down to breakfast?"

He stared into suddenly intelligent brown eyes. "Yes. Tom Rider," he said quietly without hesitation. Never again, he told himself, will I underestimate this guy. "Eve Kelsey just arrived, and everyone else was there."

Rider found the sketch, and Tomason examined it carefully. "This is very small," he judged. "It will be easy to hide in many places. Perhaps we should talk with the others." He led the way back to the breakfast table.

Allison's face was still missing from the group.

Behind the hotel, she grabbed the baby's basket with a smarting hand and walked rapidly along the path to town. Eve Kelsey had some kind of bloody nerve. If she hadn't been trapped, she wouldn't have spoken to her at all, but Eve had charged around the corner and nearly crashed into her as she was carefully negotiating Adam's hamper down the back stairs.

"Before breakfast. My, aren't we the energetic one. What's in the hamper? Picnic lunch?" Eve's voice had been tinged with sarcasm.

"I'm . . . it's a surprise. I'm putting it on the dock so I don't tip it over," she'd improvised, amazed at her cool response.

"Here, let me help."

Eve had grabbed for the hamper, and Allison had stopped her with a look. "What's inside is fragile and I don't want to take a chance it gets damaged."

Eve had blocked her path with a Cheshire-cat smile. "I insist."

She'd hesitated, then slid the heavy backpack off her shoulder and held it out instead. "I'll carry the basket," she'd said, leaving no room for discussion, unwilling to continue wasting time.

"I love surprises." Eve had given her a narrow look and led the way down the stairs and across the sand to the dock.

The boatmen were due any minute.

Eve had busied herself securing a flap on an outside pocket of the bag, then turned to stare at her. "Zachary, for instance. He was quite a surprise, didn't you find that to be true?"

Nervous, distracted with her own purpose, Allison hadn't followed. She'd positioned the hamper gently on the dock and reached for the pack. "Thank you."

Eve held it just out of reach. "I mean, for a man his age, he has an enormous sexual appetite, don't you think? He certainly kept me busy all night long, and I do mean all night." She'd watched intently, measuring the impact of her statements. "He's not all that much the morning after, but if he was as good to you as he was to me . . . after four nights, I'm surprised you can walk. Tell me, is he any better in a hut than a hotel room?"

That's when Allison had slapped her, a hard, ringing, *whop* of open palm smacking into the hateful expression on Eve's face, wiping it away entirely and replacing it with a round-mouthed O of teary astonishment as the sting set in.

It had taken Eve a moment to recover, then realize she'd have to retaliate or retreat. She'd chosen the latter. Deliberately dropping the backpack out of reach, she'd backed away. "Well, that certainly tells me the obvious. You and the well-equipped detective are getting it on."

When her face had reflected shocked denial, Eve had changed tack. "Nooo? What's the matter, dear, wasn't he all that hot for you out there all alone in the jungle? You too uptight for his taste?"

She'd hustled quickly to the top of the hotel stairs. "Maybe he doesn't like uptight women, because he sure enough liked me. All night long. According to him, I'm terrific. What'd he tell you? Mmmm?" She'd spat a last venomous sneer over the railing and disappeared down the hallway.

Trembling, Allison had shrugged the pack harness across her shoulder. She'd never hit another human being in her life and was appalled to discover that she'd thoroughly enjoyed it. Astonished and unprepared for the depth of the woman's vicious jealousy, she hurried now along the path toward the little town. She attempted to wipe the lewd challenges from her thoughts. The remarks had hit so close to home, had smashed so squarely inside the wall of murky gray fear, that even concern for the baby was held aside a full five minutes until she could bury the words in her subconscious. By then she'd reached the huge commercial fishing pier stretched out into deep ocean water and passed its processing plant.

A flurry of wooden signs tacked to a post indicated the center of Waler's Beach to her left. Goaded by the thought of Captain Tomason, certain to come looking for her, she knew there was no margin for error and hurried on. Eve was forgotten. Inland, she followed a narrow walk built over the sand, regretting she hadn't explored the town with Woodie and the others in their forays to the disco. She had no idea where to find a place to stay until she could locate a lawyer. Time was running out.

Tom Rider faced the group of curious volunteers. "One of the artifacts of great importance is missing. The ocarina. You all know what it looks like?"

As he displayed the drawing, Zachary watched their reactions; confusion and consternation appeared in the faces lined along the tables. Nowhere was caution, a hint of apprehension, eyes that would not meet his own. One by one they nodded. Yes, they knew.

"It was taken a few minutes ago from my laboratory," continued Rider. "I realize this is embarrassing, and please understand I mean no accusation, but did anyone here borrow it for any reason—to examine or photograph?"

A chorus of no's glanced around the table. Zachary saw Eve's eyes narrow in anger and outrage.

"You mean it's gone? I thought you took it to Belize City. If it's only been missing a few minutes, then it must still be somewhere here in the hotel."

"I brought it back to do some work on it," the professor admitted, apologetically. "I wish to hell I hadn't." He searched the group, unconsciously counting faces. "Who's missing? Where's Allison?"

The faces turned to Woodie, who spoke quietly. "She was dressing when I came down to breakfast, but she didn't leave the room all morning."

They'd search the room and discover her gone. It wasn't possible she'd taken it, and the search would buy her some time. Zachary decided not to interfere as Rider broke for the front stairs. Captain Tomason followed.

Zachary helped Woodie up from the table. "Everyone stay calm and we'll get back to you in a couple of minutes." He followed her slowed progress up the stairs and saw Tomason's back disappear through the door.

Rider was staring in outrage around the obviously empty room.

"How long ago did you leave her?" came the quiet captain's voice.

"I joined you and Zachary just when the cook called breakfast, as I recall." Woodie pondered. "That would be six o'clock."

Tomason poked through the abandoned articles on Allison's bunk, pushed aside her clothing, examined the notebook and a small piece of turquoise foil. A note fell out of the wrapping paper. He read it and tossed it on the bunk.

Zachary read the message, also.

> *Hi Lovely.*
> *I miss you already.*
> *All my love,*
> JAKE

Pierced by the reminder of Jake, something he didn't need right at this moment, he racked his brain to figure out where she might have gone. He wasn't concerned with Rider's missing ocarina. That would be found, or it wouldn't. Either way it didn't enter into his world with Allison. Where was she?

"What do you know about this, Mr. Cross?"

Pushing open the shutter, he had a clear view of the breakfast table. There was no doubt she'd seen Tomason this morning, unquestionably she'd overheard. Eve's face, as she sat at the table, was smugly animated. Not at all the expression of someone upset at the loss of a priceless artifact. Two minutes ago she'd been ready to fight. He turned to answer the young captain. "I haven't the faintest idea where she is," he said honestly.

Tomason turned to Rider. "Was she in the laboratory this morning? Think carefully. We do not want to make a mistake about this."

Rider groaned with effort. "No," he said reluctantly. "At least I didn't see her."

"Is it possible that she or someone could have come into the lab without your seeing them?"

"Well, obviously someone did and took the damned thing right in front of me. Maybe she was working with someone. Hell, I don't know. She can't get very far unless she took one of the boats." Rider ran out the door to check on the boatmen.

"Captain Tomason, this is ridiculous. We got back yesterday from four days in Guatemala. She was nearly killed, a woman was shot to death in front of her. She has a baby to take care of. You come waltzing in here this morning and tell me you want to take the baby away from her. She probably overheard you say it and is taking him somewhere safe. I assure you, she's not going to wait around and steal a piece of his art collection, or whatever you consider it!"

"I think you are probably right, Mr. Cross. However, she is undeniably gone with the baby, and an expensive artifact is missing within the same few minutes. Until the piece is found and until she is found, we won't know. Now, if you'll excuse me, I must telephone my office and report her disappearance."

Zachary looked again out the window. Eve saw him staring down at her from the window and glanced away quickly. "Where'd she go, Woodie?"

"I have no idea, son. She was determined, and I could see it was useless to talk to her. Ain't my business, but I don't think it's a good thing for a baby that tiny to be away from its mother." Woodie drifted to the doorway. "She said something about getting a lawyer to keep them from taking the child."

He smiled grimly. "I'll go look for her as soon as I can break out of here. We're on a caye. She can't get anywhere else." His stomach lurched. "Oh, hell. We had reservations on the charter this morning." He looked at his watch. It was all too possible. "You don't suppose . . ."

Eve pegged him at the bottom of the stairs. "What's going on? Where is she?"

"I don't know, Eve. She's not here." He tried to push past her without success.

Eve blanched. "Not here? She was at the dock a few minutes ago."

Rider came around the hotel. "She must have walked somewhere. No one saw her leave, and my boatmen are both out there."

"Her stuff's not at the dock?"

"There's nothing at the dock. What are you talking about?"

"I saw her at the dock right before I came in to breakfast. I thought she was in her room." Eve began to pace, hyper. "She had a picnic basket and her backpack. I helped her carry them to the dock. I don't believe this."

"That was twenty minutes ago. She could be anywhere by now."

Zachary studied Eve's ashen face as she walked unsteadily to the breakfast table and collapsed in a huddled mass.

"I could have stopped her," she said slowly.

"Well, it's obvious she stole it. Where's Tomason? I want her arrested." Rider strode away, looking for the policeman.

The telephone rang eleven times before the cook braved picking up the receiver. "Yes, who calls, please?" Breathless, he had talked on the phone only one time before. Concerned at the hubbub in the hotel, he did not at first hear the woman's voice as she responded. His room was at this minute being searched by Professor Rider, and he had been relegated to the kitchen to await the results. "Who calls?" he said as Allison tried again to ask for Zachary Cross. "Who?"

"Zachary Cross," she repeated urgently. "He's one of the guests in Tom Rider's group."

Captain Tomason stuck his head into the kitchen and distracted him further by pointing at the telephone, indicating his wish to use it.

"Yes. Tom Rider. Yes," said the agitated young cook.

"I wish to speak with Zachary Cross!"

"I am sorry, miss. The police are here and a big search is going on. I must hang up now. "

"Wait," she said frantically. "Do you know Mr. Cross?"

"Yes, miss. "

"Tell him 'I am leaving as planned.' Do you understand? 'I am leaving as planned.' It's important that you tell him."

Tomason was becoming impatient.

"I must hang up now." The frightened cook severed the connection, and a dial tone buzzed from the receiver.

At the charter office, Allison frantically redialed the number. It signaled busy. The pilot, middle-aged and mile-weary from ferrying tourists who wished to avoid a four-hour drive to Belize City, stood in anticipation of departure. Four other passengers, two couples, stood with him.

"We must leave now. If you wish, you can travel another time," he said determinedly, "but I must know if you are coming this morning."

She was down here to make decisions; she closed her eyes and made a huge one. "I'm coming."

Holding the covered basket with the sleeping baby, she followed the pilot to a battered pickup truck that served as the charter's free airport service, and got carefully into in the front seat. When the two young couples had climbed into the back, the truck swung slowly onto the dirt road to the airstrip.

At the hotel, Tomason took up the receiver and said to the shaken cook, "You are free to return to your room, thank you. I am sorry for any inconvenience."

The cook stepped outside. Zachary Cross was at the bottom of the stairway. "Mr. Cross," he called with importance, and crossed the sand to intercept the tall volunteer. "You have a call just now."

"Where?" His heart leaped violently—it had to be her. He walked the cook around the side of the hotel where they would not be overheard.

"She is hung up now, but she say 'Tell Zachary Cross I am leaving as planned,'" the man repeated carefully. "She say it twice. 'I am leaving as planned.' You understand?"

He did. She was taking the charter. His watch read ten to seven. The flight left at seven-thirty. Just maybe, if he didn't have to spend twenty minutes in explanation to Tomason, he could catch her. "Do you know where the charter flight takes off? The airstrip?"

"Yes." The cook's eyes were wide with curiosity.

"How fast can I get there?"

"To drive on the main street, maybe . . . ten minutes."

"And how far to the main street?" He reached into his pocket for money.

"It is a walk of perhaps ten minutes, maybe more."

"Show me." He handed the cook a ten-dollar bill. The man's eyes danced with the pleasure of the mysteriously lucrative game, and he shed his apron in one smooth motion.

"This way is fastest," he said, and pulled aside the sagging picket fence at the side of the hotel. Within two minutes they were loping through sandy backyards, scattering chickens and exciting frenzied mongrels in their wake.

At the main street the young man flagged a farm truck, and another ten-dollar bill from Zachary convinced the driver to turn around and speed in the opposite direction. With the cook urging the driver on, the man unfortunately misjudged the turn onto the dirt road to the airstrip and had to disentangle his vehicle from a local fence.

A few minutes later the proud driver came to a sliding stop in loose gravel that served as a parking lot for the airfield, and the three men watched the single engine plane clear the treetops and gain altitude until it was a speck in the clear morning sky, heading north. Contemplating the horizon, Zachary declined a ride back to the Whale. It would buy her an hour. So be it.

Jacob Tomason was duly irate. "Where have you been, Mr. Cross! I have reported you missing, also."

Pretense was pointless, so he told him. "The charter people confirmed she was on the flight. I made the reservation yesterday. She wanted to get somewhere to have a doctor look at the baby. After we talked to you last night, I forgot about it. We were prepared to stay over a couple of days until things were straightened out."

"Apparently she changed her mind," the captain said

curtly. He checked his watch. "I'll contact airport security and have her detained there."

"Captain . . ."

"Do not push me further, Detective Cross. At the moment, I'm giving strong thought to arresting you." The captain turned on his heel and sought the phone.

Zachary followed him into the kitchen and waited while he called his superior officer. Waiting for the prefect captain to come on the line, Tomason beckoned him to have a seat. "I think perhaps it is time you told me what you know of this woman and why she is determined to have this child."

Allison looked down from her window seat in the single-engine plane with Cesar Charters painted with abandon on its fuselage and refused to think about the unbroken, lumpy green carpet of jungle treetops. She released white knuckles from the arm of her seat long enough to check again on the inert baby in the hamper between her feet. He'd been sleeping two and a half to three hours at a stretch, and she crossed her fingers that the pattern would continue. She had a bottle at the ready, just in case.

Watching the carpet slide south beneath the plane, her silent voice was hoarse with agitation. *You're breaking the law! If you're arrested, they'll take the baby for sure. There'll be no chance to keep him unless you get a lawyer who can handle the authorities down here.* She dug through her purse and counted two hundred dollars. The charter fee was fifty. She would need more.

Zachary wasn't here; she would have to manage on her own until she could reach him. How? Her confidence lunged downward until she thought of Jake. Jake could wire money! The first thing to do was call Jake.

A measure of calm returned; she looked again out the window. The nubby green carpet now had an edging of turquoise-and-cobalt ocean waves breaking against a narrow strip of sandy coast in long, thin white lines of lace. The water moved out of sight, and the single engine roared and revved in the occasional cloud as they came lower and lower over the forest canopy, then the jumbled pattern of housed civilization, rusting brown tin roofs of factories and businesses, mixed with undisciplined streets and greens of individual trees and motley colors of homes.

Foremost was getting back to the United States, mother country, home and safety. Chicago. Miami, even. She would wait for Zachary in Miami. The decision helped relieve her guilt at leaving the Whale without telling him. She would call him from the airport to let him know.

If she could get to Miami, Jake could wire the money to a hotel there. In Miami she could find not just a doctor, but a proper pediatrician. And the law firm in New York that had counseled her during the trial could surely help her pursue her right to Adam. There was no purpose in staying here and taking the chance of losing him. If she could get the baby on a Miami flight, she would go.

Cesar jockeyed the light plane into a quick, bumpy landing and a long, rolling stop, then buzzed off the landing strip onto the macadam in front of the airport entrance. Cushioned in his hamper, Adam stirred as the single engine was switched off into deafened quiet.

Inside the airport, Allison felt more confident in the semifamiliar setting. The Eastern ticket window was still closed, but the flight to Miami was listed at ten-thirty, and several passengers were already in line. Adam focused on her face and stopped fussing the moment she picked him up. She held him with one arm and searched the backpack for a diaper, beaming as he adjusted his focus to the motions of her face. "Good morning, Adam. Hello there."

Mid-diaper, she stopped briefly to laugh out loud. She'd never used the highly pitched, soft voice she heard coming out of her mouth to anyone in her life. Had always thought it an affectation that adults used to talk down to small children. Now she recognized it as vocal communication with a being who could comprehend only on a hearing level that she was safe and to be trusted. The baby responded with absolute, unwaveringly wide-eyed attention, and she opened her heart to give back an equal, unsparing message—that of absolute love, of a purity she'd never experienced. A bond that would not break. Reassured, Adam resumed his nap.

She saw the Eastern agent open his window and forced herself to function. Resentfully returning to the real world of tickets and passports and departure requirements, and policemen who wanted custody, she returned the sleeping baby to the hamper and waited in line, wired with apprehension, for the next half hour.

"I don't have a reservation this morning, I'm sorry. I didn't have time to call." That was the understatement of the week. "Will I need a ticket for the baby?" If it was going to happen, it would start here.

At the other end of the building, Leon Allesandro, the airport security agent on duty, answered the phone call from Captain Tomason. He printed the name *Allison Shreve* on his notepad. Underneath he made the notations:

BLOND MAYAN INFANT STOLEN ARTIFACT

"Yes sir. Not to be permitted to leave the country. I'll notify all U. S.-bound flights immediately. We'll find her, Captain."

The Eastern agent looked his dismay, but shook his head in answer to her question about a second ticket. "Not for children under three. The fact is, our Miami flight's been cancelled. Equipment problems. At the moment, I can't even get you on Aero-Mexico to Houston." His fingers popped the computer keys as he spoke. The phone rang at his elbow.

"I can confirm you on our afternoon flight to Houston."

The phone buzzed again. This time he picked it up. "Eastern, Hicks here." Then, after a moment: "Ten-thirty's been cancelled, Leon. Passengers were moved onto Aero-Mexico to Houston a half hour ago." He hung up the phone.

"This afternoon?" Disappointment pulsed through her body, drowning relief that Adam would not have to be identified. "Surely there's something. I have to get my baby to Chicago as soon as possible." Adam whimpered on cue. She would have to feed him soon.

The agent's fingers tocked the keys, searching. He scanned the computer screen and tried again. "To get to Chicago . . ." He cleared the screen and pursed his lips. "Let me try this."

His fingers clicked away as passengers queued impatiently in a lengthening line behind her. "I show space on TACA to Mexico City. As long as you're on interconnecting flights, you can travel on your passport. You could pick up a connection from there." Three more people got in line. "But you're better off taking our afternoon flight to Houston and connecting on to Chicago. I can check you in right now and hold the seats and you won't have to travel through Mexico."

"Great. Thank you. What time does it leave?"

"Boards at one-thirty. You're already checked in. Be here a half hour early to go through customs."

She heaved a major sigh of relief and, boarding passes in hand, sought to lower her visibility. Closing herself into an empty, old-fashioned phone booth next to the bar, she gave the impatient baby a bottle.

Refusing to allow Captain Tomason, Miami, or Zachary Cross into her thoughts, she concentrated on the moment at hand, fully engrossed in the incredible, miniature person limp and trusting in her arms. She smiled into his eyes, sending love and reassurance until he closed them in contentment and emptied the bottle. When he was full at last, she placed him in the hamper and checked her watch. Five after ten. First she would call Jake, putting off the call to the Whale to tell Zachary she wouldn't be meeting him in Miami.

She forced her mind away from the emotional jolt of guilt and a fervent wish to see him, and pushed her thoughts to Jake.

The bartender, on his way to his shift at the bar, smiled in recognition as he passed the booth. "Hello, miss. I am happy to see you again."

"Mario. I'm happy to see you, too," she said with relief. The telephone demanded more local coins than she had. "I want to call Chicago and I need some change."

"I would be happy to do this for you, miss," Mario offered gallantly. Several minutes later he had managed a connection on a static-filled line and handed her the telephone.

Allison listened to the ringing phone with resignation. At the last moment Jake's gruff words came cutting through the line.

"Are you all right? What's wrong? Where are you?"

At the sound of his familiar, loving voice, she lost control. She'd forgotten how good it was to have him in her life, strong and protecting, rock steady and dependable as the sun. Oh, God, how was she going to explain all this to Jake?

"I'm fine," she sobbed, aware that she was doing a grand job of convincing him otherwise and unable to stop the spillover of tearful relief. "I know I don't sound it, but I'm great. It's just so good to hear you. Wait a minute." She abandoned the phone long enough to grab a napkin off the bar to blow her nose.

Jake's voice was shouting out of the receiver when she picked it up again, "Talk to me, damn it! How in the hell can I—"

Back under control, she broke in. "I swear I'm fine. I'm still in Belize, but I have a flight out this afternoon."

"What the hell is going on? Why are you coming back early?"

She was thrilled to ascertain that even with his concern pouring soothing calm on her spirit, her core of strength hadn't crumbled. She felt more like her old self than she had in months. Years. How to convince him—she knew she didn't have time to tell him the entire story. "I swear on Mom there's nothing wrong. Trust me."

Jake's voice relaxed a bit, but she knew he hadn't bought the entire package just yet. She would tell him about Adam, but not about Zachary Cross. Not yet. Then she giggled. For the first time her life, she was going to shock Jake Alston speechless. "I have a baby."

Jake didn't disappoint her. There was a monumental silence on his end of the scratchy line. "A what?"

"A baby." She rushed through the blank space in the line. "Don't make me go through the whole story. Just please listen. He's a beautiful three-week-old baby and he's mine. I'll tell you how and why when I see you. The problem is I can't prove I have the right to him, and the police are trying to take him away from me."

"The police? You call this nothing wrong!"

"Jake, listen. I need your help. The woman who gave him to me is dead. I can't prove I have a right to him."

There was a moderate pause on the other end of the line, then his steady voice. "What can I do? What do you need?"

"If I can get to Chicago, will you meet me at immigration?"

"Of course. What else? What flight are you on?"

"Eastern. This afternoon. I don't know the number, but—"

"This afternoon? You'll never make it. If the police contact airport security, you'll be arrested. Why don't you just—"

"No! If I give him up, I might never get him back."

"What's the next flight out?"

"A Taca flight to Mexico City. Boards in ten minutes."

"Get on it. If they think you're on the flight this afternoon, you might be able to board. I'll get you on a connecting flight here to Chicago."

She conceded to superior strength, happy to have the burden of decision leave her mind.

"If the police have contacted airport security, you may be stopped from boarding," he continued. "If that happens, have someone contact me. I'll take care of everything." The vague line still held Jake's voice. "Lovely? Are you still on?"

"I'm here." Her stomach was doing a slow roll.

"Listen, I love you. I won't let anything happen to you, you know that, don't you?"

"Yes." The announcement for the Mexico City flight made it all but impossible to hear, but she held on to the strength in his voice.

"I'll call you as soon as I land. I love you, too."

She broke the connection, relieved and terrified in the same instant. Five minutes later, minus her original ticket and ninety-two dollars, she held confirmed space to Mexico City and a connecting flight to Chicago for "A. Shreve and infant"—the last in line for the flight.

She glanced back at the bar, waved to Mario, and denied a desperate need to plunge into one of the phone booths long enough to dial the Beached Whale, hear his voice, explain her decisions. Ill-prepared for the sense of loss, she longed to talk with him, connect with his strength. Talking to Jake had solved most of the problems, but not all. Not about Zachary Cross.

She squared her shoulders and brought her waffling under control. She'd already called for help. It was up to her to keep her end of the bargain. She carefully maneuvered the baby's hamper toward immigration and the waiting exit gate. If she was to be arrested, it would happen soon. She shut down her thoughts and forced her feet to carry her forward.

Captain Tomason replaced the receiver and faced a defiant Zachary Cross. "I am sorry, Mr. Cross. Despite your explanation, there has been no official report of the things you state. You know and I know this must now be investigated. If it is as you say, she will be free to leave as soon as these things can be proved. As a police officer, you know the call to airport security was a necessary precaution."

"I understand. Now that you've taken your precaution, will you call the police in Guatemala and see if they've identified that body? Perez said he was a local drug dealer. It shouldn't take five minutes to identify him." If she was arrested, he needed to be there to take care of her. In order to do that, he'd have to be on the charter from the Reyes Hotel an hour from now.

The telephone rang and Tomason answered, listened at great length, and wrote on a pad of paper in silence. Zachary paced in frustration until Tomason replaced the receiver.

"The authorities in Guatemala have identified the body. You were correct, his name is Paulo Metan, a thief and drug dealer in San Ruiz. Killed by a blow to the head consistent with your story of the jaguar. His mother prefers to believe he drowned and does not wish an investigation. So far as Guatemala is concerned, the matter is closed."

Before he could speak, the telephone rang again. Tomason answered, listened briefly, and hung up. "That was airport security. The flight to Miami was cancelled and she is confirmed on a flight to Houston at one-thirty."

None of which told him the only thing he wanted to know: that she and the baby were safe. He chafed at having no authority. "What about Jorgé K'ayum? He could be gone for weeks. Where's Yaxchilán? Will you fly in there and talk with him?"

"It's a ruin, not a city. I don't know how long it will take him to get there. Even if I could drive to these ruins, there is no reason to assume he is also driving, or that he would be there by the time I arrived. I'm afraid you'll simply have to wait for his return. Even if the situation with the baby were settled, which it is not, there is still the matter of the missing artifact."

Zachary stopped pacing to face the captain. "You've

searched every room and everyone here and you haven't found it. What happens if Rider doesn't find it in his staff's hotel, then what?"

"Then I shall have to conclude that it is possible Miss Shreve has taken it."

"Am I a suspect?"

"No, I think not."

"Since the police in Guatemala aren't pursuing the death of Paulo Metan, then you don't need me as a witness."

"That is so." Tomason could see where it was going. "You are, however, considered a witness to the death of Luisita Chun."

"She died in Guatemala. Isn't that a matter for the Guatemalan authorities?" Zachary sped up his end of the conversation, determined to make the charter come hell or high water.

"Unless she was a citizen of Belize, that is so."

"You already have my statement that K'ayum told Miss Shreve in my presence he was granting her the right to take the baby."

"Correct."

"So, unless you have a specific reason to detain me, am I free to return to the United States?"

The captain sighed. "Do you know where she is?"

"I wish to hell I did," he answered fervently. "You have no idea . . ." He stood to leave and offered his hand.

Tomason shook his outstretched hand. "It is obvious you care for her very much. I hope this does not affect your good judgment. I will have her arrested if she does not surrender the child, and if she has taken the artifact, I will have her prosecuted."

Eve stepped quietly into the kitchen; Tom Rider, rigid with rage, stood beside her.

"She didn't take it. I did," she said uncomfortably.

Captain Tomason looked past Zachary to study the young girl, pale and tense with apprehension. "Please sit down, miss. You have much to explain."

"She says she doesn't have it," spat the furious Rider. "She gave it to the conveniently missing Allison Shreve." He was beside himself.

Tomason gestured with his open hand to quiet Rider's outburst and questioned the miserable girl. "Tell me about this, please."

Eve Kelsey was both defiant and distraught. "I knew he had it. I knew he wouldn't leave it in a safe. He always does this—hides the best things we find in his room and works on them at night. He did it last year . . . I switched the boxes this morning while he was drinking coffee."

Zachary looked at his watch. Ten-forty. The charter out of the Reyes Hotel left at eleven-thirty. It was going to be tight.

"Kindly get to the point, miss," urged Tomason.

"It was a joke," she mumbled. "It wasn't supposed to be her. I was going to put it in his room." She looked haltingly at Zachary, who stared at her in surprise. "I ran into her on the steps and I decided it didn't matter, one of them was just as good as the other."

"Wait a minute. You took the thing to put in my room and gave it to her instead?" He grabbed her wrist. "Bullshit! She wouldn't take it. She knows how valuable something like that is. Something smells, lady. Try again."

"Mr. Cross. Please."

He restrained his temper and let go of her arm.

"She doesn't know she has it."

"Oh, come on, Eve," said Rider. "You told me you gave it to her. Make up your mind."

"I thought she was going to the dock. I carried her pack down the stairs for her and put it in one of the outside pockets. She didn't see me do it. I didn't know she was leaving. I thought she'd be going to the cay with the rest of us and it would be found in her things. It was packed in a box. I wouldn't risk damaging something so valuable."

Rider nearly slapped her. "Well, what in the hell do you call this! Some ditsy broad with fifty thousand dollars' worth of pre-Colombian art in her backpack—doesn't know it's there? She'll probably break the damned thing in a thousand—" He stopped abruptly to field a menacing move from Zachary. "What?"

"The 'ditsy broad' busted her ass down here to help you find this kind of stuff and you were the jerk that didn't put it in a safe place. If it gets broken, the 'ditsy broad' isn't going to be responsible!" Zachary found a place to park some of his rage by shouting in Tom Rider's face.

"You're right. I'm sorry. Calling her names was completely uncalled for. I am culpable and there's nowhere else to put the blame. Except you." Rider turned to Eve. "You're fired. You have exactly one-half hour to get your things and get out or I'll have you arrested for theft."

Eve stalked from the room and bolted in tears across the yard toward her hotel. Rider paced in a fury. "Maybe she'll find it. With any luck, she'll find it before it gets damaged too badly. God, I hope so."

"I'm out of here."

Tomason stopped Zachary's rapid progress toward the door. "I hope you can locate her," he said quietly, handing him a piece of paper. "Before she tries to leave the country with such a thing. Authorities may not question a woman with a child, but if they search her luggage, they will surely suspect something so valuable should not be in her possession."

"Are you calling off the dogs?"

"No. But this is my phone number. I will verify she has not stolen the artifact, but she will not be permitted to leave the country with it."

"What about the baby?"

"Perhaps . . . that's a matter for Guatemala." Captain Tomason shook his hand again.

"Thanks."

He knocked on Woodie's door to say good-bye. He'd packed in record time, and Nathaniel was standing by at the dock. No answer. He looked inside. On the bunk where he'd kissed her the previous night, a corner visible in a tangle of socks and T-shirts, was Allison's journal. Unable to leave it and feeling like a thief, he stuffed it into his bag and, in an equally guilty afterthought, grabbed the two cartridges of film lying among the abandoned clothing.

He extracted the card from the turquoise foil and reread the message from Jake, refusing to acknowledge the creepy feeling trying to take hold in him. She was still here and he was still here, and "All my love, Jake" was somewhere in Chicago. What was with this guy? He obviously loved her—what was the problem? And how would "All my love, Jake" react to Adam Zachary Chun?

Now was not the time to lose by default. Energized, he grabbed his duffel and headed for the dock. With only one passenger in his boat, Nathaniel had promised to deliver him at the airfield in twenty minutes. In the hallway he met Woodie coming out of Colonel Sharp's room and kissed her good-bye on the run. "Will you see her luggage gets to Chicago? I'll love you for it," he called over his shoulder.

"Consider it done. You just find her," she called back. "And see she doesn't lose that child!" She heard his Reeboks pounding down the stairs toward the dock. "Two to one he catches her," she said to Bill Sharp as she stepped back inside the room.

When Zachary appeared at the top of the stairs, Nathaniel started the engine. At the dock he tossed in his duffel and scrambled aboard. "You said twenty minutes," he said tersely. "Fifteen would be better."

"We'll see if we can set a new record." The boatman grinned. He pushed against the dock, allowed the boat to drift backward until it was in deeper water, then pressed the throttle for full power, and the motor roared the boat into a tight horseshoe turn, lifting the nose out of the water. They raced for Mango Creek, twisting and turning through the cays.

The boatman's estimate was close. Eighteen minutes later he cut the engine and, in perfect coordination with the boat's momentum, allowed it to drift against the dock at Mango Creek. He and Zachary, at opposite ends of the boat, held contact with the dock to a small bump from the wake.

"You can captain for me anytime." Zachary pumped the grinning man's hand. "Damn fine job. Here's twenty to cover the extra gas." He pulled himself onto the dock and sprinted up the road toward the Reyes Hotel.

He caught the pilot, Cesar Cotura, leaving the hotel lobby and secured a space on board. Cesar could add nothing to what he already knew. She'd taken the seven-thirty charter and had asked him about the flight to Miami; she'd been carrying a large basket but hadn't told him she was traveling with a child.

"She was most careful with the basket," recalled the pilot.

When Zachary identified himself as a police officer, Cesar conceded it was possible to shorten the flight time to forty-five minutes. Ten minutes later they were high over the treetops, headed north in the single-engine plane.

Staring down at the nubby jungle, he realized, even if he caught up with her, he hadn't the faintest idea if their friendship would survive. If it did, it was going to take work. Plain, old-fashioned hard work.

But, then, life was hard work. If you were gonna do it, you might as well go for what you wanted. And she was definitely what he wanted.

Finally it was her turn. Exhaling a huge sigh of relief, Allison faked confidence and tossed her pack onto the examination table, opened the hamper to the security agent. The woman slipped her hand into the blue shawl lining under the baby, then passed him through. She began sorting through the backpack as Allison held her breath and fingered her mother's wedding band for luck that no one would ask why an obviously Mayan baby was in the care of a tall, blond American woman.

Skin too tight for her body, she watched the airport security agent search her backpack. Her passport was burning a hole in her sweaty palm. She shifted the blue document and their boarding pass to her other hand and wiped the dampness on her pant leg. It was eleven forty-five. The flight was getting off late.

The security woman gruffly sorted through the cans of formula and rummaged among diapers, poorly packed clothing, and the empty baby bottle. "¿*Niño o niña*?" she asked suddenly, taking Allison by surprise, making her jump.

"Uh, *niño*," she answered. She lifted the basket. "Three weeks ago." Unconsciously her eyes searched the room behind her for his craggy face, knowing full well it could not be possible to see him there.

"Oh," said the agent, uninterested, and rezipped her pack. She opened the outside pocket pouch and held up a small cardboard box with a questioning look. "¿*Esta es* . . . ?"

Allison was caught short. A box? Where on earth had it come from? She racked her memory for a few seconds and shook her head in genuine innocence. The agent opened the flap, pulled cotton batting aside, and peered into the interior. Allison leaned forward and caught sight of the rough side of some sort of clay item. "Oh, that. That's a souvenir," she ventured, forcing herself to speak in a bored professional tone. Something of Woodie's?

Her breath halted as she realized what it was. The ocarina! Why was it in her pack? Tom Rider was supposed to have taken it to Belize City four days ago. "Please be careful," came out of frozen lips and a suddenly dry mouth. "It's pretty fragile." They would think she was smuggling it out of the country. She forced a pleasant look onto her rigid face. "It's supposed to be a whistle, I think."

The agent repacked the cotton, put it back in the pouch, and pushed the pack roughly behind her on the examination table—approved. Allison walked on eggshells through the electronic gate and picked up the pack and the baby's basket without allowing her mind to think. Unable to feel any part of her body except screaming nerve endings, she moved in appalled silence to the immigration booth, flanked by green-uniformed security agents, and watched in disbelief as the precious Exit stamp was pressured against one of the pages. An aeon later she passed through the exit gate and handed the TACA agent her boarding pass.

Through the heat of the shimmering tarmac, up the shaky metal stairway to the welcome maw of the plane, she tried to get the numb feeling out of her brain. A stewardess directed her to a bulkhead seat with space for the hamper at her feet, and she managed to put the backpack into the overhead compartment. She sat down trembling, moving Adam's basket onto her lap. Fear settled in her stomach with all the subtlety of an iron anvil. Traveling with an undocumented child was bad enough, but no customs agent on the planet would accept 'I don't know' as an explanation for carrying contraband.

After an interminable wait, she watched from a remote corner of her mind as the flight attendants secured the aircraft doors; the TACA captain moved the 727 into take-off position. The seat next to her was empty, so she buckled the seat belt around the hamper for takeoff. God in heaven, what to do? Zachary . . .

Cesar brought the small plane rolling to a stop on the tarmac and waited for the late TACA flight to move onto the airstrip for takeoff before pulling forward to allow his passengers to disembark.

Zachary was first off the plane. It was too much to hope she'd still be in the airport, but he allowed it anyway. He jerked his duffel out of the luggage bay and stuffed payment for the flight into Cesar's hands, yelling his thanks over the revving TACA engines. He hustled toward the airport, paused at the door long enough to watch the lumbering takeoff of the outgoing 727, and noted the TACA insignia with an odd feeling of loss. Christ, he wished he were out of here, too. With her and the baby, and it didn't really matter where. Resigned, he turned to go inside.

He found the airport security agent with little difficulty, coming out of the immigration office, and identified himself. The agent would confirm only that Allison Shreve had not as yet been arrested. "I assure you, Detective Cross, it will not be possible for her to leave Belize through this airport without being apprehended," he said with pride. "As I informed Captain Tomason earlier, she is confirmed on the flight this afternoon. I've just alerted Immigration."

"I'm working with Captain Tomason on this," Zachary lied, "and I'd appreciate it if you'd keep me informed. I'll be here in the airport until further notice." The security officer nodded and disappeared into his office.

He settled at the bar to wait. "Hey, Mario," he called. "Give me a beer."

Mario slid a sweating bottle of beer in front of him.

"How's it going?" he asked absently. The whole thing was a mess.

"Very good. You are leaving also?"

It took a moment for the question to penetrate. "Who else is leaving?"

"The blond lady was here, but she is gone now."

"Did you talk to her?"

"Yes. I give her change for the telephone, and I help her to call long distance," he said happily. He picked up his newspaper and flipped the pages. "She call, uh, Chicago. She asked for somebody name Jake. He say come to Mexico City."

"Mexico City? Are you sure? You heard the conversation?" He could see the man's uncertainty about admitting such a thing and produced his shield. "It's important, Mario. She could be in a hell of a lot of trouble if I don't reach her. Tell me what you heard. Please."

"Okay. But I don't hear it all. She say to this Jake something about the police. And how she need help with immigration. Then she say okay, she will call him when she gets to Mexico City. And she loves him. That's all I heard."

At the Eastern counter, he collared the agent who was on her way to lunch. Two minutes later the young woman was giving her full cooperation to Detective Cross.

"The TACA agent says she got on the flight that just left for Mexico City. She was going to connect from there."

"Mexico City?" On the goddamned plane he had watched take off!

"Yes, sir, and we show her holding confirmed space on an American connection to Chicago departing at three o'clock." Computers. Miracles of modern life.

Airport security was bound to discover her destination. "How can I get to Chicago tonight?"

"We have a flight to Houston this afternoon, there's a connection—"

He tossed her a ticket and his credit card. "Get me on it."

Jake Alston couldn't explain the child and the stolen whatever. Ocarina. Zachary Cross, the tired cop from Miami, was the only one who could do that. With his help, maybe she'd get home without being arrested. He was probably being a major fool into the bargain, but he didn't care. Even if it turned out she didn't need him, he had to see her again before "All my love, Jake" was back in the picture.

On board the TACA flight, Allison settled down, her panic subsiding for the moment as she took solace in the sleeping baby. Adam slumbered quietly in his basket, safe and warm under the blue cotton shawl. Eventually she forced herself to project ahead. First things first: she'd locate her new gate and check in, then call Zachary and decide what to do about the ocarina.

Having a course of action settled her further, and she turned her mind to the artifact. She retraced the morning. Captain Tomason's arrival, her panicked decision to leave. Then she realized it had been Eve. Eve, who had insisted on carrying the pack. Eve, with her back turned too long at the dock. Eve, who'd pushed her to strike back at the stinging, jealous accusations about Zachary. Eve had wanted her to be accused of taking the ocarina. Well, she'd succeeded beyond anything she could have planned. Allison smiled at the irony of it— Eve couldn't possibly have known she was leaving; her reaction must have been worth an admission price.

Assuming she could get it home safely, returning it to Professor Rider would be a relatively simple matter. Unless it were damaged. That thought drove her to pull the backpack out of the overhead and take it to the lavatory. Afraid to look, she first made herself wash Adam's bottle and fill it with one of the remaining cans of milk. He was sleeping soundly. Then, calmer and unable to stall any longer, she retrieved the box with trembling hands; it was, she discovered with massive relief, whole and undisturbed in the sturdy carton.

With great care she allowed herself to examine the delicate artifact and knew she would never hold such an item in her hands again in all her life.

She gingerly placed a finger over one of the stops and blew softly into the instrument. Incredibly, it produced a clear, wailing flutelike note, which changed higher when she covered both stops. Clearly of museum quality, it would have to be fully protected against damage.

She pulled Luisita's purse from the pack and decided to put the ocarina inside. Its box fit almost precisely into the bottom. As she started to pad the purse with a diaper, she noticed that one side of the cheap acetate lining was flat against the outside plastic, but the other was bulkier.

Looking closer, she discovered a fine line of stitches along the enclosure and tugged at the fabric. The stitching gave way. Inside was the unmistakable green of U.S. currency. Luisita's stolen money. Only a stroke of pure inadvertent luck had kept the purse with her. Or—a shiver rippled its way up her spine—Luisita's gods. She counted four hundred eighty dollars. There was also a travel permit issued to Sara Luisita Chun.

She put the money back inside the lining, then packed the ocarina carefully into the purse, padding the extra space with diapers. Replacing it in the backpack with the rest of her clothing, she hurried to her seat. No sooner had she pushed the pack into the overhead than Adam woke with an unaccustomed wail. She jumped to see what was wrong. Taking him from the basket, she realized that the immediate solution was a dry diaper. He quieted under her touch as she laid him on the seat; she put his bottle on the armrest.

"Let me help you, my dear." The aristocratic voice came from a well-dressed, gray-haired lady across the aisle. She moved gracefully in her beige Chanel traveling suit to the adjacent seat with a tinkling of charm bracelets and necklaces, the unmistakable sound of high-karat gold against gold. Aromatic with abundant Arpàge, she was soon cooing and admiring the wide-awake Adam.

"I'm a new grandmother," said Freda St. John, with boundless enthusiasm and the unmussed elegance of older wealth. "I do hope you won't mind if I practice a bit on this adorable infant. I'm on my way to see my daughter and my new grandson."

"I'm a new mother myself," said Allison, feeling scruffy and rumpled next to Freda, who handed her the formula. Adam's eyes fixed on the bottle and he was soon pulling handily on the nipple.

"Well, he certainly looks like his father," said Freda, taking in Allison's wedding band and appraising her pale skin and hazel eyes. "He's going to be a handsome young man, that's certain."

Allison said nothing. Adam settled into mesmerized contentment, emptying the bottle. Freda introduced herself and chatted on about her trip with the cheery enthusiasm of the bored and the lonely. "My daughter lives in Tijuana," she said. "She and her husband moved there after their marriage. The baby was born yesterday. Do you know anything about Tijuana, my dear? I have reservations at the Hotel Caesar. It's supposed to be the very best in the city."

Allison shook her head and tried to tune out the monologue without appearing rude.

"Living in Mexico has its advantages—certainly the peso is so cheap that one can live quite well on very little income, American dollars, that is. Of course, there's so much corruption. My daughter tells me that they have something called 'mordita.' Everyone does it. She hasn't paid a speeding fine or a parking ticket since they've been here. Of course, being so close to San Diego, she buys everything she needs there—clothing, shoes, everything she can't get in Mexico, simply drives across the border with it."

The endless conversation ground into a headache, making it impossible for Allison to concentrate on anything else. She saw with relief the stewardesses coming down either aisle with food carts, and Freda excused herself to prepare for the meal.

"I'll see you later, dear," she chirped, and clinked and tinkled back across the aisle.

Adam finished his bottle and collapsed into sleep; Allison collapsed into relief for some quiet time to think. They would be landing in a little over an hour.

Waiting for the flight, Zachary reordered his thoughts. Truly there was no alternative at this point. No way in hell he could give it up now. He'd come too far and cared too much not to play it out. He thought of the look of terror on her face when he'd asked her to cross the river with the baby—and she'd done it without question. Yeah, this one had to play out. In Chicago, Jake or no, he'd demand the time he needed to talk with her, reason with her, convince her he could help her with the baby. No more important conversations that stopped in the middle.

His thoughts went to Jerry. If he'd kept his temper, talked it out, maybe Jerry would still be in his life. He could have helped his brother solve his drug problem. A small part of his mind paused to take note that somewhere inside, he'd known his brother had been on drugs. He'd had enough distance now to know it was no longer about the unfinished fight with Jerry; he was furious for not fighting about what was important. For not being willing to take the hard line with his brother, to nail him to the wall and make him admit his addiction. Because he'd loved him, because he hadn't wanted to risk alienating the last member of his family, it had cost him his brother.

Confronting him might have started the process, created the crisis, forced the issue. Absolutely, in the final analysis, it would have been up to Jerry to clean up his own act. But he'd done him no favors by leaving it alone until it was too late. And he would have to live with it the rest of his life on that basis. But it was not too late for her.

He dozed fitfully, needing to see her, needing to know she and the baby were safe and well. No more unfinished business. He was on the verge of sleep, drifting downward, kissing her soft lips that first time in the cave with the rain rustling outside, in the nest of red-and-black blankets where he'd spent the night next to her body . . . The call for Eastern's flight to Houston broke into his reverie, and he got in line for boarding.

The stewardesses passed out the customs and immigration forms for their arrival in Mexico City, and Allison forced herself away from the anticipation of talking with Zachary, long enough to concentrate on providing the requested information.

Freda soon caught up with her and chatted the length of the passageway to the immigration booths, stood behind her as she chose a smiling, middle-aged immigration officer. When it was her turn, she placed Adam's hamper out of sight on the floor next to the turnstile.

"May I see your passport, please?"

She handed him the blue folder that identified her to the world and summoned a professional attitude of patient confidence.

"I see you are not planning to visit this country," he said, examining the tourist document.

"No, I have a connecting flight to Chicago this afternoon." She handed him her plane ticket.

He examined the ticket and started to hand it back to her, then reread the name. "This says you are traveling with an infant."

"Yes. My baby." Nervous, she had answered too quickly.

He shuffled through the passport. "You have no documents for the child?"

"He's only three weeks old."

The man studied the date stamps. "You were in Belize for nine days?"

"Yes." Still too quickly. Calm down.

"You had no documents to take the child into Belize?"

"Due to his age, they weren't required," she bluffed.

The man's eyes searched her face and looked disapprovingly at her figure. A well-dressed American woman, obsessed with being thin. "I must have documents for this child," he said blandly.

"Well, I don't have documents for this child, and I have to catch a flight to Chicago," she insisted, not certain what else to do. If it ended here, it ended here. She had little to lose.

"You must come with me," he informed her, and closed his station.

Freda leaned close from behind and whispered, "Mordita," in Allison's ear, then she and the passengers in line behind her sought other booths as quickly as possible.

Allison followed the agent through a maze of beige corridors and concrete walls, intent on keeping the beige from closing in about her.

"You must wait in here, please," said the smiling agent, and pointed to a chair in a small cubicle of an office. "I will return in a few minutes."

Allison paced the room until Adam stirred half an hour later, warm from the shawl. She gave him the rest of the formula and was somewhere between frantic and furious by the time the immigration agent returned with a second official. The baby was awake and alert in the basket.

The second man parroted the first. "It will be necessary to have documentation for the child."

"I don't have documentation." She decided to go for broke. "What I have is a flight to Chicago, and if you'll tell me how to arrange documentation, I'll be happy to do so."

At last, a smile.

Suddenly light bulbs went off in her brain. Mordita. That's what Freda had whispered. Not mordita. M*ordida*. The bite. They wanted money. She had been brought to a private office to arrange the transaction.

No way would she give them Luisita's money. Not one red cent. She brought the backpack to the desktop and pulled out her purse. Deliberately spilling it onto the desk, she counted out the cash. "I assume there's a fee," she said with a bitter smile. "I hope it's not more than fifty-eight dollars because, as you can see, that's all I have. And if I miss my flight, I just might have to discuss this with someone other than yourselves." The second man excused himself.

The immigration agent was irritated. Americans generally had more money when they traveled in Mexico. It had been his misfortune to select a poor one. He pocketed fifty of the dollars and gravely returned eight dollars to her. Then he quickly led the way back to the immigration booth, stamped her passport with a flourish, and handed it to her, impatient to open his booth to incoming travelers. She gave him a sardonic smile.

"How much will it cost me to get out of the country?" she said, unable to contain her fury at his blatant blackmail. "If it's more than eight dollars, I'll have to tell the next person to get the rest from you." At which point the official took back her passport and wrote "24 Hours Only" before returning it to her. Watching his petty revenge, she realized she could say nothing more without running a risk of serious trouble.

Inside Adam's basket was half a can of formula. Not quite believing that she was doing it, she placed it on top of the hamper. When she lifted the basket, it slid off and found its sticky mark: the milk splashed onto one of the man's highly polished shoes.

"Oh, my."

She escaped before she gave in to laughter. Served the little toad right.

When the customs agent encountered the diapers and cans of formula, he gave her pack a cursory examination, and she located the American terminal with fifteen minutes to spare. Gambling, she managed to combine the Belize area code from Information and the number for the Whale from memory. Her heart soared when she reached the nervous cook and asked for Zachary.

"He is not here, miss," replied the cook.

One eye on her watch, she said quickly, "Do you know where he is? Can I leave a message?"

"No, miss. He is gone. He and Miss Eve this morning."

"I see. When is he coming back?"

"Tom Rider says they are not coming back. They are gone. No meal tonight. They are gone, miss."

Zachary and Eve? She stared numbly at the second hand on her watch in its mindless cruise around the dial face. Why would he leave with Eve? She shook herself. There could be several reasons. Stop this! "Thank you," she managed, and slowly pressed the lever to disconnect the line. They had left together.

Barely enough time to get to the plane, she thought woodenly. Zachary and Eve. Eve? Why! It didn't make sense!

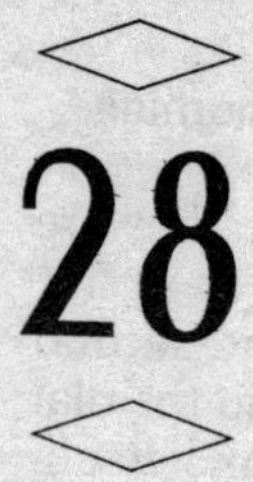

American flight 227 touched down on a perfect landing at O'Hare to passenger applause. Allison slipped into the backpack and gathered up the hamper. Outside air seeping into the jetway was cold and dry as she left the plane. She covered the baby with a shawl. Zachary and Eve. The thought had haunted her for the past hour, unceasing in its implication. Adam slept soundly, arms and legs sprawling.

The day of travel was beginning to take its toll, and she yearned for rest and an end to the tension sapping at her energy. It was difficult to think. Jake would be here. She'd have to keep it together until she connected with him. Then she could collapse and let Jake take over.

She conformed her watch to local time, 5:20, while she waited, shifting Adam's hamper back and forth between leaden arms, working her way toward customs and immigration into her own country. All about her passengers were laden with glitzy sombreros, papier-mâché piñatas, rugs, serapes, huge paper flowers— souvenir booty, Mexican kitsch.

She was tired and wanted an end to this. She would do what she had to do. If they questioned the citizenship of the child, at least she was in the United States, and if they took Adam, they damn well better be prepared to take her, too.

If they questioned her right to the baby, they would also search her pack, which would produce the ocarina, heavily padded and secreted deep in Luisita's purse. Jake was nearby. He'd be able to help her in the event the dominoes started falling. She made herself move forward as a woman and two teenagers were cleared to leave.

She was tenth in line. Adam began to fuss in the basket, waking early. He'd be hungry. Not now, she prayed; please, not now. She put her hand inside and stroked his cheek, and his little mouth made sucking motions as he quieted, eyes not fully open. She hadn't prepared a bottle, certain he'd sleep at least another hour, as he had in the past. She glanced behind her. To fall out of line now would put her back a hundred places.

The line moved forward with the steady progress of snaildom. She reached the long line of examination tables and rested Adam's basket gratefully on its top. Her foot ached from the prolonged standing; the thin skin over the cut was beginning to burn, and her back was rigid with tension.

The customs officer, young, zealous, was searching everything, questioning everyone as the baby renewed his fussy insistence. Two women down the line looked back past the man in front of her, with questioning, disapproving glances. Adam, with an uncharacteristic lack of cooperation, began to wail. Another couple was passed through the magic doors.

Desperate, Allison took the baby out of the basket and tried to entertain him, heavily aware of the contrast between his delicate coffee skin and striking Mayan features and her own pale skin and light hair. With her attention Adam quieted, and she crossed her fingers that he would stay calm five minutes more.

Sixth in line, she pushed the baby's basket forward toward the customs officer. Two young men, early twenties, were challenged, one after the other, by the officer. Reacting in anger and frustration, they shouted threats and curses, charging the officer with angry gestures. Security personnel scuffled with the men and escorted them forcibly elsewhere in the building. The customs officer was shaken. Adam set up a shrill, screeching wail.

She found herself trembling, upset by the near violence and tired to tears; her nerves were coming apart with the hungry baby's cries. Adam was inconsolable. The two women's previous disapproval melted into clucking sympathy and concern as the customs officer, now nervously twice as efficient, double-checked their items and asked for receipts on their purchases. Irritated, the women complied, one of them perversely taking forever to sift through her purse.

Having no idea how else to cope with the screeching baby, Allison laid him in the hamper, removed the backpack, and placed it on the table with the intent to feed him, period. If it cost her her place in line, so be it. The customs officer approved the two ladies' purchases and passed them through the glass doors.

Suddenly she knew what to do.

Calmly unbuttoning her blouse and unhooking her bra, as if she did this sort of thing every day, she picked up the screaming infant and thrust his head inside the blouse to her breast. It took Adam about three-quarters of a second to find her nipple, eagerly seek solace, and suckle lustily. The man ahead of her declared nothing, was quickly waved through the doors. It was her turn to face the grim officer.

"What is your citizenship?" he asked abruptly.

She fumbled the navy blue passport out of her purse with one hand. Adam pulled fiercely, seeking nonexistent milk, distracting her.

"What is your citizenship?" the officer demanded again.

"American," she responded, and finally managed to hand him the passport, flinching as Adam continued to bite her nipple. The officer finally opened the passport and studied her face.

"What are you declaring?" He put aside the passport and reached for the backpack.

The baby, she wanted to say. Some hysterical form of insanity was taking control. I'm declaring the baby. She blinked and made her mouth move. "Souvenirs . . . the basket, a shawl, uh . . ." Please God, should I tell him? He's going to find it anyway. "A clay sculpture." It was done. Her body was numb, and the baby's insistent pull at her breast receded into nonfeeling.

"Value?" The officer was scooping diapers aside and had located the plastic purse. "Where is it, please?"

"Inside the purse. It's extremely fragile."

"Value? Please, lady, I don't have all night. Value?"

"Uh, I don't know. Two hundred dollars."

The officer unwrapped the diapers from around the cardboard box and opened it to sniff inside with suspicion, obviously looking for drugs. "You have a receipt for this?"

"It was a gift." Boy, was it ever. Hysteria giggled and threatened to boil over the top. "From a woman I was staying with in Belize." Truth was truth.

The officer laid the ocarina aside in its box, next to her passport, and looked with pointed curiosity at the nursing baby as he brought out the cans of formula. One by one he inspected their labels and seams, shaking each one carefully for the liquid sound inside.

Adam chewed fitfully, unhappily; she could feel again, and the pain from her nipple was climbing in both directions from the middle of her back to the base of her brain and her spine. The officer examined every diaper, then reached again for the passport.

After an eternity of comparing her face to the photo, he asked, "Why is this document wet?"

I nearly drowned in a river in Guatemala while a woman was dying. She came close to hysterics and managed at the last instant to bite back the words and bring herself under control. "I dropped it in a bathtub," she said with a straight face.

He stamped the document at last and passed her through.

Awkwardly she closed the box on the ocarina, pushed it inside the purse and into the backpack with quivering fingers, and grabbed the strap to the pack.

Safely outside the double glass doors and around the corner, she collapsed onto a bench to detach the baby's mouth from her aching nipple and breathe again.

"You little cannibal!" she said as vast relief and adrenaline surged through her body. She refastened her bra and did up the buttons on the blouse. She'd done it. With no help from anyone, she'd done it. She hadn't crumbled. Exhilaration raced through her body. She was fourteen feet tall.

She quickly punctured a can and filled the empty bottle, vowing never, never, ever to be without it until the kid was eating pizza. "I may be your mommy, but that's the last time we play that game," she admonished him as he revved up for a new assault on her ears. She gave him the bottle and he was happy at last, black button eyes unyielding.

Jake parked his Mercedes in a No Parking zone, grabbed Allison's honey-gold cashmere wrap and a baby blanket he and Jesse'd picked up that afternoon for the baby, and charged into the terminal. Inside, a fluttery ground hostess directed him to the lounge where incoming passengers would arrive from customs. A tall man in rumpled, travel-weary Levi's, a denim jacket, and sockless Reeboks came out the one-way door into the lounge.

Jake blocked his progress. "Were you on the American flight from Mexico City?"

"No. That flight's not in?" Zachary Cross was in no mood to be polite, particularly to a tall, overdressed mannequin. Any guy that handsome ought to be stuffed and mounted, he thought irritably.

A small woman interrupted them with a pen and a slip of paper. "I never do this, but I just have to have your autograph," she bubbled to Jake. "Honestly, you're just the cutest thing. . . ."

The mannequin smiled and signed his name on the paper.

The door opened to admit a portly man and his wife, and Zachary saw her for an instant in the corridor behind, carrying the hamper. His heart rate doubled. God, she was beautiful! She was worth it. All the worry about her, missing her, gambling on the flight, gambling that he could find her in this mess. It was too good to be true. He couldn't believe she was safe. He kept one eye on her progress each time the door opened, amazed at how good just looking at her again made him feel. He anticipated her surprise that he'd be waiting for her.

She came through the door at last, and he started to move toward her when she stopped, put down the baby, and threw herself into an embrace with the tall, handsome hulk. He came to a halt, stunned. The mannequin was "All my love, Jake"? He watched with leaden feet as she kissed the huge, good-looking man.

"I brought your coat," said the guy, wrapping her in a huge, warm cloak. "And a blanket for the little guy."

His life drained away as a second kiss lasted forever. They broke apart finally, and Jake embraced her again, lifted her into the air, and held her next to him. She was radiant.

Zachary felt only the twist of a knife in his gut, too jolted to move forward, claim space at her side. He stood in limbo, bleeding at her obvious love for a man who clearly adored her. There was no way he'd be able to explain his presence, say hello and good-bye in one conversation.

He'd been right the first time. It had been too good to be true. All of it. His eyes followed them through the room, Allison wrapped in the guy's arms, face alight, animated in a way he hadn't seen in all the time he'd spent with her. Jake was equally spirited, supporting her body with one arm, carrying Adam's basket with the other.

At the last minute, he decided stonily, if she saw him, he'd stand his ground. A statue, he watched as she kissed

Jake again, aglow with laughter and excitement. "Wait till I tell you what happened," she bubbled. "You won't believe what I did. I don't believe it."

He forced himself to stand, silent witness, as she proudly handed the baby to Jake, who grinned hugely. He followed as they walked through the terminal, granting himself the ground-glass luxury of the last time he'd see her.

When Jake had walked her to the passenger door of a classy, vintage Mercedes and helped her and the baby inside, he gave it up. A few minutes later he numbly arranged a red-eye to Miami, sought the bar, bought a pack of cigarettes. Unable to open the pack, he tossed it back to the waitress and ordered a double Scotch. Damn women anyway.

The season of rain had produced shiny leaves of knee-high corn, dipping and swaying in the milpas. In the afternoon thundershower, warm and dry in her newly thatched hut, Rosa Chaya ground yellow corn for the evening meal, pleased at the secret of her impending pregnancy.

In the *t'o'ohil's* village, rain settled gently, soaking into the graves of Sara and Luisita Chun and into the newly turned earth that covered the tiny body of Och. Inside, a small dog, carved in bone, took up the duty of guiding and protecting the elder's last grandchild through the Underworld.

Jorgé K'ayum sat in his hut, smoking his cigar, listening to the rain, Little Bol at his feet.

"Can *ts'ul* ever become *häch winik*?" asked the boy.

"White men can live in the forests, they can clear milpas and plant corn like *häch winik*, they can give offerings to Hachäkyum to please him and be treated well by him, but *ts'ul* are *ts'ul*, they can never become *häch winik*. They are not sons of Hachäkyum, as was my father and his father and all his fathers before him. As are you and I." The old man was sad.

"*Ts'ul* do not realize that the roots of all living things are one. When a tree falls in the forest, a star falls from the sky. *Ts'ul* do not ask permission of Yum K'ax or the guardian of the stars when they cut down the trees. They do not know Hachäkyum has made the trees and the stars.

"Without the trees, the rains end, the soil disappears, the streams dry up. Everything dies—here, in heaven, in the higher heavens as well. It is the punishment of Hachäkyum. Soon we will all die. I am not afraid. But it is hard, very hard, to witness the loss of the trees and the death of the forest. All of the animals will die, and only the snakes will inherit the land."

"Will this come in my lifetime?"

"It is possible. . . ." Sadness filled up the old man's eyes.

A few miles to the west, high up in the offshoot to the limestone cavern, cubs were arriving, one by one. The gentle mother licked away each birth sac with her rough tongue, stimulating life, calmly, rhythmically, firmly insistent, intent on her purpose. Finally there were three mewling, blindly searching creatures seeking her milk. Two were female, fawn with black rosettes to come with maturity; the male was black on black.

In Miami it was a hot and bitchy afternoon, typically July. There was enough humidity to wilt a scarecrow, promising the kind of night air-conditioning couldn't fix, would merely exaggerate with limp, chilly air against hot, sweaty skin. After the game, Zachary decided, he'd get in the pool. At least the air off the chlorinated water would be cooler. Unwound from an afternoon with Steffie, he missed her sunny presence.

Over the interminable last three months, he'd made concentrated efforts to soften his stance with his ex-wife, and their relationship had proceeded to reasonably solid ground. She and the baker hadn't gotten to the altar. She hadn't volunteered a reason, but she'd been a hell of a lot easier to deal with lately. Maybe, for Steffie . . .

Restless, he stared at his daughter's picture on the mantel and debated whether it was too soon to call. Sue had picked her up fifteen minutes ago. "Not yet," he said companionably to the cat.

He knew he wouldn't sleep unless he was certain they'd gotten home safely, and Steffie couldn't be counted on to call. Perched on the narrow sill, the coal black cat watched him intently with implacable yellow eyes, through the window screen. It had appeared the day he'd moved in, two months ago.

He'd resisted for two and a half hours, then gotten into the Camaro and made a special trip to the supermarket for a couple of boxes of Tender Vittles; he and the cat had come to terms. It refused to come inside, even to eat, preferring to wait for fresh cat food every evening in a small dish next to the pool. "Sooner or later you'll come around," he'd promised the skittish animal. "Sooner or later, you'll trust me." The cat's name was Balum.

He looked at the picture again. The soon-to-be-nine year-old face laughed back at him from the frame. Since his return from Belize, he'd spent every spare moment with his daughter, and Steffie was blooming.

Easter vacation, they'd taken a trip to the Colorado desert—the one place he could think of where the sky was still clear enough to see galaxies. Steffie had been entranced. From a mile-high bluff he'd watched his daughter's face and shared her awe at a show of shooting stars and counted winking satellites in the pristine Colorado night.

And missed her.

In March he'd closed Jerry's apartment, sold everything, and donated the proceeds to a local antidrug clinic. The next morning, he'd uncovered the status of one Martin Bateman.

According to Attica's records, Bateman was a model prisoner with the probability of an early release. Zachary had taken supreme pleasure in altering that status by calling in a favor—a big one—and Bateman was embroiled in a messy discipline problem the following week. A guard wound up in the hospital with a broken wrist, but Bateman had drawn two weeks in solitary confinement, eight months added to his sentence. To date Zachary hadn't a shred of remorse.

The rolls of film he'd found in Allison's room had been his, taken at the ruins. They'd been incredible. In February he'd chosen a picture he particularly liked and sent a copy of it to her in Chicago, with the journal and a brief note, wishing her well.

He'd received a letter in fine, even handwriting from her, thanking him for the photo. She was working, the baby was fine, she would call him soon. She'd enclosed a snapshot of a beaming, three-month-old charmer, Adam. There'd been no mention of Jake.

He'd read the letter a thousand times and lived on hope for ninety-three days. No call had materialized. In May, packing to move, he had tucked the letter in with the balance of the photographs; when he unpacked, he'd left it there. He'd added the snapshot of Adam next to the picture of Steffie on his night table.

And missed her.

The phone rang four times before she picked it up. "Hi, Daddy." He wasn't fooling her, he was calling to check up. "I knew it was you."

"Got me! I give up." He had to laugh at her worldly annoyance that he would worry. At her age she would live forever. "I just called to make sure you're going to be nine next Saturday. I wouldn't want to get the number wrong," he teased, "because I had to notify the fire department to stand by for all those candles."

"Oh, Daaaddy!"

"Night, punkin. I love you."

"I love you, too, Daddy." The phone clicked into the hum of a dead line and the start of a long Saturday evening. He debated about going to the market and decided against it. He'd go tomorrow. He preferred food shopping when he was hungry. He and Steffie had stuffed themselves with hot dogs on the way home from miniature golf.

He was restless, filled with an unexplainable itchy feeling.

From the sill, the cat moved slightly to watch him cross the room to the television, then lowered its head on crossed paws, eyes following his return.

An hour later the Twins were pounding the Yankees and he was kicked back in cutoffs, feet bare, two cans into a six-pack of freezer-cold Dos Equis. Guidry was pounding for home in the top of the ninth. The doorbell jangled his concentration.

Annoyed, he decided he was not in the mood to be polite to a zealous Jehovah's Witness, fend off chocolate mint cookies, or whatever. Guidry was called out at the plate. He watched the replay from all four camera angles, then ABC went to their delayed commercial package. The doorbell did not ring again.

Faced with fourteen consecutive car and shaving commercials, he ambled to the door. If whoever it was was still in sight, he'd deal with it. Into the full sunset, he saw only a huge wide-brimmed hat and a cream linen dress with legs up to there. Holy shit! He'd know those legs anywhere! Chicago! She was about to get back into a Miami cab.

Out the door like a shot and down the walk in his bare feet, he caught her arm in time to prevent her from reentering the taxi. When she turned to look at him from under the hat, he stopped in his tracks. It couldn't be possible, but it was true. He had forgotten how amazingly beautiful she was. She'd gained a few pounds, the circles were gone from under the haunting hazel eyes, and she looked, in a word, sensational.

"Hey. Chicago. Hold it a second. You ought to give a guy a little more warning." Stumbling, he found a voice. "I'm sorry, but you were probably the last person . . . come in," he demanded, and ducked down to read the meter. It registered $23. Silently blessing Steffie's choice of entertainment that afternoon, he stuffed thirty dollars into the suspicious cabbie's fist, even as his eyes registered the narrow wedding band on her left hand. Damn!

He stood up to meet the unwinking gaze of a sturdy, dimpled little boy. "This is Adam," she said. He returned the little boy's stare, taking in a serene, bright-eyed, healthy child.

Married. He dived into the back of the cab to unbuckle the carrier and gather up the baby's gear, dismissing the driver's statement that he was prepared to wait. He gave him the twenty to shut up.

"We can't stay—the flight to Chicago leaves in a little over an hour," she said nervously.

"I'll drive you." The matter was settled. There was no way she was taking a taxi out of his life, married or not.

"We'd have been here sooner, but we went to your old apartment first. The woman there gave me your new address," she explained as he escorted her back up the walk. God bless his ex-landlady. Still, he was irked. Time he could have spent with her, now gone, wasted. Damn.

Inside the house, he drank her in. He killed the set, unaware of the upset win or the roar of the frenzied Yankee crowd. "You look terrific," he ventured, determined not to let her marital status interfere with their friendship or his feelings. "Motherhood certainly agrees with you." Motherhood. Not marriage.

She blushed slightly and smiled with pleasure at his open admiration as she removed the hat and shook out her hair. Two hours of torture with Sebastiani-Bernard had been worth it from the look on his face. Adam gave a restless cry and stared determinedly at his mother with a threatening face. "It's twenty minutes past his dinner time. He's really been patient, but I need to feed him."

She deftly removed jars of baby food from the diaper bag and a small spoon. He took them from her and removed the lids to zap them in his microwave for six seconds. For the next ten minutes he held the little boy while she spooned creamed corn and peaches into his unblinking face.

"How are things with you?" she asked quietly, glancing

up at him on alternate spoons of gooey yellow food that Adam seemed to love, blasting his nerve endings with clear hazel eyes.

"Not too bad. Got this place a couple months ago so I'd have a pool for Steffie. I see her a lot now. I'm a better father than I was six months ago," he said honestly, enviously, breathing her in.

"I'm a better mother than I was six months ago." She laughed.

He laughed with her, his tension easing slightly at something shared at last. "That's obvious. He looks great."

A now drowsy Adam moved his head from side to side, indicating that not even peaches could keep him awake. Allison wiped his face and pulled a full bottle of formula out of the bag, and took him from Zachary. The hair on his forearms crackled at her touch.

Cradling Adam in the crook of her arm, she gave him the bottle. "Woodie said you tried to catch me," she said, looking up at him.

Tried and failed. He was silent. There was nothing to say. The memory was pain. If he hadn't seen her face at the sight of Jake . . . He waited quietly as the little boy sucked on the bottle, willing to hear anything she had to say, still stunned she was sitting in his kitchen. Finally, to divert his thoughts, "How's the adoption going?"

"The legal battle's over. The authorities in Guatemala have conceded they can't locate the father, and there's no other family member to contest my claim to him. My attorney says it looks pretty good. Even if the father is found, we could make a case that he's unfit because of his drug activity. Jake's convinced he'll never show up."

An awkward pause while he felt her scrutiny, uncomfortable with the thought that somehow he was being tested. He glanced away, unwilling to reveal his raging jealousy even as he willed her to continue, never to leave. The baby dropped into seamless sleep, and he motioned her to follow him into Steffie's room, a mishmash of eight-year-old passion and a collection of teddy bears.

He saw her smile at the sight of the bears and survey the room while he pushed the twin bed securely against the wall. After she laid the sleeping Adam on the bed, he gently backed three chairs flush against the outside in a makeshift crib. Married. God damn her! Surely she couldn't deny the electricity he felt in the air. Why the hell did she have to be married? And in a hurry to get back to him, or she'd take a later flight. Planes left for Chicago every two hours.

He knew because he'd finally boarded one on a Friday afternoon late in April and had gotten as far as the address on her letter, an expensive complex on Lake Shore Drive. He'd walked along Lake Michigan for an hour in a miserable misting rain before deciding he was an adolescent jerk if he didn't at least say hello. He'd approached the building just as the two of them had dashed to a waiting limousine: Jake, tall and handsome, guiding her carefully, possessively.

She was laughing and gorgeous in a wonderful black flowing silk coat thing that had blown open in the breeze to reveal a dazzling cocktail gown, low cut and breathtaking, the color of the water off Waler's Beach early in the morning. They were teasing each other about being late, and he'd watched those incredible legs in sexy black stockings disappear inside the car. Jake had called her "Lovely" and slid in next to her. They were whisked away into glistening fog, and Zachary had hated him mightily.

The doorman, proud of his tenants, had confirmed they were Mr. and Mrs. Jake Alston, a brand-new baby upstairs with a nanny. It had been a long, slow weekend after that.

Adam safely asleep, they returned to the living room. She stood awkwardly at the mantel, looking at the portraits. "This has to be Steffie." She moved to the picture of Jerry. "And that's your brother," she said carefully, measuring, seeking . . . what? He couldn't fathom.

He closed the distance between them and took up her left hand to inspect the wedding band, felt her tremble as he rolled it gently around her finger, not quite in control of the bottom that was dropping out of his stomach. "How long you been married?"

"Jake and I were married when I got back to Chicago. It was easier, with the baby. The custody and all."

She was clearly skittish, uncomfortable talking about it. He didn't care. Let her squirm. Nobody said life was fair. He didn't trust himself to speak. It had been "All my love, Jake" after all. The son of a bitch. Why not? She should have the best. The guy was great looking, obviously wealthy.

He stood in silence, not sure what to do, unwilling to let go of her fingers. All he could think about were those witchy hazel eyes and how much he wanted her. And the other half of him, the raging, fried, furiously jealous half, wanted to bash her. Why in the hell was she here?

He was a little unnerved when she answered his question, and his skin jerked as she smoothed her free hand along his bare shoulder in a burning connection.

"Jake sent me. He says not to come back until I've seen you."

Then, incredibly, she stood on tiptoe and kissed him, and the kiss was open, laden with promise.

A chasm of possibility opened at his feet. Her husband had sent her? The invitation in her eyes booted caution out the window, and he shut out his disbelief. It no longer mattered why she'd come, she was here. "Oh, Christ, Chicago," he breathed. "Are you sure?"

"Trust me," from her lips into his opened mouth.

His heart was instantly too big for his chest. Somehow they were in his bedroom and he was kissing her, deeply, fervently, insistently, and undressing her, and she was kissing him back—a fully responsive, receiving, giving woman. Buttons came free under his fingers, and the crisp linen dress slid lightly to the floor, followed by thin, peach-pink silky items, baring smooth satin skin.

"God, I've thought about making love to you a thousand

times," he whispered against fragrant skin. Memory hadn't lied—her lips were open and pliant under his searching mouth, her fingers were laced in his hair. Holding her, feeling her next to his skin, he inhaled deep, life-giving breaths of the scent of her, the essence of her, moving his lips just to feel the incredible softness of her skin, then kissing her mouth again, longer and deeper, afraid to stop.

He jerked the light blanket off the rumpled bed and laid her down on faded blue sheets, drinking in pale honeyed skin. He lowered himself beside her, luxuriating as his hands explored the warm, bare length of her, and traced with his tongue the wet, butter smoothness of her mouth, tasting liquid fire, searing; he pressed the softness of her against his body at last.

This was real, and as good as it ever gets. Soft sighs and sounds, intimately explored smells, and hotly sensitive skin where fingers felt, tongues ventured, gliding mouths touched lightly, murmured vaguely of the tasting, telling, giving, swelling, silent language, lost in the timelessness that happens only once between any two people—if the gods were kind. The joyous madness of the first time.

In the filtered twilight, he molded himself to her body, unable to get her close enough. Jesus, she was incredible. She'd been too thin in Belize, and bloody great looking then. Now, she was luscious and welcome and familiar, and he wanted to hold her and crush her, and run his hands over her and touch her everywhere at once.

He gave himself over to his own pleasure as she refused his help and took a delicious forever to remove his ancient cutoffs, making him wait, slowly, deliberately, unfastening one stubborn button at a time, kissing him, her hands driving him crazy through the fabric in the process.

At last he was free to feel himself against the length of her. He kissed her breathless and with exquisite, exquisite slowness buried himself in her body, getting lost in her. Jesus! Finally! Losing the world, drowning in an ocean of forbidden, obsessive, possessive waves, he sailed on in an oblivion of rhythm and light. The only reality was her; firm, and real, and giving, and equal, and he wanted nothing else ever in his life to be this good.

In Chicago, Jake Alston, green eyes far away, sat pensively in his bedroom. Lost in thought, he stroked the arm of his favorite chair with slender fingers, rounded golden oak with smoothed staves serving as support from the back to the floor—an original by Frank Lloyd Wright, rescued from oblivion quite by accident twelve years ago from a private home in a Chicago suburb, backdrop for a fashion layout.

Allison had pointed it out to him, and he'd bought it on a whim for his bedroom. Now it would live forever. He'd made a provision in his will that it would go to the Art Institute of Chicago. Since he lacked a child, it would be his niche in history long after the photographs had disappeared.

He glanced at his watch and smiled at last, content with his decision; he'd been right to let her go. He looked up as Jesse walked out of the bath, dew from the shower glistening on damp skin in the late afternoon sunlight.

"Are you okay?"

Jake didn't answer.

"Will she be back?"

"I don't think so."

Jesse walked naked to the window and pushed it open to the late afternoon Lake Michigan breeze.

"Good," he said.

Centuries later, deliciously exhausted but unwilling to break apart from him, static trills still flashing through and across her skin from the joy of him, she wondered at this man who had transformed her to another place. She allowed him to unwind an arm from around her body long enough to lean down and hold in his mouth again a moist, peach nipple, felt him taste the salt from her body. And the other.

When he caught her close again and brought her face next to his, she reveled in kissing him, holding him close, marveling at how good he felt next to her. How right.

He laughed in irony, then raised himself to look down at her—into clear, uncomplicated hazel eyes. "I wish I'd gotten there before he did," he said, suddenly sober. A husband sending his wife to another man clearly didn't fit into the picture.

She looked her question. What on earth was he talking about?

This time he was deliberately waking the bear. "What about Jake?" It was time he understood. "Did he really send you here? Because I know you love him. I've seen you with him, it was in your face." He traced his finger across her palm and touched the wedding ring once again.

"Where'd you see Jake?" Sated, euphoric, she pulled herself to reality.

"In Chicago."

She cut him off, totally thrown. "You were in Chicago?"

"I was about two minutes late. Thirty seconds, actually."

She was incredulous. "You were there, and you didn't . . ." Confusion cleared to comprehension as she relived her reunion with Jake. Woodie'd told her about Belize City, but she hadn't known he'd followed her all the way to Chicago.

The hazel eyes sparkled, then sobered as he twisted the ring smoothly around her finger while she decided how to answer. "I do love him, and he's a part of my life. He's my family, and my best friend, and anyone in my life should know that."

She willed him to understand and witness the truth of it. "We were lovers when we were seventeen. Nothing since. We got married to gain legal custody of Adam as a family. We'll be divorced as soon as the papers are finalized. I have custody of Adam."

"I don't understand. He loves you. I've seen it."

"Yes, he does. It's not something I can explain just yet. You'll just have to trust me." She shifted slightly, with building confidence, held him close. "I've been afraid to see you—I've been terrified."

She held his face in her hands, determined to make him understand. "I was afraid you'd feel differently about me, that it was only for the time in Belize, and it wouldn't hold up. We agreed I would see you on the way back from this trip so I could show you the baby and"—she took a shuddery breath—"and make sure you still wanted me." She kissed him and ran her tongue lightly across his bottom lip, savoring the taste of him.

He kissed her back and knew what was different. Her fear was gone.

"More than that, I was afraid to make love with you," she continued, breathless. "And I was terrified," she went on, gaining strength, "that if I let us happen, what would I do if every time I closed my eyes it was him again—his face and not yours. But, it didn't happen." She smiled widely, joyously. "I had to make it real. I had to be sure I make love to you—the way I want to—and I can." Her joy was electric.

"Can you ever . . ." He leaned forward to kiss her again.

"No one controls my life but me." Her eyes danced as she looked at him. "Well, maybe you . . . a little," she teased.

Oh, God, it wasn't possible. He was going to have it all? "You said a divorce."

"It's final as soon as I get to Chicago. I was in St. Croix. You're in bed with a divorcée."

She pulled his face down and kissed him long and deep, sure at last in her heart. Then she savored his lopsided grin of joy as he removed Jake's wedding ring from her finger and tossed it over his shoulder onto the floor.

Elaborately eyeing an alarm clock next to the bed, she turned to him, impishly wide-eyed. "Oh," she whispered, rocking gently beneath him, "I've missed the plane."

He managed one kiss before he reacted with pleasure. "There's not another one for three days. Trust me."

AVAILABLE NOW

HEIRLOOM by Candace Camp

A surefire hit from the bestselling author of ROSE-WOOD, HEIRLOOM is a heartwarming story of love between a beautiful actress and a lonely Nebraska farmer.

HEARTBREAK TRAIL by Barbara Keller

A passionate and touching tale of two people, each desperately searching for two very different things when they are thrown together in the harsh frontier wilderness of Fort Apache. A stunning western romance that is sure to entice readers.

TRUST ME by Jeane Renick

Former model Allison Shreve goes to Belize on vacation to try to get her life back to normal after the shattering experience she had three years before. There, she meets the kind of man she distrusts—Zachary Cross, a Miami cop.

CRYSTAL HEART by Candace Camp

A Candace Camp classic to capture your heart. This is a story of Lady Lettice Kenton, a titled temptress with a heart of ice, and Charles Murdock, an American rebel out of place in elegant, fashionable London. They come from two different worlds, only to discover one burning passion.